HUNTER'S
PRIZE

BACKWOODS
BRIDES

BOOK THREE

MARCIA GRUVER

Print ISBN 978-1-60260-950-1

eBook Editions:
Adobe Digital Edition (.epub) 978-1-62029-002-6
Kindle and MobiPocket Edition (.prc) 978-1-62029-003-3

Scripture quotations are taken from the King James Version of the Bible.

For more information about Marcia Gruver, please access the author's website at the following Internet address: www.marciagruver.com.

Cover design: Kirk DouPonce, DogEared Design

Published by Barbour Publishing, Inc., P.O. Box 719, Uhrichsville, OH 44683, www.barbourbooks.com

Our mission is to publish and distribute inspirational products offering exceptional value and biblical encouragement to the masses.

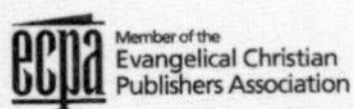

Printed in the United States of America.

Dedication

To Dorothy Faye, George Edward, and Nancy Jane—my siblings. Thoughts of you call to mind pulled hair, skinned knees, and chinaberry fights. Mud pies, cardboard forts, and side-lot baseball. Poodle skirts, miniskirts, and bell-bottom jeans. Brenda Lee, Elvis, Chubby Checker, and the Beatles. It passed too fast! I wish we could live it all over again. Never forget that I love you.

Lay not up for yourselves treasures upon earth, where moth and rust doth corrupt, and where thieves break through and steal:
But lay up for yourselves treasures in heaven. . .
For where your treasure is, there will your heart be also.
Matthew 6:19–21

Acknowledgments

Thank you, Lee, my husband, friend, and very own Superman. It's nice to have your broad shoulders to lean on.

Special thanks to Mr. John Winn of Caddo Outback Backwater Tours, my Caddo area expert, knowledgeable historian, and all-around great guy. Bless you, John, for allowing me to pick your brain. I acknowledge freely that yours are some of the best lines in the book. Find out more about John and Caddo Lake at: www.caddolaketours.com.

As always, my heartfelt appreciation goes to Elizabeth Ludwig, the first responder to my first draft carnage and the reason my Barbour editors don't tear out their hair. Lisa, dear friend, thank you for dotting my i's, crossing my t's, and chasing me down rabbit trails. I salute you!

Speaking of Barbour editors, thanks and blessings to Aaron McCarver for your knowledge, talent, and razor-sharp eye. It is a genuine pleasure to work with you.

And speaking of Barbour Publishing, Rebecca Germany and the rest of the crew, you guys are my heroes. Thank you for your unmerited favor and gracious support.

PROLOGUE

Pretoria, South Africa, November 1904

A raspy, hissing *zzzzzzZZTT* spun Cedric Whitfield toward the lone African swift soaring overhead. Whimpering, he covered his ears and stumbled away from the jarring sound. Lips tightly sealed to spare his parched throat, he ran along the hard-packed road, the hot, dry air burning inside his nose with every breath.

He skittered past Denny Currie and Charlie Pickering, arching his back and shivering at the thought of touching the scary men hired to drive them to town. In his haste, he blundered into one of the great beasts Charlie led behind him like hounds on a leash.

"Mind the oxen, sonny." The big man caught his collar, lifting him off the ground. "Unless you fancy being trampled."

Fixing Ceddy with a bulging eye, the huge animal flared his velvet nostrils and snorted.

With a shrill scream, Ceddy struggled free and shot away.

"Blimey, he's off again!" Mr. Currie shouted. "Mrs. Beale, can't you keep the lad close at hand?"

At the mention of Aunt Jane, Ceddy slowed to a trot and spun, his heart thudding against his ribs. Shuffling backward, feeling the sun on the backs of his bare legs, he watched her top the rise.

"He's frightened of your team, Mr. Currie," she called, her brows rising to peaks.

Shifting his weight, Mr. Currie dried his forehead with his sleeve. "Appears to be frightened of most things, now, don't he?"

Panting hard, Auntie pressed a silk hankie to her mouth and plodded up the uneven path, the grasping branches of the sweet thorn brush tangling with her hem as she passed. "My nephew is a child, sir. A child with uncommon debilitations. Must I remind you of that?"

Charlie frowned. "He seems right fit to me."

Mr. Currie jabbed him with his elbow and spoke from the side of his mouth. "She don't mean weak in the physical sense, you twit."

"Nor do I mean weakness of the mind, sir," Aunt Jane said. "Please don't twist my words."

Mr. Currie's smile slid away. "Whatever ails him, if he persists in playing about, we won't see Pretoria by nightfall." Spinning on his heel, he forged ahead. "Never mind catching the train."

Ignoring his growly threat, Auntie fell in behind him, dabbing her beaded forehead with the cloth. "How much farther? This pace is a bit much, I'm afraid."

Drawn to her strong, steady voice, Ceddy lagged to wait for her. . . until the long, silver wings of a snout bug teased away his eyes.

"A couple kilometers," Mr. Currie said.

"Oh my," Auntie shrilled. "Did you say *two* kilometers?"

He quirked his mouth. "Yes, m'lady, thereabout." He dragged off his battered cap to scratch behind his ear then used the hat to point. "If memory serves, once we round that distant grove, it's but a few steps more."

Staring across the rolling grassland, Auntie sniffed. "I'll try to remain optimistic."

Glancing around, she lowered her voice. "Could there be predators lurking in the brush? I'd prefer to survive this unscheduled trek."

Ceddy longed to chase the darting snout bug, but his aunt's frightened tone pained his stomach. Holding his breath, he passed the men and their oxen then fell back to match her steps.

"Predators in South Africa?" Mr. Currie's laugh rang hollow like a gourd. "There are lions in these parts, no doubt." He patted the long-handled pistol at his side. "But you need fear no four-footed creature, Mrs. Beale. It's the bloodthirsty lot who creep around on two limbs we hope to avoid."

Stopping so fast she tripped on the uneven path, Auntie lifted her eyes. "Would you care to elaborate?"

His stubby fingers cradled his sidearm. "Soulless devils lurk in the veld. The sort who slip up without warning and straddle your back. . .slit you from ear to ear without so much as a 'how do.'"

Moaning, Ceddy curled into the folds of Aunt Jane's skirt.

She clutched his shoulder with a trembling hand. "What could such men want with us?"

"Not an invitation to tea, that's for sure."

She drew Ceddy closer. "*Really*, Mr. Currie. If that's the case, I should think checking the hitch for damage before we left would top your list of priorities."

Mr. Currie scowled at Charlie Pickering. "You have my blundering assistant to thank for our present fix. He's in charge of the rigging."

"Quite right, missus." Charlie lifted his sweat-stained bush hat and bowed. "An unforgivable lapse on my part."

Guiding Ceddy with a firm grip on his neck, Aunt Jane continued up the road toward them. "You'd both better pray the train to Port Elizabeth hasn't left without us. If we don't make the coast in time to board the steamer for England, you'll be explaining your lapse to my husband."

"I'll drop to me pious knees on the spot, you daft cow," Mr. Currie muttered as she passed.

Frowning, Auntie paused and lowered her hankie. "Beg your pardon?"

"I say it's a pleasant day for a walk, anyhow."

She snorted. "Perhaps. . .if one considers a stifling greenhouse pleasant." She blotted around her mouth. "Peculiar weather for mid-November, I must say."

Charlie grinned. "Not in South Africa. November's the first month of summer 'round here."

"Is that a fact?" She tilted her head. "This time of year in London they're banking fires and airing heavy wraps."

He swiped his damp forehead. "Wish we had cause to bank a fire today. By the feel of things, we're due a scorcher."

Aunt Jane patted Ceddy's back. "I suppose the American climate will be quite the adjustment for this young man."

"The Americas, missus? I thought you were bound for England."

"We are. But I will accompany Cedric to Texas in a few months.

Should be quite the adventure"—she leaned to smile at Ceddy—"with all the buckaroos and Indians and such."

"Blimey," Charlie said, stroking his bristly chin. "I'd sorely love to see a buckaroo."

Frowning, Mr. Currie elbowed past. "We can stand about chatting all day, if you like. Only don't blame me when you miss your train."

"You're quite right, Mr. Currie," Aunt Jane said. "Let's soldier on, shall we?"

Ceddy clutched her skirt with both hands, allowing her steps to jerk him forward. Closing his eyes, he let his head drift back as he ambled along the path—listening.

The jumble of sound, at once frightening and familiar, settled around his shoulders like a favorite quilt. Resting in it, he picked out the rumble of a lioness calling her young to a meal, a yipping jackal, the trill of a sunbird, a huffing white rhino in the distance. Howls, barks, and calls that awakened him each morning and lulled him to sleep every night.

Mr. Currie sniffed, dragging Ceddy from his trance. Clearing his throat, the horrid man spat. "I understand his parents were missionaries?"

"Yes, the both of them." Auntie's voice drifted behind her, quivering like a sedge warbler's song. "Peter and Eliza devoted themselves to sharing the Gospel in this godforsaken region." Slowing, she looked up. "How thoughtless of me to speak so harshly of your country. Forgive me, gentlemen."

"Quite all right, mum," Mr. Currie said. "I find their efforts downright inspiring." He glanced behind him. "Your husband said they drove right off a cliff?"

Auntie gasped and eased Ceddy in front of her. "Mr. Currie, please!"

He tipped his grimy cap. "Sorry, missus. Just making conversation."

"Sadly, it's true," she whispered. "My poor sister and her husband lost their lives in a terrible accident."

Ceddy squirmed. Adults often talked quietly around him, as if his ears were dull. He could hear quite well, in fact, and her words rang in his head like a gong.

"The crash of a motorcar, of all things! In the wilds of South Africa. Can you imagine the folly?" she shrilled. "The silly contraption slid off-road in a muddy downpour. What was Peter thinking to bring that accursed machine to a place with naught to drive upon but rutted ox trails? For all his good intentions, Peter Whitfield had more money than good sense."

Charlie slid off his hat and clutched it in front of him. "More's the pity, that. Dreadful sorry."

Aunt Jane let go a rush of air, tickling the top of Ceddy's head. "The news came as quite a shock. The poor dears perished the way they lived—side by side in service to our Lord. Now they're together for eternity." She dabbed the corners of her eyes with her hankie. "That hope is my only comfort."

Charlie tapped Ceddy's shoulder with a bony finger. "What will happen to this poor little mite?"

Ceddy drew away with a grunt.

Gathering him close, Auntie draped her arms around his neck. "I requested the privilege of raising him, but"—her clipped words sounded stern—"his parents made other arrangements in their will. He'll spend Christmas with my family in London. Come spring, he's off to live with Aunt Priss in Marshall, Texas."

Charlie cleared his throat. "Forgive me boldness, missus, but ain't you his aunt?"

"Priscilla Whitfield is the boy's great-aunt on his father's side. To honor his parents' wishes, the old girl will take him in." Her mouth twisted. "It's what they wanted, though I can't imagine why they preferred that dried-up old spinster to me."

The lead ox stumbled on a mound of clods, nearly going down. Denny Currie cursed and stuck it with a rod, prompting the creature to bellow in protest.

With a loud wail, Ceddy broke free and ran.

"Oy! Not again," Mr. Currie groaned. "Where's he off to now?"

"It's your own fault," Aunt Jane cried. "The boy has no tolerance for sudden noise or violence of any sort."

"Violence?" Mr. Currie said. "We 'aven't—"

"Stay close, dear," Aunt Jane called, as if from the bottom of a well. "It's dangerous on your own."

"Mrs. Beale, this won't do!"

The packed dirt pounded beneath Ceddy's feet, sending vibrations along his spindly legs.

"Cedric, love, please come back," a lilting voice warbled in the distance. "Where are you going, darling?"

He stretched his arms to the sides and flew. He was a blue crane soaring over the rippling grass. A spoonbill searching for water. Cresting the hill, he shot down the other side, counting his jarring footsteps.

"He's gone!" The angry words echoed overhead. "What are we supposed to do now?"

"Don't just stand there." The fury in Auntie's tone drew Ceddy's shoulders to his ears. "Earn your money, gentlemen. Go after him."

Heavy footsteps thundered behind him on the trail as the men closed in, muttering fierce curses at his back. Cruel fingers lashed out, closing around his neck. "Come back 'ere, you little—"

Squirming, Ceddy spun and bit down hard.

Mr. Currie howled. Gripping Ceddy's arm with his other hand, he shoved him along the path. "Oy, Charlie," he growled. "When we reach the top of the ridge, mate, distract the old girl whilst I nudge this brat over the side."

"Tempting, boss," Charlie whispered back. "But we can't kill off clergy's seed. We'll roast in perdition."

Denny snorted. "I'd risk the fiery flames to be shed of 'im."

Scowling, Charlie swiped a bony finger across his neck. "Shut it. She'll hear you."

"Let her hear. I don't give a monkey's behind."

" 'Ere she comes," Charlie hissed. "Get a handle, mate. It's the only way we'll see our wages. We'll be shed of them for good and all once they board the train."

Ceddy covered his ears and moaned to escape their vile whispers.

"Did you hear me, Mr. Currie?" Aunt Jane's panting cry came from behind the hill. "Catch hold of my nephew this instant."

"Catch hold of my nephew."

"Nudge him over the side."

Ceddy's breath caught as he pulled free of their grasping hands and shot around them. Veering to the right, he tripped over a tussock of wool grass, the smooth bottoms of his shoes slipping on the bright green blades.

Flailing his arms, he scrambled for a hold, but the long fronds slid through his fingers, leaving a sharp sting. He toppled, moving so fast the ground shot past in a blur. Shrieking in fear, he dug in his heels, plowing twin rows in the earth as he slid.

Halfway down, his feet hit a rock, flipping him again. He tumbled to the bottom in a blinding rush, rolling to a stop on his back, next to the bank of a stream.

Ceddy screwed up to cry, but the wide expanse of a cloudless blue sky drew his gaze. He stilled, watching the gray belly of an osprey soaring overhead.

Arching his body, he drew away from the sharp stones biting into his shoulders. Stirred by pain and frantic voices calling his name, he rolled to his elbows and stared at the scatter of rocks and stones he'd unearthed.

One of them glinted in the sunlight. Ceddy made a grab for it as the brush parted and long shadows fell, blocking the light.

Glancing up the hill, he tensed to flee, but Aunt Jane pushed between the men, her face bright from the heat. "Heavens, child! Are you all right? Come to me, dearie. That's it, now. No more games, right? You're a good boy, then, aren't you, lamb?"

Pushing off the ground, Ceddy hobbled to the safety of her skirts.

Mr. Currie cursed aloud. "Well ain't that just ducky. Dusts 'im off and pats 'is head, she does, and after he nearly got us killed. That brat needs a strap to 'is backside."

Auntie spun. "Mind your tongue and your business, Mr. Currie. And I'll thank you to abstain from vulgar language around Cedric. He understands every word."

Mr. Currie snorted. "That ain't likely."

"It's true," she huffed. "Ceddy's quite intelligent. Brighter than most, in fact."

Charlie laughed, a muffled sputter from behind his hand. "Pardon, missus. I don't mean to make sport. I'll give it to you that he's a right handsome child. But smart?" He fell to chuckling again.

Her arms tightened around Ceddy. "Let's get something straight before we take another step. This is no ordinary youngster."

Mr. Currie elbowed his partner. "We worked out that bit for ourselves."

"Well, you've worked it out all wrong. Cedric's brighter than the two of you lumped together. A bit of a genius, really. He has difficulty expressing himself, that's all, and he's easily distracted." Her voice faltered. "It's why he's so flighty."

Auntie's white-gloved fingers closed around Ceddy's clenched fist. Glancing down, she frowned. "What have we here, lovey?"

Prying the stone from his grip, she turned it over in her hands. "Oh my. Another rock? I should think you've gathered plenty for your collection. They're weighing us down as it is."

He whimpered and scrambled for it.

Pulling away, she poised to toss it into the stream. "Leave it behind, dear. It's filthy."

"Nuh!"

"Yes, 'tis, Ceddy." She brushed her hand against her skirt. "Look how it soiled my nice, clean gloves. Let's throw it down, shall we? You have so many."

Bouncing on his heels, he tugged on her arm. "Mm-muh!"

With a sigh, she knelt at his side. "Yours? Is that what you're trying to say?"

He worked for the word. Fought for it. "Muh."

Auntie peered at him with narrowed eyes then pulled a hankie from her bodice. "Oh, all right. I suppose you've suffered loss enough for a lifetime. You may keep it." She wrapped the jagged stone, shoving it deep inside his pocket. "See that it stays tucked in here until we can wash it, right?" Pausing, she caught his chin. "If you run off again, I'll take it from you. Do you understand?"

He drew in his shoulders and turned away, curling his fingers around the bulging pouch at his side.

Auntie faced the angry men. "Shall we go back to the trail now?"

"Right," Charlie growled. "If we can find it."

Mr. Currie crossed his arms. "Listen up, Mrs. Beale. I ain't signed on to be no baby-minder. For all the trouble the lad's been, I've a notion to carry on without you."

She gasped. "You'd leave us at the mercy of wild animals and prowling natives?"

He held his bleeding hand toward Ceddy. "Five minutes with 'im and they'd set you free."

She stiffened. "He won't stray again. I give you my word." Her fingers tightened on Ceddy's arm. "He certainly won't be biting again. I'll see to that."

Charlie slapped Denny on the back. "Come along, old man. You've come this far; now see it through." He puffed his cheeks and blew a breath. "Let's get topside and mind the team before they're set upon by lions."

"No worries, mate," Denny grumbled, falling in alongside him. "If a lion dares to show his hairy face, we'll just sic that rabid boy on 'im."

Denny had never been so happy to see Church Square. Coming into Pretoria from the acacia karoo always startled him at first. The town, sitting square in the middle of nowhere, sported a richness that didn't belong in the valleys and rolling plains of the thornveld.

South Africa afforded plenty of room to sprawl in, and the capital of Transvaal Province had taken advantage of the space. The streets were wide, the buildings several stories high. Church Square, at the center of it all, was vast and gaudy.

Blindfolded and carried into Pretoria, Denny would recognize the town at once when the blinders came off. One glance at the Jacaranda trees lining the shaded lanes and the rambler roses climbing the walls would give it away. The City of Roses was a fitting name for a town strewn with colorful petals.

Drawing a deep, fragrant breath, he rested his hands on his hips. "Charlie, take the oxen and have them looked after. Once they're settled, unstrap the baggage from the beasts and meet us at Pretoria Station."

"Right, boss," Charlie said, turning the team.

Mrs. Beale sought Denny's eyes, her mouth set in a stern line. "There's no need for you to accompany us to the station. Ceddy and I can find our way from here."

Denny shook his head. "I was hired to see you safely onto the train, and that's what I mean to do."

She tugged on the fingers of her glove. "Very well, Mr. Currie. As you wish." Resting her hand on the boy's back, she struck out down the street—in the wrong direction.

"Mrs. Beale?"

She turned.

"It's that way," Denny said, pointing.

"Of course." She raised a haughty chin and pranced up the sidewalk.

Denny grimaced at Charlie in the distance then grudgingly followed the silly cow and her impish nephew.

A bicycle careened around the corner, frantically pedaled by a businessman in a suit coat and dapper straw hat.

In a burst of speed, Denny yanked the troublesome child and his aunt out of the road.

Ceddy jerked free with a sullen pout and plodded woodenly toward the station platform.

Denny ran his thumb over the ring of teeth marks on his hand. "S'aright, you cheeky little beggar," he whispered to the back of the boy's head. "I'll be shed of you soon enough."

The 132 wending its way toward them on the tracks—its big engine primed to take Cedric Whitfield out of his life for good—was a sight to warm the cockles of Denny's heart. If he never saw the wicked lad again, it would suit him fine.

"Wait up, dear. You'll be lost."

Ignoring his aunt's harried warning, the boy scurried onto the platform and ran to a row of windows. Folding his legs beneath him, he sat on the ground and reached inside his pocket. Unwrapping the stone she'd given him, he commenced to scratching on the wall of the station.

Mrs. Beale sighed then shook her finger. "Stay put, yeah? The train's almost here."

Turning to Denny, she held out a fat wad of bills. "I've decided to pay extra for your trouble."

"Not extra, lady." He raised one brow. "Double."

She drew back, narrowing her eyes.

Denny wiggled his fingers. "I earned every copper."

Releasing a huffy breath, she counted out a few more pounds. "Very well. Done."

Loud tapping pulled their attention to the boy. Kneeling before a window, he rapped hard on the glass with his silly rock.

"Oh bother. What's he doing?" Denny waved his arms. "Hullo there, sonny! Stop that, now."

Fidgeting, Mrs. Beale stared down the track, deaf and blind to the child in her charge.

"Call the lad away, Mrs. Beale, before he breaks something."

She glanced over her shoulder. "Leave him be, Mr. Currie. He's not hurting anything."

Gritting his teeth, Denny turned aside in disgust. "Right," he whispered. "What's it to you? You'll soon be rolling south, free as the wind. I'll be left to square the tab."

Charlie appeared as the hulking engine rumbled past, the squeal on metal piercing as the engineer braked to a stop.

Denny hooked his thumb in Ceddy's direction. "I'll load their bags. You go fetch the brat so he can board. We can't have her leaving without 'im."

Nodding, Charlie dropped his burden then hustled to the boy and leaned to speak to him.

Cedric pushed to his feet and ran to join his aunt.

As they climbed the steps of the passenger car and disappeared inside, Denny drew a deep, cleansing breath. He didn't relax until the rods on the massive wheels began to pump, rolling the bothersome blighters out of his life. Patting the wad of money in his pocket, he grinned and strolled to join Charlie. "Looks like we scored a profit after all."

"Maybe not, boss," Charlie said as he approached. "Take a gander at what he's done."

Denny groaned. So much for the few extra quid. "The window's cracked, ain't it?"

Charlie shook his head. "Not cracked. The little beggar left his calling card."

"What are you on about now?" Curious, he bent to stare at the pane. What he saw fired a rushing sound inside his ears.

"Blast me! Will you look at that?" Heart racing, he ran his finger over the jagged letters of Ceddy's name etched into the glass.

Charlie scratched the wiggly lines with his thumbnail. "He's done it now, ain't he? It's ruined." Standing, he tugged on Denny's sleeve. "There's still time to do a runner. No one's noticed yet."

Denny jerked off his cap and whacked Charlie on the head. "Don't you know what you're looking at, you mindless dolt?"

Clutching his reddening ear, Charlie frowned and shook his head.

"Use your loaf, mate. Nothing will cut into glass like that except. . ." His voice rose on the end, inviting Charlie to finish.

Wheeling, Charlie stared toward the train, the last car glinting on the horizon. "You mean that hulking great rock is a. . ." His words trailed off, but his eyes bulged from their sockets.

Denny gripped his arm and spun him around. "Where was that silly woman taking the boy?"

"To London for Christmas." Charlie flapped his hands as if it helped him to remember. "Then somewhere in America. Texas, I think."

"Ah yes," Denny said, the satisfying *hiss* befitting his slanted eyes. "I remember now." He whirled and stared down the tracks. "They're bound for a place called Marshall."

ONE

Galveston, Texas, December 1904

Salty spray blasted Pearson Foster as he hurdled the side of the dinghy and hauled the boat to shore. Cold, wet clothes clung to his body, and gritty sand chafed his shivering frame.

Bone-wracking fatigue wasn't new to Pearson. Neither was the disappointment weighing his heart. The latest promising lead to the treasure of Jean Lafitte had him combing deserted beaches again to no avail—after he'd sworn never to fall for the legend again.

This time he'd been so sure.

If "the Terror of the Gulf" had hidden a stash of gold on Galveston Island, he'd buried it well. The only things Pearson had unearthed in his relentless pursuit of the pirate's treasure were painful memories and deep feelings of utter failure.

Harsh sea breezes lifted his damp shirttails, waving them like flags of surrender. He couldn't suppress a shudder and a quick glance at the horizon. Since the terrible day four years ago when the worst hurricane in history swept all he held dear into the sea, he'd kept a nervous watch on any threat of foul weather.

Pearson gritted his teeth until his jaw ached. "I should've been here," he whispered for the thousandth time. If he hadn't taken a jaunt off the island the day before the storm, he'd have perished alongside his family and the six thousand souls lost that dreadful night. Some days, when loneliness and guilt came in crushing waves, he wished he had.

At times, he tortured himself with thoughts of their final moments. His mother's frightened face as the rushing water swirled under the door, higher and higher, until it lapped at the eaves. . .and beyond. His jovial little brother and innocent baby sister fearing that the shrieking wind, splintering houses and uprooting palms, would tear them from their parents' arms. Hardest to bear, his father's anguish at the terrible moment when he knew he couldn't save them.

Jutting his chin, Pearson scowled into the bank of angry clouds, staring down the Creator Himself. As sure as the pounding surf at his back and the shifting sand at his feet, he'd never stop asking why God spared him yet counted his loved ones unworthy. As long as he lived, he'd never trust Him with anything precious again.

"Ahoy, brigand!" Theodoro Bernardi's familiar voice drifted up the beach followed by his lanky body.

Wincing, Pearson pretended not to hear. He itched to push off again, steer past the breaking waves, and set sail. He'd sooner battle the restless sea than admit defeat to his closest friend. Instead, he put his head down and dragged the boat farther inland, away from the rising tide.

Grinning, Theo hustled to lend a hand, his oversized feet leaving great sucking prints in the sand. "Well?" he asked, the question Pearson dreaded evident in his raised brows.

"Nothing," Pearson said calmly, as if declining jam with his morning toast.

Theo's eyes echoed Pearson's frustration. "Too bad, Pearce. I know you were hopeful."

Abandoning false indifference, Pearson pursed his lips and sighed. "It was a good lead this time around. I really thought—"

"I told you to wait till I could join you, no? With both of us looking, the outcome might've been different."

Pearson shook his head. "Once I locked onto the site, nothing felt right. That blasted storm turned this whole island upside down."

"Then how are you sure you found the spot?"

Pearson fired him a pointed look.

Theo lifted his hands. "Sorry I asked. I still say you should've waited."

Flipping the dinghy with one heave, Pearson gritted his teeth. "Some battles a man has to face alone."

Theo hooked his neck with the crook of his arm. "Well, you don't have to drink alone. Let me buy you a stiff swig at Rosie's to warm your mulish bones."

Pearson stiffened. "I appreciate the offer, old boy, but my stand on strong drink still holds."

Questions swirled in Theo's veiled eyes, but he wisely bit them back. "In that case, I was referring to Rosie's coffee. A shot of her stout brew should thaw you out." He thumped Pearson's chest. "And grow hair on this bald, girlie carcass."

Pearson chuckled and knocked his hand away. "That's different. When have I ever turned down Rosie's coffee?"

Grinning, Theo pointed him away from the approaching wall of rain, guiding him up the beach to the outline of the wagon waiting in the distance.

Pearson understood Theo's confusion about his ethics. His life was a contradiction that baffled him as well. Consuming rage kept him from communing with the Lord, yet he carefully maintained godly standards. It made little sense, but he couldn't seem to walk another path. His upbringing by Christian parents had marked him.

By the time the buckboard pulled in front of Rosie's Café and Theo set the brake, dusk—helped along by the imminent storm—had settled over the island, and the whipping wind had nearly dried Pearson's clothes. To dry his thick, matted hair would require a bench close to Rosie's glowing hearth.

Welcoming light from the window drew them past the double doors. Pearson relished the familiar comfort of babbling voices and soft laughter, the mingled odors of good food and men who smelled of the sea. Shouts of greeting melted the lead from his careworn heart. Grinning, he shook hands all around, returning warm smiles and hearty pats on the back.

"What foul breeze blew your ugly mug across the bay?" Cookie cried over the noise. Shoving through the kitchen door, the ruddy-cheeked cook poured a steaming cup of oily coffee from a blackened pot on the counter and slid it across to Pearson. "And after we'd set our hearts on never seeing you again."

The gathered circle of men hooted, pounding on the bar until the dishes rattled.

"I never meant to come, that's for sure." Pearson pinched the man's scruffy cheek. "But I couldn't get your handsome face out of my mind."

The room erupted in catcalls and gales of laughter.

Cool fingers tightened around Pearson's arm. "What about my face?" Pearl, Rosie's daughter, had slipped in from the kitchen and pressed against him, the smell of her hair and curve of her neck headier than any sip of ale. Her sultry gaze lingered on his arm while she caressed the swell of his muscle. Pearson cleared his throat, and she pulled her eyes to his, bold appreciation flickering in their depths. "Did you think of me while you were gone?" A slow smile tilted the corners of her plump, inviting mouth.

"You know I did." He lowered his voice. "Almost every day."

She pouted her lips. "Almost?"

Beaming, he winked at her mother who had come to stand behind her. "The other days were taken with thoughts of my own sweet Rosie." He held out his arms to the portly older woman. "Come to me, vixen."

Startled, Pearl glanced over her shoulder, stepping aside as Rosie coolly slid into her place.

"Don't fret, little Pearl," Theo teased, snaking his long arm around her shoulders. "I promise to think of you every minute."

"A likely pledge, Theo Bernardi. You'll think of me alongside ten other girls." She flashed him a shy smile, but her longing gaze slid to Pearson.

Rosie held Pearson's face with both hands, planting a kiss on his lips. "What wretched folly kept you from us, darlin'?" she demanded, her booming voice rattling the rafters. "The island mourns in your absence." She tilted her head and winked. "And so does this old woman."

He grinned. "You know me, Rosie. I've been chasing my fortune to the four corners."

"The four corners of Galveston, maybe," one of the laughing men shouted to the room. "We're stuck with the great adventurer while Lafitte's gold has a hook set in him." Nodding at Theo, he gave Pearson a wicked grin. "Since your friend here hasn't offered to buy a round of drinks, I'm thinking old Jean outsmarted you again."

Pearson cringed, and a blush warmed his neck. Despite his secrecy, word had gotten out that he'd come home chasing another blind lead. Worse, that he'd be slinking off again in defeat. He flashed a look at Theo, who shrugged and shook his head.

"Don't bother denying what I saw with my own eyes, matey," the fellow pressed. "There's only one reason you'd pitch that bobbing cork of yours onto rough seas." He flashed a wicked grin. "And no mistaking the thatch of seaweed on your head, not even from a distance."

The man's companion lifted a strand of Pearson's hair. "Looks more like tentacles to me. With all the time he's spent in water, the lad's more sea beast than man."

Rosie's glare wiped the smirks from his tormentor's faces. Swiveling on their bar stools, they rounded chastened shoulders over their mugs.

Lifting her chin, she graced Pearson with a sunny smile. "Don't mind those two simpletons. They still think the earth is flat. Grab your coffee, and come take your ease by the fire." Hooking her arm through his, she led him to a table near the hearth.

Sliding onto a bench worn smooth by the backsides of faithful patrons, Pearson scrubbed his weary eyes with calloused palms. "Trouble is, the simpletons called it right. I'm a dolt to keep chasing an old fable. There's no hidden treasure on this island."

Rosie and Theo's jaws dropped as if wired by a single hinge.

Falling into a seat across from Pearson, Rosie gaped. "I never expected those words to come out of your mouth."

"Me either." Theo plopped into a chair next to her. "What's gotten into you?"

Pearson gripped his cup to still his shaking hands. "They're feeling more and more like the truth."

"Nonsense, dear boy. You just need something else to think about for a while. Something to whet your appetite. . .stir your sense of adventure." A spark of mischief lit the depths of her eyes. Lurching forward, she held up a knobby finger. "And I know just the thing."

Twisting to search the café, Rosie's roving gaze jerked to a stop on an elderly stranger hunched over an empty mug at the end of the bar.

"Hoy, mister!" She whistled and waved her arm.

The man's head came up and he frowned. Slowly, warily, he stole a peek over his shoulder.

"I'm talking to you," she called.

His throat rose and fell, and he pointed at his chest.

Rosie nodded. "That's right. Come over here, please. We'd like to speak to you."

He slid off the stool, nearly toppling, and shuffled across the room. Five feet shy of the table, he stopped and licked his thin lips, so dry they were cracked and white. His darting gaze swept Pearson and Theo, but the need driving him proved stronger than his fear. Venturing two steps closer, he pleaded with his eyes. "Miss Rosie. . .you reckon you might allow me one more on the tab?" His trembling fingers fiddled at his pockets. "I've come up a little short this week." His mouth strained at a smile. "Well, I never been tall, truth be told. What I mean to say is my thirst stretched farther than my earnings this month."

Rosie's round face softened. "I have a better idea. Pull that chair around, and we'll serve you a bite to eat on the house." Resting her arm on the back of the bench, she scanned the room for Pearl. Spying her, she beckoned. "Honey, dish up a bowl of beef stew for our friend here, with a big slice of sourdough bread."

Pearl stirred from her thoughts and slunk toward the kitchen.

Halfway there, Cookie waved her toward three newcomers sidling up to the bar. "Wait on them fellows first, gal, while I ladle the stew."

"On second thought," Rosie called, wiggling four fingers in his direction, "bring a round for the table."

"Coming up, boss," he said, spooning meat and potatoes into crockery bowls.

The old sailor's weathered face relaxed. "Well, thank you, ma'am. Don't mind if I do." A new spring in his step, he dragged up a slatted chair and straddled it, crossing his wrists atop the back. "That's mighty nice of you folks."

Rosie leaned across the table, her mischievous smile in place. "I want you to tell these gents the story you told me last night."

He tugged his anxious gaze from Pearl, who watched from the bar as she filled tall glasses with frothy ale. His brows drew to a knot. "Story?"

"You know," Rosie offered, "the sunken steamboat?"

He withdrew to arm's length, his eyes wary. "I never said nothing about a steamer."

"Sure you did. The *Mary* or *Tillie*, or some such thing. She went down carrying a fortune in gold."

Evidently, when he'd shared the tale with Rosie, his pockets had jingled with plenty of coin to quench his thirst. Whatever he'd told her, he hadn't meant to let slip. Batting bleary eyes, he gnawed his bottom lip. "You've got the wrong man," he finally blurted. "I don't know anything."

She touched his trembling hand. "It's all right. These fellows are friends of mine."

He tucked his chin and gave a firm shake of his head.

Pearl finished her appointed task then snatched the heavy tray from the counter and hoisted it over one shoulder. Dodging tables and grasping, leering men, she wove toward them.

Straightening, Rosie took the tray from her and slid it under the old man's nose. Lifting a bowl, she handed it to him with a smile. "There we go. Nice and hot."

Brightening, he lifted his head and beamed. "Much obliged, ma'am."

Pearl stood watching Pearson, her hands twisting her white apron to knots. "I made a fresh pot of coffee for you." She pointed at the steaming cup on the tray. "I hope it's strong enough."

Pearson laced his fingers behind his head and shot her a playful wink. "If you made it, I'm sure it's fine."

Blushing, she flitted away.

Rosie's careful gaze trailed her daughter to the bar. "Sorry, Pearson," she muttered over her shoulder. "She's so blinded by how she feels, she can't see you don't feel the same."

Pearson gripped her shoulder. "It's all right, Rosie. I don't mind."

She sighed. "I need a good man to marry her and take her out of here. She's better suited to raising babies than drawing ale."

Rosie watched Pearl until she disappeared inside the kitchen. Propping her arms on the table, she jutted her chin at the old man. "Now then. . .about that shipwreck." Her finger shot forward, pointing at him. "I remember now. You called her the *Mittie.*" She slapped the wobbly table. "The *Mittie Stephens.*"

He flinched and drew up his shoulders. "Have a heart, Miss Rosie. I don't know much about that old legend. Just an ear-load of wayfarer's drivel."

Rosie patted his trembling hand. "Go on, now. Tell my friends what you told me."

Releasing a weary sigh, he picked up his spoon and nodded. "If you say so, ma'am."

Details emerged with each careful bite of the hearty dish. As his stew cooled and the bowl emptied, he warmed to the story with the bright-eyed eagerness born of a worthy tale. Darkness settled over the room as he spoke, broken only by distant flashes of lightning outside and the dim, flickering candles burning in blackened jars.

Thunder boomed overhead, rattling the windowpanes. A brilliant flash exposed startled faces, followed by a violent, piercing crash as lightning struck something close by. A few of Rosie's patrons hustled for the door to seek another port in the storm.

A handful of regulars, with no better place to be, found their way to the table, curiosity getting the best of them as the old fellow's hushed voice carried across the room.

He spoke of a "lost world" in the northeastern reaches of Texas and the dreadful fate of a doomed side-wheeler steamboat. "February, it was, in 1869. The *Mittie Stephens* left Shreveport with her guards flat in the water."

"What's that mean?" Rosie whispered hoarsely.

"A full load," Theo explained, his spoon clanking. Oblivious to the patrons hanging on the old sailor's words, he chased dregs of brown gravy around his bowl.

The old man nodded. "Under command of Captain H. Kellogg, the ship pulled away from the Commerce Street wharf with her cargo, forty-three passengers, and sixty-six crewmen. Stacked on board were two hundred seventy-some bales of hay, a dozen kegs of gunpowder, and enough gold to make payroll for the Reconstruction troops in Jefferson. Now mind you"—one bushy brow peaked as he stared around the circle of rapt faces—"this shipment of hay, stacked four tiers deep on the guards, weren't just any old bales."

Pearson swallowed a sip of his coffee, the liquid hot and bitter all the way down. "What was so different?"

"Government issue, that's what. The stuff was parched as powder on account of being kiln dried."

"I've heard of this," Theo said. "They dry the hay to fight off mold."

The old boy nodded. "The water was high that night, so it was clear sailing through the channel on Caddo Lake. At the midnight hour, just below Swanson's Landing, a steersman alerted the pilot that he'd caught a whiff of smoke. Sure enough, they hadn't properly snuffed the torch baskets on the bow before setting sail. The wind lifted sparks from the basket, carrying them across to the dry bales. They went up as if doused with coal oil. The crew kept their wits about them and tossed the gunpowder overboard, but it was too late."

He leaned across the table, his haggard face ghoulish above the flickering candle. "Better than sixty folks lost their lives that fateful night. Some because they couldn't swim but most because they plain lost their bearings." He shook his head. "Blinded by the flames, the poor souls swam away from the bank. Turns out the *Mittie* was less than twenty feet from shore. She ran aground with her cargo of gold and sank into Caddo's murky depths." He shuddered then grew silent, his haunted eyes staring into the blazing hearth.

"And?" Rosie prompted.

Without warning, his chin sank to his chest and his bottom lip sagged.

Rosie clutched his bony shoulder and shook him awake. "Is that it? Nothing else about the gold?"

Jerking upright, he fixed her with bloodshot eyes. "I've blabbered all I know, though I'm sure there's more to tell." He yawned and wiped his slack mouth on his sleeve. "I'm bone-weary, Miss Rosie. Can't go no more. Ain't found a place to sleep since I left my ship." Folding his arms for pillows, he slumped to the table, resting his grizzled head.

Compassion softened her features. "Poor, wretched thing, you have now." Signaling Cookie, she gave him instructions to help the fellow to the storeroom.

Towering over him, Cookie sighed. "He's playing you for a mark, Rosie. You should charge him rent. He spends more time on free cots than he does at sea."

Rosie tilted her face up to him. "I'm surprised at you, Cookie. Where's your Christian charity?"

"Christian charity?" He snorted. "He should be keelhauled."

She frowned. "I won't turn away a man in need."

"Suit yourself, but don't expect him to appreciate it none. And while you're at it, forget any notion of collecting his tab. You won't see a nickel." He circled the fellow's chest with both arms and hauled him to his feet. "Toe the mark, you old beggar. No night watches for you."

They took a few shuffling steps before the man's drooping head lolled to the side. "There's a fellow on Caddo Lake," he said, his voice surprisingly strong for a bone-weary man. "An old fishing guide they call Catfish John. Ask for him around Marshall, Texas."

"Yes?" Theo said. "What about him?"

"Find him. He can tell you anything you want to know about the *Mittie*." He and Cookie disappeared beneath the low archway.

Rosie turned twinkling eyes on Pearson. "Well then?"

He shrugged. "Well, what?"

"It's a good lead. Why aren't you running out the door to book passage on a northbound train?"

Pearson stifled a grin and winked at the spellbound circle of men. "Sorry, honey, but he's not the first drunken sailor with a far-fetched yarn." He hooked his thumb toward the mainland. "There's a tale like his in every port of call."

Dazed, she shook her head. "No, sir. Not like this one. I sense he's telling the truth."

Pearson laughed softly. "Oh, he is. . .the truth as he believes it to be."

Rosie slapped the varnished table so hard, coffee sloshed over the rim of his cup. "How can you treat this so lightly? When first he told it to me, I wanted to round up some men and go search for the *Mittie* myself."

Pearson calmly wiped up the spill with his napkin and took a slow swig of the tepid brew. "I understand your passion, little Rosie. I used to get worked up about these old legends myself. After a while you get a feel for what's real"—he nodded toward the raspy snores coming from the back room—"and what isn't." He shot the uninvited spectators an amused glance. "Right, boys?"

Several grinned and nodded. A couple patted Rosie affectionately on the shoulder. Others shared winks and knowing glances with Pearson before drifting to the bar, their murmuring voices sprinkled with good-natured laughter.

She stared after them with blazing eyes.

Pearson slid his chair around to make room to stretch out his legs. With a wide yawn, he fisted his hands and kneaded his temples. "Are you ready to take me back to your place, Theo? I'm so tired I won't mind your lumpy couch." He grinned and winked at Rosie. "Or the musty quilt he pulled out of mothballs just for me."

Stirring from her pout, she blinked at Pearson. "Still can't bear the thought of staying in your house, honey?"

Not willing to talk about his parents' big house on Broadway Street, he shook his head.

"Well, that's all right." She patted his hand. "There's no need to suffer Theo's distorted idea of hospitality. We have the spare room upstairs." She pointed with her chin. "It's not much, but it's clean. . .and free of lumps and moths."

Pearson's stomach tightened the way it did only while on the island. The prospect of sitting upstairs alone with his thoughts seemed far less appealing than a tattered blanket. He squeezed Rosie's hand. "I appreciate the offer, sweetheart. I really do." He ducked his head at Theo. "But I'll stay with my old friend there, so his feelings won't be hurt. I hate to see a grown man cry."

Stepping gingerly over his booted feet, Pearl stopped in front of him, her crossed arms hugging her chest. "Are you sure, Pearson? It's a nice little room, and the windows face the ocean. You'd wake up to a beautiful sunrise." Blushing, she reached to fiddle with her apron again. "I washed and ironed the curtains myself." She cleared her throat. "They're yellow."

An uncomfortable silence settled like dew.

Pearl's bright flush deepened, and she lowered her lashes.

"It's no use, honey," Rosie said, coming to her rescue. "You know how stubborn men are, and I'd say his mind is made." Grunting from the effort, she pushed up and stood behind Pearson, gathering long strands of hair off his shoulders. "Do you have any plans to cut this moldy mess?" She tugged hard on a lock. "I've seen sheep with less matted wool."

Laughing, he straightened in his chair. "Speaking of hurting a man's feelings. . ."

She pulled his head back and stared upside down at his face. "There are topics I dare to raise out of love"—she scowled at the two scoundrels who were teasing him before—"and those I won't tolerate from anyone else." She grinned. "But you have to admit it's a peculiar mess."

Theo snickered. "His hair has always twisted into knots, and people have always taunted him. That's how he learned to fight like a badger."

Rosie held out a snakelike strand and tried to pull it straight. "You couldn't drag a rake through this. How do you comb it?"

Pearson preened. "Go on and scoff, but in your hands you hold the fruit of careful and deliberate neglect."

They shared a hearty laugh, except for Pearl. Casting a shy glance at Pearson, she frowned. "I think your hair is nice. It suits you."

Holding her gaze, he gave her a warm smile. "Thank you, Pearl."

Grinning like an unbalanced dolt, Theo stood and pulled Pearson from his chair. "Let's get you home so you can wash up. Lumpy or not, you can't sleep on my sofa without a soak in the tub. You stink."

Pearson sniffed his shirtsleeve. "It's not so bad. I smell better than your quilt."

Theo tugged him toward the door. "Not unless it reeks of sunbaked codfish." He grimaced. "Or the stench of a rotted octopus."

Rosie's high-pitched cackle followed them out the door.

The storm had passed, leaving a light drizzle behind and trailing dark, wispy clouds across the moon. The dim glow of the streetlamp lit their path to the wagon and the poor, wilted horse standing in a puddle of rainwater.

Stopping short of the rig, Theo slapped his forehead and groaned. "Stupido! I forgot about him."

"So did I," Pearson said. "Maybe he'll forgive us if we get him to the barn and rub him down. If not, a few oats might do the trick. A little love and care goes a long way."

Tittering like a child again, Theo nudged him. "I think Pearl would like to give you a bit of loving care. With very little encouragement, she'd have you broken and stabled before you could whinny."

Pearson balled his fist and delivered a sound blow to Theo's arm. "That's why I won't be encouraging her. I'm not ready to be gentled." He shuffled sideways to dodge the return punch. "Besides, when I'm ready to be strapped to the feed bag, I'm not looking for Pearl's brand of oats."

"Particular, aren't you? Exactly what are you looking for?"

Grabbing the wagon post, Pearson tensed to pull up on the seat. "I suppose I'll know when I see her."

Theo caught his arm before he could board. "How long will it take you to pack for East Texas?"

Pearson stifled a grin. "I never unpack my bags in Galveston. You know that."

"So when are you leaving?"

"When are *we* leaving is the question." He gripped Theo's shoulder. "I want you to go with me."

Theo's beaming face glowed in the streetlight. "I've been waiting for you to ask. Let's go!"

Pearson chuckled. "Not so fast, boy. The *Mittie*'s been at the bottom of Caddo Lake for thirty-six years. She'll be there in a few more months."

"Why waste time?"

"It's the dead of winter, Theo. Too cold to dive. Besides, we need supplies. Special gear. Let me get back to Houston and pull a plan together. I'll wire you when I'm ready to leave."

"How long?"

Scratching his sandy scalp, Pearson ticked off the facts in his head. "Well. . .it's mid-December, isn't it?"

Theo chuckled. "You don't know?"

"It's hard to keep track of the date when you're riding the Gulf in a dinghy."

Theo patted his shoulder. "Point made. It's December 15th, to be exact. Nearly Christmastime."

Pearson nodded. "Then I say we slow down and enjoy the holidays. Let the weather warm up a tad. Come spring, plan to celebrate my birthday in East Texas."

"End of April?" Theo's voice cracked with excitement. "Sounds right to me."

Pearson searched his eager face. "So it's settled? You're on board?"

Hitching up his pants, Theo frowned. "Try and stop me. What town did the old man mention before? The place where we'll find Catfish John?"

"He said Marshall." Staring toward the mainland, Pearson's blood surged hot and fast in his veins. A familiar pull in his chest urged him toward the lure of treasure. "We'll find what we need in Marshall, Texas."

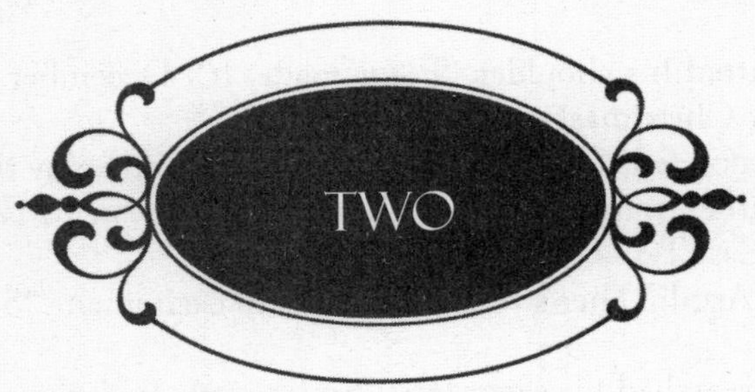

TWO

Canton, Mississippi, March 1905

Addie McRae clutched the letter to her heart with both hands. The scent of lavender wafted up from the page and teased her nose, but the smell of freedom flared her nostrils. Determination surged, and excitement gripped her chest. Placing the delicate stationery onto her desk, she smoothed the creases from the dainty bluebonnet border and stared hard at the graceful scrawl.

> *Therefore, with the tragic demise of my young nephew and his wife, I will soon find myself in dire need of a reliable governess for my new charge, their only son, Cedric. As you know, our Ceddy is an unusual child and will need special handling. My fervent prayer is that you will arrange for your lovely granddaughter to come to our aide. If this isn't possible, perhaps you know of a suitable girl of a sober and responsible character to come in her stead. In my hour of need, my thoughts turned to you, Thomas Moony. Might you help an old friend?*

Miss Priscilla Whitfield of Texas had written of her urgent need for a governess to Addie's dearest companion, Hope Moony, the granddaughter of Canton's distinguished doctor. Hope's recent engagement forced her to decline, so Dr. Moony passed the offer to Addie with a promise to recommend her for the position. From the first reading, Addie felt a sense of destiny spark in her veins.

Movement at the edge of the garden drew her eye. The abandoned kittens, a little calico and her tabby brother, crouched near the woods, watching her.

Placing the letter beside her on the bench, she wriggled her fingers close to the ground.

The kittens launched themselves past the azaleas and over the bricks lining the flower bed, tumbling over each other in their haste. Tiny claws extended, they climbed her skirt and huddled in the folds of her dress, lapping the saucer of cream she held ready. Eyes slanted in bliss, they took turns arching their bony backs toward her caress.

Addie smiled. Only weeks ago, they'd darted away each time she stepped out the door. After days of baiting them, placing bits of food a little closer each time, they'd come as near as the hem of her dress, but no farther—until the evening she'd offered bits of leftover fish from supper. Unable to resist such a tempting treat, they'd conquered their fear and crawled into her lap to eat.

The pair shared the final drop of cream in the dish then curled together, diligently cleaning their whiskered mouths on furled paws.

Addie set the empty saucer aside and took up the troubling letter. Spreading her slender fingers over the flowing script, she swallowed the lump rising in her throat. The idea of a child so brutally torn from the safety of his mother's arms, rendered an orphan by one fateful turn of events, brought her to tears. A little one left to fend for himself without the guidance and tender care of his parents seemed a tragic and lonely soul.

She glanced at the helpless creatures in her lap, waifs and strays themselves. Their plight and the boy's rose in stark contrast to her own dilemma. By comparison, struggling against the wishes of overprotective parents was infinitely better than not having them at all.

She smoothed her knuckle over the boy's name on the page. "I'm deeply sorry for your loss, dear Ceddy. Poor little tyke."

Miss Whitfield wrote that her nephew's son was unusual. Despite any sort of "special handling" he might need, Addie had never met a child who didn't respond to love.

Recalling the impish youngsters she'd encountered as a governess, she nodded thoughtfully. With a gentle hand and understanding heart, she'd taught all of them to trust her and eventually brought them into line. Cedric Whitfield would be no different.

The back door opened, and the housemaid's strident voice shrilled her name.

Addie blinked away the moisture in her eyes and spun. "Yes, Dicey?"

Chin raised, Dicey scanned the garden until her gaze fell on Addie, sitting in her favorite spot on the bench under the wicker arbor. "Breakfast, Miss Addie. Drop them flea-ridden critters and come inside. Yo' sistahs already gathered at the table, and yo' folks say hurry. They hungry."

"Tell them I'll be right along."

"All right now. . .but don't make me be tellin' no lies."

Before the screen clicked shut at Dicey's back, Addie returned the letter to its envelope and tucked it deep inside the pocket of her skirt. She'd carry it to breakfast and allow Miss Whitfield herself to sway them. The woman's expensive stationery and lovely handwriting would help drive home her impassioned plea, but reading firsthand of Ceddy's plight would go a long way in persuading them.

Addie would need all the help she could get.

Rousting the drowsy kittens, she deposited them at her feet. The tabby mewed in protest, and the calico stole a peek with one slanted eye. Sluggish from full bellies, they snuggled on the spot and fell straight back to sleep. Steeling her spine, Addie arose and crossed the yard to the steps.

At the end of the hall, she paused to eavesdrop on the family's conversation, hoping to assess the mood. By the sound of Father's gentle teasing and Mother's gleeful laughter, it appeared to be the perfect morning to state her intentions. Closing her eyes, she imagined their reactions—her horrified gasp, his disbelieving stare—when she told them she planned to move to Texas. Gathering her skirts along with her courage, she breezed around the corner.

"Here she is," Father announced, looking up from his breakfast. "Hurry and pass the corn cakes, Carrie Beth, before Addie catches sight of them." He grinned and winked at Mother. "Take some for yourself, Mariah, if you plan to have any. Once your eldest daughter gets a taste of corn cakes, it's 'Katy, bar the door.' "

Carrie and the twins, Father's preferred audience when it came to tormenting Addie, tittered like a nest of baby mockingbirds.

"I like corn cakes, too, Papa," Marti crowed, crossing her arms.

Mattie stuck out her bottom lip. "Well, so do I!"

Father grinned at his matched set of pouting little girls. "And you shall have some, my doves. I'll see to it Addie shares."

"Hush, Tiller McRae," Mother said. "There's plenty to go around. I baked extra this morning."

Addie leaned to kiss his cheek, noticing for the first time the strands of silver hair mingled with the rusty red of his sideburns. "What's this?" She fingered the smattering of gray. "Heavens, it can't be. My handsome father, losing the battle with time?"

His big hand closed over hers. "Time isn't turning my hair, Addie Viola. Fretting over your constant stream of suitors is to blame for bleaching it white."

Mother liked to boast that she'd borrowed Addie's forename from Adelina Patti, highly acclaimed opera singer. The source of Addie's middle name made her prouder. Viola Ashmore Jones was Addie's old governess and Mother's longtime companion, and Addie loved her dearly. Rendered feeble by age, poor Miss Vee seldom made it to breakfast these days.

Addie feigned shock. "What's the harm in a few suitors? A girl has to weigh her options."

Father squeezed her fingers, drawing them to his lips for a kiss. "None of the addlepated options I've chased from the porch lately are good enough for you. I'd lock you in your room until your curls grayed if I thought it would do any good."

Addie laughed, but her stomach lurched. Time to steer him to less troublesome ground. "You'd best douse your temples with Miss Vee's henna if you want to keep up with your wife." Pressing her face close to his, she pointed across the table. "Look at Mother, as young and lovely as ever. She could pass for my sister."

Father huffed. "A stinging injustice, considering she worries over you girls more than I do."

Mother blushed and ducked her head. "My Indian ancestry keeps me youthful. The Choctaw age quite gracefully."

Smiling, Father winked at her. "You're only half Indian, Mariah. The British half should have the manners to grow old alongside her husband." He tugged on Addie's arm, pulling her from behind him. "Sit down so I can ask God's blessing on our food." He chuckled.

"Especially these poor corn cakes. They're not long for this world."

Addie's giggle echoed back at her from around the breakfast table. Grinning at her sisters, she folded her hands and slipped off her shoes. She may as well make herself comfortable. Most of Father's prayers turned to long-winded chats with God.

That morning proved no different. His heartfelt pleas touched on each of them in turn, asking protection and direction for each life. When he reached Addie's name, thanking the Lord for his dutiful daughter, she squirmed in her chair.

Longing to blurt her news, she held herself in check. He'd be more receptive with a bellyful of Dicey's ham, doused with a ladle of redeye gravy.

After a heartfelt "Amen," Father shook out his napkin and smoothed it on his lap. He finished the first half of his breakfast in silence, except for quiet murmurs of appreciation for Mother's biscuits and grunts of approval for the meal in general. Her father loved to eat as well as any gentleman of the South and kept his zeal for Southern cooking finely tuned. Stabbing a forkful of ham, he tilted his chin in Addie's direction. "What's on your dance card for today, little miss?"

The endearment irked a bit. Addie might be short in stature and small-boned, but he needn't treat her like a child. "I thought I'd run into town for a spell." *To ask Dr. Moony to wire Miss Whitfield of my decision to accept—just as soon as I've broken the news.*

"What manner of mischief are you and Hope planning for our townsfolk?" Father leaned across the table and winked. "And how gravely will it impact my wallet?"

Addie's heart stirred with pride. Silver hair and outrageous appetite aside, she had the handsomest father in all of Mississippi. "Mischief indeed." Pouting her lips, she pretended to sulk. "I could stroll these streets for weeks and not find a smidgen of trouble. Canton is, without a doubt, the most boring place on earth."

Mother's fork stilled, her large brown eyes lifting to meet Addie's. "Do we need to discuss your values, Adelina? When did safe and respectable become boring?"

Since the beginning of time, at least, but it wouldn't be prudent to say so. "How's Miss Vee this morning?" she asked, wisely changing the subject.

"Feeling frail, poor old love. Her joints pain her worse every year."

Father chuckled. "If you believe half her complaints, she'll be joining

Otis in eternal rest any day now."

"Was Otis Miss Vee's husband?" Carrie asked.

"No, dear," their mother said. "Miss Vee wed Tobias Jones, God rest his soul. Dear departed Otis was Papa's closest friend. Both men passed on before you were born."

Turning, she touched Addie's arm. "I hope you'll duck in on Miss Vee before you leave for town. You always seem to cheer her."

Addie nodded. "Yes, ma'am, I will." She cleared her throat. "First, there's something I'd like you both to see." She pulled the envelope from her pocket and handed it to her father.

Creases formed between his brows, but he pulled his spectacles from his vest pocket and unfolded the letter.

The onionskin paper was so thin, Addie read along with him, her eyes following the backward letters across the page.

He finished and handed the missive across the table to Mother. As she read, he reached for Addie's hand. "I know how this must feel, sugar. It'll be hard to manage without young Hope around." He smiled softly. "We'll miss her, too, considering she's been underfoot since the age of ten. She's practically part of the family."

Taking off his glasses, he tucked them away. "Take comfort in knowing she's providing a worthy service."

"Poor little boy." Wiping her eyes, Mother placed the letter on the table. "I don't understand, Addie. How can Hope consider the offer when she's getting married soon?" She frowned. "Will her young man accompany her to Texas?"

Addie clenched her fists in her lap. The time had come. "Hope won't be accepting the position." She swallowed hard. "I will."

Stunned silence pressed her down in her chair. Wide-eyed, she watched the looks that passed between her parents.

His said, *"Here we go again."*

Hers said, *"Relax, I can handle this."*

Tightening her lips, Addie gathered her resolve. *I won't be handled. I simply won't!*

"Well?" she demanded. "Won't one of you say something?"

Mother placed her hand over the folded sheet of stationery, as if she couldn't bear to look at it. "Who gave you this letter, Addie?"

She jutted her chin. "Dr. Moony."

Father's mouth tightened. "Wait until I see Thomas Moony in town. . ."

"Now, Tiller," Mother soothed. "It's not his fault." Tears still glistening in her soulful eyes, she turned the force of them on Addie. "I feel for this poor orphaned child, dear girl, but my first concern is for you. With all the children in Mississippi, you can't find a position closer to home?" A tiny frown wrinkled her brow. "*Texas*, Addie. Do you know how far away that is?"

Addie sighed. "I didn't look for this opportunity, Mother. It fell into my lap. And I don't want another position. I want this one." Hearing a whine in her voice, she cringed. It wouldn't do to act like the child they thought her to be.

She sat forward and tried again. "I won't shrivel by degrees in Canton with never a chance to see the world. I can't settle for a loveless marriage like half the girls in town, groomed to live a dutiful life while pretending to be ignorant of intellectual opinion. I need to prove I'm capable of making a decision besides which day of the week should be washday." The final impassioned word squeaked out on her last bit of air. Drawing a fresh breath through her nose, she glared. "Surely God gifted me with talent beyond how to mend socks and maintain an organized pantry."

Her mother lowered her head. "Tending a family to the best of your ability is a gift of God, too. One that I treasure."

Her heated stand doused with guilt, Addie's hand flew to her mouth. "Oh Mother, I didn't mean to imply—"

Father cleared his throat. "We'll let this offer pass, Addie. There will be others, I'm sure."

Lurching to her feet, Addie strode to the door and spun. "I would never deliberately defy you, Father, but I feel led of God to go. I'm not asking your permission. I'm announcing my intentions."

Speechless for several seconds, Father closed his startled mouth and wagged a finger in Mother's direction. "This is your fault, Mariah Bell McRae. She inherited your willful spirit."

Mother sat back in her chair and calmly placed her napkin beside her plate. "Caroline, Martha, Matilda, go to your rooms."

Carrie, Marti, and Mattie likely couldn't understand the reason for the breakfast-hour skirmish, but the use of their proper names sent them scrambling. Carrie turned back long enough to make a face at Addie and snatch a slice of jellied toast.

Wincing, Addie glanced at her mother, bracing for a glimpse

of her fiery temper.

Respect shone from her dark eyes instead. She touched Father's arm. "The words sting because they're coming from Adelina. You look at her heart-shaped face and delicate features and see your five-year-old daughter. She's a woman now, Tiller. One who's been more than patient with us." She reached across and patted his hand. "It's time to let our little bird fly."

Addie bit her trembling lip and shot her mother a grateful smile.

Father steepled his hands on the table and sighed. "I get the distinct feeling that I'm outflanked." He quirked his mouth to the side. "I guess this means you're bound for Texas?"

Squealing, she crossed the room and hugged him around the neck. "You won't be sorry. I promise."

Standing, he gripped her shoulders. "Don't be so sure. I already regret my decision. And on one point I won't compromise. You can't leave until after your birthday. Otherwise, you'll break your father's heart."

"But sir, my birthday is over a month away."

Mother stood, her arm circling Addie's waist. "We'll write Miss Whitfield of your intention to interview. If the position is filled by the end of April, it wasn't meant to be."

Addie bit her bottom lip. She didn't view it the same way, but after the concession her parents had made, it wouldn't be fair to say so. Excitement bubbling in her chest, she turned to go. "I'll run upstairs now and write her when to expect me."

Father caught her wrist and hauled her back. "Not so fast, young lady." His green-eyed gaze searched her face. "Sometimes, with the best of intentions, we misread God's voice. That said, your mother will be traveling with you to meet your Miss Whitfield. If she doesn't approve of the arrangement, you'll feel led of God to take the next train home. Is that clear?"

Addie lowered her head and nodded. "Quite."

Mother held out the letter. "You'd better take this, honey. You may need it."

"One second," Father said, snatching the envelope. "I want to see exactly where my womenfolk are going." He stared at the return address then lifted puzzled eyes. "I've never heard of this place, Addie. Where in blazes is Marshall, Texas?"

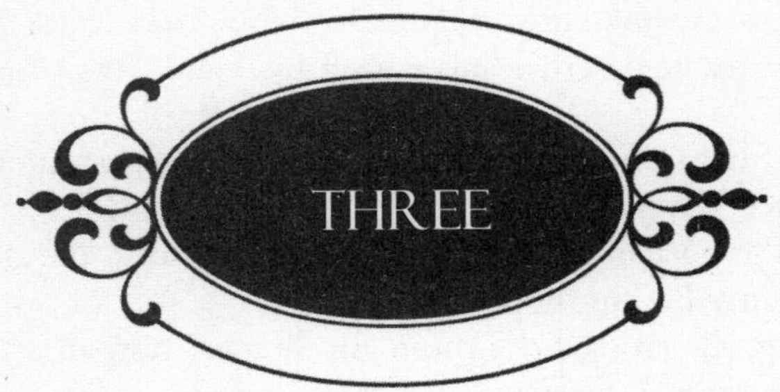

THREE

Marshall, Texas, April 1905

Ceddy trudged up the walkway to Aunt Priscilla's two-story house. Clinging to Auntie Jane's skirt, he counted the soaring white columns stretching from the porch to the rooftop like bars on a giant cage. *One, two, three, four* across the front. He couldn't see those extending around the sides of the house, but he counted them from memory. *Five, six, seven* on one side. *Eight, nine, ten* on the other.

The door swung open before they reached it, and Aunt Priscilla appeared on the stoop. It wasn't right. Wasn't right. Lilah should've answered, wearing her white ruffled cap.

"Cedric, my dear child, how tall you've grown! You're as brown as pork pie, precious." She leaned close and smoothed his hair the way she'd always done with Daddy. The skin of her face sagged, and her breath reeked of lemon tea.

He stiffened and flapped his hands, grunted, and spun away.

She sighed and stood up straight. "Hello, Jane. So nice to see you again. I suppose some things never change, do they?"

"Ever so sorry, Priscilla," Auntie Jane said. "He's in a right foul mood. Thoroughly knackered, I suppose."

"Think nothing of it. I'm used to him. You must be exhausted as well."

"That I am. It's an endless trip across the Atlantic. Days of nothing but ocean on all sides. It's enough to drive you quite insane after a time."

"Yes, it's maddening," Aunt Priss murmured. "Before the dawn of transatlantic steamers, it took months to cross. You can't imagine the ordeal."

Aunt Jane moaned. "I'd perish."

"I'm surprised you didn't, poor thing."

The driver struggled up the walkway with two bulky trunks then returned to the buggy to fetch two more. "Where shall I put these, ma'am?"

"Heavens!" Aunt Priss cried. "Are they yours, Jane?"

She shook her head and pointed at a small green case. "I won't be staying that long. I have to be back in England soon or Richard will summon King Edward's Guard."

Aunt Priss's skirt swished as she spun toward the luggage. "Then whose. . ."

"Those are Ceddy's things."

"All of this for one small boy?" Her voice grew shrill at the end.

Ceddy cowered and covered his ears.

"I'm afraid so. I had the man swing by my sister's house to pack the boy's belongings, as you requested. You can't imagine the odd assortment of toys, books, and such. I tried persuading him to leave most of it behind, but he fell into such a panic, I gave in."

Auntie continued talking as Aunt Priscilla herded them inside the great hall, their footsteps echoing overhead. "He became most unreasonable about a collection of rocks and stones." She waved her hand at the trunks as the driver carried them over the threshold. "They weighed us down until I feared the poor horse might collapse."

"I wish you'd sent for my carriage, Jane."

Auntie waved her hand. "There was no need to trouble you. Ceddy and I have traversed the African continent." Her laugh was like jangling bells. "Mostly on foot. Traveling from the station required far less effort." She lowered her voice. "At least there are no *lions* in Marshall."

Aunt Priss gasped. "You can't be serious! You'll have to tell me all about it once you're settled."

Lilah hurried down the hall and bent to hug Ceddy, her smiling cheeks smooth and dark. "How you, Little Man?" she whispered in his ear. "I'm mighty pleased you here. We gon' have us a high old time."

Ceddy pressed closer to her baked-bread smell.

Handing her shawl to Lilah, Auntie tugged off her gloves. "It's unseasonably warm in Texas, isn't it? I hardly needed my wrap."

"I wouldn't put it away just yet," Aunt Priss said, bending to help Ceddy take off his jacket. "The weather here can be quite unpredictable."

Aunt Jane glanced toward Ceddy. "Speaking of unpredictable, there are things we need to discuss about the boy. Can we talk in private?"

Aunt Priss paused with Ceddy's arm still halfway up his sleeve. "But Jane. . .there will be plenty of time for that later. Won't you have a lie-down first?"

"I'd rather not. I need to speak my piece before I can relax."

Aunt Priss blew a shaky breath. "As you wish. We can retire to the study."

Handing Lilah Ceddy's coat, she guided him into her hands. "Delilah, show the boy upstairs and entertain him for a spell. This won't take long."

Lilah shoved back the brim of her cap and smiled. "Yes'm, Miss Whitfield." She nudged Ceddy toward the stairs as the study door closed with a loud click. "Let's us go see your new bedroom, Little Man."

Ceddy frowned. His room was on North Washington Avenue from where they'd just left, not here in Aunt Priscilla's big house. Shying away, he ran his fingers along the white rail on the wall, following the smooth, shiny board to the end of the hall.

Lilah's soft footsteps trailed at his heels. "What's this, now? You don't care none to see your quarters? Well, suit yo'self, but your toys and such be there. Miss Priscilla done bought you a shiny new book. . .filled to bustin' with pictures of rainbow-colored rocks."

Spinning, Ceddy took her hand. Halfway up the staircase, the study door opened, and angry voices filled the downstairs hall.

Lilah stopped so fast she jerked Ceddy's arm.

"You're being stubborn and unreasonable, Priscilla Whitfield," Aunt Jane spat.

"I rather think *you* are, Jane. Don't you wish to honor your sister's wishes?"

"Don't bring my sister into this. Matters of earthly import can't trouble her now. This is about Ceddy's welfare." Aunt Jane's voice softened. "I'm thinking of you as well, dear lady. Do you have the faintest idea what a handful he can be? His parents shamelessly indulged the lad's whims, and it hasn't improved his behavior. You're not getting any younger, you know."

Aunt Priss huffed. "While I thank you for your concern, it's misplaced. Doddering old fool that I am, I can handle a little boy."

"Can you?" In the quiet that followed, the two words danced in Ceddy's head, bouncing, twisting, changing places until they'd lost all meaning. He counted the click of shoe heels across the floor until the door opened with a whoosh of air. "I'll take a room at the Capital Hotel. You can reach me there if you come to your senses."

"Dear Jane, is that necessary?" Aunt Priss's angry tone had eased. "You'll be far more comfortable here."

"I'm leaving tomorrow afternoon, Priscilla. Think long and hard about the choice you're making. Meanwhile, I pray to hear from you before I board the train. Afterward, it will be too late to change your mind. I won't be coming back to the States."

"Save your prayers, dear. I won't change my mind."

The door banged shut, and Ceddy tugged on Lilah's hand. With a low whistle, she squeezed his fingers then led him to the top of the stairs.

North Atlantic Ocean, April 1905

Cursing his fetid luck, Denny Currie leaned against the rail and let the brisk Atlantic wind buffet him the way life had always done. Despite months of odd jobs, pinching every farthing with grasping fingers, the run-down ship he'd managed to book would take twice as long to cross the ocean as any modern steamer, since the outdated engines still required the use of sails.

By his reckoning, he and Charlie had another week to ride the pitching, dilapidated tub before reaching New York Harbor. Another week for the ghastly boy's family to discover what he'd smuggled home in his pocket.

Denny had spent sleepless nights staring at the ceiling of his ramshackle flat, weighing the odds that the treasure might be undiscovered after so long a time. In its raw state, the big stone little resembled a diamond. Only a practiced eye would ever figure it out.

If memory served, the boy had gone to live with a dotty old aunt—a fact that increased his odds tenfold. The old girl could be using it as a paperweight and be none the wiser. After all, it had happened before.

On the banks of the Orange River, in the spring of 1866, children of Boer settlers played about with sparkling rocks picked up from the ground, tossing them aside like worthless trinkets when they were bored. A roving peddler took more than a casual glance at one of the brilliant stones then passed it along to a government mineralogist. Denny's gut-twisting quest to better himself began with the diamond rush that followed.

Since that day, he'd followed strikes across South Africa, from the Orange River to the Vaal. Griqualand. Kimberley Mine. The strike in Pretoria—his own backyard, for pity's sake.

For endless years, his weary soles had trod upon the answer to life's problems, his clumsy big feet tripping over his own destiny. Roaming the rich African soil, he'd dug, burrowed, and scoured the ground for diamond pipes until his fingers bled and muscles ached. The relentless search became obsession, aging him beyond his fifty-three years and netting him little more than frustration and dishonor.

How could there be diamonds on every farm in Africa, yet always just out of his reach?

Now a simple-minded heathen on his way to the docks in Port Elizabeth had stumbled onto a king's fortune, only the dolt and his foolish aunt hadn't realized what he held.

Blast it all! Could every blithering fool find himself a diamond? Everyone but him?

His chest swelled to draw a hopeful breath. With a clarity he'd never felt before, he sensed the earth tilting, shifting a bit of good luck his way.

Stand aside, world. It's Denny Currie's turn at last.

"Hoy, Denny!" Charlie shouted, jerking him back to the present. Clinging to his cap, the big man staggered along the rail. "I've looked everywhere for you."

"Not everywhere, have you, mate? I've been 'ere all along."

"Listen up, Den. We need to 'ave us a chin-wag."

"Go on then," Denny growled. "I'm listening." He gulped as the wind whisked the words right out of his mouth. Lowering his head, he waited for the gust to pass, but the next one plastered his thinning hair to his scalp and whipped his lashes like bloomers strung on a line.

Charlie leaned into the squall, gripping his hat with one hand and clutching his worn coat with the other. "It's cold out, boss," he yelled. "Come inside, will ya? It's important."

Denny waved him on, and they staggered along the pitching deck to the stairwell. Shielded from the bitter wind, they descended into the belly of the ship and made their way down a long corridor to the tiny, one-room cabin they shared.

Charlie led the way inside. "This is better, yeah? A man can't hear himself think out there."

"I could hear meself fine till you turned up." Wrinkling his nose, Denny glared at the dusty corners, dingy blankets, and water-stained curtain over the porthole. "Blimey, the ocean smelled less of fish."

Chuckling, Charlie plopped on the bottom bunk. "You get used to it over time."

Denny pulled out a rickety chair and perched on the seat. "There's where you're wrong, old boy. I won't ever get used to living in dustbins and fish stalls. That's why I'm bound to change my luck." He propped his ankle on his knee and leaned forward. "Now, then. . .what's all this about?"

Charlie blinked up at him. "Well, I. . ."

"Go on, Charlie. You dragged me away from fresh air to choke in this stinking hole, so where's the house on fire?"

"Ain't no house on fire." Twisting his fingers in knots, Charlie stole a guilty glance. "But our bellies may be burning once we reach land."

Denny cocked his head, staring dumbly at the squirming man. "What are you on about, mate?" His stomach coiling with dread, he stalked to the bed, shoved Charlie aside, and raised the mattress. Snatching the drawstring purse, he knew it was empty before he ever peered inside. The pleasing bulge in the bag was gone; the cloth draped his hand like a dead cat. He glared ferociously. "Where's the money?"

Charlie grimaced, drew in his shoulders, and sank deeper into the moldy mattress. "Gone."

The word thundered in Denny's head. "What happened to it?"

"Now don't go spare on me, Den. I'm awful sorry. I happened onto a game of five-card loo down in the hold. Just a couple of damp-eared deckhands, so raw I had to teach them the rules of the game." He spread his hands. "I figured to double our stakes, see? But they skinned me." He shrugged. "A streak of beginner's luck, I suppose."

Denny glared through a heated tunnel while the shabby little room whirled in a haze. They were riding the lurching barrel in the first place to save a few quid to get them to Texas. "They took you for a mug, Charlie!" he roared. "They saw you coming, you witless nit."

Confusion twisted Charlie's pasty face. "You're wrong, mate. They didn't even know—"

"Do you really think you found two sailors who couldn't play a round of loo?" Struggling to breathe, Denny jabbed at the air with his finger. "The first trick they played was on you."

Charlie frantically shook his head. "Nah, Den. I don't think so."

Denny lunged and gripped his collar, jerking him to his feet. "There's your trouble, bloke. You never think. You've got 'idiot' scrawled across your forehead. Those boys cut their teeth on dolts like you." He shoved him toward the door. "Now, go on with you. Haul your worthless bum topside and replace every shilling."

Charlie widened his eyes. "H–how am I supposed to do that?"

"Rob a few cabins. Pick some fat pockets. I don't care how you do it—just get it done."

Eyes downcast, Charlie slumped across the threshold.

Catching his arm, Denny spun him around. "You get nicked, and I'll deny ever knowing you. They can toss your rotted corpse off the starboard bow for all I'll care." He wrinkled his brows and scowled. "Mind you, it's a long swim to shore."

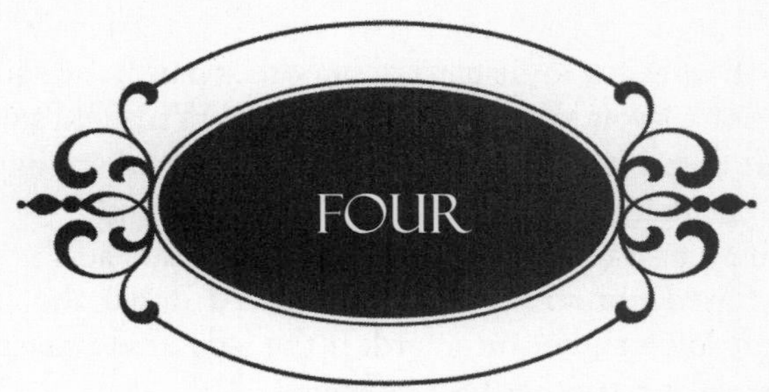

FOUR

Marshall, Texas, April 1905

Addie stepped down from the T&P railway car and took her first shaky steps on Texas soil. Nervous fingers clutching the moss-green fringe on Mother's shawl, she felt like a toddling child traipsing behind her mother on the first day of school. She couldn't pretend that if Mother weren't there, leading her wherever she went, she wouldn't be frightened out of her wits.

The porter handed down their luggage with a broad-toothed smile, tipped his cap, and moved on.

Lifting her chin, Addie stole a peek over her mother's shoulder.

The platform teemed with people of every description, all in a terrible hurry. Most ignored them, brushing blindly past in their haste. Others, all of them men, stared rudely. One young fellow, sporting pointy-toed boots and a bold smile, raised his broad-brimmed hat and winked.

Ducking her head, Addie swallowed the lump in her throat and stepped closer to Mother.

Texans are ill mannered and full of themselves, she thought—and felt like saying so.

Miss Whitfield had forwarded several points of interest about her town, neglecting to mention the improper conduct of its male residents. Marshall, known as the Gateway of Texas, was a regional education center, a major railroad hub, the cotton-marketing center for East Texas, and the first city in the state to have electricity and telegraph service—not to mention boasting a population of more than ten thousand souls.

Evidently, all ten thousand had picked that day to cluster at the depot.

Shifting the cumbersome bags to her other hand, she squirmed with irritation. "I don't know why you refused Miss Whitfield's offer to send her driver, Mother. Now we're totally at the mercy of strangers."

"We are no such thing. The Lord will be our guide."

"Can you at least tell me why you didn't wire ahead?"

Mother raised her strong chin and stared down the street. "Your father thought to catch her off guard. If the lady knew exactly when we were coming, she'd be on her best behavior."

Addie fumed inside. She had the notion there was little chance of catching a woman like Miss Whitfield at anything but her best behavior. When would her parents allow her to trust her own instincts?

Mother leaned to squint past Addie's head. "Over there, dear. The G–Ginocchio." She smiled. "An odd-sounding name for a hotel, if I've pronounced it correctly, but it looks very nice." A determined set to her mouth, she gripped the handles of her cases and straightened her spine. "Come along. Well find a bite to eat before we hire a ride to our destination. It's bad manners to arrive hungry if we're going to show up unannounced."

Worse manners to show up unannounced, Addie decided, but chose to bite her tongue.

On the walk to the hotel, weighed down by heavy bags and wearing dusty, rumpled clothes, Addie feared they resembled a pair of common laborers. Blushing, she tucked her chin close to her chest and followed the swish of her mother's skirt.

As they reached the path leading to the impressive, well-appointed building, two men rushed them from behind.

Startled, Addie spun, tightening her grip on her luggage.

A stranger towered over her, staring confidently into her eyes. "May I?" he asked, slipping her belongings from her fingers with ease.

Stifling a cry, she gaped helplessly, too captivated by the arresting figure to do otherwise.

The man was as tall as a Mississippi magnolia. His eyes were warm and smiling, the outer lashes so long they curved close to his expressive, dark brows. The skin of his face glowed smooth and dark, sunbaked to a golden brown. A narrow line of fine-whiskered hair grew from a dimpled recess beneath his full bottom lip, extending down his strong chin. But his most striking feature by far was the matted hair tumbling past his shoulders, the tips bleached by the sun.

"I—I—" Addie stammered, unsure whether to swoon or shriek for help.

"Why, thank you," Mother said, her voice sounding far away.

Addie whirled to see her blithely pass her bags to a small, swarthy man. "Mother, for heaven's sake," she hissed, "what are you doing?"

"Allowing these nice young men to render aid." Turning the force of her considerable charm on the lanky man at her side, she smiled her brightest. "And not a moment too soon. I couldn't have carried those things another step."

The fellow beside her tipped his odd little hat, freeing a dark tumble of curls. "Happy to serve, *signorina*."

Mother's laughter floated back to Addie. "That's *signora*, if you don't mind."

Swinging her gaze upward, Addie fell once more into haunting brown eyes. The color of burnt-sugar candy and as clear as a handblown demijohn, they latched onto her, and she couldn't pull away.

"We frightened you," he said. "I apologize." Some men's voices didn't suit them, despite a pleasing appearance or manner of dress. This man's deep rumble served him well, melting in Addie's ears like a match on candle wax.

Her traitorous mother had moved on, chatting with her new companion like an old friend. Addie scowled after them, her brows drawn to a tight knot.

"After you," the man behind her said, interrupting her pout.

She lifted her glare to him, and he waved his hand with a flourish, his once-friendly smile now more of an amused grin.

Before Addie reached the entrance of the hotel, her mother had disappeared.

The stranger stepped onto the boardwalk in front of Addie to hold the door.

Careful to avoid brushing against him, she slipped past and hurried inside. As she gazed around the high-ceilinged lobby, her heart sped up. Instead of weaving through the milling crowd or waiting her turn to speak to the clerk, Mother was nowhere in sight. Frantic, Addie searched the big room, her head spinning and panic crowding her throat.

The stranger touched her shoulder, nodding toward an arched doorway. Inside the dining hall, the dark-skinned man held a chair for her mother as she settled gracefully against the padded cushion.

Weak with relief, Addie reached for her bags. "Thank you. I can manage from here."

He held them out of her reach. "They're pretty heavy. Go on, and I'll carry them to the table for you."

"That won't be necessary."

"It's really no trouble."

Her jaw tightened. "I wouldn't dream of detaining you. I'll take them now, so you and your friend can be on your way."

He tilted his head, the effect on his appeal mesmerizing. "This is on my way. We were headed to the Ginocchio to eat." He glanced toward her mother, holding a menu and conversing with a waiter. "I'm guessing the two of you were, too."

Defeated more by his searching gaze than his answer, she bit back her objections and made her way to the table.

Mother seemed to miss the quizzical look Addie fired as she crossed the room. Instead, she nodded and smiled at something her new friend had said.

Incredibly, he had pulled out the chair next to her, draped a napkin over his arm, and proceeded to pour her a glass of water from a cut glass pitcher. Setting the container aside, he lurched to his feet as Addie approached.

"Say hello to Theodoro Bernardi of Galveston, dear," Mother said. "By way of Sicily, that is. Theo's family owns a restaurant near the shore. Isn't that wonderful?"

Explains his accent, Addie thought. *And his finesse with a pitcher.* She returned his nod of greeting, fighting the urge to shake her head in disbelief. Given three minutes or less, her mother had unearthed the man's family history.

Mother lifted a dazzling smile to the man at Addie's side. "According to Theo, this gracious fellow is Pearson Foster from Houston. It was his idea to help us, Addie." She held out her hand. "Allow me to offer our thanks."

Cupping her slender fingers in his palm, Mr. Foster gave a slight bow. "Like I told your sister here, it's no trouble at all."

Raising her hankie, Mother sought to hide a pleased grin. "Gracious, you do flatter. I'm her mother." She blushed prettily. "But of course, you knew that."

Genuine surprise flashed in his eyes. "On the contrary. It's obvious you're related, since you favor, but I'd never have guessed."

Mother had met her match.

She withdrew her hand. "I'm Mariah McRae from Canton, Mississippi. The pretty and much younger girl at your side is my daughter, Adelina Viola."

Addie cringed at the use of her formal name but stifled the urge to correct it. It didn't matter what name he called her.

"Sit down, dear," Mother said, "so these poor gentlemen can rest their feet."

A twinkle of amusement in his eyes, Pearson held Addie's chair while she reluctantly sat. With wide grins and a boisterous scraping of chairs, the blatant interlopers followed suit.

"There. You see, Addie?" Mother nodded firmly. "I asked God to provide in our hour of need, and He sent us these nice young men. I'm so grateful. Aren't you?"

Addie focused on shaking out her napkin but couldn't prevent her brows from rising. "Um. . .yes, ma'am. I suppose so."

"You know," Mother said, "there's a passage in the Bible that reads, 'Be not forgetful to entertain strangers: for thereby some have entertained angels unawares.'" She winked. "You two aren't angels by any chance?"

Theo chuckled, the sound so merry Addie smiled despite herself. "Mrs. McRae, I assure you, angelic behavior is a thing we'll never be accused of."

Pearson pouted his lips. "Speak for yourself, old man. You're dangerously close to hurting my feelings."

Theo burst into laughter, joined by Mother and Pearson.

Glancing around, Addie blushed.

Nearby patrons looked on, some with amused expressions, others laughing along with them. Anyone passing the table would think they were dear old friends enjoying each other's company instead of strangers who hadn't been properly introduced.

"By the way," Mother said, "Theo and I took the liberty of ordering for you both. I hope you won't mind."

Addie's cheeks warmed. Of course she minded. Only a child needed its mother to order lunch.

Pearson grinned. "I don't care, as long as he doesn't try to eat it for me, too."

Curious, Addie stole a peek at his face.

Glancing her way, he lifted one expressive brow. "Theo's well acquainted with my likes and dislikes. We've been friends since his parents first came to this country. He didn't speak a word of English for the first six months." He shrugged. "Somehow we managed to communicate."

"How long has it been?" Mother asked.

Theo pinched his bottom lip. "Let me see. . .we came to Galveston in April of '91, on Pearson's tenth birthday. I remember because his mother crossed the street to invite me to his party." He winked at Pearson. "I was his favorite birthday present."

Pearson folded his arms on the table, a relaxed smile on his face. "My only present that year, as I recall. I've tried to return him ever since."

"Your birthday's in April, then? What day?"

Addie shot a warning scowl across the bread basket. "Mother, please."

"The twentieth," Pearson said, ignoring her.

Delight lit her mother's pretty face. "For goodness' sake! You share birthdays with Addie. Isn't that a wonderful coincidence?"

Leaning back in his chair, he flashed Addie a warm smile. "I think it is."

"Of course she's a bit younger," Mother continued. "You're twenty-four by my calculations. She just turned twenty-two."

Compelled to stop her before she revealed the color of their bloomers, Addie swiveled toward Theo. "When will you be returning to Galveston?"

A hush fell over the table, magnifying the murmur of voices and the clink of eating utensils in the room. Before she could recover from her inappropriate question, the waiter delivered four lovely salads to the table, bowed at the waist, and backed away.

Addie licked her lips and tried again. "I meant to say, are the two of you here on business?"

Theo picked up his napkin. "Well, miss, the length of our stay is up to the boss here." He jabbed a forkful of lettuce and got it halfway to his mouth before Mother cleared her throat. With a startled glance, he lowered the food to his plate.

Mother tilted her head and shot Pearson a winsome smile. "Do you mind if we say grace?"

Drawing a deep breath, he folded his hands in his lap. "Not at all, ma'am." The words were right, but the slight buckling between his brows said otherwise.

His reaction surprised Addie so completely she scarcely heard the prayer. She found his discomfort so unexpected, her unruly eyes wouldn't stay off him throughout the rest of the meal—a meal that passed in a blinding flash of lively conversation and pleasant laughter.

Pearson explained that they were in the wrecker business—adding "sort of" in a most mysterious tone—and in Marshall on an expedition to raise a shipwrecked steamboat from nearby Caddo Lake.

Mother asked a few polite questions, but their answers were vague, so she tactfully steered the conversation to safer ground.

Once Addie relaxed, she began to enjoy herself. The Ginocchio salad was a first for her, but she vowed it wouldn't be her last. Both men seemed content to focus on conversing with her mother, so Addie was free to sit back and savor every bite.

"I'm mostly a meat and potatoes man," Pearson said, talking around a generous bite. "But this is really good."

Theo shoved in the last bit he could scrape from his plate. "I'm a pasta and sauce man myself, but I have to agree."

They laughed together while Pearson signaled the waiter and handed him several wrinkled bills.

Mother held up her hand. "No, dear. It's my treat. It's the least I can do after you two came to our rescue."

"Sorry, ma'am, it's taken care of." He ducked his head at the waiter. "Go ahead, sir, and keep the change."

"Well then—" Mother pushed back her chair and stood while the others followed suit. She held out her hand to Pearson with a big smile. "I don't know what to say, except thank you. You're very kind."

A faraway look crossed his face, and a tinge of sadness darkened his eyes. "You're very welcome, Mrs. McRae. I'd like to think someone would offer the same courtesy to my mother and sister." His throat rose and fell. "If they were still with us, that is."

Mother's chin jerked up. "Oh Pearson. Do you mean—?"

"Yes, ma'am. I lost them, along with the rest of my family. Almost five years ago now, in the great storm on Galveston Isle."

Addie's heart stirred to pity. She knew which storm he meant. News of the terrible hurricane that swept over the island, washing hundreds of people into the sea, had spread quickly. Shocked by the dreadful report, the citizens of Canton mourned the tragic loss for days.

Her mother reached for Pearson's hand, gripping so hard her knuckles turned white. "I'm so sorry, dear boy. It must've been a devastating loss. But how fortunate that you were spared."

Blushing, he blinked rapidly and turned his face aside. "Thank you, ma'am."

Catching Theo's sleeve, he shook him gently. "Are you ready, old boy? We have work to do, and we'd best get at it."

Mother gave his hand a final pat then turned him loose. "Yes, we need to get started ourselves. We're running late for an appointment."

Addie glanced at her. How could one be late to an appointment they'd never set?

She leaned to pick up her bags, but Pearson's long fingers closed over the handles. With a combination smirk and challenging smile, he hoisted them and nodded at the door.

Theo collected Mother's two cases, and they followed her out to the street.

Fishing in her handbag, she brought out the letter from Miss Whitfield and held up the envelope. "I realize you're new in town as well, but do you have any idea where we might find this address?"

Theo shoved back his cap and whistled. "You don't have to be around Marshall long to hear of Whitfield Manor. It's the grandest place in town."

Mother brightened. "Is it close by? Within walking distance?"

Pearson shook his head. "It's not too far, but you'll have to hire a ride." He pointed. "The house is built on a rise a few miles outside of town. You could see it from here, if not for the trees."

Theo flagged a passing carriage and announced their destination to the driver. While he loaded the luggage, Pearson offered his arm to help them board. Grinning and waving merrily, the men stood on the street and saw them on their way.

As soon as she could speak without being heard, Addie spun on the seat. "Heavens, Mother, what were you thinking? Those two weren't the sort of men we should take up with in a strange town. What would Father say?"

Mother drew back and frowned. "Theo and Pearson? What was wrong with them?"

"They were entirely too forward for one thing. And far too familiar for strangers."

She laughed. "Nonsense, Addie. I'm a fair judge of character, if I say so myself. And I believe I proved it just now." She nodded firmly. "My instincts about those two bore out. They were wonderful young men and perfect gentlemen."

Addie widened her eyes. "But they looked so. . .so coarse, for lack of a better word." The warning glance from under her mother's lashes wilted Addie's smug indignation.

"Character isn't always reflected on the surface, young lady. One look at Theo's bright smile and the sincerity in Pearson's brown eyes, and I knew we were in safe hands." She nudged Addie with her elbow. "Don't act as if they didn't intrigue you. Especially Pearson. I didn't miss how closely you watched him."

Addie's gaze leaped to the back of the driver's head. "Mother! Keep your voice down. I was only—"

"Pearson's a very attractive man, which you can't deny. If I'd judged your father on his rough-and-tumble appearance, I'd never have given him a second glance." Smiling, she stared across Addie's shoulder into the past. "I saw straight through his cocky boasts and swaggering posture to the wonderful man that he is." Back in the present, she winked at Addie. "In the nick of time, too. He almost got away."

Addie shrugged, feigning interest in a passing stand of trees. "Please don't compare your courtship with Father to a brief encounter with a strange man." She rolled her eyes. "And I emphasize *strange*." She focused on her lap, twirling a loose string on the index finger of her glove. "Besides, they'll finish their business in Marshall and go back to where they're from. Chances are I'll never see Mr. Foster again."

A knowing look on her face, Mother tilted up Addie's chin, her slender fingers adjusting the brim of her hat. "I wouldn't count on it, honey. I saw the way he looked at you, too."

Shifting away to hide the flush that warmed her face, Addie fiddled with the row of pearl buttons on her sleeves. "Don't be silly. How could he look at me when he never took his eyes off you?"

Pearson's handsome profile swam in Addie's mind, with his straight nose and strong chin, his peculiar hair, and the haughty smile he gave her—infuriating yet titillating at the same time.

Flustered, she dismissed him with a shake of her head. "I'd prefer we change the subject. I have more important things to occupy my mind." She settled against the seat with a sigh. "Besides, the whole conversation is ridiculous."

"Premature, perhaps," Mother said. "Hardly ridiculous." Her almond eyes softened. "Don't misunderstand. I'm not suggesting you cavort with strange men while you're in Marshall. Your father would have our hides." Reaching for Addie's hand, she squeezed. "Just don't limit God's ability to bring two people together." She held up one finger. "In a proper and respectable way, of course. After all, He managed things quite nicely for your father and me." Nudging Addie again, she chuckled. "Lucky for you, as it turns out. Otherwise, where would you be?"

Addie laughed and leaned her head on her mother's shoulder. "I wouldn't be, I suppose."

"The ways of God are wonderful," Mother said, caressing her cheek. "His generous heart unsearchable. It's important to keep watch at all times, allow Him to orchestrate your destiny. You never know what amazing gifts He has in store, and you don't want to miss a thing."

A large house loomed as they crested the hill, its tall white columns stark against the bright blue Texas sky.

Addie's breath caught and her stomach tensed. "Oh Mother, that must be Whitfield Manor. I can hardly believe we're finally here."

The driver took the sharp curve at the top of the rise then turned into the circular driveway and pulled up in front. The two-story, redbrick building sat off the back side of the gently sloping lot, the crawl space concealed by white lattice. Matching windows fronted the house, four on the bottom and four on top, each as tall and wide as the door and framed in bright white borders. Another lofty casement sat atop the door, with more windows and columns lined up around the corner.

Her mother sighed with pleasure. "It is quite impressive, isn't it?"

Addie inhaled sharply. "More grand than I could've imagined."

The driver helped them down to the stone walkway then scurried to the rear to unload their baggage.

Mother turned with a stern look on her face. "Now remember,

Adelina, let me do the talking."

Would there be any way to stop her? Addie wondered.

Of course, she didn't say so.

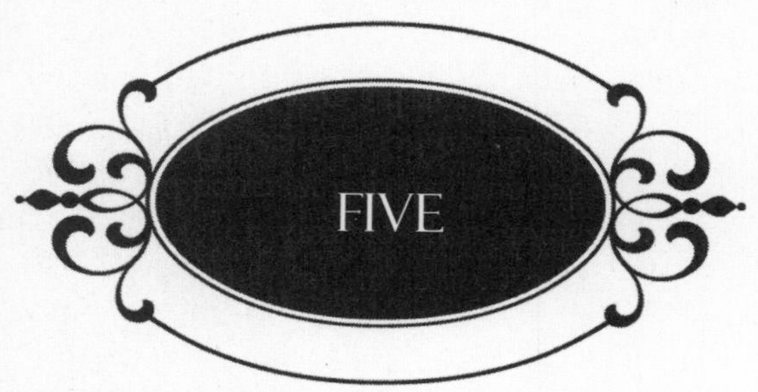

FIVE

The air in Miss Whitfield's spacious study smelled of starched curtains and leather chairs. Each time the kind-faced lady shifted in her seat, a hint of lavender-scented soap drifted across in pleasing waves. She smiled sweetly at Addie then tilted her head at Mother. "Thomas's letter overflowed with praise for your daughter, Mrs. McRae, but never once mentioned how lovely she is."

Mother sat up straighter and preened. "Why, thank you. Addie's our firstborn, the eldest of four girls. Their father and I are proud of each and every one."

Miss Whitfield clasped her hands at her chest. "Four wonderful daughters. My, who wouldn't be proud?"

The women beamed at each other across the heavy oak desk, and Addie felt the first surge of hope. If things continued to progress so pleasantly, Mother would soon be on her way back to Canton, and Addie could begin her life in Texas as Cedric Whitfield's governess. Consumed by curiosity, she had craned her neck from the moment a maid in a ruffled cap admitted them into the cavernous front hall. So far, there'd been no sign of a little boy.

"How long have you known our Dr. Moony?"

The translucent glow of Miss Whitfield's cheeks turned bright pink. "Thomas and I attended school together up north. He went on to pursue a higher education, and I wound up in Marshall. We haven't seen each other since, but we never lost touch." She smiled wistfully. "You might say we're kindred spirits."

"Oh, what a shame," Mother said. "You know he's a widower now."

Miss Whitfield's head came up. "Yes, Thomas wrote me."

Addie inhaled sharply and sat forward. She'd caught the meddling spark in her mother's eye.

The rascal reached across the desk and patted Miss Whitfield's hand. "If you enjoyed each other's company so much, why did you allow a separation?"

Groaning inside, Addie clenched her fists in her lap. Her coveted position—and the shade of Miss Whitfield's bloomers—was in jeopardy.

"What brought you to Marshall, ma'am?" she asked quickly, hoping to steer the conversation to safer ground. "Do you have family here?"

Pulling her startled gaze from Mother, a bit of color returned to the poor woman's face. "I did at the time. My father was a shrewd businessman, you see. Forty years ago, Marshall was the fifth-largest city in Texas." She lifted her chin. "A prosperous Confederate city. Somehow, despite the eventual occupation by Union forces, Daddy maintained control of his vast holdings. He built this old house, and we've been here ever since."

"He did well for himself," Mother said. "He's made a lovely home for you here."

Miss Whitfield smiled. "I haven't confessed the whole story, I'm afraid. My father didn't amass all of his fortune from that unfortunate war. We're old money, as pompous and posturing as it sounds. Daddy brought his fortune with him when he came to this country. He was quite the philanthropist, however, and I'm quite proud of the good things he accomplished with our wealth." A faraway look crossed her face. "We had hoped Cedric would one day fill his shoes. He stands to inherit all of this one day, only—"

She sniffed demurely and folded her hands on top of the desk. "Speaking of Ceddy, I suppose we should begin the interview."

Thankfully, Mother stood, gathering her parasol and gloves. "The two of you have quite a lot to discuss, and I'm sure you don't need me. If you'll direct me to the parlor, I'll wait there for my daughter."

"You'll do no such thing," Miss Whitfield said, reaching for a small brass bell.

The pleasant jangle brought a polite knock at the door, and the maid in the white cap peered inside. "Yes'm?"

"Delilah, will you show Mrs. McRae—" Her eyes widened as a small figure in khaki shorts and a striped percale waist staggered into the study, clinging blindly to Delilah's skirts.

Addie's first glimpse of Ceddy Whitfield took her breath. The boy was achingly beautiful.

Clear blue eyes dominated his delicate pixie features, and flyaway blond wisps fell over his forehead to tangle with his sweeping lashes. His graceful bottom lip dimpled, and his rosebud mouth turned up a bit at the corners. A beam of light from the hall shone through his hair, illuminating the top of his head like a kiss from God. Swinging his head dreamily from side to side, he seemed cut off from the presence of mere mortals.

Irritation marring her pleasant face, Miss Whitfield cleared her throat. "I asked you to keep him occupied until"—she glanced at Addie and her mother—"after."

Delilah caught Ceddy's shoulder to guide him from the room.

Whether her touch set him off or he'd noticed the company of strangers, Addie couldn't tell, but he moaned and grimaced, straining toward the far corner.

"I done jus' like you say, ma'am," Delilah said, scrambling to hold on to him. "I kept right on his heels the whole time, only I heard you ring the bell."

Ceddy's moans became shrill screams as he struggled to escape her grasping hands.

The older woman bent close to the hysterical boy's face. "It's all right, precious. Won't you please go with Lilah? She has a cookie for you, I'm sure. After a while she'll take you out back to dig for rocks." She glanced at the maid. "Won't you, Lilah?"

"I sho' will." She stretched out her hand. "Come along, sugar."

Ceddy eased from the corner and ambled out ahead of the maid.

Before she left, Delilah glanced over her shoulder. "I'm real sorry, Miss Priscilla."

Pulling an embroidered handkerchief from her waistband, Miss Whitfield blotted her top lip. "Never you mind. Take Ceddy to the kitchen; then come show Mrs. McRae to her quarters. Make her comfortable and bring her refreshments. It's awhile yet before suppertime."

"Yes, ma'am."

The door closed, and Mother smiled at their hostess. "That's very kind, Miss Whitfield. I'm grateful."

She waved the hankie. "No trouble at all."

Mother's dark eyes softened. "He's a lovely boy. You must be so proud."

Their hands clasped briefly. Miss Whitfield's damp lashes fluttered. "Thank you."

Mother had made another conquest.

Their heads tucked close together, the women chatted quietly until Delilah returned. With a last encouraging wink, Mother backed from the room, shutting the door on Addie and her prospective employer.

Priscilla Whitfield cleared her throat, bringing Addie to the edge of her seat. Despite the gracious smile on the lady's face, there was a change in her demeanor. "I suppose you have questions. About Ceddy, I mean."

Addie sat straighter and modestly folded her hands on the desk. What could be said to explain the wild behavior they'd just witnessed? "I'm sorry, ma'am. I'm not sure what to ask."

She nodded. "That's understandable. I'll just begin, then. Shall I?"

"Yes, please."

She settled against her high-backed chair. "As I mentioned in my letter, my nephew's son is an unusual child."

Unusual or unmanageable? If only Addie had taken the warning to heart. . .

"He was a beautiful infant. Positively angelic. People noticed he was special and commented often on his appearance." She smiled. "Peter and Eliza doted on Ceddy from the second they laid eyes on him and loved showing him off around the community." Her smile waned. "I suppose that's why they noticed his differences so early."

"Differences?"

"He didn't smile like most babies or respond to their voices. He wouldn't meet their eyes and became easily distracted."

Addie nodded thoughtfully. "I can understand their concern."

Miss Whitfield pursed her lips. "We tried to comfort them, told them the child just needed time to develop properly. When Ceddy got older and his. . .*unique* behavior grew more noticeable, his parents took him around the globe searching for answers. The closest we came to understanding his illness was in a London hospital. Doctors there diagnosed him with nervous mental disease."

Addie frowned. "What does it mean?"

Miss Whitfield glanced up from the desktop and whatever else held her anguished gaze. "I have no idea, to be honest. I can only describe his current behavior."

Addie leaned closer. "Please do."

"Well. . .he still avoids eye contact, still resists smiling. Loud noises, strong odors, and the like startle him. Any change in routine angers him. When he's upset, he flaps his hands or rocks himself. Often he sits on the floor and spins like a top. Left alone, he entertains himself for hours, with no need for human interaction."

She stared out the window at the manicured lawn, profound sadness etched on her face. "He forms attachments to objects yet won't allow cuddles or hugs." Tucking her bottom lip, she dug in her teeth so hard the skin turned white. The attempt to contain her grief failed. Large tears pooled at the corners of her eyes. "I find the last trait the saddest of all, and the hardest to accept."

"I can imagine how difficult that would be."

"No, dear," Miss Whitfield said, wiping her eyes with the tips of her slender fingers. "I'm sorry, but you can't." Her trembling voice held no rebuke. Taking a quick breath, she regained her composure. "One last thing. Ceddy becomes preoccupied—obsessed, if you will—with certain items. Rocks and stones in particular."

Remembering the mischievous charges from her past, Addie grinned. "It seems a harmless obsession for a boy. At least it's not frogs and snakes."

A smile tugged at the woman's lips. "Except he won't throw them away. His room resembles an excavation site."

Addie chuckled. "I see your point."

"As you may have noticed, he will not speak."

"No speech at all?"

Miss Whitfield sighed and shook her head. "Not for a very long time, though he spoke quite well in the beginning."

A lump swelled in Addie's throat. "So he's mute?"

"Not according to my understanding of the word. *Webster's International* defines *mute* as 'unable to speak' or 'lacking the power of speech.' Ceddy meets neither criterion."

"I'm not sure I understand."

"The doctors say he still has the faculty of speech. He simply won't use it." She shrugged. "I suppose he doesn't see the necessity."

Addie shook her head. "How could that be? Speech is the greatest tool for communication."

Miss Whitfield sobered. "You're beginning to catch on, dear. With the exception of meeting his most basic needs, Ceddy hasn't the slightest desire to communicate."

Addie struggled with an urge to abandon the conversation. She longed to bolt from the chair and join Mother for refreshments, where she'd find the topic of conversation no weightier than adding one lump or two to her cup of tea. The pretense of appearing knowledgeable on the matter of broken children left her drained. Uncomfortable, Addie squirmed in her chair.

Miss Whitfield's probing gaze flickered away. "Of course, these are just parts of his complex personality. With the passage of time, you'll discover the rest on your own." She angled her head. "If you accept the position, that is."

Staring at her hands twisting in her lap, Addie cleared her throat. "What are the predictions for his future? I mean, what are Ceddy's prospects?"

Lips pursed, Miss Whitfield studied her for several moments then slid open the shallow drawer in front of her. "I can best answer your question with an article Eliza discovered shortly after Ceddy's diagnosis. Along with our faith in God's plan, this story inspired us to hope."

Unfolding a yellowed sheet of newsprint, the creases so worn they'd torn in spots, she spread it carefully on the desk. "A child born in Dalston, London, in 1835, was labeled a deaf-mute and developmentally disabled. They called him Poor James, an appropriate name considering his family gave up on him when he turned fifteen, committing him to the Earlswood Asylum. James nearly succumbed to the bleak environment, lapsing into terrible mood swings and exhibiting violent episodes of rage."

Addie cringed. "I'm not the least surprised. How awful for him." She'd heard horrid tales of such institutions, and the thought of a helpless child locked away in a hospital for the insane pained her chest.

"Awful indeed," Miss Whitfield said. "Until a discerning employee suggested a handcrafting session for the boy. The staff introduced him to woodworking tools, and he took to it wholeheartedly, designing intricate figurines and elaborate pieces of furniture as if he'd been born with an awl in his hand. Before long, Poor James became the "Genius of Earlswood Asylum"—from discarded child to celebrated artist." She smiled. "In fact, his lovely masterpieces are on display in England still today."

Pleased with the ending, Addie sat back in her chair. "It's a wonderful story, but I don't see a connection to Ceddy's plight."

"Cedric has a similar gift in relation to rocks and stones. His father first saw it when he brought home a volume on gems and minerals. From that day, Ceddy spent hours poring over the book. At first, Peter supposed the pictures fascinated his son—until he realized Ceddy had lined up his entire collection of colorful pebbles according to the classifications in the book. He was six at the time."

"Amazing."

"From that moment, Peter began searching once more for cures. Eliza, God rest her, made the wise and heartfelt decision to stop chasing miracles and accept her son as he was. Over the protests of my brother and nephew, she ceased all interference from outside sources and began to raise Ceddy according to her instincts and God's direction. In their bumbling fashion, both men raised a stink, along with the rest of the Whitfield family, but the darling girl held her ground."

She carefully folded the article and put it away. "Once Ceddy relaxed, he flourished. His nervousness improved and his appetite picked up. For the first time in years, he seemed happy. This fact alone won my nephew over to his wife's way of thinking." She sighed. "That's when he agreed to leave Ceddy to me, should anything happen to them."

Addie leaned forward. "Because?"

"I stood in wholehearted agreement with his mama. Eliza knew she could trust me to keep the swarming horde from descending on the poor little thing." Her jaw tightened. "And I shall. As long as I draw a breath, Ceddy will be safe from those who seek to poke and prod at his fragile spirit."

"I should think the family would honor his parents' wishes."

Anger clouded her features as she struggled with unseen foes. "Certain of them feel compelled by duty to 'fix' Ceddy. I'm afraid, despite their good intentions, they'll never see him as anything but flawed."

Relaxing her chin, she drew a breath. "You're very young, Addie. I'll understand if you find our plight too much to bear, but I hope you'll consider the position. I sense in you the same loving spirit that embodied the boy's mother."

Addie lowered her eyes. "Thank you. That's a heady compliment." Heady but undeserved. She couldn't possibly accept the demanding position. Glancing up, she wrung her hands and searched for something to say.

Miss Whitfield held up her finger. "Don't answer yet. You need ample time to decide about such an important matter." Nodding as if the issue were resolved, she continued, "I'd like you to stay on at Whitfield Manor for a few weeks. You can observe Ceddy's day-to-day activities and get a better idea of what's expected before you commit."

Startled, Addie shook her head. "I'm afraid that's impossible. Mother can't stay away from home for long." She blinked rapidly, struggling to find a way out. "My father and sisters need her."

Miss Whitfield's knowing eyes studied her closely. "I'd love to have her, dear, but I'm certain a bright young woman like you can manage without her mother."

Embarrassed, Addie tucked her lips. "And if I choose not to take the position?"

"I'll arrange your passage home and accompany you straight to your doorstep. Your parents have my solemn word."

Before Addie could protest further, Miss Whitfield swiveled in her chair and stood, signaling the end of the interview. "Talk it over with your mother, dear. She appears to be a very wise woman."

Addie struggled to her feet, her knees trembling. "Yes, I'll speak to her." She held out her hand. "And thank you for considering me."

The woman squeezed her fingers, determination burning in her eyes. "I believe God brought us together for a reason, Addie. Let's sort out what He has in store for us, shall we?"

Ceddy shoved the last bite of cookie into his mouth then pulled the wooden box from under the bed. Running his thumbnail over the rows of square sections, he counted each time he passed a divider. Twenty-five across. Twenty-five down. Grunting, he hefted the case, struggled into the window seat, and settled the collection onto his lap where a ray of sunlight lit fires inside the bright stones.

There were other boxes under his bed, filled with igneous, sedimentary, and metamorphic rock. These were his favorites, the gemstones, each labeled and tucked into the special box Papa built for them.

Wriggling at the thought of his father, he started his count. *One, agate. Two, alexandrite. Three, aquamarine. Four, chrysocolla. Five, chrysoprase.*

Pausing, he smoothed his fingertips across the next one in the box. The side facing him was the color of milk mixed with water, rough and cloudy like white alum. Traces of kimberlite still clung to the edges.

He lifted the stone from the velvet lining and turned the smooth side to the dusty sunbeam. The hidden sparkle inside blinked up at him, and the words from the big book in the library trailed across his mind. *Gemstone. Mineral species. Crystallized carbon. Hardest known naturally occurring mineral.*

With a contented sigh, he returned it to its place, climbed down, and shoved the collection box into the deep shadows under the bed.

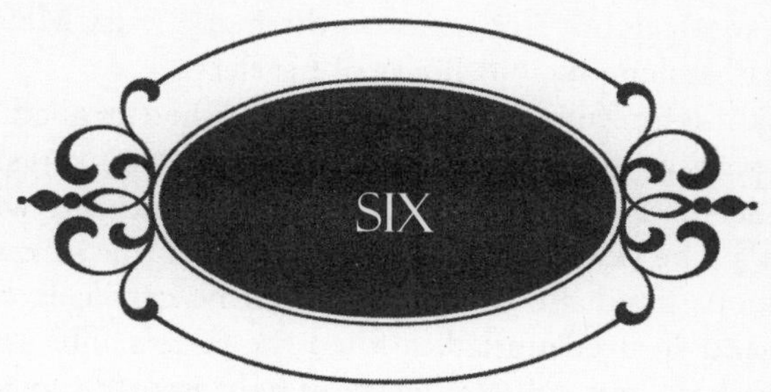

Pearson held the door of the Ginocchio Hotel for Theo then followed him onto the wide porch, the drum of their heels on the cedar planks loud in the morning air.

After seeing the women off to Whitfield Manor the day before, they'd booked a room in the hotel. Pearson had looked forward to a restful evening after traveling three hundred miles, but he'd spent a fitful night instead.

The cheerful clerk at the desk said they'd find supplies and information about Caddo Lake at a nearby store, so they'd set out early to find the place.

Yawning, Pearson gazed around with bleary eyes. "Which way, *paisan*?"

Theo shook his head. "You navigate the Gulf of Mexico in the dead of night but can't follow simple directions?"

Pearson chuckled and gazed overhead. "There are no stars to chart my course."

Theo's brows drew together. "The only stars are in your eyes. You're distracted by the pretty *bambolina* we met yesterday, aren't you? Your big feet haven't touched the ground since Miss Addie McRae wrestled you for her bags." He nudged Pearson with his elbow. "A fight she nearly won, I might add."

Pearson slanted his eyes at his irksome friend. "Which way, Theo?"

His cheeks round with glee, Theo pointed. "Dead ahead, Christopher Columbus. Washington Street to the town square." He cut his gaze to Pearson. "She was mighty pretty, though."

Catching him by the collar, Pearson herded him down the steps. He wouldn't admit it, but Theo was on the mark. Miss McRae and her dainty face had stolen precious hours of his sleep.

"Sure is a mighty fine day." Long-legged Theo strolled beside him at a leisurely pace, as if he hadn't a single care—or a sunken ship to raise.

"It is indeed," Pearson agreed, gazing at mounded white clouds suspended in a blue sky. "I'm ready to come out of this jacket."

Varied shops lined the boardwalk, and fine carriages transporting dapper men and spruced-up ladies filled the streets. The women wore tall, feathered hats and colorful wraps. Their escorts sported brushed derbies, turned-down collars, and canes.

A well-heeled couple approached from the opposite direction. The gentleman hurriedly switched sides with his lady, placing himself between her and Pearson. Lifting their noses, they offered a wide berth.

Pearson tipped his hat, giving them a devilish grin, and then nudged Theo. "Looks like we failed inspection."

Theo swatted his back. "This isn't the island, *paisano*. We stick out like knots on a whittling stick."

"Did you see all the finery they were trussed up in? It's not Sunday, is it?"

"Today's Wednesday, but I think every day's Sunday here. We'd best hurry and find our way to the swamp where we belong."

A few blocks from the hotel, Theo slowed his steps and whistled. "Would you take a look at that?"

Pearson glanced over his shoulder, expecting to see another pretty girl. Instead, the oddest contraption he'd ever seen raced along the street, darting easily between mounted horsemen and dodging rigs. It resembled a fancy wagon, complete with four wheels and a buggy top but missing a pony. Mouth agape, Pearson stared until it bounced around a turn and disappeared from sight.

Theo wagged his head. "Brother, that was something to see."

"A horseless carriage they're called. All the rage up North."

"Maybe, but I wouldn't trade in my horse for one. I can't see them ever taking hold in the South."

Pearson sniffed and shook his head. "I'm sure you're right. Still. . .it would be grand to drive one." Nudging Theo's shoulder, he jutted his chin at the building across the street. "We've arrived, my friend. There's the store we're looking for."

They crossed the rutted road, Theo reading aloud the large, painted letters on the sign. "J. WEISMAN & COMPANY—THE FIRST DEPARTMENT STORE IN TEXAS. What do you reckon a department store has for sale?"

Pulling a slip of paper from his pocket, Pearson grinned. "Hopefully, some of the items on our list." Theo reached for the doorknob, but Pearson brushed aside his hand. "I'll go first, thank you. And let me do the talking."

Theo scowled. "Why?"

"Don't you remember that time in Amarillo?"

A sheepish look crossed his face. "You're right. You'd better do the talking."

Leaving the pleasing warmth of the early spring sunshine, they strolled beneath the bell jingling over the door. The morning chill lingered inside the store, so Pearson pulled his jacket tighter, thankful he'd left it on.

The cavernous shop was like nothing he'd ever seen before. Equal parts general store, hardware store, and clothing boutique, there seemed to be something for everyone. Potent odors wafted from the four corners—familiar smells such as tobacco, spices, and soap. One wall held the usual items sold in a general store—straight razors, shaving cups, eyeglasses, hairbrushes, and looking glasses. Another offered churns, coffee mills, iron kettles, dishware, and silver utensils. Behind the glass counter, folded neatly in stacks, were woolen socks, handkerchiefs, wallets, cravats, and suspenders. In a corner along the back wall sat a brightly colored display of fabrics, buttons, and ribbons. Along the upstairs rail were racks of hats, high-top boots, ladies' shawls, and fancy dresses.

Even toys for children, Pearson thought, dodging the handle of a wagon with brightly painted slats for sides.

A stately gentleman with a heavily waxed mustache approached the counter. "Help you fellows?"

Pearson took off his hat. "Yes, sir. We're in need of a few supplies."

The proprietor swept his arm to take in the room. "I'm sure we can accommodate."

Pearson grinned. "I'm inclined to agree."

Looking eager to please, the man pulled out a pad and the stub of a pencil. "What can I get for you?"

Holding the list beneath a dusty beam, Pearson started from the top. "We'll need a healthy coil of rope, a couple of lanterns, coal oil"—he pointed to a high shelf over the man's head—"three or four of those oilcloths." He scanned the room. "You don't carry lumber by any chance?"

The clerk bobbed his head proudly. "Sure do. Stacked out back in the shed."

Properly impressed, Pearson nodded. "Well, that's fine. We'll need enough to build a platform over the water." Tapping his chin, he gazed around the room. "I suppose that's all for now. Later we'll need a couple of rowboats, oars, and a sturdy lift rig, if you have one."

The man pointed to a storage bin. "Like that Yale & Towne hoist and pulley over there?"

Pearson grinned. "Yes, sir. Exactly like that one. Now, if you can point me to a wagon for hire so we can haul all these goods, I'd be much obliged."

The man stopped tallying their purchases and straightened. One hand on his hip, he gazed from Pearson to Theo, his eyes alight with mirth. "You're headed out to Lake Caddo, am I right?"

Pearson shared a look with Theo.

Before they could answer, he chuckled. "I know what this is about. You boys are set to try your hand at the *Mittie*."

Theo squirmed, shuffling his feet like a schoolboy.

Pearson swallowed, taking his time to answer. "What makes you say so?"

Bending behind the counter, the clerk brought up a lantern in each hand and slid them toward Pearson. "You're not the first to try it, believe me." He cocked his head. "Say, where are you fellows from?"

"Down Galveston way," Theo said, grabbing a bottle of oil and adding it to the items on the counter.

"You're seamen, then?"

"Sometimes," Pearson said, dodging his eyes.

"What makes a couple of young sea dogs think they can find the *Mittie Stephens* when experienced men have searched for thirty years?"

"Well, we—"

"Your mariner skills may help you dodge sharks but won't do you a bit of good in a nest of cottonmouths." He flashed a knowing wink. "Unlike the alligators you'll meet in the swamp, you boys have bitten off a little more than you can chew." Laughter shook his body. "You'll wrestle a few gators, too, before you've earned your right to the *Mittie*."

Pearson leaned against the counter. "Well then. . .since you're onto us, maybe you can tell us where to find Catfish John."

The clerk stilled, his eyebrows lifted. "I see you've done your homework."

"How about it?" Pearson pressed. "Can you tell us where he is?"

The man opened his mouth to speak, but the overhead bell jangled, dragging their attention to the door.

An elderly gent shuffled inside, pulling off his sweat-stained hat with gnarled fingers. He moved in the slow, measured gait of the aged, men with stiff joints and nothing but time on their hands. "Mornin', folks." Wincing, he patted the door. "Ought to prop this thing open, Sam. Warmer outside than it is in here."

"That's a good idea," the clerk called. "Go on and brace it, then." Lowering his voice, he nodded at Pearson. "Must be your lucky day. There's the man you need to see."

"Catfish John?"

He grinned. "Not *that* lucky. This here's Mr. Robb, a plantation owner on the Caddo. If you ask him real nice-like, he just might tell you where John can be found."

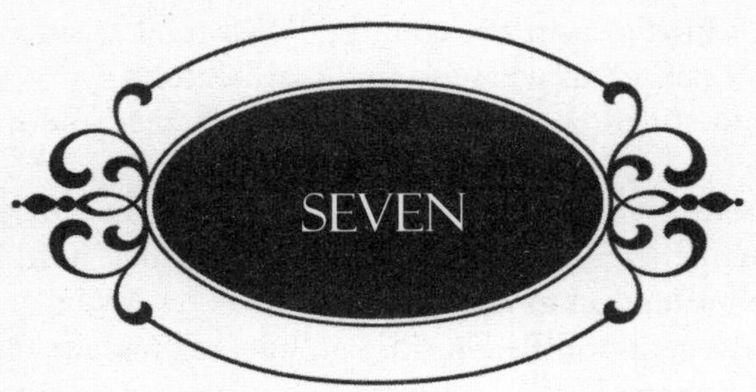

SEVEN

Addie stood at the full-length mirror adjusting the sash at her waist and marveling at the furnishings surrounding her. Her room in the big house Father built in Canton was grand, to say the least, but unimpressive compared to the opulence of Whitfield Manor.

She ran her fingertips along the gilded frame of the looking glass, touched the bronze bust of William Shakespeare on the desk. Every detail shouted wealth aplenty—with impeccable taste, of course. Yet for all the manor's lavish comforts, Addie wouldn't trade a home filled with little girls' laughter for the heartache sleeping in the room next door.

How could one endure such pain and disappointment? How did Miss Whitfield manage Ceddy every day?

At the lady's forceful suggestion, Addie slipped into his room after the meal to offer a plate of treacle tart and clotted cream. The experiment produced disastrous results, ending with the child cowering in the corner and Addie splattered with cream.

A tap on the door jolted her heart. She prayed it wasn't Miss Whitfield with another plot to help Ceddy warm up to her. She wasn't up to the task, and besides, she didn't plan to stay. When her mother left on the afternoon train, Addie would be sitting beside her, shoulders slumped in defeat.

The door opened before she reached it, and Mother peered inside. "There you are, *sioshitek*. Look at you, already dressed. I feared my knock might awaken you."

Alarm tightened Addie's stomach. Mother seldom addressed her in Choctaw. When she did, dire news often followed. She watched her mother's serene face carefully as she approached. "Oh my," she said, one hand over her heart. "What's wrong?"

Mother blinked at her. "Why, nothing, dear."

Addie shook her head. "You don't speak Grandmother's language unless you're troubled."

She chuckled and pulled Addie close. "How clever of you to notice this about me."

Drawing back, Addie tilted her head. "I've had years of practice."

Caressing her hair, Mother offered a wobbly smile. "Actually, I am quite distressed, but I have every reason to be. I'm leaving here today, traveling three hundred miles away from my firstborn."

Addie lowered her chin. "Well, cheer yourself, Mother, because I'm going with you."

"No, darling." Her knuckle curled beneath Addie's chin and raised her head. "No, you're not."

Addie had expected stunned silence. A disappointed pause. Mother's quick answer meant she anticipated the announcement. Pulling away, Addie busied herself at the mirror, adjusting her hair. "I've given it a lot of thought. I was up half the night, in fact. I regret putting everyone through all this trouble, but I'm absolutely certain it's the right thing to do."

"Addie. . ."

She spun. "I don't belong here, Mother. I have no special training for this sort of thing. I'm not the right person for the job."

"Nonsense. You're exactly what that poor child needs."

"You saw for yourself how difficult he is. I'm not sure if I. . . I don't know if I'm—"

Mother lifted one hand to cut her off then crossed to sit on the bed, patting the spot beside her. "Come over here."

Slouching like a disciplined child, Addie slunk to join her.

Mother caught her hands, wringing in her lap, and held them still. "I've watched you win the trust of innocent creatures in the past, from hurting children to feral cats. It's your gift."

"But don't you see? That's the problem. Ceddy Whitfield is both. He's a wounded boy but wilder than any beast I've ever seen."

"Not really. Unsettling behavior seems more extreme from a cherubic child."

"If you offer food to a wild animal, it won't shriek and sling it in your face." She touched her still-damp curls. "I don't think I could bear that happening again."

Mother had the nerve to laugh. "A touch of clotted cream is good for the complexion, honey. Don't underestimate yourself. You can bear more than you think."

"I'm not so sure anymore."

"Then I'll be sure for you," Mother insisted. "This is your chosen vocation, Adelina. All your work with children up to this point was to prepare you for this position. You won't tuck tail and run when it counts the most."

Tears spilled down Addie's cheeks. "You have entirely too much faith in me, and I fear it's misplaced." She met the familiar brown eyes, seeking comfort in their depths. "I'm frightened, Mama."

"Of course you are. We're all afraid when confronted by our destiny." Reaching beneath her high-buttoned collar, Mother's searching fingers emerged with the beaded necklace she wore so often it seemed a part of her. Pulling it over her head, she slipped it around Addie's neck and patted the speckled stone dangling at the end. "There now."

Addie gripped the polished bloodstone. "What are you doing? Not your mother's jasper necklace. I couldn't."

"Hush, now. They don't belong to you yet. That privilege comes on your wedding day." She squeezed the hand that held the pendant. "Just wear it for courage until I see you again. When you feel the weight against your heart, think of your grandmother. She was the bravest woman I've ever known."

Lifting damp lashes, Addie searched her face. "Are you sure?"

"I'll feel better knowing you have it."

With a ragged sigh, Addie shook her head. "I haven't decided to stay."

Mother gave her hands a final squeeze then stood and walked to the door. "I want you to pray before you make up your mind. That's all I ask. If you feel you should leave on the afternoon train, I'll help you pack."

Addie gave her a grudging nod and watched the door close at her back. Mother had best be ready to help because she'd already made up her mind. She just hadn't the nerve to say so.

Grinning like a fisherman with a bobbing cork, Mr. Robb's head wagged. "Why, sure I have time to talk to these young fellows about Catfish John." The twinkle in his eyes deepening, he motioned toward the door. "If you don't mind waiting whilst I make a quick purchase, we'll sit outside and chat a spell. These old bones can't abide the chill in here for long."

"Very good, sir," Pearson said. "We'll wait for you there." He opened the door to the accompanying overhead jingle then followed Theo out of Weisman's into the warm sunlight.

Theo braced his hands on his hips and stared down the street. "You suppose that old coot knows anything?"

Pearson shrugged. "We'll have to take our chances, won't we? Right now he's our only lead."

Theo pivoted toward the door. "I think they're playing us for ninnies." He pointed. "Listen at them in there. They're laughing at us."

Pearson pulled a wood-slatted chair around and took a seat. "Let them laugh. As long as Mr. Robb steers us in the right direction, I don't care."

"Well, I just might," Theo groused, straddling the chair beside him.

A rowdy group of young men crossed the street and hurried along the storefront, talking loud and jostling for position with their elbows. Two men in tall hats and pretentious suits strolled from the other direction, lost in a hushed conversation. A flirtatious couple rounded the corner of the building, the giggly girl blushing at being caught by Pearson's gaze, the boy intent on grasping for her hand.

The boisterous commotion in the street hadn't faded since they'd been inside the store. The denizens of Marshall hustled past in droves, oblivious to strangers in their midst, hatching a plan to snatch a prize from under their noses.

Pearson nodded at the milling throng. "Don't you wonder why they're not looking for the *Mittie*? Why they haven't already found her? She can't be hidden that well, can she? Finding a great hulking thing at the bottom of a lake is not like searching the ocean floor."

Theo nodded. "It would be something, wouldn't it? If we came all the way from Galveston and pulled up a fortune in gold, when all the time these folks were sitting right on top of it?"

Pearson leaned forward and laced his fingers. "I've wondered the same about Lafitte's gold. Why aren't there leagues of men contending with me for it? How could a man hear of a lost bounty and lack the heart to search?" He shook his head. "It's not in me, Theo. I'm not made that way."

Theo nodded thoughtfully. "I suppose most people are busy chasing the fire in their own chests. Just because a man works for years baking bread for someone else doesn't mean he's not burning inside to own the bakery."

Pearson bit his lip and nodded.

"Look at Rosie," Theo continued. "For years she served slop up and down the Strand, saving every penny she earned. Now she has a little place of her own. It took most of her life, but she chased her treasure and found it." He nudged Pearson's arm. "It's just that your idea of treasure is a tad more literal than most."

Grinning, Pearson sat back and crossed his arms. "So what about you? What hidden riches do you covet?"

Before Theo could answer, a bevy of young women sashayed toward them, their sweeping skirts, mounded curls, and brightly colored parasols crowding the boardwalk. Tittering and cooing, they danced past, lovely preening birds on display.

His attention snared, Theo tipped his cap at each smiling girl as she went by. Only when their retreating backs turned the corner did he pull his gaze around to Pearson. "I'm sorry. What did you ask me?"

Shaking his head, Pearson laughed. "Never mind, paisan. I think I have my answer."

Mr. Robb tottered out of Weisman's, paused by the door to summon his best offering for the spittoon, then joined them with a broad smile.

Pearson stood and offered the old man his seat, stepping over Theo's long legs to slide into the chair opposite him.

"Turning into a mighty fine day, ain't it?" Mr. Robb said.

Pearson leaned to nod at him. "It surely is. And Marshall's a real nice town."

Mr. Robb raised his chin. "Yes indeed. Thanks to Mr. Gould and cotton."

Frowning, Pearson glanced at Theo and shrugged. "Come again, sir?"

"Jay Gould, president of T&P Railroad. He moved his operation to Marshall in the '70s. The town grew rich overnight. Before long, we were one of the South's largest markets in cotton."

Theo smiled. "Jay Gould and cotton. I get it now."

Mr. Robb leaned over and nudged him. "Speaking of money and cotton, I could use your strong backs and nimble fingers on my farm. I'd pay you a fair picker's wage." Grinning, he lowered his voice. "You'll get rich a lot quicker that way than looking for sunken gold."

Theo slapped his knee. "The clerk told you. I knew it!"

Grinning, Mr. Robb patted his back. "He did, but he didn't have to. Why else would two strangers come asking for Catfish John?"

Pearson scooted his chair so he could see the man better. "Well then? Now that our secret's out, can you tell us where to find him?"

His unruly brows rose to peaks. "Mind you, catching up with Catfish John could be as hard as raising the *Mittie*."

Pearson shot him a slant-eyed challenge. "Try me. I'm fairly skilled at finding things." Theo cleared his throat, and Pearson scowled. "Most things, that is."

"Well, all right," Mr. Robb said, settling his back against the slats of his chair. "He lives on an island out on the lake—no one knows exactly where. He only comes to shore to sell fish and store up supplies. You could wait around one of the landings until he comes off the lake with a stringer of catfish. Otherwise, the chance of running across him is slim."

"I'll take that chance," Pearson said.

Mr. Robb shook his head. "You're on a fool's quest, you know, one even John can't help you with. Many a man has scoured the Caddo looking for that ship, men who've lived their lives working the steamboats. They know the routes, some even lived on the lake, but none of them has ever found her. What makes you think you can?"

"To be honest, sir"—Pearson winked—"I'm more determined."

Mr. Robb blinked, his jaw going slack. Sudden laughter bubbled up his throat, first as a wheezing sound then tumbling from his mouth in belly-shaking glee.

Theo joined in, draping one arm around his shoulders and patting him.

Except for the hint of a smile, one he quickly bit back, Pearson fought to stay sober lest the old man doubt his sincerity.

When Mr. Robb finally caught his breath, he clutched his knees with both hands and swiveled toward Pearson. "Son, you've given me the best laugh I've had all year. For that, and because I admire your gumption, I'm going to tell you what you want to know. You take the Port Caddo road, the Old Stagecoach Road they call it, heading east out of town. It's a good long ride. Go to old Port Caddo or the old Uncertain Landing and talk to some of the dockhands who used to work with the steamboats, loading and unloading goods. Those that are left are commercial fishermen now, guides and so forth."

He paused. "Who knows. . .you might find a leftover Caddo Indian still lurking in the woods. Then you'd have a bona fide tracker." He snorted. "You'll need one to find that ol' *Mittie*."

Theo's big eyes held a question. "Did you say you were uncertain about which landing? Because if you don't know, how can we hope to find it?"

Mr. Robb's shoulders shook again. "No, son. Uncertain is the name. The old steamboat captains had the dickens of a time mooring their vessels there, so it became known as Uncertain Landing." Beaming, he tilted his head. "Come to think on it, it's right comical that you two are headed out there seeking an uncertain treasure on the wreckage of a ship whose location is the most uncertain part of all."

Standing, the old man stretched then scratched his midsection. "If I can help you boys with anything else you're uncertain about, come out to the house and see me." The twinkle had returned to his eyes. "It's not too late to change your minds, you know. My offer to pick cotton still holds."

Smiling despite himself, Pearson stood and offered his hand. "I'm pleased you find our plight so entertaining, Mr. Robb. I've enjoyed meeting you, sir, and thank you for the information. I guess we'll pass on your generous offer, though."

"Suit yourself, young fella. You all be careful, you hear?" With a jaunty salute, Mr. Robb shuffled away, still chuckling as he turned the corner.

EIGHT

Breakfast passed in an uncomfortable blur. Every word Miss Whitfield said, every topic broached, held the erroneous assumption that Addie would stay. Her own mother behaved the same way.

Watching them, Addie squirmed in discomfort. How would she break the news to the two gaily chatting women that her clothes were already tucked inside the trunk waiting just inside her bedroom door? Resisting the urge to sit on her wringing hands, Addie stole a glance at the tall clock in the corner. Would it ever be time to leave for the station?

Miss Whitfield leaned to touch her arm. "I see you're quite fascinated by the longcase clock, Addie. It was a gift to my parents from Alfred, the Duke of Edinburgh."

She stared wistfully at the old timepiece as if remembering grander days. "Did you know they're becoming known as grandfather clocks?"

She smiled. "And all because of a song penned in 1876 by Henry Clay Work. As the story goes, there was an inn down in Piercebridge on the border of Yorkshire and County Durham called the George Hotel. Mr. Work visited this establishment and learned the legend of the elderly Jenkins brothers who once owned it. The lobby of the inn had a longcase clock that kept perfect time until one of the gentlemen died—at which point it began to falter. When the other brother joined him in death, the old clock stopped for good."

"How fascinating," Mother said.

"Henry Clay Work went home and set the story to music." She inclined her head toward the ceiling. "If you'll indulge me, it's a quaint little ditty that goes like this:

"My grandfather's clock
Was too large for the shelf,
So it stood ninety years on the floor;
It was taller by half
Than the old man himself,
Though it weighed not a pennyweight more.

"It was bought on the morn
Of the day that he was born,
And was always his treasure and pride;
But it stopped short,
Never to go again,
When the old man died."

Mother beamed over the top of her cup. "You have a wonderful voice, Miss Whitfield."

The blushing lady busied herself with the delicate lace bordering her place mat. "Oh heavens, not really, but thank you. And please. . .call me Priscilla."

"I will, if you'll call me Mariah."

"I'd be honored."

Mother glanced toward the window. "I stepped out onto the porch earlier. It's a lovely morning."

Miss Whitfield smiled. "Texas weather is as fickle as a debutante, so don't forget the whereabouts of your wrap. In all possibility, we could wake up tomorrow to a cold front." She laughed. "Then face a heat wave by Tuesday. We endure a hot summer here in Marshall once it sets in. Enjoy the cool while it lasts."

With a dainty clink, Mother set her teacup in the matching saucer. "Doesn't Cedric join you for meals? I noticed his absence last night at supper and again this morning."

Miss Whitfield lowered her chin and shook her head. "It's not possible, I'm afraid. Ceddy is far too disruptive. He takes his meals in the kitchen with Delilah." She raised her head and smiled. "I join them occasionally. . .when he's feeling calm."

Delilah slipped quietly into the room, collecting Miss Whitfield's empty plate with one hand while sliding a platter of rounded cakes onto the table with the other.

"What's this?" the elder woman asked. "Scones?"

"Buttermilk scones," Delilah said proudly. "Dotted with currants and slathered with peach jelly."

"Oh, how lovely." Miss Whitfield reached for one then paused, her cheeks ripening to apples again. "I know what you two are thinking. We eat entirely too many sweets around this house."

Giving in to temptation, she fumbled for a scone then jabbed her knife into a pat of butter. "I blame it all on Delilah. She's the best cook in town. I count myself lucky to have her"—she chuckled merrily—"until I consider the girth of my hips." She took a bite then swooned. "Light as a cloud." Picking up the platter, she held it out to Mother. "Where on earth are my manners? I should serve you first. Go on, have one, Mariah. You won't be sorry."

"They look lovely," Mother said, reaching for one of the golden-brown quick breads.

"Addie?" Miss Whitfield said, waving them under her nose.

Addie reached for one, but her hostess pulled them back. "On second thought, why not partake of yours in the kitchen with Ceddy?" Oblivious to Addie's discomfort, she placed two servings on a small plate and handed it across the table. "He's much fonder of these than he is the tarts. I'm sure he won't throw them."

Her pleading look touched Addie's heart, but that only increased its pounding. "I don't know, ma'am. He, um. . .he's not very receptive to me."

The offered plate didn't budge.

Mother quietly cleared her throat. "Go ahead, Addie. Take it."

Wishing her hand didn't tremble so visibly, Addie reluctantly reached for the treats. With a last pleading glance at her mother, she excused herself from the table and followed Delilah down the hallway to the kitchen.

Easing the swinging door open, Delilah peeked inside. "Always make sure he's not sitting right in front," she explained over her shoulder. "Many a time, I've busted inside without looking, and he wound up with a goose egg."

She stepped aside, and Addie entered the kitchen.

Ceddy lay on his stomach with his chubby cheek pressed against the floor, running one stubby finger along a polished wood plank. In his other hand, the arm crooked over his head, he held a jaunty little cap, black-rimmed velvet with a double row of silk cords stitched to the front.

"We just come in from outside," Delilah said brightly, taking the cap from his lifeless fingers.

Engrossed in tracing the line, he didn't seem to notice.

She snatched his jacket from the back of a chair and swept past. "I'll go put his things in his room."

Lifting her hand toward Delilah's retreating back, Addie swallowed the urge to ask her to stay. An ache starting low in her stomach, she pressed against the counter and watched him.

She couldn't call the noise he made a proper hum, more of a rhythmic grunt, but it was the first sound he'd made that might've come from a little boy.

Encouraged, she moved closer. "Ceddy?"

The slightest pause—then his tracing resumed.

Swallowing hard, she squatted to the floor. "I've brought you something nice, see? One of Delilah's scones."

No response.

"There's jelly inside. Peach, I think." She put the plate on the hardwood floor and nudged it toward him with the backs of her fingers. He continued to ignore her, so she edged it bit by bit until it bumped into his hand.

With barely a break in concentration, he shoved it away with the heel of his palm.

Addie sighed and sought the heavens. What was Miss Whitfield thinking? She could barely reach her great-nephew herself. How could she expect a stranger with no training in his unusual behavior to get through?

She dropped to her behind and crossed her legs in front of her, absently reaching for the strand of beads around her neck. Instead of lending her courage, they pressed against her heart with the weight of her mother's expectations.

A scurrying sound from Ceddy raised her head. He had straightened his arms and pushed up, his wide-eyed stare locked on her necklace.

Startled, Addie dropped the clattering beads to her chest.

As though mesmerized, Ceddy's gaze followed them.

Struck by sudden inspiration, she gripped the strand and rattled it.

In a flash, he scampered across the floor and scrambled into her lap. Wonder lit his delicate features as he placed his hand over hers, gently tugging them out of the way. Palming the jasper pendant, he lifted it close to his face and smiled.

Of course! Addie thought. *I've been using the wrong bait.*

In a surge of understanding, she saw the orphaned kittens snuggled in the folds of her skirt, straining toward her caress as if desperate to be touched. Just as bits of cold fish drew them against their wills, Ceddy, responding to what he loved most, couldn't resist her. He perched close to Addie, allowing himself to be touched by the only thing that moved him.

What had Mother said? That winning the trust of innocent creatures was Addie's gift? For the first time since she'd heard the words, she began to believe them.

Unable to stop herself, she smoothed wispy strands of hair off the child's forehead with trembling fingers. She expected him to withdraw, but the stone held him transfixed.

"Ceddy?" she whispered, desperate to have him look at her.

He batted his long, tangled lashes but didn't glance up.

In a blinding flash, in a jumble of thoughts coming so fast she couldn't have put them into words, she saw the parallel to God cut off from His creation by a yawning gulf of sin, shut off in the same way Ceddy had locked out the world around him. Her breath caught on a sob. Compassion welled in her chest, so deeply felt her untrained heart could only express it as love for a feral creature who couldn't acknowledge it—at least not yet. But she knew in her heart that he would.

Just as certainly, she knew that when the northbound train pulled out of Marshall with her mother aboard, she wouldn't be sitting beside her.

NINE

Pearson stood on the dilapidated dock overlooking Tow Head, where the Big Cypress River fed into Broad Lake, and stared into the murky depths of the Caddo. Surrounded by acres of cypress swamps, bayous, waterways, channels, and sloughs, the enormity of the task he'd so boastfully shouldered hit his stomach like a blow.

Beside him, Theo whistled. "Now I see why that old sailor called this region a lost world."

Pearson nodded. "And why the clerk at Weisman's said we'd bitten off more than we could chew."

Theo's gaze jerked to his face. "Are you thinking we have?"

Giving his head a little shake, Pearson squatted close to the water. "I'm not ready to quit just yet."

Kicking a pinecone off the end of the dock, Theo sighed. "Everyone we've talked to today said we'll be lucky to find Catfish John. Without him, we're as sunk as the *Mittie*."

"We asked each of them to pass the word to John if they see him. That's all we can do for now. Besides"—he glanced over his shoulder—"we may not need him. All of the old hands agreed that this is about where she rests."

Theo pointed with his chin at the widening rings fanning out on the surface of the water where the pinecone went down. "You heard them, Pearce. That overgrown sinkhole is twenty feet deep in some places."

Pearson gave him a sideways glance. "But it averages eight. And it won't be that deep where we'll be searching. The *Mittie* sank close to the bank, near the shallows."

Twisting his mouth, Theo tapped his bottom lip. "Hmm. The shallows. Where the gators live?"

"Only the babies. The big ones go deep."

"Except when they're hunting a meal. And why are you ignoring what the one fellow said?"

"Which fellow?"

"The man at Port Caddo who told you the *Mittie* burned to the waterline. That her safe, bell, and boilers were salvaged right after she sank."

Pearson waved him off. "That man didn't believe the words coming out of his own mouth. Besides, they never recovered the gold. So if the safe was found, the gold wasn't in it." Pushing past him, Pearson stalked off the dock to the water's edge. "Ready to get wet?"

"What?" Theo whirled, his voice cracking. "Now?"

"We might as well take a look while we're here. Find out what we're dealing with."

"Don't we already know what we're dealing with?" Grasping Pearson's shirtsleeve, he pulled him around. "Nests of angry cottonmouths." His eyes bulged. "Remember?"

Hiding a smile at Theo's hysterics, Pearson spoke calmly. "I intend to give this lake every ounce of respect it deserves, buddy boy, especially the cottonmouths. Now come on." Pearson strode along the shoreline for several yards to a spot where the bank sloped gently to the water.

Theo ran along behind him, still fussing like a flustered woman.

Sitting on the ground, Pearson slid off his boots and socks then stood and peeled off his sweat-dampened shirt. The wind felt good on his bare chest.

Walking into the water up to his ankles, he sighed. If he closed his eyes, ignoring the dank smell and the mud squishing between his toes, he could almost imagine himself back on the coast. After two more steps, bringing the frigid lake up to his calves, he stopped and glanced behind him.

Theo still dawdled on the bank, fully clothed.

"Aren't you coming?"

He licked his lips. "I realize your skin's like a whale's. You can't live long without getting wet." Breaking eye contact, he gazed at the dark water lapping his boots. "But I'm not like you, Pearson. I wasn't born with gills."

"You don't like getting those prissy curls wet is all. Stop grousing. You sound like your grandmother."

"Nonna is a wise and cautious woman. It's why she's lived so long." He shook his head. "I'll wait here this time."

"Suit yourself, sissy boy."

Theo gawked. "You're really going in there? What do you hope to accomplish?"

In up to his waist now, Pearson looked over his shoulder. "I'll let you know the answer when I figure it out. But I can truthfully say I prefer sand and salt water." With a sharp inhale, he dove.

So this was how it felt to be blind. Opening his eyes in the pitch darkness got him little more than a burning sensation from silt and debris. Feeling his way along the bottom was none too pleasant either, with slime so deep, his groping fingers buried to the wrists, never hitting solid ground.

Aware of small fish darting in all directions, Pearson kicked his legs, skimming the lake bed for several feet until it dropped sharply from beneath him. From somewhere below a bubble rose, tickling his stomach as it bounced off him. The exhale of a large animal, one that would soon rise for another breath.

Spinning, he fought through a tangle of underwater plants, swam as far as he could, and then forced his way to the surface. Gasping for breath, he pushed back his hair and sought the bank.

Theo paced like an anxious mother, biting what was left of his stubby nails.

Grinning, Pearson paddled toward him until he found his feet, emerging from the swirling water with mud up to his knees.

"There you are," Theo said. "What took so long?"

"It seemed only seconds to me." He pointed behind him. "It's dark and cold down there."

Crossing his arms, Theo slouched to one side. "What did you expect?"

Pearson laughed. "That it would be dark and cold, I suppose." He sobered. "We're going to need a drag, Theo, and it won't be easy going. We'll have to find a couple of rough-and-tumble men with strong arms and backs, preferably as familiar with this lake as we are with the Gulf."

"Men like Catfish John?"

He nodded. "Exactly like him."

"How do you plan on finding them? We've been asking around since we got here. No one seems interested."

Gripping Theo's shoulder with a muddy hand, he shook him. "Let's worry about the details later, all right? For now, I'm anxious to get back to town and clean up."

"And have dinner?" Theo rubbed his stomach. "I'm starved."

Pearson nodded, leading him to where they'd tethered their rented horses. "I could eat a bite myself." He patted Theo's back good-naturedly. "As long as it isn't catfish."

Smiling and waving, Mother boarded the train out of Marshall, her eyes red from crying, her chest puffed with pride.

Standing beside Miss Whitfield at the station, Addie struggled with all her might not to cry. She wasn't a child anymore, for goodness' sake! Her parents had sheltered her far too long. She'd fought hard for independence and the respect due her twenty-two years. Standing on the train platform, waving good-bye to her mother, she had it at last. Why then did it seem so hard?

"Oh Adelina," Miss Whitfield said, her arm circling Addie's waist, "you have the most forlorn expression. Don't worry, dear. You'll see her again."

Addie swallowed the growing lump in her throat. "I know I will. It's just that. . .well, it's the first time we've ever been apart."

"I know how you feel, honey. I remember when my parents sent me away to school for the first time. I thought my heart would break." She sighed. "Soon I made new friends, met your Dr. Moony, and before long, my father was scolding me for neglecting to write home." She tittered. "I got so wrapped up in my new life, the pull of my old one lessened."

Addie shook her head. "I can't imagine that happening."

"It will though." Miss Whitfield patted her waist. "You'll see."

Addie stood on tiptoe at the edge of the platform, watching the train until there was no longer even a speck visible down the track. Shoulders slumped, she rejoined her new employer, waiting patiently with her hands clasped and a fringed reticule dangling from her wrist.

"Are you ready now?" Miss Whitfield asked.

"I suppose so." She tucked her bottom lip. "I want to thank you for coming with me, ma'am. I didn't relish facing this alone."

Clucking her tongue, Miss Whitfield tapped her hand. "Nor should you. I was more than happy to be here. Let's get back to the carriage and we'll take you home."

Home? Addie's heart sank. The word had taken a whole new meaning. Instead of the two-story house in Canton, Mississippi, with her loved ones gathered inside, home meant a stately manor house in Marshall, Texas, where she dwelled with utter strangers.

"Are you hungry, dear? Delilah will have supper about ready when we arrive. I believe she's frying chicken for us tonight. Won't that be nice?"

Addie's mouth felt as though she had cotton bolls tucked into her cheeks. She grimaced. "Oh yes, ma'am. It sounds lovely."

Miss Whitfield prattled on about all the foods she hoped Delilah would serve alongside the main dish.

Not sure how she could stomach one bite, since the mere mention of supper made her queasy, Addie tuned out her chatter and gazed around at the nearby shops and houses.

Marshall's a pretty town, she thought as they neared the carriage. A prosperous town by the look of it. People dressed very nicely and kept their homes and yards in first-rate conditions. She would miss the familiarity of her hometown but decided on the spot to give Marshall a fair shake.

Two horses approached, trotting side by side along the opposite edge of the road. The riders' merry voices carried on the afternoon breeze—one shrill with mock indignation, the other gently teasing.

Addie's breath caught even before she glimpsed the tanned face and tangled hair beneath the hat. She couldn't mistake his smooth, rich voice.

Despite Pearson Foster's wet shirt and a layer of dried mud on his bare feet and rolled-up pants, he sat the saddle with the self-assured grace of a man in frock coat, button boots, and cashmere trousers.

He didn't see her at first, so she got a good long look at his handsome profile as he passed. At the last second, he whirled in the saddle and stared.

Addie blushed and ducked her head. Then, unable to resist, she met his gaze.

Pearson's eyes lit up, and a wide smile graced his face. He lifted his hat and nodded. "Well, well. Good afternoon."

Before she could think how to respond, or if indeed she should, Miss Whitfield took her arm and spun her around. "Shameless rabble," she muttered. "No better breeding than to address strange women in the street?" She rushed Addie into the carriage and tapped the driver's shoulder with her parasol. "Drive on, please. The streets aren't safe for decent women these days."

The man flicked the reins, and the horses moved away from the station. As they made the turn, Addie stole a peek.

Pearson and his funny little friend pulled up to the hotel and slid off their horses. Halfway up the walkway, he turned, bumped his hat off his forehead, and gazed in her direction.

Theo continued walking then stopped and doubled back. Clutching Pearson's sleeve, he hauled him toward the door.

Covering her smile with two fingers, she forced herself to focus on Miss Whitfield and whether candied yams or mashed potatoes were the best complement to Southern fried chicken. Unfortunately, she couldn't offer much to the conversation, considering the only accompaniment to supper she desired wasn't welcome at the table.

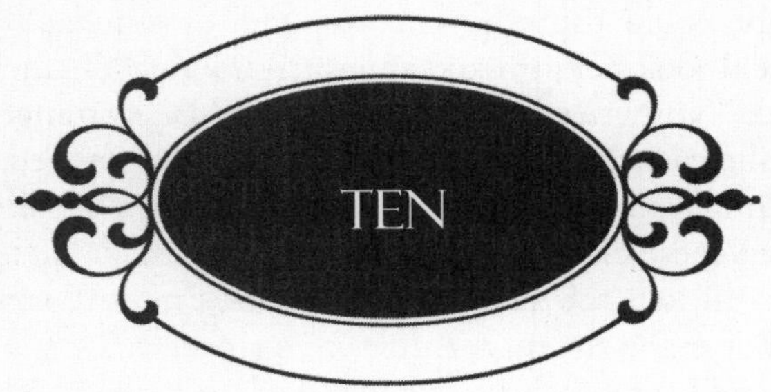

TEN

Pearson dried himself off then wrapped the towel around his waist. Despite the endless pitchers of water he'd poured over his head, muddy streams still dripped from his hair.

He'd sloshed through sludge as thick as gruel over the past three days in Caddo Lake, but today was the worst. He didn't look forward to doing it again, but he'd have to if he wanted to raise the *Mittie*.

"Won't you hurry, *principessa*?" Theo called.

Grinning, Pearson peered around the doorway, choking on laughter at the sight of Theo, his impatient dance rattling the boards of the bathhouse floor. Mud covered his face like a mask with cutouts for his mouth and eyes. "I'm the princess? I'm not the one who was afraid to go into the water for the last two days."

"I was afraid today, too," Theo countered, "but I went. I'm not accustomed to swimming with alligators, you know."

"The trick is in the dodge, my friend."

Theo chuckled, but his voice rose in irritation. "Hurry out of there, Pearson. The mud is beginning to harden on my skin. Pigeons are circling my head." He slapped his arms. "And I'm cold! What fools we were to come so early in the year. The warmth of the sun is deceptive. Two feet down in that lake and you'd swear it was winter."

"I'm almost done." Pulling on his britches and lifting his shirt from a hook, Pearson glanced at the tub. "Have the chambermaid bring a fresh bath. You don't want to dunk yourself in this muck soup. You'll come out worse off than you went in." He slipped on his boots and rounded the corner, settling his hat on his head. Lifting it again, he nodded at the fetching young maid crossing the courtyard of the Ginocchio Hotel. "Afternoon, miss."

She shot him a sweet smile and lowered her lashes.

Tossing the towel across his shoulder, he tipped his head at Theo. "I hope you'll excuse my grubby friend. He's been making mud pies again."

Theo shot him a threatening look then bowed to the maid, his smile bright against his mud-smeared face. "If it's not too much trouble, pretty lady, I'd appreciate a fresh tub of water. I make it a rule not to bathe after hogs."

She ducked her head and giggled.

Pearson yanked the towel from around his neck and swatted Theo with a loud *pop*.

"It's true," Theo insisted, dodging the end of the towel. "He cleans up well, but this man isn't kosher."

"Whatever you say, sir," she managed through her laughter. "I'll bring your water right away." Tittering, she scurried down the walk toward the back door of the hotel.

Watching her go, Theo yawned and stretched. "I hope she hurries. I need a hot meal and a soft mattress."

"I agree. We'll find something to eat before we go, and we'll turn in the minute we return."

Theo's hands, busy squeezing water out of his curls, stilled. "Return from where? I'm plenty tired, Pearson. I had no plans to go anywhere."

Pearson averted his gaze. "I thought we'd ride out to Whitfield Manor. You know. . .check on our new friends and see how they've fared."

Theo flashed his crooked grin. "By 'friend' you mean Mrs. McRae's daughter."

Pearson lifted one shoulder. "They're both very nice ladies." He wouldn't admit it to his merciless comrade, but in the four days since he'd met her, Miss Addie's big eyes and dainty chin hadn't left his mind.

Theo smirked. "Indeed. I thought you weren't ready for the bridle, stallion."

Tossing the towel, Pearson nodded toward the bathhouse. "Go wash the mire from your body. . .and rinse the sass from your big mouth while you're at it."

Laughing, Theo lobbed the wet cloth back at him and ducked inside the door.

With a hopeless shake of his head, Pearson ambled to their room.

Theo appeared a few minutes later, just as ornery, but looking more like himself. Pausing in the doorway, he gave Pearson a long look. "Are you spit and polished enough to go see this girl? I won't have you embarrass me."

Pearson tilted his head. "For a man who didn't want to go, you seem mighty eager."

He grinned. "Once I cleared the mud from the seat of my trousers, I felt better. Must've been weighing me down."

The buggy ride to Whitfield Manor was short but pleasant. The well-traveled road out of town soon turned into a winding uphill lane beneath spreading oaks.

In the circular drive, Pearson gave instructions to the driver to wait and then climbed to the ground.

Bailing out the other side, Theo passed behind the rig and came to join him. "What will you say to her?"

Heading up the stone walkway, Pearson shrugged. "I'll figure that out when I see her." At the stately front entrance, he took a deep breath and rapped with the gleaming brass knocker. Immediately the door swung open with such force, it startled him.

Theo gripped his shoulder and pulled him back a couple of steps.

A small boy, so wraithlike and spry he put Pearson in mind of a fairy, gazed with hollow eyes past them to the yard.

With a wry smile at his jumpy friend, Pearson stooped to eye level with the child. "Hello there. I'm Pearson, and my friend here is Theo." He offered his hand. "What do they call you?"

Ignoring Pearson's hand, the boy grunted and angled his body to see around him.

The intensity of his stare raised the hair on Pearson's neck. Instinctively he twisted to see behind him.

"What's he looking at?" Theo whispered.

"I was wondering the same."

A woman in a starched white apron and cap appeared from the shadows and latched onto the boy's shoulders. "Sorry, suh. He ain't supposed to answer the door, but he do it anyway. Can I help you?"

Pearson stood. "We're here to pay a call on Mrs. McRae."

She blinked up at him. "Did you say *Mrs.* McRae?"

He lifted a brow. "Mrs. Mariah McRae? I understand she's a guest here."

The boy began to moan and sway, so she nudged him gently down the hall. "Oh, yessuh. She was a guest, but she lef' on the train two days ago."

Regret sank like a stone to the pit of Pearson's stomach. He'd tried to wait a respectable amount of time to come calling, but now it appeared he'd waited too long. "May I ask where she went?"

"Gone back to Mississippi, I think." She pointed behind her. "I can go ask—"

"No, don't bother. We won't intrude." No sense disturbing the old lady.

"All right then," she said. "You gentlemens have yo'selves a nice day."

She stepped inside to close the door, but Pearson raised his hand. "Miss?"

The crack in the door widened. "Yessuh?"

"If I leave a note, will you see that Mrs. McRae gets it?"

"I'll do my best."

He fumbled at his pockets. "Let's see. . .I need something to write on."

"I'll bring you something, suh."

"And an envelope, if you don't mind."

"Yessuh. Wait right here."

The woman returned quickly and passed him a sheet of frilly stationery and a pen. The paper had bluebonnets around the border like a watercolor painting and smelled of flowers.

Pearson held it up and wrinkled his nose.

Smiling slightly, she shrugged. "That's all I could find."

Using Theo's bony back for a desk, Pearson jotted a few lines and signed it, then sealed it in the envelope. "Will you ask Miss Whitfield to send this?"

She nodded. "I'll ask."

"Much obliged."

Tipping his hat, he yanked at Theo's sleeve. "I guess that's all we can do. Let's go."

His heart a pulsing lump in his chest, he trudged down the steps. Mississippi seemed worlds away from Texas, which meant it might take a miracle to see Addie McRae again. On the way to the rig, he decided there were drawbacks to being on the outs with the One who specialized in miracles.

Ceddy sailed toward Addie in the upstairs corridor then whisked past her in a blur. Whirling, she called his name, but he ignored her. Wheeling around the corner, he burst into his bedroom and slammed the door shut behind him.

Two days ago she might've followed, but she'd grown accustomed to some of his behavior. Most anything could set him off, and seldom was it anything she'd done.

"Very well. I'll bring your afternoon snack," she announced to the empty hallway and then smiled. "Might get one for myself as well. Delilah's been baking again."

Smoothing her crisp linen skirt, she preened before the mirror as she passed. She'd worked for many families around Canton, caring for their children, but Miss Whitfield was the first employer who supplied a smart uniform.

Adjusting her white cap, she stepped closer to the upstairs window, her gaze drawn to someone milling in the yard. Pressing her nose to the glass, she gasped. Incredibly, Pearson Foster, the man who'd haunted her thoughts for days, and his Italian friend had come to call.

It took a second glance for her to realize they were at the end of the walkway climbing aboard one of the hired buggies from town.

"Great heavenly days!" she shrieked, hurling herself for the stairs. She reached the bottom landing and bolted for the front door. "Wait, don't leave!" she cried as she ran across the porch. Teetering at the top step, she slapped her hand over her mouth, shocked at her shameless lack of decorum.

No matter, they hadn't heard. The wagon turned at the grove of trees and disappeared down the lane.

Part of her flooded with relief that no one had witnessed her bellowing like a weaning calf. The other part shriveled inside with disappointment.

"Missy McRae? What is you doing?"

Spinning, she stared dumbly at Delilah.

Delilah hitched her shoulder toward the drive. "You know them boys?"

"Yes. Well, not exactly. What did they want? What did they say? Why on earth did they leave so soon?"

Delilah placed one hand on her hip. "Which of them questions you want me to answer?"

"All of them, please."

Biting her lip, she nodded. "Well, they wanted your mama. That's about all they said. And they left on account of she ain't here."

Addie stared. "They asked for my mother? Are you certain?"

"Yes'm. Called her by name."

"Did they say anything about me?" The second the words tripped off her tongue, heat crawled up her neck and flaming fire lit her cheeks. "I mean. . ."

"Sorry, Miss Addie. Your name ain't come up." Grinning, Delilah gathered her skirts and turned from the door. "Now, if you be done with questions, I got to take this letter to Miss Whitfield like I promised."

Seconds later, the import of her words pierced the troubled fog in Addie's mind. Racing inside, she caught up with Delilah, knocking at the door of the study.

"Come in," Miss Whitfield's muffled voice called.

Addie tugged on Delilah's sleeve. "Wait, please," she whispered. "Do you mean to say those two"—she pointed toward the front of the house—"the men who were just here. . .left a letter for Miss Whitfield?"

"No, ma'am."

"Oh." The breath left Addie in a rush. "Well, all right then." She waved with her fingers. "Carry on."

Delilah turned the knob. "They left a letter for your mama." Pulling an envelope from her pocket, she stepped inside the study and closed the door.

Pearson watched a robin flit by the buggy and perch on the edge of its nest. Tracked a cat squirrel up a tall pine. Considered the bald spot on the back of the driver's head. Anything but meeting Theo's mournful gaze.

"Sorry, old man," he finally said.

Embarrassed, Pearson shrugged. "For what?"

Theo widened his eyes. "Don't try pretending with me. I know you too well." The tip of his tongue appeared in his cheek. "You're pretty disappointed, aren't you?"

"Don't get sentimental, Theo. She's just a girl like all the rest."

"Is that so?" He dug his elbow in Pearson's side. "Then why do you look like you're about to cry?"

Growling, Pearson returned the favor, except with more force. "You don't know what you're talking about."

Theo wagged a finger in his face. "I've seen that expression before. Many times, in fact. You look this way after every bum lead on Jean Lafitte's gold."

"What?" Angry with himself for the girlie shrill in his voice, Pearson crossed his arms and turned his back on his friend. Much more lip and he'd be tossing him over the side.

"What is it about this one, Pearce?" Theo continued, oblivious to the danger he was in. "You didn't take on this way when you left Pearl behind at Rosie's."

"Do yourself a favor, pal. Change the subject."

His gruff tone sounded so ominous, the driver glanced nervously behind him.

Laughing, Theo held up his hands. "All right, just tell me one thing." He pressed his face dangerously close and raised his brow. "What did you write in that letter?"

"Let it go, Theo. I'm warning you."

He chuckled. "Very well. I'll leave you to mourn in peace." His voice lowered dramatically. "Just remember. . .I'm here for you."

"That's supposed to cheer me?"

After a last hearty laugh, the maddening Italian settled against the seat humming an off-key tune, his big eyes taking in their surroundings.

Left to his thoughts, Pearson questioned his reaction to the news that the woman he'd known so briefly had departed Texas.

Miss Adelina Viola McRae had affected him more than he cared to admit. . .to Theo or anyone else.

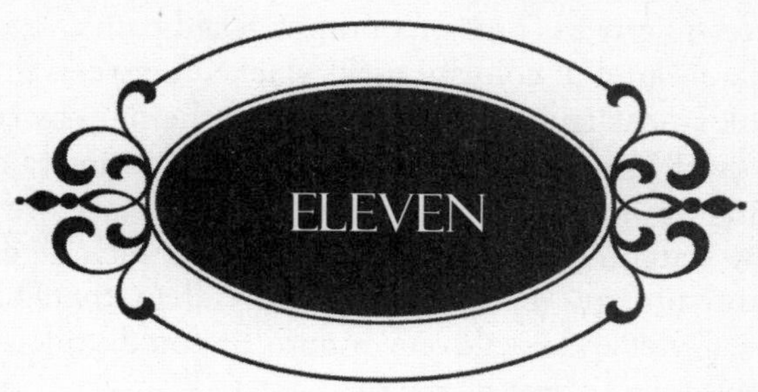

ELEVEN

Her mind consumed by thoughts of Pearson's visit, her curiosity piqued by the mysterious letter, Addie found it hard to concentrate on her job. Balancing a tray with Ceddy's afternoon snack and a generous serving of milk, she bumped open the door of his room with her hip and stepped inside.

Her first day as Ceddy's governess, she'd knocked before entering his inner sanctum. Flustered when he never answered, she'd gone to Delilah for advice.

Finding more humor in her display of common courtesy than Addie felt was warranted, Delilah took pleasure in demonstrating the futility of the gesture. She stationed Addie inside the room so she could see for herself that when a knock sounded on Ceddy's door, he pressed his ear to the other side and listened.

Addie wondered if he failed to recognize the sound as a request to enter or if he didn't bother to care. The accepted customs of polite society seemed wasted on his simplistic view of life.

Delilah may have said it best once she'd opened the door and peered inside, laughing. "He don't know no better!"

Mr. Uncomplicated sat on the floor behind the bed when she entered, the back of his blond head the only thing visible.

"Good afternoon, young sir. I've brought your goodies."

Not a whisper of response. No hint of notice.

"Look here. Lilah used her last jar of dewberries to make you a cobbler."

The little shoulders rounded over his task.

"Ceddy?" Addie placed the tray on a table and walked around the bed. He played quietly in front of a humpbacked trunk, legs splayed to the sides and a mound of colorful rocks stacked between them. One at a time, he took stones from the pile and lined them up by color.

She observed him for a spell, burning with curiosity about what might be going on inside his pixie head. Over the last two days, she'd come to enjoy watching him immensely. He was such a beautiful boy, looking at him brought her pleasure. More than that, his behavior fascinated her. Quiet and docile one minute, he could explode in motion or erupt in frightened cries the next.

Picking up the tray, Addie placed it next to him. With the hem of her skirt, she waved the aroma of the fresh-baked treat in his direction, smiling when he dropped the rock clutched in his hand and made a grab for the cobbler.

She'd rather he'd reached for the fork. Still, it was progress.

Squatting to his level, she held out the milk. "Don't you want to wash it down?"

He raised both shoulders and leaned away from her.

"All right," she said, sliding the tray closer. "I'll put it where you can reach it when you're ready."

Reaching blindly behind him, he felt for the glass and shoved it over.

"Why did you do that?" she cried, whipping off her apron to use for a mop. "Look at this mess."

The door squealed open and Delilah blinked at her from the hall. "Miss Priscilla be looking for you."

Startled, Addie shot to her feet, wiping her wet hands on her skirt. "Oh gracious. Tell her I'll be right along."

Delilah shook her head. "No, Miss Addie, she right out here in the hall."

Addie whirled as Miss Whitfield squeezed past Delilah. "Not looking anymore. I see I've found her."

"Ceddy's having his afternoon snack," Addie announced stiffly. The silly words echoed in the room.

Thankfully, Miss Whitfield smiled. "With his usual flair, I see." She shook her head at Ceddy's sticky hands and face, the berry stains like terrible bruises. "Wipe up this milk, please, Delilah, and bring a wet rag to clean him up." She grimaced at Addie. "He doesn't like to take his milk, but I suppose you've figured that out."

Addie released a breathy laugh. "He managed to communicate his wishes fairly well."

"We should've warned you, I suppose. We have to beg and bribe him. But it's quite good for his health I understand."

"Yes, ma'am. So it is."

Miss Whitfield's demeanor changed. "I suppose you're wondering why I'm disrupting your workday." Deep creases appeared between her eyes. "I wanted to discuss your mother's recent visitors."

Addie's stomached tightened. Before she could think how to respond, Ceddy howled, the sound so piercing she cowered and covered her ears. "What on earth?"

He had finished the rows of stones, laid out in front of him in a patchwork of color. The square they formed lacked a corner, one empty slot marring the perfect symmetry. Screaming as if in pain, he tapped the space with his gooey pointer finger.

"What is it, dear?" Miss Whitfield asked, her voice taut and anxious. "Merciful heavens, what does he want?"

Delilah returned at a run, and Miss Whitfield spun toward her. "Bring another dish of cobbler. Quickly!"

"Yes'm," she cried and dashed away.

"Wait, don't you see?" Addie said. "He doesn't want to eat. He wants—"

With a frustrated grunt, Ceddy bent over his design and forcefully swept it away with his forearm. The rocks scattered in all directions, one striking the windowpane so hard it cracked.

"Oh blast! Look what he's done. Addie, can't you do something?"

She'd been asking herself the same question. On instinct, she dropped to the floor in front of Ceddy and rattled her mother's beads.

Their effect was immediate. The shrieking died on his lips, and his head whipped around to face her. A sweet smile softened the lines of his face, and he swiped at a lingering tear.

Clutching her hands together, Miss Whitfield plopped onto the bed. "For pity's sake. Have you ever seen the like?"

Delilah burst in waving a mottled scoop of cobbler on a saucer. "I come as quick as I could."

Addie's hand shot up. "Wait, please. Not yet."

Ignoring the treat and everything else in the room, Ceddy scooted closer to smooth his fingertip over the polished jasper.

Addie crowded her finger beside his to stroke the stone along with him. "It's very pretty, isn't it?"

Disappointment filled her heart as he abruptly pulled away. In rash impatience, she'd stumbled over one of his boundaries.

Dismay turned to wonder as he tugged a big book from under the bed and set to frantically flipping the pages. Stopping on a dog-eared sheet, he crab-crawled into her lap, dragging the book behind him. "Uh," he grunted, jabbing one of the small photos on the page. Catching the necklace in his curled fingers, he jangled the pendant.

"Is he—" Miss Whitfield started.

"I believe he is," Addie said. "He's showing me they're the same." She touched the little square; the stone in the picture was medium green with flecks of red scattered throughout. "Jasper. Also known as bloodstone. You're exactly right. Very good, Ceddy." She beamed at Miss Whitfield. "Very good indeed."

Just as fast as he'd come to her, Ceddy scooted from Addie's lap and gathered his stones, this time aligning them in the order they appeared on the page.

Delilah advanced with the saucer, but Miss Whitfield shook her head. "Take it back to the kitchen. He doesn't want it."

She crooked her finger at Addie and strode to the door. "Stay with him for a spell, Delilah. Should you need us, we'll be in the study."

A lump in her throat, Addie followed Miss Whitfield down the hall. Just inside the door, the woman abruptly turned and embraced her. "I knew it," she whispered against Addie's ear. "I knew my instincts about you were good." Pushing her to arm's length, she smiled. "You're going to be wonderful for Ceddy."

"But I didn't do anything."

"Oh, my dear, but you did. And I'm grateful." She pointed at the straight-backed chair. "Now on to less inspiring topics. Take a seat, please."

Sitting across from her stern-faced employer, Addie fought the urge to loosen her collar.

Slipping on her spectacles, Miss Whitfield leaned across the desk, one brow drawn to a peak. She placed a sealed envelope between them. "As I said before, I have a few questions about the young men who came to call earlier today."

Addie nodded. "Yes ma'am?" The woman's silence pressed her to continue. "To be honest, I don't really know much about them." Bending closer to the letter, she frowned at the faint outline of bluebonnets. "I don't understand. Isn't that your stationery?"

Miss Whitfield nodded. "Delilah provided it for them."

She turned the envelope over, and Addie stared at her mother's name scrawled in large, neat letters. Surely Pearson Foster had written the letter. The forward act was just the sort of thing she could imagine him doing. But why?

"Does your mother know these men?" Miss Whitfield asked, interrupting her thoughts.

Addie swallowed. "Not exactly. We met them at the station when we arrived."

She gaped at Addie over the top of her wire frames. "Did you say *met* them?"

"I mean, they just suddenly appeared and offered to help with our luggage."

The poor woman's eyes bulged. "Why would your lovely mother give those two ruffians the time of day? They looked so"—she wrinkled her nose—"unkempt."

"You saw them?"

Miss Whitfield waved toward the front window. "A glimpse is all, but it was enough." She stared thoughtfully. "I had the oddest sensation that I'd seen them somewhere before. . ." She shook her head. "But that's not likely."

Shriveling under Miss Whitfield's air of disapproval, Addie didn't dare jog her memory. If she knew they were the same men on horseback in town, she'd bust a stitch.

She wrung her hands in her lap. "They were really quite nice."

"Nice? Well, they certainly don't look it. What are they doing in Marshall?"

"They're here to raise a shipwrecked steamboat or something of that nature. I believe he—Mr. Foster, the tall one—said they were wreckers."

A glint of understanding flashed in Miss Whitfield's narrowed eyes. "Wreckers indeed. I know just the steamboat they hope to raise, and I know why." She snorted scornfully. "Those two aren't wreckers, dear. That at least is an honorable profession in most circles. They're treasure seekers, Addie. A vulgar pursuit at best, not to mention a reckless waste of time."

Addie sat forward in her chair. "Treasure hunters?"

"They're after the gold that went down with the *Mittie Stephens*."

Now that Addie thought about it, Pearson Foster had sounded vaguely mysterious about their intentions. "Ma'am, is the steamboat you mentioned in a nearby lake?"

Miss Whitfield lifted her head. "Lake Caddo." She nodded. "I'm right, then, aren't I? They're after the *Mittie*." She absently worried the corner of the letter with one tapered nail. "Oh Addie. What do you think they want with your mother?"

Addie shrugged. "I can't imagine. We spent a very short time with them. After lunch they escorted us to hire a rig, and that was the end of it."

"You took lunch with total strangers?" Miss Whitfield snatched a small crocheted doily from the corner of her desk to fan herself. "Oh my, I hope no one saw you. What was Mariah thinking?"

Addie's spine stiffened, and she drew up her chin. "My mother may be a bit unconventional at times, but she's ever the lady. There was nothing improper about our behavior."

Biting her bottom lip, Miss Whitfield lowered her makeshift fan and leaned to touch Addie's hand. "Forgive me, dear. I never meant to imply otherwise. I'm a bit concerned, that's all."

Her eyes drawn to the letter again, Addie cleared her throat. "This mystery is easily solved. I have errands in Marshall this afternoon." She reached across the desk. "I'd be happy to forward this on to Mother. I'm sure she'll send a timely explanation."

Snatching the envelope before Addie's fingers reached it, Miss Whitfield shook her graying head. "Don't trouble yourself." Her stern voice left no room for argument. "I'll take care of it."

As she stared at Mr. Foster's bold handwriting, her brows knitted above her glasses. "I need to give the matter more thought. To be honest, I haven't decided if I should mail it at all."

"But ma'am, is that—" Shocked by her own boldness, Addie tucked her chin and stilled.

Miss Whitfield shook herself from her thoughts and drew a breath.

"My place to decide? I'm convinced it is. If not for me, you and your mother would never have come to Marshall. Consequently, you'd never have met those two peculiar men." She opened a drawer and slid the letter inside. "That's all for now, dear. You may go."

Firmly dismissed, Addie rose from her chair and turned toward the door.

"Adelina?"

She slowed to look over her shoulder. "Yes, ma'am?"

"Take some time while Delilah's with the boy." She motioned with her hand. "Change into a fresh uniform. I'm afraid you're wearing a good portion of Ceddy's milk." A smile warmed her eyes. "Get in a nice nap if you'd like. I imagine Delilah's urging your charge to do the same. You'll find our pace slows down considerably this time of day."

Touched by her thoughtfulness, Addie ducked her head. "Thank you, Miss Whitfield."

Passing Ceddy's door to her own, she glimpsed Delilah tucking the covers under his chin, heard her deep, rumbling voice humming a quiet lullaby.

Inside her room, Addie quickly shucked to her dainties and pulled on a dressing gown. Wrapping it around her, she sank into the comfortable chair beside the bed and breathed a relieved sigh.

She was tired lately, as the bags under her eyes bore witness. She always found the early days of a new assignment tedious, what with getting a firm grasp on things and learning her employer's expectations. This job made the rest seem paltry.

As her tense muscles eased, her thoughts swirled in a drowsy fog, centered on Mr. Foster and his troublesome letter. Three points of interest tickled her scattered mind, roiling from the mists and taking an ugly shape: One, Mr. Foster seemed quite taken with her beautiful mother the day they met. Two, he'd made a special trip from town to call on her. And three, the most scandalous act of all, the blackguard had written a note to her mother on Miss Whitfield's lavender-scented stationery with the bluebonnet border.

Addie sat up gripping the arm of her chair, all possibility of a nap driven away by outrage. These truths led to one inescapable conclusion. Pearson Foster wasn't drawn to Addie. The unscrupulous rogue had designs on her mother!

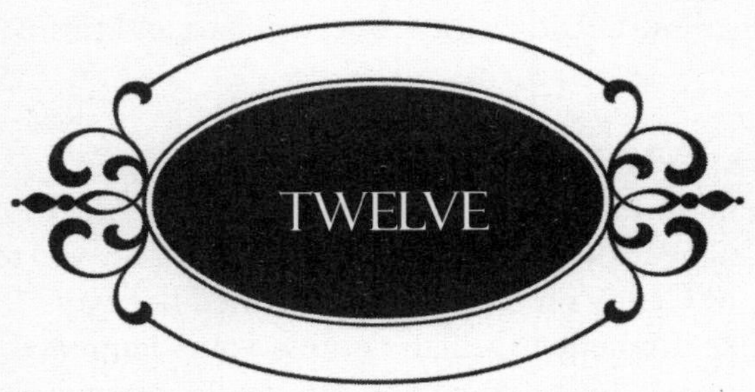

TWELVE

After a restless night pondering the shocking revelation about Mr. Foster's indecent intentions, and a stressful morning coaxing Ceddy to eat his porridge, Addie had little patience with his refusal to drink his afternoon glass of milk. Why Miss Whitfield seemed so adamant for him to have it, she couldn't fathom. Surely they could remove from his diet a beverage he so fiercely detested.

They sat together at the breakfast nook in the kitchen. The sun, muted by the magnolia tree near the window, shone patches of mottled light across his face.

"Please, honey," Addie pleaded. "Have a few sips, and then you can leave the table."

He swung, but she snatched the glass away in time.

"Mercy! It's not that bad, is it?" She wrinkled her nose and stole a taste of the frothy drink. The creamy liquid slid over her tongue, cool and refreshing. "My goodness. It's actually very tasty." Her stomach growled, but she resisted the urge to drain the glass. Shrugging, she placed it out of his reach as Delilah entered the room.

Leaping up, Ceddy ran to bury his face in her apron.

Delilah smiled. "I'm glad he don't drink it no better for you, Miss Addie. I's startin' to think he jus' be spiteful."

"I can't imagine why he doesn't want it." Addie swiped away the white mustache clinging to her top lip. "It's delicious."

Ceddy moaned and tugged on Delilah's skirt.

"Poor mite. He hungry, too."

"I know," Addie agreed. "Miss Priscilla thought with an empty stomach he'd be more receptive to the milk." She smiled wryly. "It didn't work."

"Why you don't feed him?"

"We're going into town for lunch today." Addie beamed. "We're having the Ginocchio Salad. Have you ever tried one?"

Turning to the sink, she snorted derisively. "No, and I don't care to. Whoever heard of putting pecan meats in lettuce?"

Addie spun on her heel. "Why, I'm surprised at you, Delilah. You're such a creative cook, I would've thought you'd appreciate diversity in food preparation."

Delilah blushed. "Thank you, Miss Addie. I don't understand them big words you always spoutin', but thank you jus' the same." She took the milk from Addie and poured it in the dishpan. "When Miss Priscilla asks if he took it, you let me answer. I'd sooner have a lie on my conscience than see Little Man pestered anymore."

Addie grinned and patted her arm.

Miss Whitfield swept in wearing a wide-brimmed hat and a lavender dress with velveteen trim. Delilah had laced her corset so tightly, the contraption forced her torso forward on top and her hips backward, creating the silhouette of a stuffed pheasant.

She glanced at the empty glass in Delilah's hand, and her mouth flew wide. "He drank it? How wonderful." She smoothed the back of Ceddy's head. "There's Auntie's good fellow. I knew you could do it."

Ceddy pulled away and slid behind Delilah.

Addie cast her co-conspirator a secretive look and hurried to change the subject. "My, don't you look lovely, ma'am."

Miss Whitfield's lips pushed outward in a pout. "I simply hate to be called 'ma'am,' Addie. Makes me feel like a crone. And 'Miss Priscilla' just reminds me that I'm an old maid. Can't we dispense with formality? I'd like you to call me Priscilla, if you don't mind."

"Yes, ma'am." Addie grinned and brought her hand to her mouth. "I'll try to remember."

Priscilla patted her arm. "Good. Shall we go then? That salad of yours is sounding better by the minute."

Pearson stabbed at his plate and brought up a forkful of pecans and lettuce covered in thick mayonnaise. "This was a good idea, Theo." He shoved in the bite and proceeded to talk with his mouth full. "It's the first time since we left the lake that I can't taste mud."

Theo nodded. "Enjoy it while you can. You'll get another mouthful once we hire a couple of hands and head back out there." Closely studying his plate, he avoided Pearson's eyes. "You're not going to turn this into another search for Lafitte's gold, are you, Pearce?"

Pearson wiped his mouth. "Now, what did I say? We'll give it a good effort, but if we don't have any luck, we'll call it a wash. Didn't I promise?"

Chasing a sliver of pecan around his plate, Theo nodded. "You did, but I know you. You're like a blind bulldog. Once your teeth are buried in something, you don't know when to turn loose."

Dropping his fork with a clatter, Pearson sat forward and stared. "I don't know about blind, but I am seeing things." He pointed. "Isn't that the lovely Miss McRae?"

Theo spun around. "Oh yeah, that's her. I'm not sure about the mourning dress, but there's no mistaking that heart-shaped face and those big eyes."

Accompanied by an elderly woman, Addie stood with one hand on the shoulder of the odd little boy they'd briefly seen at the mansion. The stiff, black uniform she wore tried hard to hide her charms but couldn't succeed. She stared around the room, most likely watching for the maître d' to seat them.

"Looks like we were lied to," Theo said.

"Yes, it does." Pearson stood. "Let's find out why."

"Wait!" Theo called, reaching a hand toward him.

Ignoring his friend's caution, Pearson strode across the room and bowed to each of the women in turn. "Good afternoon, Miss McRae. What an unexpected pleasure."

The color drained from Addie's complexion, and the big eyes in question rounded in surprise. "Mr. Foster, I didn't expect to see you again so soon."

He smiled. "I didn't expect to see you at all. You're supposed to be in Mississippi, aren't you?"

The older woman stiffened and stared down her nose. "I beg your pardon." Her tone, more than her words, invited Pearson to return to his table and to his lowly station.

He shot her his most charming smile. "Forgive me, ma'am. I'm acquainted with Miss McRae here, but you and I haven't been introduced. I'm Pearson Foster, of the Galveston Fosters."

She relaxed slightly and nodded, good breeding getting the best of her. "Priscilla Whitfield."

He caught her hand and lightly kissed it. "Dear lady, you're a legend in Marshall, and I'm honored to meet you."

"Yes." The single word wavered with doubt.

"My friend and I rode out to your lovely home the other day." He studied her face for recognition. "We spoke with your maid. I assume she told you?"

She sniffed. "I'm well aware of your visit."

He turned a shaky smile on Addie. "We came to call on you, to be exact."

"On me?" She lifted her chin, ice in her voice. "Or my mother?"

Thrown off by their chilly reception, Pearson searched his mind for something to say.

Miss Whitfield beat him to the draw. "If you'll excuse us, we'd like to be seated now."

Jumping at the chance, he spun and pointed behind him. "Won't you join us? The hungry-looking fellow in the corner is my business partner. We'd be happy to share our table."

Theo, leaning over the back of his chair, grinned and raised two fingers in a jaunty wave.

"Well, I. . ." As flighty as a snared grouse, Miss Whitfield searched about the room for an avenue of escape. "We appreciate the offer. Perhaps another time."

Pearson opened his mouth to protest, but the boy, standing docile and quiet until then, let out a shrill cry and darted behind the old girl.

Turning one way then the other like a dog chasing its tail, Miss Whitfield tried to pull him in front of her. "What is it, Ceddy? Come here, child."

The piercing howl grew louder, and tears flooded his eyes.

Catching his arm, she bent to look at him. "Heavens! His face is deathly pale. What happened?"

"I can't imagine," Addie said. "He seems frightened, doesn't he?" Concern clouded her face as she knelt in front of him. "Ceddy? What is it, darling?"

Forgetting herself, Miss Whitfield spoke her mind. "Could it be Mr. Foster's hair? I'm sure he's never seen the like."

Flustered and embarrassed, Pearson gathered the strands off his shoulders.

"I told you this wouldn't work, Addie." Miss Whitfield stood, glancing around at the staring diners. "Whatever has him bothered, it's obvious we can't stay now." She guided the boy toward the exit. "Come, let's get him home. Your salad will have to wait for another day."

Desperate, Pearson caught Addie's sleeve. "If not lunch today, maybe a picnic tomorrow? The hotel will provide a nice basket, if you know of a sunny spot."

She tugged her arm free. "No, thank you. Now, if you'll excuse us. . ."

Pausing on the threshold, she turned. "By the by, Miss Whitfield decided to mail your letter. In fact, we've just left the post office." Tilting her head, she gave him a knowing smile. "You'll be happy to hear that your missive is probably on its way to my mother as we speak. I'm certain my father will find it most entertaining." Nose to the sky, she flounced out the door.

When the stunned haze cleared, Pearson slunk to rejoin Theo at the table.

Glee in his eyes, Theo cleared his throat. "A picnic?"

Pearson released a ragged sigh. "Don't start. It was all I could think of at the moment."

"Sorry, old man," Theo murmured.

"Stop saying you're sorry for me, will you? You said the same the day we left Whitfield Manor."

"I couldn't help it. You looked so dejected when you thought she'd gone." He pointed. "Pretty much the way you do now."

Balling his napkin, he tossed it at Theo's face. "Forget about her. I plan to." Shoving away the salad that seemed so appetizing just moments before, he sat back in his chair. "Let's get out of here. It's time we focused on hiring a couple of hands. The sooner we're done and out of Marshall, the better."

Theo pointed over Pearson's shoulder. "What about those two? They have an out-of-work look to them."

In the far corner, a couple of men sat hunched over their plates, one short and gaunt, the other portly and balding. Both stared out the window with bulging eyes.

Following the direction they gazed, Pearson saw Addie and Miss Whitfield outside the glass, still trying to calm the sobbing child.

"Will you look? They're gawking at Addie."

Theo shrugged. "They're men, Pearson. They're going to watch a pretty woman."

"I don't like how closely they're watching."

"Is that so? I thought we were going to forget about her." Theo nudged his shoulder and stood. "Come on, they're leaving. Let's see if they're interested in work. Or if they know someone who is."

The bony man with the hollow eyes glanced up fast when they neared his table. Tensing, he lowered the money he'd been counting out for his bill into his lap.

Theo ducked his head. "Afternoon, sir. My name is Theodoro Bernardi. We don't mean to intrude, but my friend and I are looking for a couple of locals with idle hands and strong backs."

The men looked ready to bolt for the door.

Pearson edged Theo aside and held out his hand. "Pearson Foster, gentlemen. Forgive my blundering associate. He's trying to ask if you might be seeking gainful employment. We're hoping to hire a pair of laborers."

The meatier of the two waved them off. "Barkin' up the wrong oak, mate. We ain't lookin' for work."

His companion's hand shot up. "Not so fast, Charlie." Grinning up at Pearson with tobacco-stained teeth, he shrugged. "We ain't locals, guvnah. If that don't worry you none, we might 'ave a go. What sort of job are you peddlin'?"

Denny gnawed his bottom lip as Mr. Foster and his clownish friend strolled away from the table. Once they passed through the archway and left by the double doors, Charlie clutched his sleeve. "What in blazes are you doing? Why'd you take the job?"

Denny shoved his hand aside. "Think, mate. Those two were talking to the old girl, which means they likely know where she lives. And Charlie, me boy, where she lives is where we'll catch up with that snivelin' brat."

Charlie nodded, a light in his eyes. "And where the brat is. . ."

"I'll find me blessed diamond."

Charlie cocked his head and scowled. "Yours, Denny? We're in this together, you and me."

Denny glanced away. "Sure, that's what I meant."

"Why don't we just follow them home?"

"Well, that was me plan before that strapping big bloke loomed over the table."

"I see your point." Charlie rubbed his bristled chin. "You think the woman recognized us?"

"How could she? She ain't the same one as before."

"You sure about that?"

"Yeah, mate. This girl is younger. . .prettier. Did you notice the uniform? She's a governess to the lad, or some such."

Charlie blew a breath. "The boy knew us right off. Nearly choked on me nosh when he set to squawking."

"Yeah? Well, he's mute. Who's he going to tell?"

Pretending a sudden interest in his food, Charlie swirled cold potatoes with his fork. "You promised not to hurt him, right? No matter what?"

Denny's hand snaked out and caught him by the scruff. "You leave the planning to me. If it was down to you, we'd be on that sinking washtub still, swabbing the deck to pay our passage home."

Drawing his hulking body into a shrunken knot, the big oaf looked like a scolded child. "Sorry, Den. I don't want him hurt, that's all. He's just a wee tyke, after all." He glanced up. "And an orphan, remember? Like you."

Denny shoved him against the back of the chair. "Like me?" He snorted. "Did you see his frilly white shirt with the ruffled collar and cuffs? Those leather shoes with the perky bows? Just one of those shoes cost a month's wage for the likes of us, Charlie Pickering." He pointed a trembling finger, his voice shaking. "That boy's life is nothing like mine."

Reclining against the seat, he crossed his legs and stared out the front window. "We'll take that job all right." He absently stroked his chin. "We'll bide our time, get close to those two blokes. Maybe they'll lead us right inside the house." A slow smile crept over his face. "Who knows? We could be sipping tea and nibblin' biscuits at Ceddy Whitfield's table."

Charlie leaned closer. "You reckon?" He beamed stupidly. "I'd like that."

"Meanwhile, we'll follow them wherever they go. The first chance I get to lay me hands on that boy, I'm takin' it."

Pearson strolled onto the porch ahead of Theo, searching the street for signs of Addie McRae. Spotting the back of her carriage turning toward the hill, he let go a deep sigh. Why did that little girl persist in running away from him? Even more distressing, why did he care?

"Why'd you go and hire those men?" Theo demanded behind him. "They know less about the *Mittie* than we do."

"You're the one who marched us to their table."

"It's a little hard to tell a man's foreign from across the room."

"We need help," Pearson said over his shoulder. "They looked able to haul a dragline. Right now, I'd hire old women."

"Old women might be more helpful. We don't know what we're doing, Pearson. Or where to start. We need locals."

Pearson turned and swept his hand up the street. "Find me a local, and I'll hire him."

Theo stood in front of a bulletin board nailed against the wall, his fists on his hips. "I hope you mean that." Motioning to Pearson, he moved aside to make room. Planting his finger against a handwritten notice tacked to the board, he nodded. "Here's where we'll find all the laborers we need."

Pearson read the first few lines then scowled. "A church social?"

Theo nodded. "Of course. It's perfect."

Feeling smothered, Pearson stalked away. "I don't think it's perfect."

"Sure it is, Pearce. The whole town turns out for these things."

Waving his hand behind him, he drew a deep breath. "If you want to, go ahead. But count me out."

"It's just a church service, buddy. I remember a time when you wouldn't miss one."

"That was a long time ago."

Theo stood quietly for too long. It didn't bode well. "Come on, paisan. What happened to you?"

First Addie's stinging rebuke, and now this? Could the day get any worse? "I know you mean well, Theo, but change the subject."

Theo shook his head. "Not this time. Look, friend. . .you've kept this feud with the Almighty going for five years. Don't you think it's time you made peace?"

Anguish washed over Pearson, as fresh as the day his family died. Gripping the arm of a nearby bench, he lowered his body before his trembling legs gave out. "Mind your own business."

Theo spun closer, surprising Pearson with tear-filled eyes. "It is my business. I spent more time in your house than my own, more time at your mama's table than mine." A wobbly grin slipped through his grief. "We both know it wasn't because of her cooking."

"So?"

"So I know the thing that made them proudest of you was your faith. I also know that if Mama Foster was here, she'd be sad to see you've shut God out."

Pearson's throat threatened to close on his pain. When he could speak, his protest came out a croak. "But she's not here, is she? Neither is Pa, my brother, or my sister." He swiped at his eyes. "That little girl was three years old. She never had a chance at life."

"Thousands perished that night, Pearson. God didn't single out your family to die."

"I never said He did."

Theo splayed his hands. "Then what? What do you blame Him for?"

Leaning over, Pearson gripped his head in his hands. "For singling me out to live."

Scalding tears dripped onto his boot and slid over the side, washing the dust away in little rivulets.

Theo crossed the porch and gripped his shoulder. "I'm going to that service tomorrow. I really hope you'll join me. It's time you forgave yourself for being alive."

FOURTEEN

Addie hurried downstairs and lit out for the dining room, late for breakfast again. She hadn't quite settled into life at Whitfield Manor, and her duties to Ceddy kept her jumping. There seemed never enough time in the harried mornings to wash up, air out her uniform, arrange her curls, and find her place at the table before Delilah appeared with the food.

Dreading her employer's disapproving glance, Addie slid to a stop outside the door to check her hair and smooth her apron.

"Addie, is that you? You're not dawdling behind the doorpost again."

Addie's shoulders drooped in defeat. "Yes, ma'am." She sighed. "I mean, yes, it's me."

"Stop lurking, dear, and come inside."

Drawing a quick breath, she charged into the fray. "Morning, Priscilla. So sorry I'm late."

The woman's forehead drew to a troubled knot. "What are you wearing, Adelina?"

Addie paused with one hand on the back of her chair and gazed down at her skirt. "I'm sorry. I tried to press out the wrinkles, but my time grew short."

"I don't mean the state of your clothing, child. I'm referring to what you have on. Are you going to church in your uniform?"

Addie gave her a vacant stare. "Oh my. Today's the Sabbath? I completely lost track of the days."

Priscilla picked up her knife and spread a thin layer of butter over a slice of toast. "Get back on track, if you please. I'd like you to accompany me this morning." Her head tipped toward a vacant place at the table. "Sit down before the grease on your eggs congeals any further, and then you can go upstairs and change. I promised your mother I'd see to your spiritual welfare, and I always keep a promise."

"What about Ceddy?"

"He's going with us. Delilah won't be here to watch him. She worships with her family on Sunday mornings."

Addie fingered the folds of her uniform. "As Ceddy's governess, shouldn't I leave this on if we're going to town?"

Priscilla wiped her mouth. "In one of those pompous homes up north, perhaps. We're far less formal around here. I won't require you to wear that dour old thing to God's house."

"Well. . .if you're sure."

"Yes." Priscilla nodded firmly. "I am. I should think you'd relish the chance to show off those pretty spring dresses in your wardrobe. I must say your parents provided well for you." She flashed a sweet smile. "Besides, Addie. . .you're not just Ceddy's governess. I consider you a friend."

Heat rose to Addie's cheeks. She slid into her seat, unfolding her napkin in the same motion and laying it across her lap. "I'm honored. I want you to know I feel the same."

"Then it's settled. I'm going to show off my new friend to my church fellowship."

Addie beamed. "That sounds lovely."

Delilah bustled in, snatching up serving trays and wiping away scattered crumbs. She startled, one hand on the coffee decanter, when Priscilla abruptly cleared her throat. "What are you doing, Delilah? Leave those, please. We're not done eating."

Delilah licked her bottom lip and glanced over her shoulder at the grandfather clock. "You ain't?"

"As you can clearly see, we've hardly touched our plates. I know you're in a rush to be on your way, but allow us to finish our breakfast, please, before you clear the table. In the meanwhile, lay out warm clothing for Ceddy. It actually resembles a winter morn outside, though I doubt the chill will linger past noon."

Addie swallowed a bite of toast and nodded. "The weather has been quite mild and pleasant. I hate to see it end."

Delilah still hovered, thoughtfully gnawing her bottom lip.

"Didn't you hear me, Delilah?" Priscilla swirled her index finger, motioning her out of the room. "Go on with you now and allow us to eat."

"Yes'm." Settling the platter of bacon with a wobble and replacing the silver urn, Delilah backed toward the kitchen door, a troubled frown on her face.

Priscilla sat back in her chair with a sigh. "Oh, for pity's sake. Fry a fresh egg for Addie then go on and leave. This mess can wait until you return. I won't be held accountable to God if the St. Paul Baptist choir lacks a contralto."

"Yes, ma'am," Delilah said, stressing both words with equal fervor and a bright smile. "I'll bring that egg right away." She left in a rush, leaving Addie and Priscilla chuckling after her.

They ate quietly, accompanied by the clink of silverware on china and the steady tick of the tall clock. Growing increasingly aware of Priscilla's watchful eyes, Addie glanced up. "Do you need something, ma'am?" *Priscilla, Priscilla, Priscilla,* she chided herself. Why was it so hard to remember the woman's preference?

Studying the delicate face, etched with concern, Addie realized the reason why. Miss Whitfield reminded her very much of Miss Vee, her childhood governess and family friend. She held such respect and reverence for the old dear, she couldn't call her Viola if she tried. Not only that, but Addie's parents had distilled in her a proper respect for the elderly. Priscilla Whitfield's request was in opposition to years of parental training.

Thankfully, whatever was on her mind seemed to take precedence over how she should be addressed. "I've been thinking all night about Ceddy's. . .episode. . .in the hotel restaurant." She crinkled her brow. "What do you suppose got into him?"

Addie cleared her throat. "His behavior was that much out of character?"

Priscilla nodded. "Indeed, even for Ceddy."

Addie laid down her fork and rested her elbows on the table, her hands folded under her chin. "He seemed afraid of something."

"Yes, I agree. Terrified, in fact." Pain flashed over Priscilla's face. It twists my heart in knots when that boy has a need he can't communicate and I can't cipher. I feel as though I've failed him."

Addie leaned to touch her hand. "You mustn't think that way."

"It's hard not to. I'm responsible for a boy who's a riddle, and I lack intuitive skills." She glanced up. "Unlike you, Addie. Just a few days with Ceddy, and already you sense when his cries are because of a stomachache or when his fits are due to frustration. It's quite a gift, dear."

Flattered, Addie lowered her lashes. "More experience than a gift, I think. I've worked with children from an early age, and my house is filled to the rafters with younger siblings."

"Call it what you will. I consider it an answer to prayer." She turned her hand over and squeezed Addie's fingers. "Thank you for staying."

Their eyes held until Delilah burst in, sliding a golden-topped egg onto Addie's plate. With one quick motion, she scooped the ruined egg onto the same dish and scurried for the door, untying her apron. "Thank you kindly, Miss Priscilla," she called over her shoulder. "I'll be back as quick as I can."

Priscilla sat up and stared. "Mercy! I've seen lightning move slower. Yet when I ask her to hurry, she creeps about moaning and clutching her back."

Addie grinned. "Is she like this every Sunday morning?"

Priscilla reached for a triangle of toast and dipped her spoon in the jam. "Yes, she is. I've often wondered what they've got going in their house of worship that we're missing in ours. Personally, I've never been in such a rush to get to church." She winked. "Maybe we should abandon our plans and join Delilah?"

The grandfather clock let out a series of no-nonsense gongs, drawing Priscilla's eyes to its ornate face. "I suppose you'd best get that egg down and go dress. Our service starts in one hour."

Suddenly starved, Addie obediently tucked into her food, finishing with a last bite of buttered biscuit and the dregs of her glass of milk.

In her room, she laid out her favorite dress, the pale blue taffeta with lace collar and sleeves, so striking against her dark hair. It was her father's favorite, too, and she smiled fondly remembering his proud grin when she wore it.

The thought of his dear, trusting face pained her stomach and made her furious with Mr. Foster all over again. The thought that anyone would seek to dishonor her parents' marriage boiled the blood in her veins. How dare the pompous dandy? Did he presume to think his attention would flatter her mother? That she would for a single moment think to hide the note from Father?

Before, Pearson's arresting good looks drew her wistful thoughts to him. Now he seemed dark and ugly despite his sun-washed hair and the golden glow of his skin. What mischief had he been about in the restaurant with his ridiculous invitation to a picnic? Wasn't the clandestine note to a married woman bad enough? Did he think to use Addie to get to her mother?

Priscilla had been shocked that they'd shared a lunch with two strange men. If she ever realized what Addie knew about the letter she'd mailed, she'd be scandalized.

"Addie?" Her tinny voice echoed from the stairs, jerking Addie's head toward the door.

One thing was certain. . .Addie wouldn't tell her. The thought of such behavior burned her cheeks with shame. She couldn't imagine voicing her suspicions aloud. Stopping briefly at the mirror to pin on her hat and straighten her sash, she grabbed her parasol and hurried down the hall.

Priscilla peered up from the bottom landing and smiled. "Are we ready?"

Addie gave a jaunty nod. "We're ready. I've dressed Cedric in long pants. Just let me get him from his room."

Downstairs, Priscilla led the procession onto the wide porch and down the steps where the carriage waited.

Despite the predicted chill in the air, warm sun rays on Addie's shoulders promised it wouldn't last. She drew her light shawl around herself and smiled. They were in for a beautiful day.

The ride seemed over before it started as the driver pulled up to a handsome brick building overlooked by a tall steeple. Leaping down, he helped first Priscilla then Addie and the boy to the ground.

The sidewalk leading to the steps was empty. Except for a cluster of men hovering over a smoking pit out back, the grounds were deserted. Tables with bright, checkered cloths dotted the grassy yard on both sides of the building. Beneath the trees, colorful quilts were spread.

An usher opened the door, nodding a welcome. Strains of music and voices raised in song floated to them from inside the foyer.

"Gracious, I suppose we're later than I thought. I'd hoped to introduce you before the service started, but it looks like that will have to wait." Priscilla winked and took Ceddy's hand. "Might be more fun this way. We get to make an entrance and set them to whispering."

Addie grimaced. The last thing she wanted was to cause a stir in church. Gulping, she followed Priscilla to a vacant spot on a pew near the front, squirming as their passage down the aisle provoked upturned faces and curious stares.

At the end of the hymn, the minister raised his head, a big smile on his face. "So glad you could join us, Priscilla. As you can see, we saved your place."

Unfazed by his banter, Priscilla nodded and settled regally on the pew. "Morning, Reverend."

Friendly chuckles followed.

Much to Addie's discomfort, he swept his arm her way. "I see you've brought a guest. Who might this lovely young lady be?"

Catching Addie's hand, Priscilla stood, dragging her to her feet. "This is my friend Adelina McRae, formerly of Mississippi. She's going to be living in my house and helping me with Ceddy."

"Fine," the minister boomed. "We're so glad to have you. Congregation, please welcome Adelina McRae to our midst."

The room erupted in a round of hearty nods and friendly voices. Beside her, Ceddy moaned softly and clapped his hands over his ears.

"The Lord has richly blessed us with guests today, hasn't He?" He turned his smiling eyes on the front row. "I see we have two other newcomers right here. Stand up, please, gentlemen, and introduce yourselves."

Addie's intake of air sounded so loud in her ears she thought those around her were bound to hear. There was no mistaking the tops of their heads, one dark and curly, the other twisted coils.

They stood, Pearson's shoulders so wide they blocked sight of the organist. His delighted eyes were fixed on Addie, and likely had been since he'd first heard Miss Priscilla call her name. "My friend here is Theo Bernardi, and I'm Pearson." His simpering smile mocked her across the sea of curious people. "Pearson Foster from Galveston."

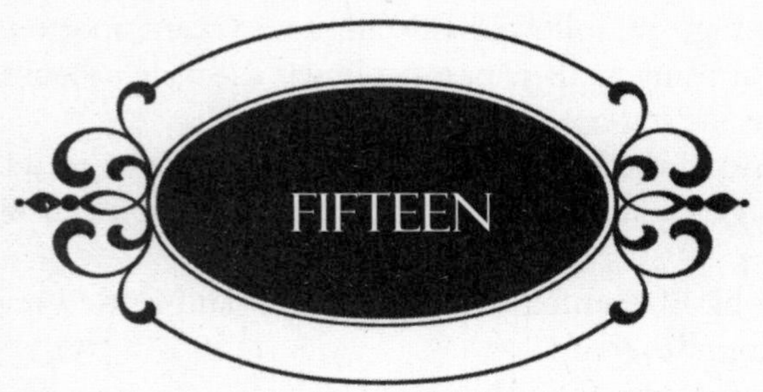

FIFTEEN

I don't believe it!" Priscilla leaned to whisper. "Can you imagine the gall?"

"No." Addie scowled and pulled her gaze from Pearson's searching eyes. "I certainly can't."

They sat in a rush of satin and crinkle of petticoats.

"What are they doing here?" Addie murmured as the preacher went on with the service. "Do you suppose they followed us?"

Her friend shot her a look. "Highly unlikely, dear, considering they were inside when we arrived."

Flustered, Addie busied herself with soothing Ceddy while her troubled thoughts swirled among the rafters.

Pearson Foster in church? She feared for those sitting in close proximity to him, for they were surely in danger of lightning bolts. Remembering the day they met and his annoyed reaction to blessing the food, Addie nibbled her bottom lip.

Unable to contain herself, she inclined her head for a peek past the person in front of her. Sure enough, Pearson sat twisted in his seat, boldly staring her way. She drew in her chin and inched closer to Ceddy on the pew, out of his line of sight. In all her experience with the opposite gender—albeit limited, thanks to overprotective parents—she'd never met a more vexing man.

Between Ceddy's bored wiggling, her own troubling thoughts, and Pearson's furtive over-the-shoulder glances, Addie hadn't a clue what the minister's message contained. She thought it may have been a cautionary discourse on the perils of judging your fellow man, but she couldn't say for sure.

Distracted by her musings, she failed to stand for the closing prayer until Priscilla tapped her shoulder. Humiliated by Pearson's quick glance and knowing smile, even more embarrassed that he'd caught her looking again, her cheeks glowed with heat. Dismissed with a hearty invitation to stay for the social, they stood and waited their turn to file outside.

The pastor had approached Pearson and Theo, engaging them in a lively discussion as they passed. Addie couldn't resist watching Pearson go by. The trouble was, he stood out wherever he went. His unusual good looks drew the eye of everyone around him. With his golden skin and hair, the man seemed to glow.

Priscilla stepped into the aisle. Catching Ceddy's reluctant hand, Addie slipped in behind her and followed her out. In the yard, a flurry of Priscilla's cronies descended in a cackling rush. Eager to introduce her to each of them in turn, Priscilla tugged her this way and that until Addie's arm grew sore from the press of her fingers.

Throughout the session of greetings and the endless string of polite questions, Addie remained acutely aware of Pearson, still in quiet conversation with the minister and several other men who had joined them. She told herself his soaring height was the reason she couldn't keep her eyes from wandering his way.

The tone of the men's conversation had somehow turned. Instead of lighthearted banter, two of the men seemed to be teasing Pearson and his friend unmercifully.

A dark cloud of resentment had settled over Theo's face. Smiling and nodding good-naturedly, Pearson seemed to take it in stride.

Noticing Addie gazing past her shoulder, the young woman across from her turned to see what held her attention. "Very handsome men, wouldn't you say, Adelina? Especially the tall one."

Her older companion wrinkled her brow. "Mind your tongue, Dora. You're on church grounds."

"Sorry, Mother. Just stating the obvious."

Pretty is as pretty does goes for men, as well, Addie thought, but she wouldn't say so.

After another round of boisterous laughter, the men dispersed. Theo and Pearson were immediately swept up by a second group of curious folks, but the minister strolled Addie's way. "Miss McRae, wasn't it?"

Addie smiled and nodded. "Yes, sir, but you may call me Addie."

"My pleasure, considering we'll be spending every Sunday afternoon together. I have a standing invitation to lunch at Whitfield Manor." He raised his brows. "Although today it appears you're my guests. I'm Reverend Abner Stroud, in case our dear Priscilla failed to mention." A good-natured grin lit his face. "Part-time barber, full-time preacher. I can trim a man's hair and save his soul all from the same chair." He leaned closer and winked. "Of course, it's not me doing the saving, you know. I'm just an instrument in the Master's hands, much like a straight razor's a tool in mine."

Narrowing one eye, he tilted his head. "Which brings to mind a scripture, if you'll indulge me. 'For the word of God is quick, and powerful, and sharper than any two-edged sword'"—his sudden swipe through the air with an imaginary weapon made Addie jump—" 'piercing even to the dividing asunder of soul and spirit, and of the joints and marrow, and is a discerner of the thoughts and intents of the heart.'" He offered a wide grin. "Pretty much says it all, doesn't it?"

Glancing at Pearson, Addie squirmed. Should the sword of the Spirit happen to pierce her anxious heart, dark rage and deep distrust would spill out.

Priscilla nudged the reverend with her elbow. "Speaking of discerning a person's thoughts and intents"—she nodded toward the lively circle surrounding Pearson and Theo—"I see you've met Marshall's latest opportunists."

Reverend Stroud checked over his shoulder. "Yes. Yes, I have. *Wonderful* fellows, in fact. Pure-hearted, honest men."

Addie and Priscilla blinked at each other.

"Th–they are?" Addie stammered.

Lacking an ounce of decorum, Priscilla extended her arm and wiggled a bold finger. "I'm referring to those two ruffians. The newcomers with the odd hair."

"Yes, indeed," the reverend said. "Fine Christian men, the both of them."

Priscilla gaped. "Are you quite sure?"

He nodded firmly. "I have a sense about such things. Knew it from the moment I looked into their eyes." He twisted around to gesture with his nod. "Especially the tall fellow. Very sensitive to godly matters." He frowned. "Something holds him captive though. I'm not sure what."

Priscilla smoothed her gloved fingers over her mouth. "Well, I'll be. . . I took him for a cheap, money-grasping treasure seeker."

Reverend Stroud laughed aloud. "Priscilla Whitfield. Didn't one word of my sermon penetrate?"

"I'm not judging, Reverend. For a fact, they're in town hoping to make a fast dollar."

"My dear lady. . .you can't possibly know their motives for wanting to raise the *Mittie*."

Disappointment furrowed her brow. She'd lost her edge in the debate. "They told you what they're up to?"

"Seemed to have nothing to hide." He smiled. "A good thing, since Sam Donley from the department store and a few of the others were giving them quite a hard time just now." He studied her pursed lips then rested his hands on his hips. "I'll admit to knowing less about women than most crusty old bachelors, but why should their interest in a downed steamboat so offend you ladies?"

Addie nibbled her bottom lip, unable to answer. She dared not mention her reason for disliking Pearson.

She needn't have worried. Priscilla had no such qualms. "Plundering shipwrecked vessels and digging for lost treasure isn't exactly an honorable profession," she said. "I would think they could find better use of their time."

"It's a dangerous pursuit, Priscilla. One that takes a tremendous amount of courage and faith. Given half their fortitude, I'd trade in my shears for an eye patch and blade." He winked at Addie. "Instead of a preaching barber"—his invisible sword slashed the air between them—"I'd be a swashbuckling minister."

"You, Reverend?"

"Yes, indeed. The lure of lost gold drives many men. In most cases, it's due to a heightened sense of adventure rather than greed. Whatever the cause, the trait can work in their favor in the end. Such men have a great appreciation for the abundant reward promised to the believer."

His dancing gaze jerked past them. "Here come our fortune hunters now. I admonish you two to make them feel welcome."

Confusion glued Addie's tongue to the roof of her mouth while Pearson and Theo descended. The reverend's words clashed against recent events with the force of sparring horns. How could the man who sought to woo her mother's affections be the one Reverend Stroud described?

Rocking on his heels behind Pearson, Theo grinned foolishly. "Afternoon, ladies."

Pearson stood straight-backed and tall and nodded her way. "Miss McRae, it's nice to see you again so soon." A winsome smile warmed his face. "It's interesting how we continue to cross paths in a town of this size." He gave her a penetrating look, his bronzed forehead creased. "Do you believe in destiny?"

Before Addie could gather her wits to speak, her companion swept closer and held out her hand. "Mr. Foster, isn't it?"

Still watching Addie, Pearson dutifully took hold of Priscilla's fingers. "Miss Whitfield." He withdrew his gaze. "We had no idea this was your place of worship."

Addie studied him through lowered lashes. *He's telling the truth.*

"Oh yes," Priscilla said. "For many years. We're pleased you decided to join us this morning."

We are? The warmth of her voice and genteel manner were entirely too friendly.

Priscilla patted Pearson's hand. "Reverend Stroud was just telling us what fine Christian soldiers you are."

He arched expressive brows. "He was?"

She raised her chin and drew a deep breath—as if she'd made up her mind on an important matter. "Gentlemen," she said brightly, "I'd be honored if you'd accompany our party to Whitfield Manor after the social for coffee and conversation. I'd like to get to know you better."

Pearson's startled gaze darted to Addie, likely to gauge her reaction. Unfortunately, she didn't disappoint.

Ceddy squatted in the cover of the hedge surrounding the churchyard. Too cool in the shade, but at least he was out of the sun. He didn't care for sunshine on the top of his head. Did not like it one bit.

He dug with the ragged edge of an oyster shell, searching for colorful stones and scratching his name in the dark earth between his knees. Drawn by the musty smell, he tossed the shell aside and buried his fingers in the soft, black dirt.

The evergreen branches behind him stirred, teasing his back. The faint crack of a broken branch reached his ears.

Ceddy stilled. Waited. Then sniffed and went on digging.

The stir became a rustle, and fear slid up his spine. Ever so slowly he turned. Afraid to look, he lowered his eyelids and peeked through shiny lashes.

Sunken eyes. Skeleton teeth. A twisted face leered through the bushes. "Boo!" its gravelly voice barked.

Ceddy opened wide to shriek, but a row of dirty fingers clamped over his face. Cruel hands dragged him through the hedges to the other side and rolled him to his stomach. His nose, so close to the ground, sucked dust that tickled his nostrils as he struggled to breathe.

"Hold him tight, Denny. Don't let him wail."

"I've got him a'right. You do like I said and search his pockets. Pat him down good, now."

"Don't fret, mate. If it's on him, old Charlie will find it." Rough hands slapped at Ceddy's clothing and fumbled with his pockets. Heavy breathing. A labored sigh. "Nothing this side. Help me flip the little beggar."

Ceddy's body lifted as though weightless and spun, landing him on his back. The creepy eyes of Mr. Currie bore down on him. "Search every nook and cranny, Charlie," he snarled, still watching Ceddy. "Leave no stone unturned." He smiled, his dark teeth and crinkled skin a horrid sight. "You catch that? I made a funny. No stone. You get it?"

Ignoring him, Charlie sat back on his heels. "It's not here. Must be stashed somewhere."

Mr. Currie muttered a vile curse, words Aunt Priss never allowed uttered, his hurtful grip tightening on Ceddy. "Blast the luck!" He sighed. "Well, no matter. We'll get our hands on it yet."

"How you reckon to do that?"

"You leave that to me." Holding the oyster shell against Ceddy's neck, Mr. Currie jerked it in one quick motion.

Ceddy gave a muffled cry of fear and pain.

"You see that, boy? If you tell, that's what will happen to you, only for real. I'll come in the night and slit your throat. Bleed you like a butchering hog."

Charlie spun on him. "Aw, Denny, don't hurt him. And stop spewing such awful things. The boy can't understand a word."

"Don't be so sure. Look at the fear in his eyes. His aunt said he was smarter than most."

"Remember, the poor lad's mute, so who's he going to tell?"

"I'm making sure he don't find a way."

The scary man leaned close, his smelly breath hot on Ceddy's face. "Listen real careful-like, little pollywog. I'm going to turn you loose now. You're to stand up and stroll across the yard like you 'aven't a care in the world, yeah? Hands in your pockets, whistle a tune if you like. No trouble now, right?"

Staring past the grimy calloused hand over his mouth, Ceddy tried to nod but couldn't summon the strength.

Mr. Currie shook him so hard his bones ached. "Right?"

"Leave off him, Denny! You know he can't answer."

"All right then. You just do like I say, or I'll slice up your old auntie before I cut out your gizzard. The governess, too, and I'll make you watch." Jerking Ceddy to his feet, Mr. Currie shot him a final warning glare then slowly withdrew his hands.

Ceddy stared at the ground while the evil man roughly brushed dirt off his clothes.

"Off with you now," he whispered, shoving him through the hedge. "And not a word."

Longing to dash away to Aunt Priss's skirt, Ceddy drew his shoulders to his ears and walked stiffly to the carriage, resisting with every ounce of his strength the urge to run.

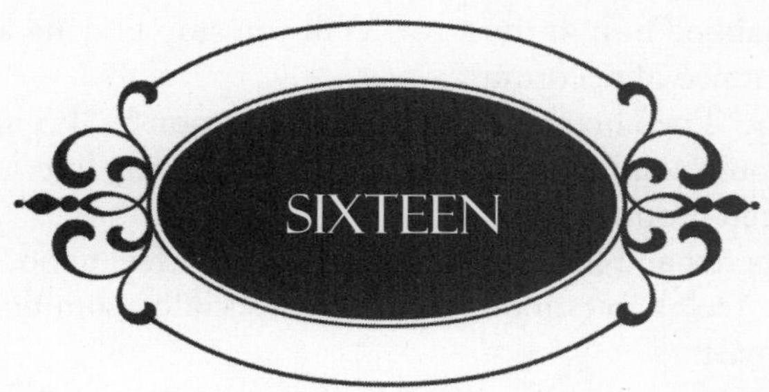

SIXTEEN

Pearson drove his hired rig up the hill behind Miss Whitfield's fancy carriage. Lilting voices drifted to his ears, those of their hostess and Reverend Stroud. As near as he could tell, Miss McRae hadn't spoken a single word since they'd left the churchyard.

Theo nudged his side. "You sure you're not Irish? You're the luckiest man in Texas."

Lifting his brows, Pearson grinned. "Why's that?"

"In the span of a church service, the old lady went from despising you to loving you." He splayed his hands. "And you didn't have to do a thing."

Pearson laughed. "I used to think of it as God's favor. Unmerited grace. Nowadays, I'm not so sure. Whatever it is, I don't deserve it, but I won't turn it down." His gaze drifted to the back of the carriage, and warmth spread through his chest. "Especially in this case." He grinned. "Besides, I knew my charm and good looks would eventually sway her."

"Don't get cocky. You still haven't won the trust of her pretty governess."

His elated mood dampened at Theo's words. Addie had carefully avoided him at the social, an impressive skill considering he sat right across from her while they ate. She'd picked at her food, not in the dainty way of a self-conscious woman but as if she'd lost her appetite and he was the cause.

He frowned and glanced at Theo. "Why do you suppose she finds me so disagreeable?"

Theo's booming laughter echoed off the trunks of a passing grove, drawing looks from the party up ahead.

Pearson jabbed him in the arm. "Will you stop braying and pretend you have an ounce of decorum?"

"I'm sorry," Theo howled then covered his mouth. "It's just funny to hear those words coming from you. That's usually my line."

"Well, keep it down."

Theo sobered and his eyes softened. "Doesn't feel good, does it?"

It didn't feel a bit good, in fact. Especially coming from this particular female.

"Take heart," Theo said, grinning. "Your charms are still in working order. You've got the old lady's devotion, and every unattached girl at the social is at your beck and call."

Pearson flashed a wry smile. "I wish I'd had as much luck befriending the men. As soon as they heard we were seeking the *Mittie*, they lost all interest in taking a job. Most backed away as if we'd uttered a curse."

"Maybe we did." Theo raised a brow. "Maybe the *Mittie* herself is cursed."

Pearson jerked his head to scowl at him. "That's absurd."

"Is it? It would explain why she's still out there."

The buggy up ahead rattled over the uneven ground and pulled to a stop in the circular drive. Pearson pulled in behind them, set his brake, and climbed down.

"Welcome, welcome," Miss Whitfield called, waving them up the stone path. "Please come inside."

The boy pulled free of Addie and bolted, taking the steps so fast he tripped. Scrambling onto the porch, he pounded the door with clenched fists. When it opened, he scurried past the maid and disappeared inside the house.

"What pulled his tail?" she asked, hands on her hips.

"Oh good, Delilah, you're home," Miss Whitfield said. "Put the kettle on, will you? And slice up some pie. We have guests."

"Right away, ma'am," Delilah said, taking their burdensome coats.

Pearson had shed his hours ago as the weather grew warmer and felt relieved to be free of it.

Theo leaned close to Pearson. "Look at the size of this foyer. Pull in a table and bed, and I could live in here."

He'd meant the comment for Pearson's ears only, but his voice carried in the vast room.

Miss Whitfield smiled over her shoulder. "It's far too much room for one crotchety old lady, and a shameful waste of space." Her gaze shifted to Addie climbing the spiral stairs, likely following the child. "Having dear Addie move in and my great-nephew underfoot helps ease my conscience at the vulgar pretentiousness of such a dwelling."

Pearson nudged Theo.

He shrugged and made a face.

"Let's retire to the parlor, shall we? Delilah will be right in with our refreshments."

Filing into the splendid room, Pearson rubbed his stomach. After the lavish spread on the church grounds, he wondered where he could cram another bite. By the uncomfortable look on Reverend Stroud's face, he guessed he felt the same. The man looked due for a tonic.

The afternoon passed in pleasant conversation. Confirming Pearson's suspicions, the reverend requested a ginger tea instead of coffee and pie. After his second cup, and several discreet belches, a livelier glow appeared on his cheeks.

Propping his arm on the back of the velvet couch, he beamed at Pearson. "So you're after the *Mittie*. As I told Priscilla here, I'm quite envious. What I wouldn't give to go along on the search."

"Really?" Pearson placed his coffee on the low table between them. "You're the only man in Marshall who feels that way."

He waved his hand. "Oh, don't mind them. They're bound by fear and superstition." He chuckled. "A fact that works in your favor, I suppose. Otherwise, she wouldn't still be out there somewhere."

His face aglow with interest, Theo sat forward. "What are they afraid of?"

The reverend sobered. "No one knows unless they're from the area. Those who do aren't saying. It's like they're afraid to talk."

Theo nudged Pearson. "I told you it was cursed."

Reverend Stroud's attention jumped to him. "Cursed, eh? That's what the Caddo Indians believed. They'd walk a mile out of their way to avoid the site."

Excitement firing in his chest, Pearson scooted to the edge of his seat. "Which means they knew the exact location?"

"Yes, I suppose they did."

"Where could I find a Caddo Indian?"

He smiled and shook his head. "If you found one, Pearson, it would do you little good. Those remaining few along the lake feel the same as their ancestors did. Bad medicine, they call it. I doubt they'd help you." His eyes sparked with remembrance. "However, there is one person. The fellow's not an Indian, mind you, but he may as well be." He paused. "But I'm afraid he might be just as hard to find. They call him—"

"Catfish John," Pearson and Theo finished for him.

Laughing, Reverend Stroud sat back and crossed his legs. "I see you're already acquainted with Marshall's own Daniel Boone."

"Not yet, sir," Pearson said, "but I hope to be."

Settling into the cushions, the reverend turned the warmth of his smile on their hostess. "Priscilla? I believe I'll take a slice of that rhubarb pie now, if there's any left."

"Of course," she said, laying aside her plate and standing. "Boys, would you care for more?"

Theo held out his saucer. "I could go for another piece. Best pie I've had in years."

Pearson stood, handing the dish to Miss Whitfield. "None for me, thanks. But I could use some fresh air."

"Help yourself to the back porch swing. I want you all to make yourselves right at home. I simply won't have it any other way."

Rounding her chair, she motioned for him to join her. "Come, I'll walk you into the hall and point the way. I adore lazy Sunday afternoons, don't you, Mr. Foster?" Pausing, she gripped his arm. "Oh pooh. I'm going to call you Pearson, if that's all right?"

He smiled. "Of course."

Following her instructions, Pearson navigated the hallways until he reached the double doors at the back of the house. Pushing past the screen, he stepped onto a wide, covered veranda overlooking a whitewashed gazebo and a lush garden that sloped downhill and out of sight. From this vantage, atop the rise, the whole town of Marshall lay at his feet. His soul at ease, he drew a deep breath and braced his hands on the high back of the swing.

Too late, he noticed the small black pair of sensible shoes placed neatly beneath the contraption. It swung sharply forward then rocked dizzily back.

"Oh!" Addie cried. Struggling to sit against the motion of the seat, she clutched her book with one hand and grasped the cushion under her head with the other, dragging it to the ground.

Horrified, Pearson rushed to her aid, trying to steady the swing while he helped her up.

"Mr. Foster!" she shrilled. "What are you doing?"

"I'm so sorry," he croaked. "I didn't see you."

Her eyes had the sleepy glaze of one just awakened from a nap. "How could you not see me? I'm right here. If I didn't know better, I'd think you were trying to launch me into the daffodils."

Leaning to pick up the cushion, he used the time to wipe the smile off his face. "I assure you I had no designs in that direction." Unable to resist, he added, "Though you would be a charming addition to the garden."

Addie huffed and crossed her arms. "Flattery will not earn my forgiveness."

Pearson handed her the pillow. "Tell me what will, and I'll get right on it."

She shot him a sullen pout and tucked a curl behind her ear.

He motioned to the empty spot beside her. "Do you mind if I sit while you think it over?"

She gathered her book and shawl. "You may take my place. I really should—"

He lifted a staying hand. "Please don't go."

Her mouth set in a firm line, she turned up her fetching face and studied him.

"Unless you have to, of course." He smiled. "Otherwise, I'd really appreciate your company."

Settling against the cushion, she gave a curt nod. "I suppose I can stay until Ceddy wakes from his nap."

They sat quietly, Pearson gently rocking the swing with one foot. He stared across the misty miles stretching toward town, trying to regain the sense of peace he'd felt before. The woman sitting beside him stirred him to anguish instead. He'd never desired the acceptance of a person so strongly. Never craved a woman's interest so dearly. His stomach pitched when she shifted toward him on the seat.

"So. . .um. . .do you like Marshall so far?"

An effort at small talk. It was a start. "I do. The townsfolk seem to be goodhearted people, and the weather's nice."

A smile twitched her lips. "And which hour's weather would you be referring to?"

Pearson laughed, a little too loudly. "You make a good point. I'm used to the fickle nature of the climate though. It behaves the same in Galveston." He raised one brow. "Is Mississippi a little more predictable?"

This time she nearly grinned. "Not in the least, although we don't boast of the fact as often as you Texans do."

He'd already taken note of her eyes, of course. They were her best feature. Wide most of the time, as if soaking in her surroundings. Intelligent and strikingly brown. But he hadn't noticed the dark rings circling her pupils, lending a depth to her gaze that pierced right down to his soul.

"You don't much favor your mother, Miss McRae," he blurted. "Except for the color of your hair. I suppose you take after your father?" Leaning, he lifted his finger toward her face. "Did you know that your eyes—"

She stiffened and drew back. "What do you mean I don't favor her?"

He lowered his hand. "Well, nothing, really."

"What were you implying?"

He squirmed at her angry tone, the motion jostling them. "It's just that, with your fair complexion"—he smiled and pointed at her nose—"and that little smattering of freckles, well, you're—"

"Not nearly as pretty?"

Pearson's gut twisted. "That's not what I'm suggesting at all." His unpracticed foray into the art of flirtation wasn't going well. "Your mother's a beautiful woman, but—"

Addie stood, cutting him off midsentence. "You've said quite enough."

Struggling against the ridiculous, pitching swing, Pearson pushed to his feet. "I'm only trying to say that I find you quite attractive."

"Oh stop! Honestly, Mr. Foster, I won't have you use me this way. Secondhand flattery is a low-class, despicable ploy to get to my mother. You should be ashamed." Gathering her skirts, she marched to the door. Pausing on the threshold, she turned. Her pretty features were twisted with rage, but the glint of a tear shone from the corner of her eye. "And just when I'd started to doubt my suspicions. . ." Jerking the screen nearly off its hinges, she swept inside.

Pearson gaped after her, speechless. She couldn't really believe what she'd just said. He didn't know much about Mississippi women, but if they went to these lengths to discourage a suitor, he'd stick with Texas girls.

Angry with herself for her threatening tears, Addie charged up the stairs.

Only moments before, when her drowsy lids closed on the pages of *Villette*, her mind had replayed the events of the day. She'd finally concluded that if her employer and Reverend Stroud vouched for Mr. Foster, then she must be mistaken about him. She would defer to their good instincts and put all her suspicions aside. How foolish Addie felt now to consider trusting him. All the man could find to talk about was her beautiful mother.

Outside Ceddy's room, Addie paused to compose herself. As sensitive as he was to change, he would notice her distress right away. She didn't want to upset him. Wiping her eyes and smoothing her skirt, she put a smile on her face and opened the door.

On the threshold, she frowned. Ceddy wasn't sitting in the window seat, his favorite spot, or sprawled on the floor surrounded by rocks. His bed, where she'd left him huddled under the quilt, was empty. His shoes and stockings, always the first things off when he entered his room, were no longer scattered across the rug.

Spinning, she rushed along the hall calling his name and checking every room and closet. Finding nothing, she hurtled down the stairs and bolted for the kitchen, praying she'd discover him tracing planks on the kitchen floor.

She recruited Delilah, and together they searched the bottom floor. Addie peeked discreetly inside the parlor, smiled and backed out again when Priscilla glanced up.

Hurrying upstairs in a panic, she went over the top floor again while Delilah scoured the yard. Her heart pulsing in her throat, she met Delilah on the bottom landing and questioned her with frantic eyes.

Trembling, Delilah shook her head and pulled Addie into her arms. "It's time, honey," she whispered, her voice breaking. "You can't put it off no mo'."

Cringing, she nodded. Breaking free of Delilah's comforting arms, Addie marched woodenly toward the parlor, praying for the strength to tell Priscilla that Ceddy was gone.

SEVENTEEN

His head whirling, Pearson pushed out of the swing and opened the door. Spotting Theo striding toward him, he pointed over his shoulder. "You won't believe what just happened."

He bit back the rest when Reverend Stroud rounded the corner, white-faced and shaken.

Theo clutched his shoulder. "Pearson, the little boy is missing."

Pearson looked past Theo into the hall, half expecting to see Ceddy crouched at the foot of the stairs. "Are you sure?"

"The women have searched every inch of the house," the reverend said, "and called until they're hoarse."

Spinning, Pearson stared toward the garden. "I saw the maid running over the grounds, but I never imagined. . ." He firmed his jaw. "The boy's got to be here somewhere. He couldn't get far on foot."

A tearful Miss Whitfield pushed past the reverend and Theo, wringing her hands. "Ceddy's simply gone. We've looked everywhere. In the pantries, closets, and storerooms. The bedrooms, sitting rooms, and his late grandfather's den." She shuddered. "Even the abandoned servants' quarters. There's no sign of him."

"Has he ever done this before?"

She shook her head emphatically. "Never. He's a slave to routine and seldom varies his actions. This time of day he's always in his room, napping then playing with his rock collection." Her hand twisting intensified. "Poor Addie. She's distraught. Blames herself for leaving him alone for so long."

Guilt twisted Pearson's stomach. She'd tried to go to the boy, but he'd held her. "Don't fret, ma'am. We'll find him." Spurred into action, Pearson directed the reverend to search the front of the estate and Theo to scour the thick woods to the right of the property. "I'll take the garden slope and the stand of trees to the left."

"I suggest double duty, gentlemen," the reverend said.

"How's that?" Theo asked.

He set his mouth in a grim line. "Pray while you look."

Pearson nodded then vaulted past Addie's daffodil beds into the grassy yard. With the onset of dusk, the serenity of the well-laid garden became a shadowy, ominous maze. Meticulous in his method, he crisscrossed the yard, checking the limbs of every tree and the base of every hedge. Topping the slope, he trudged downhill to the property line then cut along the picket fence and ducked into the trees, calling Ceddy's name. Theo's voice, and the reverend's, echoed back to him in the distance.

For the second time that day, he said a prayer. *God, please watch over Ceddy. Help us find him.*

The first stole into his mind that morning in church, the sermon washing over him in waves of healing oil, the scriptures in his ears like soothing balm. Taken by surprise at how he'd missed God's house and the fellowship with believers, tears had threatened and a plea rose unbidden. *Help me to forgive You.* It seemed a forward, sinful prayer, but it came from the depths of his wounded soul.

Show me the way back to Your side. Would God honor such a prayer? Pearson hoped so, because without help he'd never find his way through all the pain.

Exhaustion and thirst, more than the closing darkness, drove him toward the house. They'd wasted enough time. They'd have to go for help.

Theo and Reverend Stroud stood in the foyer speaking in low tones as he walked in. They spun with questioning eyes.

Pearson shook his head, and they slumped in disappointment. "Sir, can you round up a search party from your congregation?"

He nodded. "We're of like minds. I was just telling young Theo the same."

"Then we'd best go get them. It's getting dark and cold out there. We may be running out of time."

Delilah appeared, running halfway down the stairs, her heels loud on the steps. "Miss Priscilla," she shrieked, "you best come quick."

The woman burst from the parlor with a startled glance then ran up the staircase faster than Pearson thought possible for a woman her age.

Tight on her heels, they spun into the boy's room.

"Thank you, merciful God!" she shouted.

Addie sat on the floor, holding the sobbing boy close to her breast, rocking him gently. He appeared drained, his head drooping, his arms hanging limp.

"Is he hurt?" Priscilla asked.

Tears shining in her eyes, Addie released a breath. "I don't think so. He was under his bed the whole time, cowering in fear."

"How could that be?" Miss Whitfield asked, as if she couldn't make sense of the words.

"On impulse, I lifted the quilt and found him rolled into a shivering ball. Something has frightened him half out of his wits."

Pearson knelt beside her. "Do you want us to go for a doctor?"

"That might be a good idea."

Miss Whitfield shook her head. "There's no need, Pearson. I'll send my carriage."

Ceddy's hand fell open, and a large white rock slipped from his fingers, rattling across the floor. He whimpered and stirred.

Glancing up, Addie sought Pearson's eyes. "Will you get it for him, please?"

Pearson picked up the milky white stone, surprised by its weight, and offered it to the boy.

His small fingers closed around it possessively, his breath catching on a sob.

Miss Whitfield motioned toward the door. "Leave us alone with him, gentlemen, if you please? I'd like for Addie to dress him for bed."

"Of course," Pearson said, pushing off the floor. Realizing Addie couldn't rise with the boy in her arms, he bent to gather the frail, still body to his chest. Cradling Ceddy's head, he gently carried him to the bed and laid him down. On impulse, he smoothed the hair off his forehead then patted his cheek. "Rest well, little fellow."

"Oh my," Miss Whitfield whispered, her fingers working the lace collar at her throat. "He won't usually allow strangers to touch him. You must be very good with children."

He gave her a tight smile. "I had a brother his age."

She touched his arm. "Had?"

"I lost him five years ago. In the Galveston storm."

Miss Whitfield tightened her hand. "I'm so very sorry, dear."

Ceddy stirred, almost asleep, winding his arms above his pillow and lolling his head to the side.

Addie gasped and rushed to the bed. "What on earth is this?"

"What is it, dear?" Miss Whitfield scurried to join her.

When she gasped, too, Pearson and the others crowded close to see. From ear to ear, an angry red line marred the skin of his neck. Droplets of blood had oozed and dried in tiny pearls along the ugly scratch.

Grabbing the lantern off the table, Miss Whitfield held it over him then groaned as if in pain. Ugly bruises covered his cheeks like black and blue fingers stretched over his mouth. She lifted his shirt, revealing more bruising on his stomach and along his sides.

Addie gently probed the wound on Ceddy's neck, and he moaned in his sleep. "What could have done this?" she demanded.

"You mean who," Reverend Stroud said. "Was he playing with anyone at the social? A ruffian or bully perhaps?"

Miss Whitfield glanced over her shoulder. "Oh Reverend, another child couldn't have done this."

He shrugged. "You'd be surprised."

"It wasn't here before we got home," Addie insisted. "I would've seen it."

"Not necessarily," Theo said. "Not with the cut tucked under his chin like that. And it takes awhile for bruises to show."

"That's why he 'fraid," Delilah announced from the doorway. "Some fool been hurtin' him."

The circle of people gazed around at each other.

Straightening, Miss Whitfield clenched her fists at her sides. "I don't know who did it, but when I find out—and I will get to the bottom of this—there will be swift reckoning." The rage burning in her eyes left no doubt of her sincerity.

"I'm relieved we found him, at least," the reverend said. "Poor little mite."

"Do you really think this happened at the church?" Pearson asked.

The man shrugged. "Anything is possible these days, and if you don't mind my saying, it would be preferable to the alternative."

"Which is?"

Reverend Stroud's throat worked furiously before he spoke. "That someone in our midst is the culprit."

Addie opened Ceddy's door and stole another look. By the light of the lamp she'd left burning, she watched him sleep. His long lashes fluttered occasionally, and his rosy mouth puckered. A beautiful boy awake, he seemed angelic at rest.

Backing from the room, she pulled the door closed and leaned her head against it. What had happened to him that day? How could she have allowed it? She should have watched him more closely instead of Mr. Foster. "If only I could go back and change it," she whispered.

"Wishing won't make it so, dear."

Startled by the voice behind her, Addie jumped.

"Forgive me," Priscilla said, drawing her dressing gown tight. "I couldn't rest either. Is he all right?"

"He seems to be."

"Good." She stretched, twisting her head back and forth, as if working out the kinks. "It's not your fault, Addie. I don't want you thinking so."

"Of course it is. He's my charge."

"A lot took place today, most of it out of his normal routine. You can't be prepared all the time. I neglected to watch him, too." She frowned and nibbled the corner of her lip. "The thing I can't put out of my mind is this: we were with trusted friends the whole time. It just doesn't make sense, unless. . ."

"Go on."

She glanced up. "Follow me, if you please. I want to talk to you in private."

A deserted hallway in the dead of night seemed private enough, but Addie wouldn't say so. She followed Priscilla to the end of the hall and into her large, ornate bedroom. The scent of lavender met her at the door, and soft rugs cushioned her feet. Uneasy to be in her employer's private space, she paused just inside and waited.

"Come along," Priscilla said, patting a striped divan. "Have a seat right here."

Addie trudged obediently to the sofa and perched on the edge.

Priscilla climbed into an overstuffed chair and tucked her bare feet beneath her. "The matter I want to discuss will require strict confidence, Addie. I wouldn't dare broach the subject unless I felt you were mature enough to keep a secret."

She nodded. "Yes, of course."

With a sharp inhale, Priscilla leaned forward and began. "What if I told you I suspect Mr. Foster of harming Ceddy?"

Addie's heart lurched. "Why would you think such a thing?"

"I don't like having these thoughts, believe me." Priscilla fell against her chair. "But you heard Reverend Stroud. 'Someone in our midst,' he said. Addie, you've been around Mr. Foster more than I have. Do you think it's possible?"

"To be honest, I can't imagine it." Addie's first instincts were to shout down her accusations. Yet she suspected Pearson of something nearly as vile.

"How well do we really know him?"

How well indeed? Addie raised her head. "Wait, he was with me on the swing, so how could he be guilty? He didn't have the opportunity."

"I'm afraid he did. That's what haunts my thoughts. I directed him to the back door and then went out to the kitchen. He was standing at the foot of the stairs when I left him. Who's to say he went directly to the porch?"

Weakness swept over Addie's limbs, leaving her feeling helpless. Why did the urge to defend Pearson surge so strongly through her veins? "It seems preposterous. Why would he hurt a little boy?"

"You heard him say he lost his brother in the storm. Perhaps it twisted his mind."

Staring thoughtfully, Addie confessed the truth. "Actually, he lost his entire family that night. Pearson alone was spared."

Priscilla's eyes widened to deep, troubled pools. "There. . .you see? I've heard of these kinds of cases—the most charming and agreeable men living double lives, eventually found culpable of murder and mayhem. Like those two in London, Dr. Jekyll and Mr. Hyde."

"But Priscilla. . .they're a work of fiction."

She blinked. "They are?"

"Of course."

She waved dismissively. "Still. . .think about it, Addie. Both times when Ceddy grew so frightened, at the restaurant and again today, Mr. Foster was present. The boy has never acted in such a distraught manner before. It's the only conclusion I can make."

Addie held out one last shred of hope. "But you saw for yourself, Ceddy was totally relaxed with him. Even allowed the man to carry him to bed."

Priscilla touched her bottom lip. "Yes, there is that. But he was drifting in and out. Perhaps he didn't realize who held him." She sat forward and folded her hands. "I know it's a lot to take in. Believe me, I've struggled with the idea for half the night, and I hardly believe it myself." Her lips tightened. "However, my first responsibility is to Ceddy. I won't expose him to a dangerous man." She sighed. "But now that I've befriended Mr. Foster, it does present a perplexing set of circumstances."

Addie nodded. "To say the least."

Priscilla curled her fingers at her temples. "It's a dreadful failing of mine, Addie. I tend to become familiar with people entirely too soon. It's my trusting nature, I suppose."

Addie knew another impetuous lady with the same weakness. If her mother hadn't allowed the two men into their lives, they wouldn't be having this strange conversation. And Addie wouldn't be battling an attraction that made her uncomfortable. "How can we prove that Pearson is innocent?" Addie asked, certain that he was.

Priscilla gripped her knees and stared at the darkened window. "I don't know at present. But I assure you, I won't let the matter rest until I uncover the truth."

EIGHTEEN

A week had passed since Pearson last saw Addie. His reason for wanting to had drastically changed. After the accusation she made, of his improper interest in her mother, he wanted a chance to deny her charge.

The previous Sunday, Reverend Stroud accepted their offer of a ride home from the mansion, and on the way they'd waged a lively debate on the treasure of Jean Lafitte. The man seemed drawn to the legend and was quite knowledgeable of the details, a fact that forged a bond between them.

Since that day, Pearson spent hours at the bachelor's table, breaking bread and sharing ideas on where the pirate's bounty and the *Mittie* might be found.

As Pearson left the parsonage the day before, the reverend milked a promise from him that he would be in church, a promise he meant to keep. "Almost ready, Theo? We're about to be late."

Theo pulled on his boot and stood, shaking his pant leg until the cuff slid down. "Have you counted our money lately?" he asked, clearly distracted.

Pearson glanced at the bright sun outside the window and laid aside his coat. "Why should I? You're the bookkeeper for this operation."

Theo winced then met his eyes. "Not such a good one, I'm afraid. Somehow we've gone over our budget."

"Meaning?"

"We won't be able to stay in this hotel much longer and still afford to eat."

One hand on the door, Pearson stilled. "Let me see, die of exposure or die of starvation. Those are the options you're giving me?"

He nodded. "If you want to keep paying our help, it is."

Drawing a deep breath, Pearson shook his head. "There are a couple more alternatives, neither one very pleasant."

"Let's hear them."

"We could get part-time jobs."

Theo frowned. "I'm so tired after dragging the bottom of the lake every day, I couldn't do justice to an employer. What's the other idea?"

"We find somewhere else to stay."

"Such as?"

"I don't know yet. Reverend Stroud would take us in, but there's barely enough room for him in that little cabin."

Theo's eyes narrowed. "The light's beginning to dawn, brother. I know what's brewing in that reckless head. You're hoping to wheedle an invitation from Priscilla to stay at the mansion."

Pushing him into the hall, Pearson laughed. "That wouldn't be proper, would it? Not with two unmarried ladies inside." He winked. "But there's always the servants' quarters."

"Those gloomy shacks haven't been lived in for twenty years. Braving the elements might be better."

Pearson laughed and patted his back. "I'm surprised at you. You've slept in worse places, like the cot in Rosie's storeroom, sharing a bed with rats as long as your arm."

"I was younger then. And foolish. I'm a man now and partial to comfort."

"Like lumpy sofas and musty quilts?"

Theo nudged him. "You've slept in worse places, too."

They entered the Ginocchio's bustling lobby, Theo beaming and raising his hat to an attractive woman at the desk. She blushed prettily, but her companion glared and moved closer, sliding his arm around her waist.

"Uh-oh," he whispered, hurrying his steps to the door. He strolled along the boardwalk beside Pearson, quiet for a change. Just as Pearson had begun to enjoy the silence, he cleared his throat and glanced up.

"Don't get me wrong, paisan, I'm happy we're attending church again, but. . ."

"Why am I going?"

He nodded. "I'm not your judge or anything, but I'm fairly certain a desire to see a woman isn't a scriptural reason to go."

After the trouble with Ceddy at the Whitfield place, Pearson thought better of mentioning his skirmish with the vexing Addie McRae, who could teach a thing or two about the art of judging people.

"Though I do mean to have a word with Miss Addie at my first opportunity, I assure you I'm not going to church to see her. I promised the reverend I'd be there, and I'm bound to keep my word."

Guilt burdened his soul as they walked from the hotel to the church. The truth was he hadn't told Theo the whole story. His decision to attend the service had nothing to do with Addie, but there was a lot more to it than keeping a promise to Reverend Stroud.

Since the church social, Pearson couldn't shake the desire to return. The need to feel the serenity he'd experienced consumed him, both in the service and afterward, while standing on Miss Whitfield's back porch.

Too many years had passed since he last felt calm inside. Having stumbled onto a taste, he craved it more than food and drink. If God's house was the source of that peace, it's where Pearson wanted to be.

The towering walls of the Kimberley Mine threatened to close in on Denny, and the soaring blue sky above the big hole spun his head. Sweat beaded on his top lip, tickling his nose. To wipe it off would attract attention. The blighters watched always, suspected everything.

He tried not to look at Tebogo, the big black wandering a half morgen away on a patch of weathering blue ground. The Cameroon cigars Denny used to bribe him had cost him dearly, but if the duck-footed bloke pulled off his trick, Denny could buy a passel of stogies.

Tebogo had done it before and succeeded, risking his hide to make another man rich, and for paltry recompense. Whatever drove such shortsighted behavior, Denny was glad the foolish man was willing to take the risk.

Without breaking his stride, Tebogo strolled into the unsorted field where Denny had spotted a brilliant flash. With the barest wrinkling of his toes, he snatched the kimberlite rock with his foot then meandered past Denny.

In a convincing show of clumsiness, Denny dropped his spade. Bending at the waist, he snatched the stone and promptly swallowed it.

Excitement swelled his chest, and he bit the inside of his lip to hold back a smile. At last! Boundless treasure had lain in wait for luckier blokes than he, far less deserving men growing rich and powerful in droves. Now his turn had come.

Casual as could be, he shouldered the spade and made for the huddle of shacks serving as an office. He'd turn in his tools and collect his wage, then—

A firm grip on his neck halted him in midstep. Cruel fingers dug in and spun him around.

The guard's leering grin shot fear to his chest, and he lost the power to breathe. . . .

Denny's eyes flew open. His heart pounded so hard, he feared for his life. Working to slow his breathing, he gazed around at the tattered rug and torn wallpaper of the rooming house.

When would he stop dreaming of that terrible day?

The attempted theft earned him a stay in the compound, bound in handcuffs, force-fed castor oil and stewed fruit until his traitorous body returned the stolen property.

His ill-fated assistant fared worse. He paid for his folly with the loss of his foot.

Denny rolled out of bed and sat on the side, holding his aching head. The bottle he'd drained the night before mocked him from the floor. Drawing back his foot, he gave it a swift kick then howled as pain shot from his toe to his throbbing temples.

Charlie reeled over and fixed him with a bleary stare. "Have you gone spare, mate? What's the good of all that racket?"

"Shut it and go back to sleep."

Growling, Charlie sat up instead. "Too late. Me heart's pounding out of me chest. What's eatin' you?"

Denny cast a surly glance around the room. "I'm sick of this rotted slum of a flat. We should be living like kings by now. Riding a luxury liner to an island in the Pacific."

Charlie's mouth grew slack, and he stared dreamily. "Yeah? That sounds nice, Den. So why ain't we?"

" 'Sounds nice, Den. Why ain't we?' " Denny mocked, throwing a pillow at his head. "Why do you think? We ain't got that blooming rock yet, now, have we?"

Charlie ducked and shook his head.

"We've been working our fingers to nubs for those two blokes, braving snakes and gators and dragging all manner of rubbish up from the deep." He spat on the floor. "Not a thing to show for it but short fingers and aching backs."

Charlie shot him a sullen glare. "You said we'd follow them so's we could find out where the boy lives, but we ain't done it."

Tapping his forehead, Denny grinned. "I don't tell you everything, now, do I? We don't need to follow them because I already know where the boy lives. It don't take long in this town to find out who Miss Priscilla Whitfield is or where her big mansion sits."

Confusion flashed on Charlie's face. "Then why ain't we gone after the diamond?"

Denny vaulted from the bed and slapped a hand over his mouth. "Pipe down, will ya? These walls are like onion peels. You want to compete with half the blokes in this seedy dive?"

Staring with frightened eyes, Charlie shook his head.

Settling to Charlie's lumpy mattress, Denny heaved a sigh. "I got a wee bit distracted, I suppose." Staring thoughtfully, he slipped his arm around Charlie's shoulders. "You see, I can't help wonderin' why those two are dragging the bottom of a lake." He gave Charlie a shake. "They take us for a couple of mugs. Think our accents make us stupid." He gave a harsh laugh. "We ain't stupid, are we, Charlie?"

The idiot shook his head. "We ain't stupid."

"That's right. And as long as nobody knows what the boy has, we've got time to help our friends find what they're looking for, maybe see what other trinkets there are in that big house. If my hunch is right, we'll be leaving town with more than a big white rock."

Charlie's shoulders slumped. "What if the boy don't have the stone no more? He could've lost it. Or chunked it away."

Denny shoved him against the wall, bumping his head so hard the window rattled. "Don't you say that, Charlie. You hear? He's still got it, all right." Squinting his eyes, he stared toward Whitfield Manor. "But he won't keep it, you can bet on that. If I have to kill somebody to get it."

The week since Addie last saw Pearson passed in a dizzying blur. It took days to settle poor Ceddy into his comforting routine.

As happy as she felt to see the Sabbath roll around again, she dreaded it with equal measure. What challenges might the day hold? How would Ceddy react to returning to church, the most likely place where he'd been harmed? Or to seeing Pearson, who Priscilla believed to be the culprit?

As for Addie, she didn't think for one minute that Pearson had hurt Ceddy. He might be a cad in matters of the heart, but his gentleness with the boy was genuine. Whoever the vile person was who cut and bruised Ceddy, nothing could convince her that it was Pearson.

She heard the boy whimpering before she turned the corner into his room.

Delilah stood over his bed, holding a warm cloth to his bare stomach while Ceddy rolled back and forth.

"What's wrong with him?"

"He got a touch of misery in his belly, that's all. It happens on occasion."

"Like this? How frequently?"

"Oh, 'bout twice a month, I s'pose."

Addie frowned. "Come to think of it, the same thing happened last Wednesday. The poor dear lost his lunch. What do you suppose is causing it?"

"I cain't say, Miss Addie. I ain't no doctor."

"Have you called one?"

"Oh yes'm. Lots of times. He say nothing wrong, near as he could tell."

"Well, it's happening too often to ignore." Addie crossed to the bed and smoothed his forehead. "What did you give him for breakfast?"

"He wouldn't eat this mornin'. Miss Priscilla got mos' his milk down, but that's all he had."

Addie jerked her gaze to Delilah. "He drank milk?" She returned to watching Ceddy. "And this was the outcome?"

"Yes'm, I s'pose."

Priscilla swept in, tugging on her gloves. "Are we about ready?" Pausing at the door, her eyes flashed to Ceddy. "Oh my. What ails him?"

"His stomach again, Miss Priscilla," Delilah said.

Hands on her hips, Addie faced her. "Did Ceddy drink his milk last Wednesday?"

"I don't recall," she said, her brows furrowed. "Wait. Yes, I do." She beamed proudly. "I coaxed him to finish every drop."

Bracing for battle, Addie stamped her foot. "You're not to give him any more milk. And no sugary sweets."

Both women gaped at her.

Delilah straightened. "But he love his treats, Miss Addie."

"No more, I say."

Worrying her bottom lip, Priscilla approached the bed. "Oh Addie. Are you certain? Sometimes Delilah's cookies are all that will settle him."

"Do you trust me, Priscilla?"

She thrust her shoulders back. "Implicitly."

"Then let me try this, please. It's my theory that a constant diet of sugared foods may be contributing to Ceddy's bad behavior. He's always much worse after he's eaten a treat."

"But the milk? It's good for him."

Addie shook her head. "I don't think so. He holds his stomach and moans for hours after ingesting milk. It's why you have to force him to drink it." Moving to the bed, she patted his flushed cheek. "Poor dear. He's smarter than all of us."

Priscilla stared at Ceddy, her eyes dazed. "If it's true, then it's very astute of you to make the connection, dear."

Crossing the room, she stood over Ceddy's bed. "He does look miserable." She sighed. "Very well, Addie. You'll have a chance to test your theory." She turned, a determined set to her jaw. "Delilah, no more desserts. And no milk."

"But Miss Priscilla. . .what do I do when he come pulling on my skirt and moaning like he do?"

"Give him dried apples instead," Addie said. "Or a spoon coated with honey." Bolstering her courage, she voiced her next concern. "And we should stop treating him like an invalid. He can do many things for himself, but we've allowed him to become lazy. He's perfectly capable of combing his hair and dressing, yet he stands like a limp doll and lets Delilah do it for him."

"Are you sure, Addie?"

"Quite sure. And another thing. . .everyone talks over him, past him, about him. Hardly ever directly to him. We must start addressing him as though we expect a response. He understands very well, whether he appears to or not."

Delilah huffed. "I talks to him all the time, but he don't say nothin' back. How you gon' converse to a body who don't answer?"

Addie briskly nodded. "Yes, he does. Granted, not vocally. You have to watch him closely, but in his own way, he answers."

Priscilla slid her arm around Addie and leaned to kiss her forehead. "I can't tell you how grateful I am for your keen insight and concern for Ceddy."

A blush warmed Addie's cheeks. "I'm very fond of him."

"And it shows." Priscilla patted her shoulder. "Go dress for church. You could use a day out of the house. I'll sit with him this morning."

Addie shook her head. "I couldn't allow you to miss church for me."

Priscilla stole a glance at Delilah. "Perhaps we could both go, then, if only. . ."

Delilah's big brown eyes rounded.

Smiling, Addie walked to the door and held it wide. "I won't have either of you missing your service. Ceddy is my responsibility, and I'll sit with him today."

Truthfully, she felt immensely relieved. While she hated for Ceddy to suffer, staying home with him solved both of her problems. She wouldn't have to deal with his reaction to being at church, and she wouldn't have to deal with her own scattered emotions about seeing Pearson.

NINETEEN

Standing with Reverend Stroud on the steps of the church, Pearson's heart pitched at the sight of the Whitfield carriage. His disappointment when the lady of the manor climbed down without Addie stung more sharply than he cared to admit. Happy to see his new friend nonetheless, he smiled broadly as Miss Whitfield approached. "Morning, ma'am. Good to see you again."

"Good morning, gentlemen." Her wary eyes slid to his and then away so fast, Pearson's stomach clenched. Something was obviously wrong.

"Priscilla, I hope you intend to remove your hat for the sake of those seated behind you," Reverend Stroud teased. "Mercy is a virtue, you know."

Her trembling hand reached for the sky blue contraption sprouting assorted feathers and bows. "Do you really think I should?"

He chuckled. "Why break with tradition? Besides"—he nudged her—"haven't you noticed? No one ever sits behind you."

Instead of laughing with him or offering a barbed retort, she edged toward the door. "I'd best go inside. The service will be starting soon."

The reverend's brows rose. "I hope not, dear lady, since I'm an integral part."

With a tight smile, she slipped inside and disappeared.

Pearson and the reverend exchanged looks.

"What was that about?" Pearson asked.

The man shook his head. "I've never seen her like this." He chuckled. "Perhaps I can figure her out by the close of service. My sermon is rather lengthy, I'm afraid. I'll have plenty of time to observe."

Pearson followed him inside then joined Theo on the front pew. The sensation of someone staring at the back of his head persisted so strongly throughout the singing and the message that followed, he gave in a few times and stole a glance behind him. Each time, he met Miss Whitfield's startled gaze.

He caught only snippets of Reverend Stroud's discourse on the importance of loving your neighbor and lending a helping hand to those in need. Based on their earlier conversation about the servants' quarters, he suspected the reverend had directed his sermon, at least in part, to Miss Whitfield. Too bad she didn't seem to hear a word.

Her odd behavior so distracted Pearson, it robbed him of the peace he sought. After the closing prayer, unlike the week before, he didn't feel as if he'd even been to church.

Outside, a welcoming committee—self-appointed no doubt—of Marshall's unmarried daughters and their mothers descended on Pearson and Theo. To Theo's delight, they brought baskets of baked goods and pretty smiles. Beaming like a cat in a birdcage, he bowed as they filed past, whispering promises to each of them that he'd taste their gift first.

Grinning and shaking his head, Reverend Stroud strolled to where Priscilla stood anxiously wringing her hands. After a hushed conversation that didn't appear to end in her favor, he waved them over.

Pearson pried Theo from the circle of tittering girls and urged him toward the carriage.

"Gentlemen, we're graciously invited to the manor for lunch, if you have no prior plans."

Pearson ducked his head, trying to read the lady's face. "Are you sure, ma'am? We don't want to intrude."

She drew herself up and took a deep breath. "Of course, Mr. Foster. I wouldn't have it any other way."

Seven days ago, she'd insisted on calling him Pearson. Something was definitely wrong.

The milk Priscilla forced on Ceddy that morning would trouble him no more. Most of it now splattered the front of Addie's uniform; the rest puddled on the floor.

With one hand she held a damp cloth to the poor child's forehead; with the other she tried to work his arm free of his nightshirt. "It was a wise move to abide by my suggestion, Ceddy," she told the drowsy-eyed boy. "Otherwise we'd face a skirmish to rival First Manassas the next time you're offered milk."

He groaned and rolled to one side.

She hadn't the heart to jostle him further, so she tucked the covers around his thin shoulders and left him be.

The sound of footsteps on the stairwell, too slow and heavy for Delilah's yet too quick for Priscilla's, stirred her heart to pounding. Before she could react to her fear, Priscilla hurried into the room.

Addie's hand went to her heart. "It is you! Heavens, you frightened me silly."

"Addie, you won't believe this," Priscilla whispered. "He's downstairs."

"Who?" she asked, but she already knew. "Not Mr. Foster?" Snatching the rag from Ceddy's head, she swiped self-consciously at the sour mess on her skirt.

Closing the door quietly, Priscilla whirled, a frantic look in her eyes. "The very same. Only it's even worse than that."

Addie didn't see how it could get any worse, but she didn't bother making the point. "What happened?"

"He's going to be living here."

Her hand stilled, clutching the cloth. Pointing at the floor, she frowned. "Here? In this house?"

"Nearly as bad. In the servants' quarters out back."

Addie knew the place she meant. The row of crumbling buildings along the back corner of the property.

Many questions raced through her mind. Only one made its way to her lips. "Why?"

"Are you asking why they want to or why I let them?"

She waved the back of her hand. "Yes, both of those."

"If I understood right, they're trying to conserve money so they might continue their search for the *Mittie*."

"And?"

Priscilla's face flushed, and she paced the room. "Reverend Stroud pressed me to allow it. The man is simply thick when it comes to social graces. He asked me right in front of those two. I had no choice but to agree."

Addie bundled the rag with Ceddy's soiled clothing. "What are we going to do?"

"That's what I asked myself the entire ride home."

She stopped walking and faced Addie. "It's all so perplexing. When I spend any length of time with that young man, the idea of his hurting anyone seems outlandish."

Addie nodded. "I know just what you mean." Except for his fixation on a married woman, Pearson seemed a most agreeable man. She didn't hold it against him for finding her mother attractive. He wasn't the first to fall under the spell of Mariah McRae. The unforgivable part was his seeming determination to follow his wayward heart.

"And I trust Reverend Stroud's instincts completely, or I would never have agreed. Yet we can't lose sight of the fact that *someone* hurt our boy. To answer your question, dear, here's all we can do—we'll welcome Mr. Foster and his friend to the estate. After all, some hold with the notion of keeping one's enemies near enough to watch." She offered a tight smile. "You can't get much closer than your own backyard, now, can you?"

Dazed, Addie shook her head.

"There's more bad news." Priscilla grimaced. "Until repairs are made, they'll be taking their meals with us and—"

"Excuse me?"

"Freshening up inside, too."

"Oh my, that seems too close."

"Don't fret, dear. Between you, me, and Delilah, we won't let Ceddy out of sight for a moment."

If Priscilla knew the true reason Addie felt uncomfortable around Pearson, she'd be stunned.

"I don't want you to worry, honey. Together we'll see this through." Drawing away, she wrinkled her nose. "Oh my. What's that horrid smell?"

Addie held out her skirt. "I fear it's me, courtesy of Ceddy."

Priscilla waved her toward the door. "Go on and freshen up for lunch. I'll stay with him until you return. Delilah is laying the table, but I'll send her up the minute she's finished."

"Where are the men?"

"In typical male fashion, they couldn't wait until after the meal. They're tramping through the cottages out back, deciding which one is fit to occupy."

"Can't Delilah bring a tray upstairs for Ceddy and me? Surely you don't need me at the table."

A shocked look crossed her face. "Of course I do. I'll need you to spend as much time as possible with Mr. Foster, Addie. How else will you help me decide if he's to be trusted?"

Pearson patted the beam in the center of the room, flinching when plaster rained down on his head. "She warned us they were in disrepair. I'm afraid she wasn't kidding."

Theo, far handier with a hammer and nails, scurried around the room like the only ant at a picnic. "They're not so bad. Nothing that can't be fixed."

"So this is the one, boys?" Reverend Stroud asked.

"Yes, sir," Theo said. "It's the most structurally sound of the three."

Pearson dared to look up again. "Can you do something about this ceiling? I don't relish paint chips as a complement to my meals."

The reverend laughed. "Oh, but you heard Priscilla, son. You won't be taking your meals out here."

Pearson studied his face. "I think the lady said a lot of things she didn't want to say. Are you sure we're welcome to stay?"

The reverend patted his shoulder. "Don't mind her quirky ways, son. I've known Priscilla for many years, and her heart is good. If I had to guess, she's worried about how others will view your presence on the estate. I'm sure she's intent on protecting the reputation of that pretty little governess."

Pearson nodded. "That's high on my list of priorities, too, sir. If you think there's any chance of talk in town, we'll make other arrangements."

"It's not like you're sleeping under the same roof." He shook his head. "Leave the gossips to me. Once I place my seal of approval, no one will dare speak a word against them." He motioned toward the door. "I think we've seen enough. Now that you've picked your cabin, I suspect I can commandeer a work force from the congregation."

Theo grinned. "That would be a big help, sir. I won't get much out of Pearson."

"I'm sure they'll be happy to lend a hand." He patted his stomach. "Fellows, by now the table is groaning with platters. Delilah's the second-best cook in Harrison County. Let's go sample her wares, shall we?"

"Second?" Pearson asked. "Who's the best?"

He waved his index finger. "Never mind, for now. I may let you in on the secret someday. For now, let's keep that comment between us."

Miss Whitfield met them in the hall and ushered them to the dining room.

Addie, already seated, glanced up as they entered, offering a smile to Reverend Stroud and Theo, a curt nod for Pearson.

True to his word, the reverend seemed eager to try every steaming dish as soon as the 'Amens' were said.

Not to be outdone, Theo took a healthy serving from every bowl passed to him.

His conscience raw from feeling he'd forced himself on the gracious lady seated at the head of the table, Pearson had no appetite.

"Is everything all right?" she asked, her troubled gaze on his hands, lying still next to his plate.

He ducked his head and picked up his fork. "Oh yes, ma'am. It looks delicious."

She watched him for several minutes, her mouth fidgeting as if she couldn't find the words she wanted to say. "If there's anything else you need, please say so, and I'll get it for you. Delilah is busy with Ceddy today. He's ill, I'm afraid, and confined to his room." She studied his face, as if waiting for his reaction. "The poor child isn't the same after his frightening ordeal. Of course, we won't be leaving him alone anymore." She cleared her throat. "That is, there will be someone with him at all times."

Pearson felt the need to squirm under her attentive gaze. "I think that's a wise idea."

She took a bite of sweet potato and nodded thoughtfully. "Can you imagine the sort of man who would deliberately injure a child?"

He met her eyes. "No, ma'am, I can't."

"It's a deplorable act, don't you agree?"

"I do indeed."

"You mentioned a little brother. . . ."

Pearson laid down his fork.

"If anyone had ever harmed him, how would it make you feel?"

The room stilled. The others stopped eating to watch the exchange.

"I can answer that question from experience."

Her brows peaked. "Oh?"

"You see, someone did harm him. In fact, he lost his life."

"I don't understand," she said. "I thought your family died in a storm. No one is responsible for that."

He shrugged. "Maybe not. Then again, they might not have died if I'd been there to help."

"Oh, Mr. Foster," Addie said from across the table, "you mustn't think that."

Her unexpected sympathy surprised him. He longed to look at her, but shame kept his eyes on his plate.

Theo leaned past him to see Miss Whitfield. "No one could've saved them. Not a soul from the neighborhood survived. If he'd been there, instead of on holiday with my family, he wouldn't be sitting here today."

Reverend Stroud reached across the table and gripped Pearson's hand. "I'm sure Pearson knows that in his head. Sometimes the heart is slow to follow."

Embarrassed and angry with himself for displaying his emotions so openly, Pearson cleared his throat. "I'd love a piece of that cake now, if nobody minds."

Her cheeks damp with tears, Miss Whitfield stood. "Coming right up, dear. Along with a nice hot cup of coffee to wash it down."

TWENTY

Addie sat quietly in the parlor, the first peaceful moment she'd had all day. Muted sunlight, peeking around the edges of the drapes, a single lantern, the wick turned down low, and a waning fire in the fireplace provided meager light in the heavily shaded room.

After the meal, the others retired to the coolness of the garden. Addie hurried upstairs to relieve Delilah. Finding her napping on the floor by Ceddy's bed, she'd covered her with a blanket then tiptoed out and shut the door.

Addie tried hard to match the mood of the house, but her restless heart was anything but quiet. She didn't want to ache for Pearson Foster's plight, didn't want her mind consumed by thoughts of a man attracted to a married woman.

The parlor door swung open. Pearson stood on the threshold, blinking against the dimness. His squinted eyes came to rest on her then widened. "I'm sorry. I didn't realize anyone was in here."

He began to back out the way he came, but she held up her hand. "It's all right. Can I get you anything?"

He smiled, the sight of it stirring her heart. How could a man with such an appealing face be capable of any wrongdoing?

"They're asleep." He pointed toward the garden. "The reverend nodding in a chair, Miss Whitfield in the swing, and Theo sprawled on the ground in the sun. I didn't want to wake them, so I thought I'd wait inside."

She motioned. "Won't you come in?"

He cocked his head. "You don't mind?"

"It's a little too quiet in the house. I could use the company."

The shock on his face pained her, but why wouldn't he be surprised? She'd been anything but cordial. "Besides, there's a matter I'd like to discuss with you."

He propped the door open with the stop and crossed the room. "Fancy that. There's a matter I'd like to discuss with you, too."

"I suppose the only question now is who shall go first. Have a seat, please."

Settling into Priscilla's overstuffed chair, he stretched out his long legs and crossed his ankles. "No question there." He waved in invitation. "Ladies first."

Not nearly so confident with him sitting so close, she folded her hands in her lap. "This is awkward. I'm not sure where to begin."

"If you start by apologizing for last Sunday's outburst, it will save us a lot of time. Then we could dispense with both of our topics at once."

She gaped at him. "You're joking."

He shook his head, not a hint of teasing on his somber face. "That's my first rule. When it comes to my reputation, I never jest."

Scowling, Addie crossed her arms and sank against the sofa, at a loss for words.

He suffered no such impediment. "What is it with you, Miss McRae? How have I so thoroughly offended you?"

Her chin jerked up. "I should think it would be apparent."

"Well, it's not in the least."

The passion in his tone startled her. She pressed deeper into the cushion.

"If I knew what I'd done"—suddenly smiling, he drew in his feet and sat forward—"I would shower you with apologies until you forgave me."

Surprised, she glanced away.

"A word of warning, Miss McRae. The more you withdraw, the more determined I become to win your friendship."

She raised flashing eyes. "I can see how some women find your flattery appealing, but I assure you, it won't work with me." The burning in her chest intensified. "Or with my mother."

He cocked his head. "Your mother again? What does she have to do with anything?"

As absurd as it seemed, his offhanded attitude toward Mother made Addie madder than ever. "Have you so quickly forgotten her charms? What do they say? Out of sight, out of mind?"

"Mrs. McRae is a delightful woman. A kind and gentle soul. I haven't forgotten her at all."

Addie pushed off the couch and stormed to the hearth. "I suppose you penned all those compliments in the letter you sent her?" She hugged her waist. "Mr. Foster, sir, what were you thinking?" In the silence that followed, tiny hairs stood up on her neck.

Pearson angled his head. "So that's what this is about?

Insufferable blatant arrogance! She spun. "Do you presume to suggest I'm jealous of my own mother?"

Pearson's eyes flew wide. "Jealous?" He scooted to the edge of the chair, his wide stare closing to slits. "I think I'm beginning to understand now. When was the last time you heard from her?"

"Not since she left, if it's any of your business."

He nodded slowly then stood. "I expect you'll be hearing from her soon. At that time you may regard me in a different light, but I fear this conversation will be the source of stinging embarrassment." He drew a shallow breath. "For both of us." With a curt nod, he strode for the door.

"You're just going to walk away?" Addie called. "Without bothering to explain your deplorable behavior?"

"That's my second rule, Miss McRae. On the matter of my honor, I never stoop to defending myself. I let my actions do the talking."

Ceddy shot up in bed and stared. His chest burned from holding in a scream, and his stomach hurt. Eyes darting, he took in every corner of the room, terrified of what he might see.

Lilah lay beside him on the floor, breathing loud in her sleep. Scary Mr. Currie and big, ugly Charlie were gone. He clawed around his neck, but the sharp white shell cutting his skin was gone, too.

He slumped against his pillow, panting hard. Safe. In Aunt Priss's house.

The fog began to clear, and his heart slowed. Were the men only there in his dream?

Cold without his nightshirt, he drew up his knees and cuddled deeper into the mattress. Feeling for the quilt he'd kicked off in his sleep, he jerked it over his shoulders. The white stone flew up, crashed to the floor, and then rolled into Lilah.

She sat up rubbing her head. "Who done walloped me?"

Ceddy spun out of bed and slid on his knees to where Lilah sat. Shoving on her shoulder, he felt around the blanket and in the folds of her dress. "Mmm-muh."

"Now, jus' hold on, lil' mista. Don't go meddling about with me. I got nothin' of yours." She chuckled and held her hand over his head. " 'Less you hankerin' after this old thing."

Feeling up her arm, Ceddy's eager fingers closed over the rock. Fumbling it away from her, he sat back on his heels. "Muh."

"Yes, yours, and that be jus' fine with me. I got no use for that shapeless old paperweight."

Ceddy's middle rolled and growled. Clutching his stomach, he tapped his mouth with his knuckles.

She laughed. "I reckon you is hungry." She stroked the back of his head. "Trouble is I don't think what you want is what you bound to get."

He pushed her again.

Struggling to her feet, she groaned. "Wait jus' a minute. Old Lilah don't move so quick no mo'." Patting his hand, she picked up the blanket, folded it, and tossed it on his bed. "Let's get you dressed so we can go down to the kitchen." Her growly voice lowered to where he barely heard the rest. "See if we can't stir up some old, dried-out fruit. Maybe dip you out some honey or some fool thing. Never in all my days have I heard of giving a poor child—"

She twisted around. "Well, looky. Here's Miss Addie now with your snack. You shouldn't've troubled yourself, miss. I was on my way downstairs."

"It was no trouble," Miss Addie said. She swished past Ceddy with a tray and set it on the table. "I needed something to busy my hands."

Something besides strangling the life out of one Pearson Foster, Addie thought.

"I have a new treat to try today. One of my mother's old recipes, and I think Ceddy will like it." She lifted the dishcloth off the saucer of hasty pudding.

Delilah eyed the sticky-topped dish. "I thought you said no more sweets."

"There's no sugar in the batter and only a touch of honey on top. We'll see how he does."

"I can tell you how he gon' do," Delilah mumbled, "before he ever lay eyes on it."

Ignoring her nay-saying tone, Addie crossed to the wardrobe. Nodding at the pitcher and bowl atop the washstand, she pulled out his clothes. "Wipe him down so I can dress him, please."

With Ceddy scrubbed and combed, Addie sat beside him on the floor, his favorite place. Pretending far more confidence than she felt, she placed the dish in front of him. As an afterthought, she turned the saucer so he could reach the spoon, an addition to his mealtime routine he had finally accepted.

Ceddy wrinkled his nose and nudged it away with his knuckles.

Delilah's low hum said, "I told you so."

"Ceddy, please try some," Addie pleaded. "I truly feel it's for your own good."

"He missing his treats, Miss Addie. Powerful bad. He cry and moan and hang on my skirts till he wearies me fit to be tied."

"He'll get used to the change." She eased the pudding toward him again. "We have to give him time."

Delilah sucked a breath through her nose, the cords in her neck protruding. "I don't mean no disrespect, miss. I swear I don't. Only I never heard such an outlandish notion. How could a little cane sugar hurt a body? Children grow up on they mama's cakes and pies. I cain't see how—"

Addie lifted one hand to shush her. Smiling, she tilted her head at Ceddy.

One small finger hooked the edge of the dish, teasing it closer. Gouging a hole in the pudding, he carefully tasted it. Swaying side to side, intent on spinning the white stone, he picked up another gooey scoop and crammed it in his mouth.

"Oh my, his spoon," Addie said. Grinning at Delilah, she shook her head. "I don't even care. We'll work on etiquette the next time."

Priscilla appeared at the door suppressing a yawn. "Here you all are. Where is Mr. Foster? The reverend is ready to leave, and I've summoned the carriage."

Pushing to her feet, Addie crossed to the basin and dipped the corner of a towel. "I don't know where Mr. Foster might've gone. I saw him briefly in the parlor, but he left before I did." She dropped to her knees and wiped Ceddy's hands. "Maybe he returned to looking at the servants' quarters."

Delilah picked up the empty saucer from the floor. "I'll look in the kitchen, Miss Priscilla. If he in there, I'll send him out front."

"Thank you," Priscilla said as she slipped past.

Taking a backward step, Priscilla gazed down the hall until Delilah's footsteps echoed from the stairs. Then she entered and closed the door.

"Addie, I've made a decision about Mr. Foster. I don't see him capable of evil in any form." Her brows rose in a hesitant question. "Don't you agree?"

Choosing her words carefully, Addie shook her head. "I don't think he hurt Ceddy, if that's what you mean."

Priscilla clutched her hands. "I'm so happy you concur. He's such an agreeable young man." She smiled. "Actually, both he and Theo are a pleasure to be around. I do enjoy their company." She chuckled, staring over Addie's head. "They tell the most amusing stories about growing up together on the seashore. I laughed at their antics until I grew hoarse." Sobering, she glanced at Ceddy. "Of course, I'll continue to watch his interaction with my nephew. . .just in case." She placed a hand on Addie's shoulder. "But my heart tells me we should look elsewhere for our culprit."

Addie nodded and tossed the soiled towel toward the hamper. "I think that's a wise decision, Priscilla."

TWENTY-ONE

Reverend Stroud went straight to work the next morning and convinced a few members of his congregation to lend their idle hands to something other than the devil's workshop—evidenced by a six-man crew descending on Pearson and Theo as they were beginning to tear out the rotted interior walls of the chosen servants' cottage.

Glancing up as the reverend appeared on the threshold, Pearson offered a warm smile. "The cavalry?"

"I'm a man of my word, son." He flashed a crooked grin. "Come to think of it, I'm a man of God's Word. Either way, I have to keep my promises." Shaking Theo's shoulder playfully, he picked up a jellied biscuit from the platter provided by Delilah. "Ever notice how similar the word *cavalry* is to *Calvary*? Both are instruments of rescue, and in your case"—he pointed at the members of his flock—"both terms are appropriate."

"And I'm grateful to God for both," Pearson said, ducking his head when Theo shot him a startled glance.

The reverend rolled his shoulders and flexed his hands. "Now then, gentlemen. . .what can I say to help?"

Grinning, Pearson braced his knuckles on his hips. "You can start with a prayer, sir. Nothing else will get this place livable."

The unflappable man nudged him. "Oh ye of little faith. These fine men can raise a barn in an afternoon. They'll have this done quick as a wink."

Patting his back, Pearson laughed. "They have considerably more time than a wink. We're paid up at the Ginocchio through the next two weeks."

The reverend drew back and stared. "Two weeks? They can restore the whole wing in that amount of time. You'll each have a place of your own when we're done."

Caught off guard, Pearson gazed around at the crowd of men. "You'd do that for us?"

"We would, though Priscilla will benefit as well. She's been worried about the state of these old houses for too long."

Pearson offered his hand. "I'm humbled by your kindness." Nodding at the circle of beaming faces, his chest swelled. "And by your sacrifice."

The men filed past, smiling and shaking his hand, then set to work.

Last in line, Reverend Stroud caught Pearson's fingers in a firm grip. "It's what we do. And speaking of one's vocation, how will you two raise a lost steamboat while you're swinging hammers and sawing boards?"

Pearson handed him another biscuit then took one for himself. "We planned to get a start here and then head on out to the lake. Our hired hands should be on their feet and ready to go by then." He grimaced. "Those two have a hard time finding the floor in the mornings."

"Late sleepers?"

Pearson nodded. "Something like that."

The reverend nodded thoughtfully. "In this case, you have to take on whoever's willing, I suppose."

Through the hammering and ripping of old lumber, a knock sounded at the open door. A timid Delilah peeked around the jamb, searching the dim room. "Reverend? You be in there?"

He strode toward her. "I'm here, Delilah."

"Miss Priscilla saw all those rigs pull around back and knowed you had a hand in it somehow. She sent me out to fetch you up to the house for breakfast." Her eyes cut over to Pearson. "She say to bring all of you." A worried frown creased her brow. "You'd best throw down those trifling biscuits and don't tell Miss Priscilla I brung 'em out here. She say to come hungry."

Addie stood before the gilded mirror and stared at her ashen face. Since the moment she'd spotted Pearson from her window, her heart had fluttered near her throat. The sight of him likely marked the first of many mornings she'd need to battle her rage.

Calling on a lifetime of breeding, she took a deep breath and steeled her spine. At Priscilla's request, she'd go to breakfast and treat him civilly at the table. Civil, in this case, had little to do with warmth, and Pearson would understand the difference very soon.

He said the more she withdrew, the more determined he'd become to befriend her. "Humph! Prepare to become most determined, sir," she told her scowling reflection.

She turned at a knock on the door. "Yes, come in."

Delilah poked her head inside. "Miss Priscilla say hurry down those stairs. You have guests to entertain."

"Where's Ceddy?"

"Fed, clean, and spinning wooden soldiers in his room. Never saw a child play in such a peculiar way with his toys."

"Thank you, Delilah. Will you be able to sit with him while I'm at breakfast?"

"That's where I be headed now." She grinned. "Reckon I'll sit and spin right along with him."

Addie laughed and gave her hair a final pat before starting for the door. "Well, mind you don't get dizzy."

Mingled voices greeted her as she descended to the hall. Swallowing hard, she opened the door on the long dining table and Priscilla's boisterous laughter.

"Here she is now. Take a seat, please, Addie, so these fellows can start." She unfolded her napkin onto her lap. "They've waited so long for you they're bound to be starved."

Two men leaped up at once to pull out her chair. Though seated right next to her, Pearson wasn't one of them.

Gritting her teeth, Addie pasted on a broad smile. "My apologies, gentlemen. I didn't mean to take so long."

"Quite all right, young lady," the reverend said. "You're a vision this morning and worth the wait."

Nods and mumbles of agreement circled the table, Pearson conspicuous in his silence.

Addie flashed a smile. "Why, thank you. Now who can pass me the jelly?"

Reverend Stroud held up his hand. "May we ask God's blessing first?"

Cheeks flaming, Addie folded her hands in her lap. The reverend would think her an infidel, and it was Pearson's fault. He kept her in a constant state of distraction. Her humiliation wasn't fair, considering the true heretic seated at breakfast was Pearson, given his aversion to prayer—a fact witnessed the day they met.

"Pearson?" Reverend Stroud glanced his way. "Would you mind offering our thanks?"

Addie's stomach sank. Despite Pearson's insufferable arrogance, she didn't want him to be embarrassed. A man like him likely didn't know how to pray.

His cheeks colored a bit, but he promptly bowed his head.

Addie followed suit, waiting breathlessly to see what he could possibly scramble to offer.

"Great and gracious heavenly Father—"

Startled, she jerked her head up. Feeling like the word *infidel* might be an appropriate description for her, she hurriedly lowered it and closed her eyes.

"—we thank You for Your bounty and ask Your blessing on this food and those who partake of it. We humbly ask for guidance and protection as we start another day."

He said more, closing by invoking the Savior's name, but Addie's fevered mind had strayed. How was it possible? The person who squirmed uncomfortably through a prayer the day they met had offered an eloquent, heartfelt blessing.

She glanced at the reverend, his cheeks bulging with food. Had the man of God wrought a miracle in such a short time?

Priscilla passed the scrambled eggs to Reverend Stroud. "What's the state of our repairs, then? Are the buildings worth saving?"

"Ah, dear lady, you ask this of a minister? Everything and everyone is worth saving." Smiling, he handed off the bowl to his right. "I can tell you this much, our project supervisor is worthy of his hire." He winked at Theo. "With this young man at the helm, we'll build a structure you can be proud of."

The tips of Theo's ears turned bright red. "Thank you, Reverend."

Until that second, Addie hadn't taken Theo very seriously. Seated across the table from her, he squirmed beneath the attention, chewing on his bottom lip to keep from smiling. The humble gesture touched her heart.

Upon closer inspection, he was actually a nice-looking fellow. Some would even say handsome. His dark clownish curls and peculiar manner of speech drew attention from the delicate arch of his brows and the pleasing shape of his mouth. His wheat-colored skin and brown eyes. His—

A heaping platter jutted in front of her face. "Pork?"

Pearson, anger etched on his face, held the tray of ham. Something besides rage flashed in his eyes. He'd caught her staring at Theo and didn't like it. Did he find her unworthy of his best friend?

She shook her head. "I don't partake of unclean beasts, Mr. Foster." She tucked her chin and lowered her voice. "Or pork."

Deliberately crowding her, he leaned to offer the meat to the man at her left.

She lightly shoved him.

He jabbed her with his elbow.

Furious, she twisted in the chair, offering him her back. "Priscilla, tell your guests the story of the grandfather clock."

Giving encouragement, the clock struck the ninth hour.

Priscilla smiled and launched into the charming tale, complete with the song at the end.

While she spoke, Pearson gradually inched closer until she could feel his warm breath on her neck.

Flustered, she swatted the swirling, tickly hairs.

He laughed, low and throaty.

She imagined the satisfaction of dumping her plate in his lap.

"Miss Priscilla?" Delilah whispered from the threshold.

Priscilla glanced up from buttering her flapjacks. "What is it, Lilah? You're interrupting breakfast."

Her eyes were wide. "Little Man need Miss Addie."

Priscilla glanced at Addie and back. "Something you can't handle?"

She shook her head. "Not this I cain't."

Addie pushed back her chair, the harsh bump it gave Pearson's leg bringing warm satisfaction. Served the gangly rogue right for scooting improperly close. "I don't mind, Priscilla. I'll go see what he needs."

She followed Delilah up the stairs, curious questions pressing at her lips. Before she had time to voice them, Delilah pushed open the door and stood aside.

Ceddy sat in his usual place, his favorite box of rocks on his lap.

Nothing seemed out of the ordinary.

Addie shot Delilah a puzzled frown. "What's the urgent problem? He seems fine."

"Oh, he fine enough." Her brows rose, wrinkling her forehead. "Only your special necklace ain't."

At Addie's openmouthed stare, she nodded. "Go on. See for yourself."

Dread crowding her throat, Addie hurried over and dropped to her knees beside the boy. Her darting gaze scanned the box in Ceddy's lap, and her heart pitched to her throat. "Oh Ceddy," she breathed, tears blurring the terrible sight, "what have you done?"

The small jasper stone he once kept in the box was gone. Grandmother's polished pendant jutted from its place. The clasp and beads were gone.

TWENTY-TWO

Pearson rubbed his throbbing shin beneath the table. Blast that infernal female! He'd never met a more vexing woman. Each time he gained the upper hand in their curious game, she played a marked card.

Blistering under the heat of another's stare, he looked up.

Theo watched him, a teasing grin on his face.

In no mood for his taunting, Pearson challenged him with a raised brow.

Still smiling, Theo shook his head and tucked into his scrambled eggs.

"So, Pearson," the reverend said, "tell me more about your drowsy hired hands."

Pearson folded his napkin and laid it beside his plate. "There's not much to tell. They're an odd pair, I know that much. Aimless drifters, I think. Full of questions, but fairly closemouthed about themselves."

The reverend bit off a corner of his biscuit. "Most drifters are."

"They're foreigners," Theo said. "Fresh off the boat from South Africa." He held up his spoon. "With accents as thick as these grits."

Knives and forks stilled their clinking, followed by shared laughter.

A wrinkle creased Theo's forehead. "What's the joke?"

Pearson chuckled again. "That's a funny observation, coming from you."

"What are you saying? I speak plain enough."

Pointing at the white mound in Theo's spoon, Pearson grinned. "Not that bad, but close."

Theo thumped his chest. "Now you hurt my feelings."

"Mercy sakes, we're out of syrup." Miss Whitfield added the last thick drops to her skillet cakes. Peering into the hall, she heaved a sigh. "I suppose Delilah's still upstairs." Pushing back her chair, she plunked her napkin on the table and stood. "Excuse me, gentlemen. I'm a little shorthanded this morning. I'll have to run out and fetch it myself." She waved at their plates. "Carry on. I won't be a minute."

As though anyone would have waited.

She slipped into the hallway leading to the kitchen.

The reverend turned to Pearson. "I didn't want to say anything in front of Priscilla. She's so easily flustered."

Dread settled in Pearson's stomach. By the look on the man's face, his next words weren't good news. "Go on, sir."

"It's probably nothing to worry about, but there's a lot of talk around the church about a series of petty crimes taking place in town. Folks are getting nervous and starting to point the finger." His gaze flitted to the window then returned, his stare direct. "You and Theo are the only strangers living in town. People have noticed, and they talk."

Theo's fist came down on the table. "What?"

Incensed, Pearson half rose in his chair, but the reverend waved him down. "A conclusion I promptly squashed." He forked another flapjack and idly spread it with jam. "Your workmen never crossed my mind until just now. They're recent additions to our fair town as well."

Theo sat forward in his chair. "It's true, they are. They must be the ones who—"

Reverend Stroud held up his hand. "Careful, son. You didn't appreciate the finger pointed in your direction without cause. You don't want to be guilty of the same." He shrugged. "I'm only suggesting you keep a watchful eye on them." A small frown creased his brow. "Unless you have reason to trust them, of course."

Pearson shook his head. "There's nothing about their conduct so far to encourage trust."

He gripped Pearson's shoulder. "Then I repeat my caution. Be careful."

Addie sat on the floor with her hands clenched in her lap, tears coursing unchecked down her cheeks. Mother had entrusted her with a precious possession. Two weeks in her care, and it existed only in scattered pieces. Finding those pieces had become the most important task in Addie's life.

A frantic search of her jewelry case, the floor in her room, Ceddy's room, and the hallway in between had revealed nothing. With Delilah's help, they looked in every likely place inside the house—with no luck.

She turned to her young charge and dropped to his level. "Ceddy?" she whispered. "Please show Addie where you left the beads."

Moaning softly, he spread his fingers over the collection box and shrank away.

Delilah slumped on the side of the bed. "He feel your anger. You won't get nothin' out of him while he do."

Addie swiveled to look at her. "Anger?" Spinning to Ceddy, she held out her hands. "Oh honey, I'm not angry with you." But was she?

He offered her his shoulder.

"I only want to make it right again." She nodded at the top of his unresponsive head. "To fix the pretty necklace." She sniffled. "It doesn't belong to me, you see. It's my mother's, and it's very, very dear to her." Her voice broke, and she turned away, unable to fight the sobs shaking her.

Delilah drew in sharply. "Don't you cry, Miss Addie. We gon' find it somehow."

Addie covered her face and let the bitter tears fall.

A timid little hand ventured into her lap and closed around her finger. Ceddy tugged, grunted, and tugged again, trying to pull her to her feet.

Amazement penetrated Addie's heartbreak. Gathering her legs beneath her, she pushed off the floor and followed him from the room.

They descended the stairs. Addie shot a questioning look over her shoulder at Delilah.

Eyes wide, Delilah shrugged.

At the base of the staircase, Ceddy veered right instead of left toward the main rooms of the house. A hallway Addie only vaguely knew existed led to a single door.

Ceddy opened it and pushed into the room, hauling her with him.

A large, inviting space drew her in, filled with high shelves and wall-to-wall cases lined with books in various bindings and muted colors. A massive desk, framed by floor-to-ceiling windows, dominated the room. The heavy brocade drapes were open, and beams of dusty sunlight slanted to the floor.

Addie raised her brows at Delilah.

"This be Masta Whitfield's den before he passed," she whispered. "Miss Priscilla's brother. Nobody come in here no more except me, for to dust, and Little Man on occasion." She nodded at the walls. "He like to study inside these books."

Ceddy pulled a tall, rolling ladder from the corner and climbed to a shelf over Addie's head. Panting from the strain, he pulled out a large book and struggled to tuck it snugly against his chest.

Addie crowded close to the ladder, her arms lifted to catch Ceddy if he fell. When he struggled down the last rung to the floor, she stepped back and sighed with relief. "Oh my, Delilah. Should he be allowed to do that? It seems dangerous."

Delilah wagged her head. "Ain't no stopping him. We done tried."

Running across the room, he heaved the book on the desk, opened the cover, and thumbed through the pages.

Addie peered over his shoulder. "Oh look. It's a Bible."

Delilah grunted. "Yes'm, the family Bible. He love the old pictures. 'Specially David and Goliath."

Ceddy stopped flipping and stepped aside, scrambling into the high-backed leather chair.

Addie's heart leapt. Mother's beads lay tucked inside the worn pages. She picked them up with trembling fingers, cupping them in her palm. The clasp that held the pendant was undone but thankfully still attached.

Delilah nudged her. Smiling, she opened her hand and gave Addie a peek at the pendant, evidently plucked from the collection box before leaving Ceddy's room.

With all the parts in one place again, the burden lifted from Addie's shoulders. She hugged Delilah, this time fighting happy tears.

Ceddy bounced several times in the chair then sprang to the floor. Closing the Bible, he lifted it and scurried for the door.

"No, Little Man. You ain't supposed to be carrying books out from here."

Paying Delilah no mind, he rounded the corner and disappeared.

Her shoulders slumped. "He determined to keep us busy today." She patted Addie's arm. "I'm glad you found your necklace, Miss Addie."

Addie gave her a trembling smile. "So am I. I prayed so hard."

At the top of the stairs, Delilah followed Ceddy while Addie rushed to her room. Pulling a chair around, she climbed onto the seat and took her canvas bag from the top of the tall wardrobe. Slipping the button free from the loop, she opened the bag and shoved the beads and pendant to the bottom. There they would stay until she saw her mother again. It wouldn't do to let Ceddy see them anymore. Her heart several pounds lighter, she returned to his room.

He lay on his stomach on the floor, his raised feet crossed behind him and the family Bible propped open in front. Taking stones from his collection box, he carefully placed them, one at a time, on the page.

Intrigued, Addie knelt beside him. "What's he doing?"

Delilah turned from emptying Ceddy's basin into her mop bucket. "He do that all the time." She pointed with her chin. "Matches up his rocks with the picture there."

On one side of the book, the page header read EXODUS CHAPTER 28 over twin columns of text. On the facing page, the picture Delilah indicated was a muted lithograph of the high priest's chest adorned in his breastplate. *Aaron,* Addie's memory supplied.

A wiggly tongue tucked in the corner of his mouth, Ceddy worked diligently, lining up colorful stones to match those in the Bible.

"Come and see, Delilah. They're all here. Topaz, sapphire, emerald, amethyst. . ." She gazed up in wonder. "Surely these stones aren't actual gems?"

Delilah tilted her head. "Cain't say, Miss Addie. I reckon most of them are. For years, folks been helping Little Man collect rocks for that old picture. Old Masta Whitfield took uncommon pleasure in it."

Pointing, she laughed. "I see the old one is back in its place 'stead of your pretty pendant, and he ain't even squawked. Seem like he don't care to see you cry no mo'."

Awed by the display, Addie ran her fingers down the page. "They're a perfect match." She paused. "Except for this one." She pointed at the rough white stone at the end of the second row and laughed. "You could never mistake this old thing for a diamond."

Leaning to peer where Addie pointed, Delilah snorted. "Lordy, I s'pose not. Looks like it come off a crick bottom."

Ceddy sat up and swiped his arm across the picture, raking his handiwork into a jumbled pile. Patiently, one by one, he picked them up and started over making the rows.

"What on earth?" Addie said.

Delilah glanced at her. "Don't that beat all? Left to it, he gon' do that over and over all day long."

As she watched him, sadness nearly brought Addie to tears. "Why do you suppose he does it?"

"Why Little Man do anything he do, Miss Addie? In six years working for the Whitfields, I never saw no rhyme or reason to the boy." She lifted the handle of the bucket and crossed to the door. "I finally decided to accept him like he be."

Once she'd gone, Addie returned her attention to Ceddy, still drawn into his obsessive game. Wasn't acceptance what all living souls craved?

In her initial interview, Priscilla said Ceddy's mother made the decision to stop chasing miracles and accept her son as he was. She shared how the boy relaxed and flourished in an atmosphere of love and approval.

Chewing her thumbnail, Addie pondered this truth in comparison to the ways in which she felt led to help him through mental stimulation and dietary changes. In doing so, was she going against the express wishes of his mother?

Ceddy took a long, lazy glance from the Bible to his pile of stones, his lowered lashes and the dreamy look in his eyes signaling the onset of a morning nap. Giving in, he folded his arm beneath his head and released a sleepy sigh.

His innocence and beauty stirred powerful emotions in Addie's heart. Couldn't she be a source of unconditional love *and* a teacher and guide devoted to a better life for him?

With gentle fingers, she smoothed the silky hair off his forehead and prayed for wisdom. More than anything else in the world, she longed to see him soar.

After two irksome weeks of hammering, loud men's voices, wagons rumbling past the windows, and a hectic breakfast table, the servants' quarters rose from the rubble and ascended to their former glory—at least according to Priscilla.

Amid the chaos of construction, Addie and Pearson waged a war of sorts, he bent on childish taunting and she pretending to pay him no mind, but ignoring him became harder every day.

In the years since she'd first noticed an attraction to the opposite gender, Pearson Foster—an impossible candidate for suitor—attracted her the most. It seemed a terrible injustice.

Avoiding him had been the only help for Addie's frustrating affliction. Once he moved his belongings into the little house outside her bedroom window, an event scheduled to happen any minute, she'd have to scramble for another solution.

As if on cue, a rig rolled around the side of the house and pulled up to the refurbished dwellings. Addie tried to look away, struggled to move from the window. Instead, she stepped aside and peeked from behind the curtain.

Pearson lowered his long-legged body to the ground, stretched like a bear emerging from its winter lair, and yawned indelicately.

Theo spoke from the driver's seat, drawing his attention.

Lit by the morning sun, Pearson's upraised face was, without question, the most glorious sight she'd ever seen.

She imagined her mother's voice, the way it sounded when she scolded. *"Adelina Viola McRae! What are you thinking?"*

She stiffened her spine. "Mother, I do not know!" Clenching her fists, she whirled and stalked from the room.

Priscilla met her on the stairs. "There you are. Don't fret about being late. Ceddy's already washed and fed. Delilah's with him in his grandfather's den." She smiled. "He has her scaling that monstrous ladder bringing down books." Her smile became a chuckle. "Last I saw of her was the ruffled hem of her bloomers."

Sidling past, Addie laughed, too. "I'll go and rescue her."

Priscilla caught her sleeve. "They're fine for now. Breakfast is waiting."

Blast, Addie thought. She'd nearly made good her escape.

"Pearson and Theo are here," Priscilla continued. "They're unloading their belongings out back, and then they'll be joining us."

Addie shuffled her feet. "Um. . .I'm really not hungry this morning."

As if she found the concept astounding, Priscilla drew back and stared. "Of course you're hungry. Breakfast is very important, dear. How do you expect to chase after Ceddy all morning on an empty stomach?" Taking her by the shoulders, Priscilla nudged her gently into motion. "March into the dining room, young lady. We'll have no more such talk."

They reached the bottom of the stairs as the screen squealed open and footsteps sounded in the back hall. Addie's stomach churned.

Rounding the corner, Theo smiled a greeting. "We came right in without knocking, just like you said, ma'am."

Priscilla nodded. "You did exactly right. Come along; the table is spread."

Pearson smirked at Addie over Priscilla's head. "Good morning, Miss McRae. I trust you slept well."

Addie held his mocking gaze. "A clear conscience brings peaceful rest, Mr. Foster." She flounced in front of him and fell in behind Priscilla and Theo.

"What kind of rest does a judgmental spirit bring?" Pearson whispered, trailing close on her heels.

Gritting her teeth, she took her usual place at the table, praying he would sit anywhere but at her side.

Answering her prayer, Theo slid into the next chair, and Pearson sat across from her. She immediately regretted her rash request. Seated in a position where he could watch her every move was infinitely worse.

Priscilla asked the blessing then shook out her napkin. "How are you finding your accommodations, gentlemen? I trust you'll be comfortable."

Pearson shifted his intrusive gaze from Addie to her, his expression softening. "You've provided us all the comforts of home, ma'am. I'm not sure how we'll ever thank you." He lifted his brows, sincerity shining from his eyes. "I insist you allow us to pay something for room and board."

She smiled. "Nonsense. The hard work you put into the reconstruction more than pays for your stay."

Pearson opened his hands to take in the bountiful breakfast. "But all this. . ."

"It's my pleasure, dear." She handed him a platter of crispy bacon. "You can thank me by eating hearty. Since my brother passed, I've missed having a hungry man to feed."

Theo leaned across the table and took the tray from Pearson. "Look no further for a big appetite, ma'am. I'll be happy to oblige."

Amused by his enthusiasm, Addie shot him a bright smile.

Grinning around stuffed cheeks, Theo winked. A muffled ruckus stirred under the table, and Theo's eyes widened. He gulped his bite of food and frowned at Pearson. "Easy, paisan. Take care with those big clumsy feet."

The picture of innocence, Pearson ducked his head. "My apologies, friend."

Watching the scene unfold, Addie frowned. Unlike the last time Pearson reacted to her interest in Theo, it didn't appear he disapproved of her as a possible match for his friend. If she didn't know better, if it wasn't an impossible conclusion, it would seem like Pearson was jealous of Theo. She shook her head to clear the unsettling thought.

"Are you all right, Addie?" Priscilla asked. "You've gone a bit pale."

Addie blushed and dropped her gaze to her plate. "Yes, ma'am. I'm fine." She stole a peek at Pearson.

He watched her with guarded eyes.

The rest of breakfast passed without incident. Pearson's and Theo's appetites didn't disappoint. Between them, they ate enough for four men.

Priscilla and Theo launched into a discussion about the wallpaper pattern she had planned for his room. Before Addie could catch her breath, the two excused themselves and left the dining room, still chattering about the appropriateness of flowers for a gentleman's boudoir.

Dabbing honey on a biscuit for which she had no appetite, Addie carefully avoided looking at Pearson—until the toe of his boot tapped her ankle. She tucked her legs beneath her chair then glanced up. "First Theo, now me? His comment on the size of your feet may be justified."

Crossing his arms, he settled against the chair and shrugged. "It does take a lot of leather to cover them, I suppose."

She squirmed to the side. "Since you're aware of their considerable range, kindly confine them to your side of the table."

"I'll confine my feet if you'll contain your icy disposition. I'm getting a chill over here."

Addie sat upright. "You are without question the most insufferable man I've ever known."

"Oh really?" He cocked his head. "Then why do you find my company so pleasurable?"

She suppressed a shriek. "I don't find your company pleasurable in the least."

A smile twitched his lips. "Yes, you do."

Addie shot to her feet. "How dare you?"

"What? Tell the truth? I'm an honest man, Miss McRae, with myself and others. It might be time you do the same."

She gaped.

"I'm also a busy man. I don't have time for deception."

She gripped her napkin so tightly her knuckles ached. "You're confusing our roles, Mr. Foster. I haven't deceived anyone."

Leaning forward in his chair, Pearson pinned her with solemn eyes. "If you believe that, you deceive yourself most of all. If you don't enjoy my company, you'd have left the table the minute Miss Priscilla left the room." He waved his arm. "Do you see anyone left to impress with your painstaking show of false manners?"

Chest heaving, she couldn't speak.

His gaze intensified. "Tell me. . .if you dislike me so much, why are you still sitting here with me, playing with food you don't intend to eat?"

Sick with fury, Addie stalked around the table, unsure until the last second whether she was going for his eyes with her nails or heading for the door.

He caught her in the hall, his big hand closing on her wrist. "Addie, wait. . . ."

"Let go of me."

"Not until you listen."

"To more insults?" She struggled, but his grip held her fast. "You have nothing more I want to hear."

"I'm sorry. Truly sorry. I didn't intend to go that far." He released a labored breath. "Your silence has driven me crazy for weeks. I only tapped you with my boot to get you talking."

Fighting tears, Addie refused to look at him. "Only you did most of the talking, didn't you?"

He shook his head. "That wasn't me. No more than the proud show you put on is the real you. Addie, you like me. I know you do."

She seared him with a glance. "Now who's deceiving themselves? Nothing could be further from the truth." Jerking free, she ran for the stairs.

Pearson's stomach twisted into knots. He'd set out to tease Addie, draw her out, but the game got out of hand.

He watched her climb to the second floor, her face averted, white knuckles gripping the rail, and a lump swelled in his throat. He longed to run after her, make her hear him out, but it was improper to go upstairs uninvited, and morally questionable to follow a lady to her bedroom.

Concerned about morals, sonny boy? After what you've just done?

Clenching his fists, he spun away from the stairwell and stalked to the back door.

The best he could do for Addie McRae was to steer clear of her. Given his strong feelings for the lady, it would prove a daunting challenge—even if he didn't live in her backyard.

Somehow Addie survived the twenty-four hours since Pearson's humiliating display. She'd managed by avoiding him like an infectious plague the day before. He made it easier by staying gone all afternoon and then declining Priscilla's invitation to dinner.

Arising early, she wasted hours of dread and a well-practiced speech intended for Priscilla should she try to force her to breakfast again. She'd gladly brave hunger, thirst, and whatever else was required to avoid Pearson Foster for the rest of her days.

Luckily, Pearson had a speech of his own prepared and left for the lake without crossing the yard to eat. Remembering Theo's dejected scowl and slumped shoulders as the wagon rumbled from the yard, Addie felt a twinge of guilt and wondered where they were taking their meals.

"Adelina!" Priscilla's shrill, panicked voice echoed through the house from behind the study door.

Addie swiveled on the kitchen stool and gaped at Delilah. "Oh my, she sounds distraught."

Delilah's eyes bulged with dread. Hurrying over, she yanked the fork from Addie's hand. "You'd best run on. Last time she squealed like a butchering hog, the smokehouse be on fire."

Ceddy, who'd been squirming through lessons on dining etiquette, moaned and flapped his hands.

"Calm him, please," Addie called as she rushed from the room. Crossing the hall, she burst inside the study.

Priscilla sat behind her desk, her eyes wide, peering through her reading glasses at a sheet of paper. The off-white stationery with the pretty scalloped edges was Addie's mother's.

Addie's knees wobbled and heat flooded her face. "What's wrong, Priscilla? Has something happened to my family?"

Priscilla's vacant gaze shifted to her. "They're fine. Sit down, please."

Hurrying across the room before her weakened knees caved, Addie settled in her seat and tried to still her pounding heart. "Is that a letter from my mother?"

Her white-rimmed lips drew to a firm line. "It is." Shuffling the papers on her desk, she pulled out a sealed envelope, a match to the one in her hand. "There's one for you, too," she said, handing it across to Addie.

Addie caught hold of the precious missive, but Priscilla held on to the corner.

"Kindly wait to open it. I think you'll want to hear what she wrote to me first."

Addie swallowed her protest, the letter a hot coal in her hand.

Priscilla glanced over the top of her rims. "Shall I proceed?"

Addie nodded.

Clearing her throat, she started to read.

Dear Priscilla, my gracious new friend,

I pray the weather in Texas is still fickle, as I find the notion simply charming. I want to thank you for having me as a guest in your home. I can't remember ever feeling so welcome and look forward to the chance to reciprocate someday soon.

I'm most grateful to you for forwarding Mr. Foster's letter. I can't tell you how pleased I was to learn of his intentions. From the day we met, I developed a fondness for him and sensed he felt the same.

Addie sat forward, clenching her fists.

Priscilla glanced up. "Do you want me to continue?"

"Yes," Addie croaked in a voice she didn't recognize.

Adjusting her glasses, Priscilla lifted the paper with shaking fingers.

You may find this difficult to understand, but I learned from a trusted old friend how to listen for the voice of God. I experienced what some might call an inkling about Pearson, but I prefer to think of it as a divine nudge. That said, I won't make a hasty decision about something so precious without more information.

I feel, dear lady, that you and I made a similar connection. Would you be willing to meet Mr. Foster, spend some time with him, and report back to me on what manner of suitor you feel he would make?

Addie held up her hand. "Please don't read any more." She sat quietly for several minutes, fighting tears. "I don't know what sort of trick is being played here, but that. . .that brazen request did *not* come from my mother."

Priscilla turned the page over and held it close to her face. "Well, her name is signed at the bottom." She held it up for Addie to see. "Is it her handwriting, dear?"

Addie leaned to stare at the familiar script until the letters blurred. "It certainly looks like hers, but it can't be." Her wounded heart shouted a firm denial. "Priscilla, I'm horribly embarrassed. What must you be thinking at this moment? Of me, my mother, my entire family?"

Priscilla's mouth quirked to the side. "I'll admit it's a little unorthodox, and a touch scandalous for my taste, but you shouldn't become so distraught, Addie."

The conversation had taken a dreamlike turn. Common sense told Addie there was a terrible mistake. The notion that Priscilla Whitfield would agree to weigh Pearson as a possible suitor for her mother was preposterous.

Priscilla leaned over the desk. "I'm sorry. You're upset. I suppose I should've asked you from the start how you feel on the subject."

"To tell you the truth, ma'am," she said—forgetting in her angst how Priscilla detested the formal address, "I don't really know what's happening."

Propping her elbows, Priscilla stared blankly at the single sheet of stationery. "Well, there's more, but if you don't understand by now, I doubt it would serve to clarify." She nodded at the envelope clutched in Addie's hands. "Perhaps you should read yours now. Maybe it will help."

Addie accepted the letter opener from Priscilla and cut a slit in the top of the envelope. Unfolding the note with trembling fingers, she read silently to herself.

Dearest Addie,

How pleased I was to receive a letter from Pearson. Pleased, but not necessarily surprised. I told you to allow God to orchestrate your destiny. Isn't He a gifted maestro?

I had a feeling about young Pearson from the start. I sense a kind and sensitive heart beats in his chest, and I saw you as a woman for the first time, my lovely daughter, through his admiring glances.

At last, a worthy suitor for you! I pray our Pearson passes Miss Whitfield's scrutiny. I can think of nothing I'd like better than agreeing to his request to spend time with you.

Addie's hands shook so hard, the paper rattled. "Pearson asked permission to spend time with me?"

Priscilla's slender eyebrows lifted. "Well, of course. Whom did you think? I'm decades too old for him."

Quivering inside, she read the last line.

Proceed with caution, Adelina, but trust your instincts. They're a gift from your ancestors.

Much love, darling,
Mother

Drained, Addie slumped against the chair. Trust her instincts? Hardly. It seemed the wisdom of her ancestors had skipped a generation.

When she'd confronted Pearson, he said she'd see him in a different light once she heard from her mother. How right he'd been. He also said their heated conversation would be the source of embarrassment. Touching her flaming cheek, she wondered how she'd ever face him again.

"Still with me, Addie?"

Glancing up, she met Priscilla's worried gaze and tried to smile. "Just barely."

"Did she clear things up for you?"

Addie sighed. "As clear as a hog wallow."

The lady smiled. "I know it's difficult. Whether you're expecting it or not, the first approach of an interested suitor can set a girl's head aflutter. As hard as it may be to believe, I had my share of inquiring young men in my day. None who I ever warmed up to, unfortunately."

A thoughtful look stole over her face. "Do you suppose we have only one opportunity for love, Addie? Only one other soul destined just for us?"

"I surely hope so."

Her lips drooped into a frown. "If that's the case, life becomes quite difficult should one of the parties take a misstep."

Remembering the poor dear's fondness for Dr. Moony, Addie's heart panged.

Priscilla folded the letter in her hand in half and then in quarters. "At any rate, Addie, I should think you'd be pleased with Pearson's interest."

"Oh? Why is that?"

She colored slightly. "Forgive me for making the observation, honey, but you do watch him rather closely. And you sort of"—she waved her hand in front of Addie's face—"light up when he comes into the room."

Addie stood, her fists clenched at her sides. "I most certainly do not *light up*!"

Priscilla puckered her lips and shifted her weight. "Of course, dear. Whatever you say." She pushed to her feet with a grunt. "If it helps, I feel I've observed Pearson well enough to sanction your courtship, if you're agreeable."

Suppressing hysterical laughter, Addie held up her hand. "I don't think—"

"I'll write to your mother right away. Meanwhile, your duties await you. Where is Ceddy?"

Addie pointed behind her. "In the kitchen. Delilah took over his lesson on holding a fork."

Priscilla smiled. "Then you'd best run along. He'll have her pinned to the wall with it by now. Table manners have never been his strong suit."

Addie eased toward the door, her mind struggling for the words to protest. How could she explain why a courtship was impossible without telling Priscilla how she'd misjudged Pearson?

More importantly, why did a part of her pray it wasn't too late to make amends?

TWENTY-FIVE

The sunshine reflecting off the rippling water bored through Pearson's eyes and bounced to the back of his head. Now it hunkered inside, throbbing to get out.

Their dragline had proved very effective at snagging almost everything off the bottom, including stumps, logs, anchors, and bottomed-out dinghies. Exhaustion and frustration combined had driven Pearson and Theo to take a break.

Long ago, Denny and Charlie had tied up their boat and left for the day, complaining as always about the long hours and low pay.

Pearson sat in the bow of the boat.

Theo reclined astern, idly flicking the surface of the water.

Addled by pain, Pearson decided to confide in him. After several false starts, he gathered his nerve and looked up. "Have you ever loved someone who didn't love you back?"

"But of course." Theo gripped his heart. "Every pretty girl I see."

"Stop. I'm serious."

Theo shrugged. "I don't think I've really fallen for a girl yet. Not the way you feel for Addie. Like my papa always said, *amore* is a fickle beast."

Pearson nodded. "I loved my family, of course, and they returned my affection. Then your parents, after the storm. They drew me in and made me one of their own. It's only natural to open your heart in a case like that."

Theo nodded. "True."

Pearson stared at the crisscrossed branches of a red oak tree bending close to the water. "I've been thinking about Pearl lately."

Theo's head came up. "Rosie's Pearl? One girl at a time, Pearce. Unlike me, that's all you can handle."

"I'm talking about the way I disrespected her. If you think about it, I'm facing a similar situation. I can't help how I feel about Addie the same as Pearl couldn't with me. She didn't even try to hide how she felt."

"Tshh! She couldn't. The girl was well smitten."

"And I didn't bother to care." Pulling leaves from the oak, he tore off pieces and scattered them over the water. "It grieves me now how lightly I treated her feelings." Shame burning in his heart, he stared out over the lake. "Do you remember what I said the last night I saw her? That I had no interest in the likes of her?"

Theo inhaled. "You meant no harm."

"I meant nothing, because I was too cocky and full of myself to realize I was hurting another human being." He sighed. "I suppose I'm reaping what I've sown."

"You can't help who you love, pal. Or who you don't."

"True." He jutted his chin. "But you can help how you conduct yourself. Instead of flirting and leading her on, I could've treated her with respect." He stared across the top of the trees. "This time, I care completely about a person who doesn't feel the same about me." He flung the bare stem at the water. "I need to walk away, forget about her, but for the first time in my life, I'm not in control of my emotions."

Theo whistled, low and ominous. "Not a safe place for a man to be."

"I might've agreed with you before." He shook his head. "Not now. The truth is, you realize deep down that you'll love this person, need to protect them, and long to be with them whether they return your devotion or not." He fixed on Theo's searching gaze. "Learning this, I know the reason it happened to me."

"There's a reason?"

The truth burned on Pearson's lips, but it was holy fire. He nodded. "There is, because once you love a person without conditions attached, you get a glimpse of how God feels about us."

Twilight etched the trees on the darkening sky like drawings in black ink as Pearson and Theo rode their rented mounts up the hill toward Whitfield Manor. They'd worked at the lake until hunger hollowed their bellies and thick mud seeped from their pores.

Pearson scowled at the thought of missing another meal at Priscilla's well-laid table. If she issued another invitation to dine, he intended to accept, the troublesome Miss McRae be hanged.

Feeling Theo watching him, Pearson turned and raised his brows. "What are you trying not to say?"

Theo shrugged. "Just wondering how much longer you're planning to drag the lake. I'm pretty sure we've struck bottom by now."

Pearson chewed his lip. "It doesn't make sense. We're dragging the spot where the locals claim she went down. I felt sure we'd hit her by now." He sighed. "It's like Lafitte's treasure all over again."

"You don't think. . . ?"

Pearson smirked. "That I'm bad luck?"

"No!"

"Then what?"

"I hesitate to say." Theo glanced to the side of the lane. "The last time I accused them, the reverend shamed me." He sat up straighter. "Blast it all, I'll say it anyway. You don't suppose those two fellows we hired have already found something?"

Pearson frowned. "We'd know if they had."

Theo shook his head. "How easy would it be for them to cross off one section of the grid, tell us they found nothing, then return later and claim their findings for themselves? We'd never be the wiser."

"They're not even sure exactly what we're searching for."

Theo snorted. "You're fooling yourself. They know something. That's why they won't ask. All their pretend stupidity is getting mighty suspicious."

He made a good point. Pearson lifted one shoulder. "I wouldn't put anything past those two. All we can do is keep a watchful eye."

"No, paisan. There's something else we can do. We could get rid of them, continue searching on our own, even with double the work on our shoulders."

They pulled into the Whitfield driveway and slid off their horses. Pearson gathered his reins and handed them to Theo. "I'm not ready to send them on their way just yet."

Theo wrinkled his brow. "Why? Those slackers are deadweight."

"They're more valuable than that, buddy. They're men who've led a hard life." A little embarrassed, he stared over Theo's shoulder. "I'm planning to ask them to church. Introduce them to Reverend Stroud."

"What for?"

"Have you ever seen a couple of fellows who could use a fresh start any worse than Den and Charlie?"

Properly chastened, Theo hung his head. "Yes. You and me—before we received one." He patted Pearson's shoulder. "You're a good man."

Pearson chuckled. "I'm a starving man. Go tend these animals. I'll find our hostess and plead for food."

Theo struck out for the barn.

Pearson made his way around to the back of the house. Stamping his feet in the yard to rid his cuffs of lumpy clods, he tiptoed onto the porch and knocked at the screen door.

Delilah appeared, her mouth dropping wide at the sight of him. Humming low in her throat, she studied his muck-covered feet, filthy clothes, and mud-plastered hair. "Land sakes, Mr. Foster. What you done fell off into?" She shook her head. "And where is it, so's I don't fall in, too."

Pearson grinned. "Don't worry. Our mud hole is hours from here. You'd have to ride out there and fall in on purpose." He nodded behind her. "If we promise to bathe first, do you suppose we could have a bite to eat?"

"Of course you can," a singsong voice announced behind her. "We'll fix you a late supper. I won't have it any other way." Delilah moved aside, and Priscilla took her place at the door. She raised the glasses hanging from a chain around her neck, and her startled gaze raked him head to toe. "Oh, but you'll have to clean up real nice, Pearson."

He held his arms out to the sides and laughed. "Are you saying I'm welcome as long as I leave the bottom of Caddo Lake outside?"

A prim smile puckered her lips. "That is exactly what I'm saying, young man."

"Then I'd better get started. It could take awhile."

He moved to bound off the porch, but she held up her hand. "Wait, son. I have a matter of utmost importance to discuss with you."

He frowned. "With me?" Dread pricked his heart. Had Addie said something? "Shouldn't I wash up first, ma'am?"

She peered behind her into the darkened hallway. "I'd rather speak my piece while we're out here alone." Reaching into a pocket on her skirt, she pulled out an envelope and tapped it with her finger. "I suppose you know what this is?"

He gulped. "I–I'm afraid not." He gave her a furtive glance. "Should I?"

Whether he should or not, she didn't bother to say. "This is the answer to the inquiry you made to Addie's mother." Turning her head to the side, she narrowed her eyes. "You know. . .the *special* request."

A dragline snagged Pearson's heart and plunged. He'd waited weeks for the answer. Now, when it didn't matter anymore, Priscilla held it in her hand. He stared at the letter, speechless.

"I want you to know," she whispered, "the decision about you has been left in my hands."

"The decision?"

"About whether you're a fit suitor for Addie."

After what he'd done to her, Pearson felt the most qualified to decide, and the answer was no.

"Given the unusual circumstances, Mrs. McRae asked me to get to know you better and report back with my opinion."

Two days ago, such an arrangement would've been the best possible outcome. Despite her quirks, Priscilla Whitfield seemed to genuinely like and respect Pearson. He felt confident she'd deliver a positive report to Addie's mother.

Now, it wouldn't matter. The girl wanted nothing to do with him, and he couldn't blame her.

Priscilla tucked away the letter and clasped her hands. "So. . .I wasted no time in penning a prompt response, telling the McRaes that I've come to know you quite well and wholeheartedly offer my endorsement." Beaming, she watched his face, clearly waiting for his response.

"Have you already mailed the letter, ma'am?"

Her bright smile lit up the back porch. "I have indeed. I sent my driver to town this afternoon. By now it's on a northbound train, wheeling its way to Mississippi."

The dragline dipped lower, hauling his busted heart deeper than Caddo Lake. Now, not only would Addie despise him, but her kind-hearted mother would know him for the cad he was.

Pearson backed off the porch. "Theo will have water heating by now. I'd best get a start on all this dirt."

Flustered, she reached a faltering hand. "But. . .aren't you going to say something?"

He nodded. "Thank you, Miss Whitfield. I appreciate your faith in me." *However misplaced.*

Brightening, she waved. "Think nothing of it. I wish you and Addie the best possible outcome." She turned to go inside then paused. "Hurry, if you can. I'm sure Delilah's already setting the table."

His big feet hauled him to a stop. Gripping his forehead, he drew a ragged breath. "Um, on second thought, I'm not feeling so well. I'll just send Theo over, if you don't mind."

The screen squeaked shut, and she hustled to the edge of the porch. "Are you all right, dear? Shall I call a doctor?"

"I'll be fine."

She clucked through thin lips. "Are you certain? Just minutes ago you were anxious to eat."

"Too much sun, I suppose. Please don't fret."

She sighed. "Very well, if you're sure. I'll send something out with Theo, in case you change your mind."

"Thank you."

"If I don't see you again, have a nice night." She touched the back of her hand to her chin, and her blush seemed to glow in the dim light. "Considering the good news about courting Addie, I trust you'll have pleasant dreams."

Pearson scowled in the approaching darkness. By rights, his dreams should be agreeable, since his waking hours had turned to a nightmare.

In the three days following the arrival of Mother's letter, Addie, Pearson, and Priscilla tiptoed about one another in a dance to rival Anna Pavlova's dying swan, though not nearly as graceful. Addie and Pearson took great care to avoid being alone. Priscilla, blushing and smiling, seemed determined not to miss anything should the courting commence.

Shared meals in the dining room were intolerable. Addie abandoned the back porch swing, her favorite spot, in favor of a private haven on the opposite side of the house—a wicker chair tucked into a corner of the front porch. Seated there in the late morning hours, she watched the antics of a pair of mating squirrels racing along limbs and bounding off knobby pine trunks.

Addie could learn a few tips on the art of wooing a man from the feisty little female. The moment her pursuer's interest in the chase seemed to wane, she'd rise high on her haunches and swish her bushy tail until she caught his eye again. Then off they'd go in their frantic chase, madly chattering.

Addie sighed. Why were matters of the heart so less complicated in the animal kingdom?

Dark-bellied clouds rolled in overhead, and lightning struck in the distance. Perhaps the approaching storm would postpone Pearson's workday at the lake and bring him home. Questioning why she cared, she decided the time had come to find the answer.

The very first day she'd met Pearson, when his hand closed over hers on the handle of her luggage, a fierce attraction fired in her heart. From that point on, her emotions raced out of control. No matter how diligently she tried to resist, his rumbling voice and handsome face invaded her thoughts.

She'd heard of such things in whispered conversations with other girls, her closest friend, Hope Moony, for instance. When Hope's beau began to court her, she burned Addie's ears with tales of stolen kisses and tender glances.

Remembering how hard Pearson had tried to woo her, and how determined she'd been to misjudge his efforts, Addie's conscience ached. No wonder he'd resorted to childish and rude behavior.

Far less experienced than the little female squirrel, Addie had bungled any chance of a beautiful romance. Instead of displaying her feminine wiles, she'd thrown acorns.

Sliding forward in her chair, she gripped the arms. Was it too late? Surely, despite the aloofness he displayed toward her lately, he had to feel a spark of his original interest. If Addie swished fast enough, could she fan the spark to a flame?

The steady clop of hooves drew her gaze. Just as she guessed, Theo and Pearson rode up the front drive and disappeared around the side of the house.

Addie stood, determination surging up her spine. The little squirrel had stretched high on her haunches until her mate found her. Addie didn't know if Pearson could forgive her, but part of standing tall so he might see her again would start by offering an apology.

Theo rubbed his shoulder. "I told you rain was coming. If you'd listened to my stiff joints, we could've slept longer."

Laughing, Pearson braced his foot in the stirrup and slid to the ground. "I thought only old men predicted the weather with aches and pains."

Theo dismounted. "Old bones or old injuries, they work the same." His head jerked up, his eyes wide as he stared over Pearson's saddle.

Pearson's fingers, loosening the strap on his saddlebag, stilled. "Is someone standing behind me?"

Theo nodded. "She will be in five, four, three, two. . .hello, Addie."

The last person Pearson expected. He swiveled on his heel.

Addie stood with her hands behind her back, her pale features carved in flint. "May I speak with you for one minute, Pearson?"

Anger he thought had cooled flared in his belly. "One? I suppose I can spare that."

Her slight wince shamed him.

"I mean, of course I can," he said in a softer voice. "Just let me stable the horse."

"I'll take him," Theo offered, reaching for the reins.

Pearson bowed to Addie and gestured toward the house. "In that case. . ."

Addie took the lead. Lifting her ruffled hem past her tiny shoes and stocking-covered ankles, she gracefully navigated the stone path to the porch.

Pearson followed her up the steps, surprised when she perched delicately on the swing and patted the seat beside her. He dutifully sat, trying hard in his confusion not to gawk at her.

She took a deep breath and faced him. "I'll get right to it." Her breath quickened, and her hands twisted in her lap. Despite her declaration, she couldn't seem to get right to anything.

"Pearson. . ."

He shifted in the seat, bracing the dizzying motion of the swing with his feet. "Yes?"

Gently rocking, she nibbled on her bottom lip and stared with frightened eyes. "I owe you an apology. I misjudged you, insulted you, and accused you of unspeakable behavior, all without just cause. I based my suspicions on how things appeared, not how they really were. I made decisions about you without thinking them through." Her pretty chin trembled. "From the second we met, I cast moral judgment based solely on your appearance instead of what was in your heart." She shook her head. "I've behaved like a spoiled, willful child."

Doubting his ears, Pearson stared.

Addie puckered her lips, working her mouth nervously. "Aren't you going to say anything?"

He sniffed. "What's wrong with my appearance?"

Amusement shone from her eyes. She covered her mouth but

couldn't hide her smile. "After what I've done, that offends you the most?"

He cocked his head. "I suppose that seems vain."

She chuckled. "Perhaps a touch."

Pearson braced his arms on his knees and laced his fingers. "It's just that"—he shot her a crooked grin—"my looks have never bothered a lady before." He left off the part that, of all the ladies he'd ever known, her opinion mattered most. He couldn't look at her pretty lips still twitching, glee tucking deep dimples in her cheeks, without laughing. "Addie, it's easy to defend my honor, because I've never acted dishonorably with a married woman." He lifted a strand of his hair. "Not so easy to defend this."

Drawing in her shoulders, she shrank against the seat. "I never said I found your appearance unpleasant." Her shy smile surprised him. "Quite the contrary."

His spirits soared. "Really?"

She nodded.

They sat together, both blushing, both fighting silly grins.

Pearson broke the silence. "You heard from your mother, then."

Her pink-tinged cheeks flamed red. "Yes." She stared at her fingers, twisting in her lap. "And you were right." She buried her face in her hands. "I'm very embarrassed."

He longed to pat her shoulder. "Don't be. I say we put the whole thing behind us. Forget it ever happened."

She made fists in the folds of her skirt again and looked away. "Because we both live on the grounds, and we're forced to take our meals together?" She nodded. "I suppose a truce would make life easier."

Pearson gently touched Addie's arm, and she lifted her chin. Uncertainty danced in her eyes. "No, Adelina Viola McRae. I want to forget because I still want to court you, and if you say yes, life won't just be easier. It may never be the same."

Addie said yes.

Bursting into her room, she ran breathlessly to her wardrobe to thumb through her frocks. What did a girl wear to a picnic?

High wind had whisked the plump black clouds away to the south, taking the threat of rain with them. The sun, as bright as the promise of the future, had peeked out to take their place. Pearson decided it was high time they went on the picnic he'd once invited her on, and what better place than the beautiful gardens of Whitfield Manor?

Tittering like a girl, Priscilla gave her permission for Addie to go unchaperoned—not much of an indulgence on her part, since she could see them on the lawn from any room in the house.

Addie chose a high-collared white tea dress with lace inserts and contrasting linen panels at the front, sleeves, and hem. Tea dresses, according to an article in the *Ladies' Home Journal*, were designed to "display a woman's femininity, charm, and grace." Twirling in front of the mirror, she hoped Pearson would see in her any one of those attributes.

While she slipped upstairs to dress and arrange her hair, Priscilla and Delilah scurried to the kitchen to prepare a basket filled with food. They met her at the foot of the stairs, wide-eyed and beaming.

"You look lovely, dear," Priscilla gushed.

Delilah added a brisk nod. "Jus' as fresh as a flower, Miss Addie."

Addie felt her cheeks warm. "Thank you both." How odd, and somewhat sad, to be stepping out for the first time with a gentleman caller without her mother present to share the occasion.

As if she'd read Addie's thoughts, Priscilla wrapped her arm around Addie's shoulders and squeezed. "I shall write a letter to your mother tonight describing how wonderful you look. She'll be so proud."

Addie turned into her embrace. "Bless you, Priscilla. That would mean so much."

A knock rumbled from the rear of the house. Priscilla spun toward the sound, clutching her collar. "Oh my, that must be Pearson. Lilah, answer the door." Delilah hurried to comply as Priscilla straightened the sky blue sash at Addie's waist. "Normally it would be scandalous for a man to come calling at the back door." She grinned. "But under the circumstances. . ."

Fighting a sudden impulse to hide behind the woman's skirt, Addie swallowed hard and stood up straight like Mother had taught her. Unsure of what to do with her hands, she clasped them behind her then brought them around to steady her fluttering stomach.

Pearson ducked around the corner looking a little unsure of himself, too, his tall, sturdy build dwarfing the wide archway. Blushing, he produced a small bouquet of yellow roses and presented it to Addie. "I hope you don't mind, Priscilla. I saw them on the way across the yard and thought of her."

Priscilla laughed. "I don't know, Pearson. . .magnolias might be more fitting for this Mississippi girl than a Texas yellow rose, but they are lovely." She patted his arm. "And I don't mind a bit."

Addie accepted the flowers, the stems bundled in a man's handkerchief. "Thank you, Pearson. They're beautiful."

A smile lit up his handsome face. "Are you ready to go?"

She nodded.

Delilah hefted the covered basket. "Hope you folks is hungry, Mr. Pearson. Miss Priscilla had me pack enough for Jesus to feed the five thousand."

Priscilla swatted at her. "Hush, Delilah. Don't you go blaspheming the Savior." She winked at Pearson. "Your lunch won't feed the masses, but I expect you two will eat your fill."

Raising the basket to his nose for a sniff, Pearson grinned. "Do I smell fried chicken?"

"You sho' do, Mista Pearson, with all the trimmin's. There's a hearty slice of chocolate loaf cake for each of you, too."

He offered Addie his arm. "Shall we go?"

Her breath caught. Smiling into his eyes, she placed her hand on the crook of his elbow and let him lead her through the hall and out the back door.

"You children have fun!" Priscilla's voice echoed from inside the house.

Stopping to pick up a folded quilt he'd left hanging over the gazebo railing, Pearson draped it over his arm and shepherded her over the grounds. Past the waist-high maze of hedges, wisteria bushes, and Texas sage, they ducked between a pecan tree and a tall stand of honeysuckle vine.

Pearson spread the quilt on a patch of bright green grass and placed the basket in the center. Turning to her, he held out his hand. "May I help you sit?"

Addie accepted his aid and perched demurely on the ground. She marveled at the myriad sensations she felt, all new and every one distressing. Her stomach quaked, her fingers trembled, her head felt light, as if the slightest breeze might send it bouncing over the lawn like a bubble.

She had no idea that nurturing a budding relationship was so stressful. How did generations of people before her survive the perils of courtship?

"Are you all right?"

As she glanced up, her heart lurched. She wasn't the least bit all right, and his voice, as rich as clotted cream, didn't help. She crossed her fingers. "Yes, of course."

He gazed over the slope of the grounds. "This is a real nice view, isn't it?"

She nodded. "Peaceful."

His head whipped around. "That's it, peaceful. I noticed it the first time I stepped out the back door." Leaning close to her, he pointed in the distance. "See the way the horizon stretches on forever? It sort of draws you in. . .makes you forget about everything else."

Addie smiled. "So that's why you didn't notice me in the swing the other day."

He grinned. "Not until you squawked."

She straightened her back. "Sir, I never squawk."

Laughing, he reached for the basket. "Are you hungry? Let's see what those two put in here."

He unloaded dishes and silver wrapped in napkins first, carefully arranging them as if he were setting the table for a Thanksgiving feast. Next came a platter of fried chicken. Lifting the tea-towel covering, he wiggled his brows.

Giggling, Addie took it from him and served both their plates.

Carefully inspecting each offering, he placed Delilah's "trimmin's" in a circle around them then rubbed his hands together. "Let's give thanks for what the Lord provided."

The irony of his words, considering Delilah's comparison, turned Addie's giggle to a belly laugh.

Pearson caught it, too, and joined in. "No loaves and fishes, but I'm just as grateful, aren't you?"

Her heart surging, she nodded. She happened to be grateful for much more than fried chicken, but of course she wouldn't say so.

The meal passed in a pleasant haze of delicious food and delightful companionship. Pearson charmed her with stories of the Gulf Coast and his exploits there, of Rosie's Café and Jean Lafitte's gold. He told how deeply he loved Galveston Island before grief drove him to the mainland.

Addie told him about her home state since he'd never been to Mississippi. She described small-town life in Canton and how much she missed her family and friends.

Laughing like children, they sat face-to-face on the quilt and played rock-paper-scissors.

The afternoon passed too quickly, though Addie wished it would never end. Eventually, her responsibility to Priscilla and sense of duty toward Ceddy lured her thoughts to the house. Gathering the remains of the picnic into the basket, she stood. "I really should go inside now, Pearson. It's getting late."

Drowsy-eyed and leaning on the trunk of the pecan tree, he roused himself and stretched.

Addie held up her hand. "Please, don't trouble yourself. Sit and stay awhile. Enjoy the view."

Pushing off the ground, he reached for the basket. "Don't be silly. I'll help you into the house."

She held the handle away from him and shook her head. "I'll be fine. I promise." The warmth of his chest against her shoulder quickened her breath. Glancing past him to the row of second-floor windows, she stepped back, imagining Priscilla's watchful eyes at every one. "There's no reason to cut short your relaxing afternoon. Besides"—she smiled—"I believe I can find my way home."

He inclined his head. "Are you sure?"

She nodded. "Quite."

He gave her a lazy smile. "I'll see you at supper then."

Ducking to hide her delighted grin, she nodded. "I enjoyed myself very much, Pearson."

"Mm-hmm." He tipped her chin with his knuckle, spine-tingling warmth in his dancing eyes. "I enjoyed myself, too. You're very pleasant company."

Breathless, her cheeks flaming, she pointed over her shoulder. "I really should be. . ."

He caressed the skin of her throat with his finger while his gaze seemed to drink her in. "You'd better run along now, sweet Adelina."

With a jaunty wave, she slipped past the honeysuckle vine and tripped lightly up the stepping-stones to the house. Her feet barely touched the ground.

Hunger drove Ceddy from Grandfather's den. Tracing his finger along the slender strip of wood on the wall, he turned right at the end of the hall where the strip ended instead of left toward the kitchen as he usually did. Drifting toward a square pattern of light on the floor, he reached the screen door and pushed his way onto the porch. Walking the narrow crack between two broad planks, he reached the top step and teetered on the edge.

Mama's voice echoed in his head. *"Dangerous on your own, Ceddy. Hold my hand, darling. My hand or Daddy's."*

Only. . .where had those hands gone?

Covering his ears, he bailed off the porch and burst into the bright sunlight, running with all of his might until his side hurt too much to go on. Hugging himself, he glanced over his shoulder at the house, troubled by how far away it seemed.

Without reassuring skirts nearby, the unfamiliar garden and the great blue sky overhead scared him. He ducked between the hedges, staring at the comforting ground and waiting for the pounding in his chest to stop.

A row of tiny ants marched between his feet, stretching into the distance in front and disappearing behind him. Crouching, Ceddy followed alongside the line with his finger until he could no longer reach then took two clumsy, squatting steps forward to trace it again.

A long shadow fell across the ground, and terror gripped his stomach.

"Ceddy?"

Lurching away from the tall figure blocking the sun, he scrambled to find his feet but fell flat on his stomach instead. His mouth went dry, and the pounding in his chest sped up. Try as he might, he couldn't gather the strength to run. Helpless tears blurred Ceddy's eyes, dropping to the ground in a silent spatter.

Big hands gripped his shoulders and set him upright.

His breath caught on a sob, and his body tensed, but he couldn't move to struggle free.

Strong arms scooped him high, carried him to a nearby bench, and set him down. "Don't be afraid, little fellow. I won't hurt you."

He knew the gentle voice. He'd heard the same one drifting up the stairwell in Aunt Priss's house.

The man with peculiar hair sat beside him. "Are you supposed to be out here by yourself? Does Miss Addie know?" His long fingers ruffled Ceddy's hair. "I expect she doesn't. You're trying to cause a stir again, aren't you, young man? If those three women find you gone, you'll have the devil to pay."

The rise and fall of Ceddy's chest began to slow. Pressing his ear to the man's warm side, he stilled to listen to the hollow thumping sound. Burying his face in the soft shirt, Ceddy took a deep breath. He smelled like Daddy.

"Tell you what. . .how about we hurry you back inside before you're missed. If you promise not to do this again, there's no need to tell them, is there?" The man stood, easing Ceddy to his feet. Taking his hand in a firm grip, he led him through the garden, up the steps, and across the porch. At the door, he crouched and dusted the dirt off Ceddy's hands and knees.

"There you are. Now get inside before they catch us." He patted Ceddy's cheek then stood, opened the screen, and nudged him inside. "Good-bye, buddy," the man whispered as Ceddy meandered toward the kitchen to find Lilah.

TWENTY-EIGHT

Denny slipped up behind Charlie and jabbed him hard in the side. Charlie's satisfying jump and shriek sent Denny into gales of laughter.

Charlie scowled. "Why would you do that to a mate, Denny? I reckoned you for a gator."

Denny hitched himself up on the back of the wagon and elbowed Charlie in the ribs. "I did it for a lark. And who says we're mates?"

"Aw, you're not still cross with me?"

"Except I am, ain't I?" He pulled at the legs of his trousers. "Look at me, will ya?"

Charlie lowered his chin to his chest. "Come on, Den. I never meant to land us in the drink. I lost me balance is all."

"Why in blazes were you standing in the first place? A boat is no place to pitty-pat around, Charlie. Suppose I'd landed on one o' them viper's nests?"

Charlie snickered. "I like what they call 'em." He stared over Denny's head and smiled. "Cottonmouth. Sounds nice, don' it?"

"Well, they're not," a gruff voice behind them warned. With a clatter that shook the wagon, Pearson Foster tossed a shovel and chain into the bed. "You'll not find a nastier snake."

Denny grimaced and shot him a furtive glance. It wouldn't do that he'd caught them slacking again. He smiled, pretending interest. "Worse than the coral snakes we heard about?"

"The coral's venom is worse, but he's less likely to bite you. A cottonmouth is more aggressive."

"And there are really nests of them in the water?"

"Not nests exactly, but large groups will ball up during mating. You don't want to fall into one of those."

Charlie shuddered.

"Sounds bloomin' awful," Denny said.

"And you don't have to fall on one to be bitten," Pearson continued. "They'll chase you down."

Charlie gaped, his mouth slack.

Denny tilted his head. "Are you having us on, mate?"

Pearson gave him a blank stare. "Come again?"

Charlie smiled. "He's asking if you're having a laugh."

Staring toward the lake, Pearson shook his head. "There's nothing funny about a cottonmouth."

The other fellow, the bloke called Theo, strolled toward them. "I'd sooner face a snake than another giant fish." His eyes widened. "I think the one we saw this morning swallowed Jonah."

Pearson laughed. "He was as big as a baby whale, but that's not likely in these parts."

His eyes widening, Charlie whistled. "That large, was he?"

"Stretched as long as two grown men," Theo said. "When he surfaced alongside the boat, I almost bailed out the other side."

Denny cleared his throat. "I can't make out why you fellows are risking your hides out here. Must be something special hid down in that mud, eh?"

Pearson's mouth tightened. "What one man considers special wouldn't carry the same weight with another."

Denny shrugged. "Still. . ." Leaning closer, he narrowed his eyes. "How weighty is this prize you seek?"

Dodging the question, the blighter tossed Denny's words back at him. "You two are risking your hides just the same, aren't you? And for as little as a day's pay."

Not willing to push too hard, Denny laughed and slapped his leg. "You're a tough one to crack, you are. Well, you can't blame a chap for trying, can you?"

Gripping the end of a rope, Pearson wound it around his arm. "We'll call it a day, gentlemen. It's been a long week. I'd like to be home in time for supper."

Theo smiled. "Now there's an idea. Besides, we're getting nowhere."

Hopping to the ground, Denny swatted Pearson's back. "Whatever you say. You're the boss, ain't you? Besides, there's always tomorrow."

Pearson shook his head. "Not tomorrow. It's the Sabbath."

Since the start of the job, the man's silly observance of a holy day had cheated Denny and Charlie out of a day's fair wages. Struggling to hide his impatience, he nodded. "Right. My mistake."

Laying aside the rope, Pearson gripped his arm. "Say, Denny, I've been meaning to invite you to join Theo and me for church. If you'd like to come tomorrow, you'll be properly welcomed to the community, and Reverend Stroud prepares a soul-stirring message."

He smiled over Denny's shoulder. "You, too, Charlie."

Fighting a sly grin, Denny thoughtfully nodded. "You know, that sounds right nice, Pearson. Charlie and me, we'll be there."

Charlie frowned. "But Den—"

Slapping him hard on the back, Denny laughed. "The walls may cave when we walk through the door, but you can look for us, all right." He shook Charlie's shoulders. "We'll be there, won't we, Charlie?"

The old fool scowled but managed a nod.

"Good," Pearson said. "That's good." Tipping his hat, he pulled his horse around and climbed into the saddle. "When you get to town, unload the equipment behind your boardinghouse and turn in the wagon. There's no sense paying the extra day's rent. We'll hire it again on Monday."

Denny saluted. "Sure thing, boss."

Returning the salute, Pearson rode away beside Theo.

Charlie jabbed his arm. "Why'd you go and tell him we'd be in church? I don't want to go."

"Oh yeah? Well, you're going, so get used to the idea."

"But why?"

"Why do you think, Charlie? Use your noggin, will ya?" He ticked off the reasons. "We show up at church. Meet the Lady Whitfield, all proper-like." Grinning, he wiggled the last digit. "Next stop, the old girl's mansion for tea." He pretended to hold up a cup, his little finger extended. "I can see meself hobnobbing with Marshall's finest, can't you?"

Finally catching on, Charlie beamed. "I reckon you're the smartest chap I know, Den."

Hitching his thumbs in his collar, Denny struck a noble pose. "Charlie, old boy, I just might be."

Twisting in the saddle, Theo stared behind them, his face set in an ugly frown.

Pearson whistled for his attention. "What's so interesting back there?"

He lifted the side of his cap and scratched his head. "I don't trust those two."

"Save your eyesight, friend. I doubt they'll do anything crooked while you're watching."

Theo sniffed then settled to the front. "You really think they'll be in church?"

"I hope so. I really do."

The reins slid in and out through Theo's fingers. "Pearce, you may not like what I'm about to say."

Pearson slumped in good-natured defeat. He hadn't liked it the first three times Theo said it, but it didn't sway him. "Let me guess. You're certain we're hunting in the wrong place for the *Mittie*. That, or else Denny and Charlie have already found her."

Theo winced. "We've wallowed in mud for so long, I'm starting to snort and squeal." He spread his hands. "With nothing to show for it."

Staring off into the tangled brush and low-hanging trees, Pearson nibbled inside his cheek. "I admit it's getting harder to believe she's down there. But everyone we talked to pointed us to Tow Head."

Theo shook his head. "That's pretty vague. It's a big area."

"It's a big lake. I'm starting to fear we jumped in the water too soon."

They shared a wry grin.

Pearson sighed. "We need more information."

Theo cut him a doleful glance. "We need Catfish John."

"I'm beginning to think Catfish John has a lot in common with Santa Claus."

Theo chuckled. "I'm beginning to think the *Mittie Stephens* has a lot in common with both of them."

They rode in silence for a few yards before Theo looked his way. "There's something else I've been meaning to say. You want to guess this one, too?"

Thinking the quiet was too good to last, Pearson smiled to himself. "I've run out of guesses. Just say it."

"I don't know." Theo winked. "You get all grumpy when I sweet-talk you."

Wishing he'd been less accommodating, Pearson groaned. The twinkle in Theo's eyes scared him. "Do I want to hear this?"

"No, but listen anyway." The teasing gone from his voice, he leaned forward in the saddle. "I just want to say that I'm proud of you."

"Me? What for?"

"For working through your anger with God."

Running his thumb along a seam in the pommel, Pearson smiled. "I don't have all the answers about that night, buddy. I probably never will. But I'm ready to trust God without answers."

Theo wiped his eyes with his sleeve. "I'm glad, Pearce. And happy for you. Do you mind if I ask what changed your mind?"

Pearson released a cleansing breath. "Reverend Stroud helped me realize something I'd been missing." He met Theo's earnest gaze. "My family died tragically, and I lived. Most folks would say I'm the lucky one. Only I didn't get the better outcome. They've tasted heaven and wouldn't trade places with me now. I'm the one left to slog through life until it's my time to enter glory." He laughed. "I used to feel guilty because I thought God took my family in death and spared me. Now I'm tempted to be angry because He left me behind."

Theo smirked. "He left you here for my sake. He knows how much trouble I get into without you."

"If I thought that was true," Pearson said, feigning a threatening glare, "you'd be in so much trouble."

TWENTY-NINE

Addie barely noticed her supper, though the heaping plate sat right in front of her. She took a bite or two of pork roast, a swallow of sweet potato, and nibbled the corner of her muffin, but it all tasted the same.

Eating, along with other mundane activities, had taken a trifling place in her life. Only breathing and being with Pearson held any importance now, and not necessarily in that order. Thoughts of him consumed her waking hours, visited her at night in pleasant dreams.

How glorious the act of falling in love! How soul consuming! She couldn't fathom how she'd lived thus far without knowing such bliss. Surely she was the first since the dawn of time to love so deeply. Otherwise she'd have heard the virtues of love extolled, the aching beauty of sheer emotion shouted from lofty places.

Pearson's dining-room behavior hadn't changed. He still jabbed her with his elbow, pulled his chair too close, and whispered playful taunts, his breath warm in her ear. The difference was in how it made her feel.

Priscilla cleared her throat, pulling Addie from her fog.

The sound lacked the same effect on Pearson, who seemed engrossed in tracing the crocheted pattern on Addie's sleeve.

Embarrassed, she pulled her arm into her lap and nudged him.

Glancing up with glazed eyes, he nodded at Priscilla. "Yes, ma'am. I agree."

She covered her mouth and tittered. "I appreciate your agreeable spirit, dear, but I haven't said anything yet."

Addie sucked in her bottom lip, biting hard to keep from laughing.

Theo, showing less restraint, nearly spewed a forkful of meat.

Squaring his shoulders, Pearson pressed his napkin to his mouth—more likely to wipe off a guilty grin than food. He seemed less interested in eating than Addie did.

Priscilla pushed aside her plate and smiled. "There's a wonderful baked custard on the sideboard, Theo." She glanced at Addie and Pearson. "I doubt these two are interested, but I'll cut us a slice, if you'd like."

"Oh yes, ma'am," he said. "I'd like."

Addie sat back and idly propped her elbow on the chair arm.

Drawn to her crocheted pattern again, Pearson ran his finger along her sleeve.

"As for you two," Priscilla said, swiveling their direction, "I suggest you step into the parlor and wait for us."

Pearson stood, perhaps a little too fast, and pulled out Addie's chair.

Narrowing her eyes, Priscilla shot Addie a pointed look. "Sit on opposite sides, please."

"Yes, ma'am," Pearson said, ushering Addie across the room.

"And leave the door open," Priscilla called as they ducked into the hall.

Laughing uncontrollably, they burst into the parlor, Pearson holding his side. Offering his arm, he strutted to the sofa and eased her down. With a lively bow, he marched to the chair across from her and sat. He angled his head, a pleasing grin stretching his full lips. "You look nice tonight."

Satisfaction warmed her heart. The extra time she took while choosing a dress had paid off. "Why, thank you."

"What about me?"

She glanced up. "Pardon?"

"Don't I look nice?"

She giggled. "Oh, Pearson!" He looked much better than nice, but Addie dared not say so.

Pearson laughed at his own joke then sobered, staring at something over her head. He sat quietly for so long, the click of the parlor clock began to wear on her nerves.

She strained to see where he looked. "Um. . .is something wrong?"

He scooted to the edge of his seat. "How do you feel about the ocean?"

The question caught her off guard. "I've never given it much thought."

He raised his brow. "Will you?"

She tried to swallow, but her throat was dry. "Will I. . . ?"

"Give it some thought. I'd be interested to know if you'd consider living on an island someday."

The vague nature of his question, confusing yet fraught with insinuation, left her at a loss. He'd told her he never intended to return to Galveston, so why should her opinion of the ocean matter? "I'll think about it." She tucked her chin. "But I'd like to know why you're asking."

He grew silent again, but this time it felt different—like the hush after the last chord of a beautiful song.

"Addie, look at me."

Cheeks warming, she tilted her face.

Pearson smiled, mostly with his eyes. "That's better. I don't want to say this to the top of your head."

Her insides quivered until she feared he'd notice her shaking. "Yes, Pearson?" Her voice came out barely a whisper.

"Addie, I—"

A scream echoed through the house. Footsteps thundered down the hall from the dining room.

Addie and Pearson bolted from their seats and dashed for the door. They met Theo and Priscilla near the stairs.

"Merciful heavens!" Priscilla shouted. "That was Delilah."

"Where did it come from?" Pearson asked.

They didn't have to wait long for the answer. She screamed again, and the door behind the stairwell flew open, striking the wall with a bang.

Addie ran around the banister with the others on her heels.

Delilah met them running down the hall. She shook violently, and her eyes were wide and staring. "There's somebody out there," she shrieked.

Priscilla gripped her shoulders. "Calm down. Where?"

She pointed a shaky finger at the wall. "Right outside. They peered through the glass at me."

Pearson and Theo needed no further information. They spun as one and rushed down the back hall.

As they turned the corner, Theo's voice carried to Addie. "Did you know there was a room back there?"

Their voices faded out of reach, and Addie prayed for their protection.

Priscilla's eyes grew wide. "For heaven's sake, Delilah, where is Ceddy?"

She lifted her gaze to the top of the stairs. "He up there in bed."

"What were you doing in the den? You should be with him."

"He mighty restless tonight. I come to fetch him a book."

"Well, go to him. I'm sure he heard you bellowing. Poor child is probably frightened out of his mind."

Delilah hustled to obey, tripping over the bottom step in her haste.

"I'll be up soon," Addie called as Delilah reached the top landing and sprinted out of sight.

The screen door opened and closed. She and Priscilla gawked at each other then clung together in fear while they waited to see who would appear.

Addie breathed a sigh of relief when Pearson's dear face rounded the doorpost.

"Whoever it was, they're gone now."

Theo chuckled. "I'd have cut and run, too. Delilah has a healthy set of lungs."

"Do you mind if we take a look inside?" Pearson said. "I'd like to see the window they were looking through."

"Of course," Priscilla said. "Right this way."

Their footsteps echoed in the narrow passage. In a hushed voice, Theo repeated his earlier observation. "I didn't know there was a room back here."

Addie smiled, "Neither did I. Not for the first two weeks I worked here."

"It's my brother's den," Priscilla provided. "He designed it this way on purpose. The man coveted his privacy."

Inside, the spaciousness of the room struck Addie afresh, especially given the fact that it was so well hidden.

Evidently thinking the same, Theo softly whistled.

Priscilla nodded at the large window behind the desk. The drapes were drawn aside with ornate ties. "Had to be that one. The others are on the slope. Too high off the ground."

Pearson strode to the desk and peered out into the darkness. Turning, he studied the room as if from the intruder's eyes. "Do you keep any valuables in here, ma'am?"

Priscilla crossed her arms. "I honestly don't know what my brother kept in here. I don't enter often." She winced. "Too painful." She gazed around her. "I suppose that's why I haven't changed anything. This way it seems he'll amble through the door any minute and light a cigar."

Addie squeezed her arm.

Pearson pushed off the edge of the desk and joined them. "I'm afraid there's nothing more we can do tonight. At first light, we'll search for prints and see if we can track them."

Her eyes bulging, Priscilla looked over his shoulder at the window. "Do you think they'll come back?"

Pearson shrugged but offered an encouraging smile. "Theo and I will take turns watching the house. Will that make you feel better?"

She clenched her hands at her midriff. "Oh, much. Thank you, boys. I'm ever so glad you're living on the grounds. I feel protected knowing you're right outside the door."

Her heart thudding, Addie scurried behind the desk and lowered the blind. As an added measure, she undid the ties.

"Thank you, Addie," Priscilla said. "We'd best say good night now and go see to our boy." Wringing her hands, she started for the door. "I do hope he wasn't frightened by all the commotion."

Pearson tugged on Addie's sleeve as they left the room. She peeked over her shoulder, and he mouthed the words "*Good night.*"

"*Good night,*" she mouthed back, her heart aching to hear what he'd planned to say in the parlor.

THIRTY

Sunday dawned bright but a little cool for late May. Addie leaned, bottoms-up, over her canvas bag, searching for a shawl to wear with her dress. She'd taken great pains to pack the perfect one, the style a little dated, but it would wear well with her linen gown and matching bolero jacket. Not that it mattered. She wouldn't need it past ten in the morning.

"Not a very ladylike pose, Addie."

She spun toward the door. "Priscilla! You startled me."

"I knocked, dear. I was beginning to get concerned."

Addie laughed. "I'm sorry. I didn't hear you. I was rummaging inside this bag."

"Are you nearly ready? It's time to go."

"Yes, and I'm sorry it's taking me so long. I'll be right there, I promise."

"We'll wait for you downstairs. By the by, you did a lovely job dressing Ceddy. He looks so dapper."

She beamed. "Thank you."

The door closed on Priscilla's smiling face.

Addie bent over her luggage again and snatched the folded shawl from the bottom, tugging it free. Spotting the jasper pendant, she took the time to wrap it along with the beads in a white lace handkerchief and then tucked the bundle into a corner. Before closing the top, a peculiar sight caught her eye.

Disbelief flooded her heart as she lifted Ceddy's ugly white rock, the rough edges snagging her favorite blue blouse. Balancing the stone in her hand, the significance of its presence struck a blow.

Ceddy had been in her room. He'd opened the bag where she'd hidden the pendant yet left it untouched. Even stranger, he'd placed his own prized possession alongside hers.

But why? To keep it safe?

Inhaling sharply, she stared dumbly at the wall. *Dear Lord, what could it mean?*

Hearing voices in the hall below the stairs, she tossed the stone inside the bag and slipped the loop over the big button. Scrambling onto the chair, she shoved the bag into the shadowy recess atop the wardrobe and climbed down.

Draping the shawl over her shoulders, she hustled from the room.

Priscilla stood downstairs, her hands on Ceddy's shoulders. Addie smiled at the sight of him. Standing tall and straight beside his great aunt, he looked the fine young gentleman in a suit jacket, ruffled blouse, short pants, and stockings.

Delilah hurried over with a silk scarf, knotting it around his neck with practiced hands. "There you be, Little Man. Now you won't take a chill."

"I invited Theo and Pearson to ride with us this morning." Priscilla bumped Addie's arm with her shoulder. "I thought you might be pleased."

Addie tried to hide just how pleased she was, but the twitching corners of her mouth gave her away. "Oh Priscilla! Don't you tease."

Her shoulders shook with laughter. "I don't mean to, honey, but you two are the cutest things." She picked up her pretty lace parasol and gloves from the entry hall table. "Unfortunately, they had to decline. It seems Pearson invited guests to church this morning. He and Theo rode out early to meet them and walk them over."

Disappointment weighed Addie's heart, but she pushed it aside and replaced it with pride. Pearson cared deeply for others. It was a trait to be admired.

Delilah excused herself and hurried out, late for choir practice again.

Priscilla herded Ceddy toward the door, waging and losing a brief skirmish over a handful of colorful rocks peeking between his fingers. "Very well, young man," she said when he started to cry. "But you'll keep them in your pocket inside the sanctuary."

Addie wanted to pull Priscilla aside and tell her what she'd found in her room but decided not to spoil the mood of the day. There would be plenty of time after church to ask her opinion on the bewildering find.

The morning was lovely, despite the cold lingering beneath the fringed cover of the carriage. Riding down the gently sloping hill, Addie remembered the first day she'd arrived, excited and frightened, with Mother at her side. It seemed like a scene from another lifetime.

Seated between them, Ceddy nodded drowsily until Priscilla eased him against her side. Gazing down at him, she took advantage of his grogginess and lovingly caressed his pink-tinged cheek. The gesture pained Addie's heart.

"We'll have to watch him carefully," Priscilla whispered. "Don't take your eyes off him for a minute."

Addie smoothed a stray wisp of his hair. "Not even for a second."

Ceddy slept the whole way, his chubby mouth slightly parted, his lashes grazing his cheeks. Moved by his innocence and beauty in sleep, Addie shared teary-eyed smiles with Priscilla for the rest of the ride.

Pearson and Theo stood on the steps of the church with Reverend Stroud and several others. As the carriage rumbled up, Pearson turned his head, his searching gaze finding Addie. Pausing in midsentence, he flashed a dashing smile.

Addie's stomach tumbled.

Beside her, Priscilla cooed like a mourning dove.

"Priscilla, please!" Addie hissed.

Pearson seemed to have eyes only for her. Excusing himself, he strolled to meet them at the end of the walk. Offering his arm, he handed her down. "Good morning."

"Yes, it is," she said.

As if remembering his manners, he turned to greet Priscilla. "And how are you, kind lady?"

She gave him a bright smile. "Very well, thank you."

Nodding at Ceddy, he lowered his voice. "Looks like somebody didn't sleep well last night."

"After all the ruckus, I'm amazed he slept at all." Priscilla cuddled him closer. "Poor lamb. I almost hate to wake him."

"May I carry him inside for you?" Pearson offered.

She waved her hand. "Oh no. You two run along. I'll let him rest for a few more minutes, and then we'll join you."

"Are you sure?" Addie asked. "I could wait with you."

"Go ahead with Pearson, dear. No sense in both of us being late."

Beaming, Pearson offered Addie his elbow. He escorted her inside, up the aisle, and to her usual seat in Priscilla's pew. Leaning, he dropped his voice to a whisper. "There are a couple of fellows I'd like you to meet after the service."

Aware of several sets of envious female eyes, Addie nodded and lowered her head.

She longed to sit up front next to Pearson, but such behavior wouldn't be proper, especially with Priscilla absent. She comforted herself by studying the pleasing width of his shoulders, the ripple of cloth against his broad back, and his valiant attempt at combing his hair.

Of course, she made her observations with furtive glances, timed when the women surrounding her directed their meddling curiosity elsewhere.

Priscilla appeared at her side with a rumpled Ceddy in tow.

Scooting aside to make room, Addie eased the dazed boy between them and urged him to sit. She winked over his head at a grim-faced Priscilla.

Ceddy clung tightly to the rocks she'd warned him wouldn't leave his pocket. Knowing her stubborn little charge, Priscilla must have decided giving in was the only way she could coax him inside. In the end, indulging him worked in their favor. Instead of the usual fidgeting and whining during the song service, Ceddy passed the time lining up the stones on each side of his legs.

At the close of the final hymn, Reverend Stroud took to the podium with a broad smile. "Good morning, congregation."

He waited for the answering rumble of pleasant voices.

"We have guests among us today." Gazing down at Pearson, he nodded. "Pearson, if you'll do the honors."

Addie breathed a prayer, confessing pride as her tall, handsome suitor stood. Was there a more striking man in all of Texas?

"Good morning," Pearson said to the worshippers. "I'd like to introduce Mr. Denny Currie and Mr. Charlie Pickering, my special guests this morning."

Beaming, Addie nodded along with the others at the two men standing with him.

Beside her, someone drew a frantic rush of air, the gasping sound after holding one's breath too long.

Glancing down at Ceddy, Addie felt her own breath catch.

His eyes were wild and impossibly round. Heartrending terror masked his pale face. Before Addie could call Priscilla's name, he leaped to his feet and shrieked with all his might.

THIRTY-ONE

Bedlam.

Familiar with the word, Addie had never witnessed it in action until now. Stunned silence had reigned a moment, until the last echo of Ceddy's guttural cry faded to the rafters. Wasting no time with the steps, Reverend Stroud bounded from the platform, fast on Pearson's heels.

Concerned people filed into the aisle behind them as they passed, their heads bobbing as they tried to peer past each other's shoulders.

Ceddy screamed louder as Pearson and his friends approached. A mindless, feral creature, he launched his body over the back of the pew, clawing to escape.

Addie caught him midair, the strain on her arms pulling her off her feet. As she teetered across the back of the pew, panic chilled her limbs.

Pearson's arms wound about her waist, saving her from toppling into the lap of the wide-eyed woman behind her. He set her on her feet while she fought to cradle Ceddy's rigid body.

"Is he hurt?" the reverend shouted over the noise.

"I don't know," Priscilla cried. Tears streaming, she took Addie's arm and herded her and Ceddy toward the exit, carelessly shoving the crush of curious people aside.

Pearson, Theo, and their friends followed them into the midmorning sunlight. Hurrying to the carriage, Priscilla opened the door while

Pearson lifted Addie—Ceddy and all—into the seat.

Burying his face in Addie's neck, Ceddy sobbed uncontrollably. After a moment, he spread his fingers to peek out from behind them, his frightened blue eyes lighting on Pearson and his friends. "N–nuh!" he screeched, squirming against Addie. "Nuh, nuh, nuh!"

"Gentlemen, please!" Priscilla shouted over the din. "Leave us so we might calm him."

"Of course, ma'am," Pearson said. His anxious gaze studied Addie's face. "Are you all right?"

She nodded, and he backed away.

"Driver, take us home," Priscilla called, kneading Ceddy's tense back.

The man shouted at the horses, and the carriage circled in the lane and rumbled away from the church.

They were nearly home before Ceddy's frenzied sobs quieted to whimpers. Smoothing his hair with trembling hands, Priscilla lifted haunted eyes to Addie. "In all these days since Ceddy's attack, has he once been exposed to Pearson?"

The question caught Addie unprepared. "What do you mean? Of course he has." Grasping Priscilla's train of thought, she shuddered. "Well, he must have been. Pearson's been in the house as much as we have."

Priscilla shook her head. "I've given it careful thought, and I don't think so. Ceddy was always upstairs or in the den with Lilah."

"Are you sure?"

"I believe I am."

Addie racked her mind. "Is that possible? I don't. . .I honestly can't remember."

Falling against the padded seat, Priscilla heaved a ragged sigh. "Have we done the unthinkable, Addie? Have we offered Pearson our approval without allowing Ceddy a voice?"

Addie's hand came up. "Stop it now. Pearson's not capable of hurting Ceddy, and you know it."

"I thought I did." She gestured at Ceddy. "But look at him. You saw how he reacted to the man."

Desperately shaking her head, Addie cringed at the terrible thought. "No." She held up both hands. "I'll never believe what you're suggesting. Please don't leap to judgment without proof. I've made that mistake, and it's not fair."

Priscilla caught Addie's fingers and held them to her cheeks. "I'm sorry, but we must think of Ceddy. I know how fond you are of Pearson, but it's time we faced the bitter truth."

Pulling free of Priscilla's grasp, Addie shifted in the seat. She needed time to think things through, time to find a way to exonerate Pearson. Because no matter what the "bitter truth" turned out to be, Addie wasn't fond of him—she was completely, hopelessly in love with him.

Ceddy shuddered against her, and she drew him close, her feverish mind replaying the terrible scene at church.

One troubling memory niggled away at her mind. In the midst of the fracas, while Ceddy had been so distraught, one of the men with Pearson watched with an odd smirk on his face. It seemed a cruel reaction to a child's pain. Whatever else happened, she didn't relish seeing the horrible man ever again.

Pearson sat on the back row of pews, his heart thudding painfully in his chest. He'd never witnessed a child so frightened, and it shook him to the core. The awful sight also stirred the recurring nightmare of what his precious siblings had endured before the rush of water closed over their heads. Running his hands through his hair, he struggled with the jarring comparison.

Theo slid in beside him, his normally olive complexion bleached white with shock. "What happened to him?"

Pearson shook his head. "I'm still trying to figure it out."

Reverend Stroud paused on his way up the aisle. "Fellows, there's no sense going ahead with the service. No one's able to pay attention. Let me close with a prayer for young Ceddy; then we'll retire to the parsonage for lunch."

Nudging Theo, he smiled. "Yes, I can cook. I'm a bachelor. I had to learn or starve."

With the service officially closed, no one seemed in a hurry to leave. Groups of people stood around in clusters, whispering and shaking their heads.

His lips drawn in a firm line, the reverend took to the podium again. "I'm comforted by knowing none gathered here today will yield to gossip and malicious speculation, neither here nor outside this building. Let's show our sister a bit of Christian charity."

Passing sheepish glances, the congregation broke from their cliques and ambled quietly to the door.

A grim smile on his face, the reverend crossed the room to join Pearson and Theo. Gripping Pearson's shoulder, he gave him a little shake. "Are you all right, son?"

Pearson sighed. "I'm worried about Ceddy." He bit his lower lip. "Addie and Priscilla, too. Did you see their faces? I feared Priscilla might faint."

"No one likes to see a child in distress, and it's even harder in Ceddy's case. Since he can't express himself, you're left trying to guess what ails him." He patted Pearson's back and glanced around the building. "What happened to your guests?"

Pearson shrugged. "They saw no reason to stay. I think they felt out of place and a little rattled, besides."

The reverend nodded. "I'm sure they did." He stared over his shoulder at the podium. "It's a shame really. I prepared a nice message on forgiveness of sins. They looked the sort who might need to hear it." He exhaled. "Maybe another time, huh?"

"I hope so."

Theo, his mind forever stuck on food or pretty women, tugged the reverend's sleeve. "Let's hear more about this hidden talent of yours."

Reverend Stroud chuckled. "My cooking?" Motioning at Pearson, he wound his arm around Theo's neck and walked them to the door. "Why waste time talking when I'm prepared to prove my claim?"

Inside the parsonage, the man wasted no time showing off his skill. He whistled while he built a roaring fire. Then, excusing himself, he left the cabin with an ax and returned with a freshly plucked chicken. Singeing off the pinfeathers on the open flames, he took a cleaver and split the bird like the parting of the red sea. He wasted no time cutting it into pieces, handling the knife like an expert. Afterward, he floured, spiced, and fried them to a golden-crusted delight.

Delegating tasks to Pearson and Theo, they spread a well-rounded meal over the table and settled down to enjoy the fruits of their labor.

"You didn't lie, sir," Theo bragged. "You can cook."

Reverend Stroud forked another leg onto Theo's plate. "Flattery has its rewards, young man." He peaked his brows. "And I'm not allowed to lie, remember?"

Groaning, Pearson pushed back his plate. "That was as good as anything I've eaten at Priscilla's. In fact, I tasted Delilah's fried chicken on Friday. It didn't hold a candle to yours."

The reverend touched his finger to his lips. "*Shhh.* Don't let her hear you utter such sacrilege. Delilah's known as the best cook in the county and takes pride in her reputation. If she knew she was only second place, it would crush her fragile spirit."

Light dawning on his face, Theo pointed. "It's you! You're the best cook in Harrison County."

The reverend's laughter rumbled. "Keep that fact close to your chest, please. If the truth gets out, my congregation will stop inviting me to meals."

Pearson took a big mouthful of creamed potatoes. "Given your talent with an iron skillet, I don't know why you'd care."

The reverend winked. "Because I can doesn't mean I like to." Leaning back in his chair, he patted his rounded belly. "I'm a little lazy, you see, a vice that's gone a long way toward nurturing and cultivating this shameful paunch."

They laughed together, Pearson enjoying the comfortable absence of decorum shared only with other men.

He and Theo insisted on helping to clear the table and wash dishes. Theo noticed the dwindling wood box and went outside to split logs.

Hanging the dried and oiled skillet on a hook by the stove, Pearson glanced at Reverend Stroud, busy drying and stacking plates. "Sir, what do you think happened to Ceddy?"

He raised his eyes. "Are you reading my mind now?" Sobering, he reached to place the clean dishes on a shelf. "I was just pondering the same. It came on so suddenly and seemingly out of nowhere."

"Forgive me for asking, but was his outbreak so unusual? He's a sweet boy, but he does have a nervous disposition."

"Ceddy gets in a lather quite often, but never without cause. He's set in his ways and doesn't cotton much to change." He shook his head. "But in all the years I've known him, I've never seen him like he was today."

Pearson shrugged. "So we're back to my original question. What could've happened?"

Reverend Stroud folded the dish towel and leaned against the washstand. He seemed to be weighing his words before he spoke. "I've chewed on whether to mention this or not, but. . ."

Pushing the crock of melted grease to the back of the larder, Pearson turned to give the reverend his full attention. "Go on."

"Perhaps by divine inspiration, I happened to be looking directly at Ceddy when he cried out. I watched him go from serenity to shock and then to terrible fear in the space of an upward glance."

His grim expression shot prickles of dread up Pearson's spine. "A glance at what?"

Compassion in his eyes, the reverend placed a hand on Pearson's shoulder. "You, son. When you stood up with your guests, Ceddy was staring straight at you."

Denny plopped on the thin mattress and pulled off his boots. "For the love of—" Scowling, he tossed one of them at the wall. It hit with a dull thud and slid to the floor. "Up before the sun to wash our merry faces and slick back our hair." He cocked his arm and threw the other boot. "And all for naught." He twisted to see Charlie better and frowned. "Didn't even get an invite to the mansion."

Charlie gaped at him. "What did you expect? The whole muddle was our fault." His jaw slack with dread, he glanced at the ceiling. "We shut down a church service, Denny. What's the penalty for that?"

"They'll never pin it on us, you dolt."

"I don't mean them." Charlie pointed toward the ceiling. "I'm talking about Him."

Laughing, Denny grabbed a pillow from behind him and hurled it across the room. "You're a right ignoramus, Charlie Pickering."

Charlie dodged, a sheepish grin on his face. "I sure was scared. Suppose all those people find out why the lad was squealing?"

"Well, they won't, will they?" He swung his legs over the bed, a thrill surging inside. "Do you know why they won't find out?"

Charlie shook his head.

Leering, Denny drummed his fingertips on his forehead. "Because we're too smart for 'em."

Standing, he walked to the window and leaned on the sill. "I'll tell you another thing. We weren't invited to tea at the mansion today, but we're going anyway. I won't be cheated out of it by that sniveling boy."

Charlie's jaw dropped. "Again?"

"That's right, old boy."

"But they almost caught us the last time."

"We'll have to be more careful, won't we?" He pivoted on his heel. "It's time to make our move, Charlie. I'm done wading through muck to see what those blokes mean to pull from that accursed lake. We're going to Whitfield Manor, invited or not. Only this time we're going inside." He clenched his fists. "It's high time we got a look at our bauble."

THIRTY-TWO

Addie sat with Priscilla at Ceddy's bedside. The poor child sobbed piteously and would not be consoled.

Delilah, wringing her hands in the corner, wiped her eyes on her apron and slipped toward the door. "I–I'll be back, Miss Priscilla."

Priscilla looked over her shoulder. "Where are you going?"

"To the den for jus' a second. I got an idea."

She returned quickly as promised, lugging the family Bible, and shoved it into Addie's hands. "Try this, Miss Addie. His mama used to read aloud to him all the parts where it talk about stones. It soothe him somehow."

Priscilla nodded. "That's right, Lilah, she did. How clever of you to think of it."

Ceddy wailed again, and Addie arched her brows. "I'll try anything at this point." Taking the book from Delilah, she spread it open on the bed. "Does anyone remember a passage right offhand?"

Priscilla leaned across and flipped the pages, coming to a stop in the book of Revelation. Sliding her finger along the margin, she came to rest on the twenty-first chapter and tapped the page. "Read this."

Addie held the Bible up to the light. " 'And he carried me away in the spirit to a great and high mountain, and shewed me that great city, the holy Jerusalem, descending out of heaven from God, Having the glory of God: and her light was like unto a stone most precious, even like a jasper stone, clear as crystal.' "

Priscilla tapped again. "Now this."

" 'And the building of the wall of it was of jasper: and the city was pure gold, like unto clear glass. And the foundations of the wall of the city were garnished with all manner of precious stones. The first foundation was jasper; the second, sapphire; the third, a chalcedony; the fourth, an emerald; The fifth, sardonyx; the sixth, sardius; the seventh, chrysolite; the eighth, beryl; the ninth, a topaz; the tenth, a chrysoprasus; the eleventh, a jacinth; the twelfth, an amethyst. And the twelve gates were twelve pearls; every several gate was of one pearl: and the street of the city was pure gold, as it were transparent glass.' "

Ceddy, his clenched fists buried in his eyes, grew still. His heart-breaking sobs quieted to shuddering hiccups.

"More," Priscilla whispered.

"Where?" Addie said, her mind scrambling for pertinent scriptures.

Delilah's nimble fingers swiftly turned back to chapter four. "Right here."

Addie inhaled deeply and began. " 'And immediately I was in the spirit: and, behold, a throne was set in heaven, and one sat on the throne. And he that sat was to look upon like a jasper and a sardine stone: and there was a rainbow round about the throne, in sight like unto an emerald.' "

His eyes still hidden, Ceddy's lips, red and swollen from crying, tilted at the corners. The beginning of a smile.

Addie inhaled sharply. "It's a miracle."

"He like this one, too," Delilah said, swiftly turning the thin sheets of paper.

Leaning closer, Addie read in a breathless voice. " 'Behold, I lay in Sion a chief corner stone, elect, precious: and he that believeth on him shall not be confounded. Unto you therefore which believe he is precious: but unto them which be disobedient, the stone which the builders disallowed, the same is made the head of the corner, and a stone of stumbling, and a rock of offence, even to them which stumble at the word, being disobedient: whereunto also they were appointed. But ye are a chosen generation, a royal priesthood, an holy nation, a peculiar people; that ye should shew forth the praises of him who hath called you out of darkness into his marvelous light.' "

Ceddy lay quietly asleep at last, the hint of a smile still gracing his face.

Addie closed the big book, her hands folded on the cover. "Who would've thought just hearing these words would bring such comfort?"

Delilah touched her shoulder. "Forgive me, Miss Addie, but them ain't jus' any words. They been comfortin' folk for many an age."

Smiling through her tears, Addie nodded. In a rush, the stress of the day overwhelmed her. Compassion for a scared little boy, mixed with fear and sorrow for the man she loved, brought her to tears. Needing the same comfort for her wounded heart, she folded her arms on the Bible and wept.

Priscilla pushed off Ceddy's mattress and hurried around the foot of the bed. Gathering Addie close, she helped her to her feet. "Delilah, stay with Ceddy until I return."

"Yes'm." Uncertainty thick in her voice, she added, "Don't cry, Miss Addie. He gon' be all right now."

Priscilla led Addie down the hall and opened a door. Even blinded by tears, she knew by the scent of lavender that they'd entered the lady's boudoir. Guiding her over soft rugs to the striped divan, Priscilla eased her down.

Addie hadn't been inside the big room since the first time they'd discussed Ceddy's attack and the possibility of Pearson as the culprit. It seemed ironic to be revisiting the bedroom and the horrible topic at the same time.

"Dear, sweet Addie. . . ," Priscilla began.

Addie held up a hand to stop her. "I'm sorry, but whatever you say, whatever circumstance is causing you to think the worst of Pearson, I can't possibly agree. Please don't ask me to."

Priscilla reared back, her shoulders stiff and her hands folded primly. "Adelina, I care for him, too," she said quietly. "Has it occurred to you that I want to see him exonerated as much as you do?"

Addie frowned. "You do?"

"Of course! Pearson has come to mean a lot to me." She studied the fingernails on one hand. "But you see, if he's not who we think he is, I've not only failed Ceddy; I've failed your mother's trust. And most especially, I've failed you."

Addie slid to the floor at Priscilla's feet, resting her cheek on her knee. "If Pearson is not who we think he is, then your Dr. Jekyll and Mr. Hyde story has come to life in our midst, because the loving, gentle man I've been spending time with could never, ever hurt a child."

Reverend Stroud pulled out a chair, nodding at Pearson to take the one opposite. "Is there anything you'd like to tell me, son?" He took a deep breath. "I'm a good listener, and I've seen a lot in my years behind the pulpit. It's very hard to shock me. Perhaps I can help you."

Ignoring the offered chair, Pearson scowled. "It sounds like you're inviting me to confess something."

The reverend rolled his tongue inside his cheek. "That option's available, but I'm merely offering you a chance to talk things through."

"What *things*?"

He shook his head. "I can't break a confidence, but there are still a few people in Marshall who question your integrity."

"I thought you'd put those rumors to rest."

"I did." He paused. "Those concerning thievery and malicious mischief." He drew in his lips as if chewing on the rest. "It's the new allegation I'm concerned with, made by a trusted source." He waved his hand. "I took the charge lightly when I first heard." He gazed into Pearson's eyes. "Maybe too lightly."

A chair to hold him up became a good idea. Pearson pulled it out and dropped into the seat. "Since you obviously believe I've done something, I think I deserve to know what it is."

Reverend Stroud placed a gentle hand over his. "That's the peculiar part and the hardest part for me. I haven't really known you long, but I'm having a difficult time believing it, despite compelling evidence of your guilt."

"Guilt?" Angry now, Pearson pounded his fist on the table. "Don't you think you need to tell me what I've done before pronouncing guilt?"

"Did you lift a hand to harm Cedric Whitfield?"

Pearson's head roared. He gripped the sides of the table to still the spinning room. "Why would you think me capable of such a thing?"

"Because the night we found that poor boy, tormented and bruised, there was no one in the house with us but you and Theo, and Theo was with me all evening. Now today. . .in church. . .the moment Ceddy's eyes lit on you, he screamed like he feared for his life."

Shaking his head slowly from side to side, Pearson fought to breathe. "If Priscilla thought I could hurt that little boy, she'd never have let me stay on her property."

Pain flashed on the reverend's face. "She would. . .if a trusted friend and pastor vouched for you, swayed her to trust you."

"You mean Priscilla thought—"

The reverend looked away.

A wealth of hurt clogged Pearson's throat. "And Addie?"

Before he could answer, Theo pushed the door open, his arms loaded with split wood. Rolling the logs into the wood box with a bump and clatter, he turned with a proud smile. "I filled the box outside, too. Is there anything else you'd like for me to do?"

Pearson bolted from the chair and breezed past Theo so fast he spun him around. Outside on the porch, he stared with wild eyes, a wounded animal unsure where to run. He'd once told Addie, in a show of bravado, that he never stooped to defending himself. The truth was he'd never had to until now. His ethics and moral character were part of who he was, and no one had ever questioned them.

Since he'd come to Marshall, he'd been accused of one unspeakable deed after the other, and the accusations cut deep. For Addie to think him a wife-stealing lothario was bad enough, but for good people like Reverend Stroud, Priscilla Whitfield, and his darling Addie to suspect he could harm a child was too much to bear.

Behind him, Theo cautiously placed a hand on his shoulder. "Pearson? What's wrong, buddy?"

Shame coursed through him for running out like a coward instead of standing his ground. Wheeling, he marched to the door and burst into the reverend's home.

Reverend Stroud raised his head, sadness etched on his face.

"Sir," Pearson said, his chest heaving, "I don't know how, but I'll prove my innocence to you and the others. I'll win your confidence again or die trying."

The reverend nodded. "I pray you can, son."

Pearson turned to leave, but the man of God called his name.

He paused with his hand on the knob. "Yes, sir?"

"Where are you going?"

Pearson hadn't considered it until he asked. "We'll be camping out at the lake. I need hard work to occupy my hands and a quiet place to think. After today, I doubt we're welcome at the mansion."

"I'll be praying, Pearson. If this turns out to be a mistake, I hope you'll be able to forgive me."

Pearson's shoulders slumped. "I already have."

Motioning to Theo, he walked out and closed the door.

Denny sat in the back of the hired wagon and stared up at the grand old house. A thrill surged through him as he considered the mansion up close and in the daylight. He nudged Charlie. "Look at her, mate. To think that I'll have a house like this one day soon. . .only bigger and finer."

"You mean we will, right, Den?"

He frowned. "Yeah, yeah, that's what I mean." As he gazed at the tall white columns, impatience squeezed his chest, and he found it hard to breathe. "The only thing standing in our way lies somewhere behind those walls, just waiting to be found." He elbowed Charlie again. "Pay the driver and ask him to wait."

Charlie leaned to offer the man his fee then followed Denny off the rig. "Are you sure we should be hanging around here in broad daylight? I don't think it's such a good idea."

Denny straightened his collar and tugged on the hem of his new coat. "Good on you that no one needs your ideas. Shut it, and let's go." Approaching the imposing entrance, Denny pulled back his shoulders and puffed his chest like a pigeon. "Yes, sir. I could get used to the high life, old boy. I surely could."

Charlie chuckled. "I reckon we'll have to before long, won't we?"

"You've got a point there," Den said, reaching for the brass door-knocker. "I mean, besides the one on your head."

Charlie started to grouse, but Den punched his arm hard as the door cracked open.

A stern-faced maid in a ruffled white cap stood on the stoop. "May I help you gentlemens?"

Denny yanked off his hat. "We're here to see the lady of the house." At her slight frown, he pasted on a bright smile. "It's a business matter."

"On a Sunday? She expectin' you?"

He tilted his head. "Not exactly, but it's very important."

Doubt soured her face. "Who should I say is calling?"

"Mr. Currie."

"And Mr. Pickering," Charlie added then lowered his eyes at Denny's scowl.

"Tell her we're friends of Mr. Foster," Denny said.

She jutted her bottom lip as if trying to make up her mind. "Wait here," she said and closed the door.

By the time she returned, Denny had started to doubt she ever would. "Right this way," she ordered, shuffling aside to let them in.

Denny's breath quickened. Stepping over the threshold, he drew in sharply, filled with a sense of wonder. He never imagined that money would smell of lavender.

The maid led them down the hall to a set of double doors. Thrusting them open, she motioned for them to enter. "Jus' have a seat on the sofa. Miss Whitfield be right in."

Denny raised his brows at Charlie.

With a gap-toothed grin, Charlie winked.

Strutting across the room, they sank together into the plush upholstery.

Denny ran his hand over the satin-covered arm with a whistle. "You ever feel anything like this?"

Charlie shook his head, beaming like a mug.

The clatter of footsteps in the hall stiffened Denny's spine. Sidling to the edge of the couch, he summoned his false smile and practiced what to say under his breath.

The white-haired lady stepped into sight under the arched entryway, the picture of class and old money. She crossed the room and offered her hand. "Good afternoon. I'm Priscilla Whitfield. I understand you have business with me?"

Denny stood to shake her hand, and Charlie followed suit. "Yes, ma'am. My friend and me, we've come to inquire about a room to let."

A tiny frown creased her brow. She backed into a big chair near the window and lowered herself down. "A room? I'm afraid you've been misinformed, sir. This isn't a boardinghouse."

Denny shook his head. "Oh no, missus. I never meant to imply that it was." He gave a shaky laugh. "I reckon I'd best explain meself. You see, we're associates of Mr. Foster, Charlie and me."

Unless Denny had lost his touch, the lady winced at the mention of Pearson's name. "Of course." She peered at them sideways. "Now I remember. You were his guests at church today."

"Yes, missus." Thrown off a bit, Denny swallowed hard and continued. "Therefore, we're privy to the fact that you've recently restored a set of houses out back."

Understanding sparked in her eyes. "I see." She ran her birdlike hands over the neck of her blouse, fiddling with the pleated fabric. "Well, regretfully, you've still been misled. I have no intention of offering those houses for lease." She stood. "I'm sorry you wasted your time coming all the way out here. In the future, Mr. Foster should be careful not to misrepresent the facts." Standing over them, watching expectantly with crossed arms, she left them nothing to do but take their leave.

Denny squirmed with irritation. His plan to use Pearson's name to gain favor had gone bust. He pushed off the sofa, dragging Charlie up with him. "Well, despite this unlucky turn of events, I'm ever so glad to have met you."

Her smile seemed more forced than his. "Likewise."

The maid appeared, as if she'd been standing outside all along.

Miss Whitfield nodded at her. "Delilah, show these gentlemen to the door, please. We've finished our visit."

Dejected, Denny followed the maid's starched white bow and swishing black skirt down the hall. Remembering his real reason for being inside the house, his gaze darted to the staircase and the three doors past the entrance to the back hall, making mental notes of the layout. Odd that he didn't see the boy or any sign that a child even lived there. "Nice place," he said casually.

"Yessuh," she said, her hand on the knob.

"I suppose there are plenty of rooms, yeah? How many all told?"

"Ain't never counted 'em, suh."

He laughed. "The bedrooms, then? Surely you know how many bedrooms there are."

"Six, I reckon. Four upstairs and two down."

"Six bedrooms!" Charlie cried. "Can you feature that?"

"And you have people to fill all those rooms?" Denny pressed.

"N–no suh." Biting her bottom lip, she shifted to the other foot.

"So how many are actually used?" He smiled innocently. "I suppose those downstairs for sure, right?"

She stiffened and jerked open the door.

He'd gone too far. Blundered where he shouldn't. Smoothing the brim of his cap, he dropped it lightly on his head. "I reckon we'll be on our way. Much obliged to you, miss."

She nodded curtly. "Yessuh."

On the way to the rig, Charlie glanced over at him. "I didn't know we wanted to let a room from the old girl."

Seeking the heavens, Denny sighed. "Just come with me, and try not to ask stupid questions."

"Where we going?"

"Back to the boardinghouse to scrounge a bite to eat, since Whitfield hospitality don't exactly measure up to what we've heard." He scowled. "She didn't exactly invite us to tea, now, did she?"

"And after that?"

"We'll pack our gear and sneak out on the tab." He lowered his voice as they neared the rig. "Then we'll make our way back here, find out for ourselves who sleeps where." He tugged on Charlie's sleeve. "One thing's for certain. . .I won't leave this house again without my blasted diamond."

Ceddy shoved against the cold glass pane. Toppling backward out of the window seat, he fell on the floor and bumped his head. Clawing his way under the bed, white spots swam with his tears.

In the house.

He gasped.

In Aunt Priss's house.

His breath came so fast his head began to swirl. Scrubbing his eyes with his fists, he tried to erase the terrible sight.

Gone now. Gone. The wagon took them away.

Hadn't it?

The window drew him. The need to be sure. He stole a peek over his shoulder but couldn't get his arms or legs to move.

The dark space beneath the bed didn't feel safe anymore. He wanted Daddy. Daddy's voice, his hugs, his smell.

Ceddy stilled, and his head came up. He could find Daddy's smell if he looked hard enough. But first he had to stop shaking.

THIRTY-FOUR

After picking up a buckboard from the livery, Pearson dropped Theo at Weisman's Department Store with orders to buy enough supplies to last a few days out at the lake. Turning in the middle of the road, he headed up the lane toward the hill.

Dread weighed his heart at the thought of going to the mansion, but he needed to pick up a few changes of clothes for him and Theo. He wouldn't run from a confrontation with Priscilla or Addie, but he didn't think he had the nerve to initiate one.

Not that he was scared. Only guilty people feared the finger of blame pointed in their direction. But until he had proof of his innocence, he knew he'd regret the things he'd find to say, especially to Addie.

The first time he forgave her for thinking the worst of him—they didn't know each other then. Now, only days later, she believed him capable of another terrible deed, this one much worse than before. Well, this time, he couldn't let it go. Not after she'd made him think she loved him.

He turned in at the drive and slowed the horse. If he could slip in and out without being seen, it would suit him just fine.

Driving up to the old servants' quarters, he set the brake and climbed down. Glancing toward the house, his heart settled to the pit of his stomach. He'd spent many happy hours inside the walls of Whitfield Manor. He didn't like thinking he might never be welcome again.

A pang of homesickness weakened his knees. For the first time in years, he longed for Galveston, where he'd known only love and acceptance, no questions asked. He missed Rosie, Pearl, and Cookie more than he could say. The sooner they settled their business with the *Mittie Stephens* and pulled anchor, the better he'd feel.

Turning from the house, Pearson went inside to pack. Moments later he returned to the rig, an overstuffed bag slung over his shoulder. He tossed it into the bed. Reaching for the post to climb aboard, he paused at the sound of his name.

Addie hurried toward him, dressed in his favorite white dress, loose curls framing her pixie face.

She looked so beautiful his stomach ached. Gritting his teeth, he wondered why she'd gussied up to accuse him.

She gave him a bright smile. "I'm so glad you're home." Glancing at the bag, she frowned. "Are you going somewhere?"

He gripped the wagon rail until his fingers hurt. "Yes, for a few days."

She studied his face. "Weren't you going to say good-bye?"

He lifted one shoulder. "I didn't think it was necessary."

She blinked, a crease growing between her brows. "Forgive me, but I don't understand."

He averted his eyes. "Spare the false manners, Addie. We're past that, remember?"

Her throat rose up and down. "What?"

"Reverend Stroud told me what you think of me. You and Priscilla."

Eyes rounded, she opened her mouth to speak, but Pearson held up his hand. "Don't say anything, please. I just want you to know that I came back to life after meeting you." He ran a trembling hand through his hair. "After you melted my heart, I even came back to God. For that, I'll always be grateful I came to Marshall."

He braced his foot and pulled up on the seat. "I told you once that I let my actions defend my honor. For the first time in my life that's not enough." He untied the reins from the post. "As soon as I figure out how, I'll prove my innocence. Once I do, I'll be leaving this town for good."

He clucked at the horse, and the buckboard started to move.

Addie ran alongside, grasping for a hold on the rig. "Pearson, please stop. I never believed it for a second. I promise."

"Go inside, Addie," he called. "I need time to think. We'll talk more when I return." With the sound of her sobs ripping the walls of his heart, Pearson turned onto the lane and rattled downhill.

THIRTY-FIVE

Addie stumbled through the back door, blinded by tears.

Delilah caught her just inside the screen and gathered her into comforting arms. "Hush now, sugar. You jus' hush. Ain't no man worth all this."

Priscilla rushed into the hall. "Delilah, what happened?"

"I seen the whole thing, Miss Priscilla. Mr. Pearson rode off with this lil' ol' thing scramblin' after the wagon, crying and pleading for him to stop."

Priscilla rounded her eyes. "Heavens, Addie. Why would you do that?"

Addie stiffened, anger easing some of the pain. "Because I love him, that's why. And because he's innocent. I know he is."

A hush fell in the hall. "How do you know?" Priscilla asked at last.

Addie tapped her chest. "I feel it in my heart."

Priscilla shook her head. "A heart in love can't be trusted. You're viewing him through gilded lenses." She crossed her arms and walked to peer outside. "I take it you confronted him. What did he have to say for himself?"

Addie glared. "I didn't mention a word. As a matter of fact, he broached the subject." Remembering her upbringing, she softened her gaze. "Priscilla, how could you tell Reverend Stroud such an awful thing without proof?"

Priscilla spun. "How did you—" She touched her trembling fingers to her mouth. "Oh my. That's who told Pearson." A thoughtful look crossed her face. "I never asked the reverend not to tell, but I'm quite surprised he broke my confidence. I suppose he had his reasons."

"What reason could he have for bringing me into it?" Pacing, she wrung her hands. "Pearson is so angry with me. I don't think he'll ever forgive me."

"Adelina, may I remind you that man more than likely hurt my nephew? Why should you care if he's angry?"

"Until I have undeniable proof of any wrongdoing, I can't help but care. Pearson insists he didn't hurt Ceddy, and I believe him."

Priscilla glanced at Delilah. "Speaking of Ceddy, where is he?"

Delilah inched toward the stairs. "I looked in on him awhile ago. He still asleep."

"Go see to him again. He must be starved. He slept straight through lunchtime."

Delilah raised her brows. "You want me to wake him?"

"Yes, and then go fix him something to eat."

"Yes'm," Delilah said.

Addie glanced up in time to see the back of her skirt disappear around the corner.

Priscilla slid her arm around Addie's shoulders. "I know how hard this must be for you, dear. You had no reason to mistrust Pearson, and now you've set your affection on him." She tightened her hug. "For your sake, I pray we discover the whole thing is a terrible mistake." She pressed her cheek to Addie's. "Let me take you into the parlor. We'll have Delilah bring in a nice cup of tea."

Passing the staircase, Delilah's moans jerked them to a standstill. She stood on the top landing, twisting her apron into knots. "Miss Priscilla. . .Ceddy, he ain't in his room." She looked behind her as if hoping to see him there. "I even peeked under the bed."

"He's probably just in the den."

"No, ma'am. I was in there dustin' before I heard Miss Addie squawking outside."

Mildly alarmed, Addie pointed up the stairs. "Go and check my room. I recently discovered he likes to go in there."

She whirled and slipped from sight.

They waited for what seemed an eternity, passing worried glances between them and staring at the place where Delilah had stood.

When it seemed she'd never return, she popped into view. "He ain't in there." Twisting her apron even harder, she shook her head. "I scoured all four bedrooms. Closets, too."

Priscilla waved her handkerchief. "Go look again. You know how well he can hide."

"Nowhere left for him to hide. 'Less he done crawl up under a rug, he not up here."

Her face pale, beads of sweat popping out on her lip, Priscilla clutched Addie's arm. "I'll see if he's in the kitchen."

Addie's heart raced. Lifting her chin, she waved for Delilah. "Come help Priscilla search the house. I'll go look in the garden. He may have slipped past while I was talking to Pearson."

Frantic, she raced out the door and sailed off the end of the porch, taking no time for the steps. Gathering the hem of her dress, she ran through the hedges calling Ceddy's name.

By the time she'd covered every inch of the backyard, Priscilla stood on the porch wringing her hands. "Delilah's looking out front, but nothing so far. I can't believe he's gone missing again, Addie. Where could he be?"

"Don't worry, we'll find him just like the last time, in the last place we'd expect." Her brave words were for Priscilla's sake. Inside, her stomach trembled.

Delilah bustled around the side of the house. "Did you find him?"

Gnawing her bottom lip, Addie shook her head.

"What's that?" Priscilla called.

Addie's gaze followed the direction she pointed. A cloth lay on the ground, its bright white hue in sharp contrast with the rutted drive. "I don't know."

Veering away from the bottom step, she hurried over. "It must be something Pearson dropped."

Standing over the bit of cloth, partly driven into the dirt by a wagon wheel, Addie covered her mouth to hold back a scream. She whirled, and her panicked gaze found Priscilla through a blur of tears.

"What is it?" Priscilla repeated, this time in a frightened voice. Nearly toppling over the edge of the porch, she staggered to the ground and hurried toward Addie with Delilah on her heels.

"It's my white lace hankie," Addie said. In a flash she realized she'd never told Priscilla about finding Ceddy's stone.

Priscilla slowed. "Is that all? For heaven's sake, you scared me."

Addie bent to pull the handkerchief free. "You don't understand." Holding it aloft, she gaped at the muddy track. "The last time I saw this, it was wrapped around my jasper pendant inside my canvas bag—alongside Ceddy's treasured white rock. He slipped into my room and hid it there to keep it safe."

Priscilla blanched. "Then. . ." She stared down the drive, making the very presumption Addie prayed she wouldn't, the same deduction Addie struggled against. Terror darkened Priscilla's eyes. "Ceddy was out here." She swallowed hard. "With Pearson."

Addie held up her hand. "Now, Priscilla. . ."

"Where was he going?"

"He didn't say."

Wild-eyed, she gripped Addie's arms, mostly to hold herself up considering how hard she trembled. "We have to call the sheriff immediately."

"The sheriff? No!"

"We must. He could be taking him anywhere." She gasped. "You don't think he's headed for Galveston, do you?"

"Pearson left here alone. I watched him go."

"Did you search the wagon?"

Pushing the large cloth bag out of her mind, Addie shook her head. "For heaven's sake! Listen to yourself. Don't you see it doesn't make any sense? There's no reason Pearson would take him."

Her lips pursed. "I'll look for Ceddy first and try to make sense of it later."

She began to stalk away, but Addie snatched her arm. "Please don't call the sheriff. Not yet. Ceddy could still be here somewhere. We haven't finished searching the grounds or the woods."

Priscilla didn't look convinced.

Addie waved her hand to take in their surroundings. "Wouldn't you hate knowing you went chasing a wild goose and left Ceddy out there somewhere, alone and frightened?"

Her frantic gaze darting around the perimeter, Priscilla sighed. "You're right. Either way, we need help." She started for the house again, talking over her shoulder. "Delilah, have the driver swing the carriage around. I'm going to see Reverend Stroud."

Still displeased with the reverend, Addie cringed. "Why him?"

"He'll call out the congregation to form a search party." She gave Addie a pointed look. "And he's the last person, besides you, to talk to Pearson. Hopefully the reverend knows where he's going."

"And if he does?"

Her mouth set in a determined line. "I'm going after him."

"Wait for me," Addie cried, hurrying her steps to catch up to her. Priscilla frowned, and Addie raised her brows. "I want to be there when you find out you were wrong."

THIRTY-SIX

Ceddy lay still under the wagon seat, counting the big brown stitches running the length of the tan-colored bag. Reaching the last thread, he ran his finger to the other side and started over again.

The cloth bag smelled funny. Partly of the sea—like the great rolling ship he rode with Auntie Jane—and partly of Daddy. Only it wasn't really Daddy's smell. Just the man with the odd hair.

He drew farther into the shadows as the wagon came to a creaking stop.

The springs above his head moaned as the man climbed down.

Laughing voices. The squeal of the tailgate. A thud shook him, then another, as crates came sliding toward him. Holding his breath, he waited for the noise to stop.

The seat groaned.

One, two, three, four boots in front, a wall of boxes in back. The man who hugged like Daddy, close enough to touch.

Ceddy tightened his grip on the crystallized carbon gemstone and held Miss Addie's jasper next to his cheek.

Safe.

Pearson drove northeast out of town and took the road to Caddo Lake. The sun overhead felt wrong, the gentle breeze out of place. The day seemed like any other pleasant Sunday afternoon, instead of the second worst day of his life.

Shouldn't the sky be overcast? Lightning striking? A foul wind whipping the trees?

Seated next to him, Theo talked until his voice grew hoarse, chattered until he made no sense, blabbered until his life hung in the balance.

Pearson nudged him hard with his elbow. "Take a breath, would you? It's not working."

Theo grimaced and clutched his arm. "What was that for?"

"I didn't meet you yesterday, paisan. You've done the same since we were kids." He laughed. "Come to think on it, it never worked then either."

Propping his boot, Theo reclined in the seat and folded his arms. "I hope you know you're talking in riddles."

"I hope you know I'm onto you. You're trying to distract me from my thoughts, but you're wasting your breath. That, and robbing me of the will to live."

Theo cast him a worried glance.

Pearson forced a smile. "Don't fret. Things will never get that bad again."

Theo nodded. "So. . .do you want to talk about it?"

Pearson blew a shuddering breath. "If you can explain to me what happened, I might." He shook his head. "How could I have gotten it so wrong? Addie had me convinced she cared about me."

"She does, and you won't persuade me otherwise."

Scowling, Pearson quirked his mouth. "If you're right, I don't understand her brand of caring. There's no loyalty in it."

Theo pursed his lips. "Wait a second. . . . How did Addie come into this? I thought we were talking about you and the reverend."

Pearson snorted. "The reverend brought it out in the open, but she's in on the whole thing."

Theo propped his arms on his knees and stared at his laced fingers. "You do realize I have no inkling of what you're talking about. One minute we're enjoying the reverend's company; the next you're tearing out of the house and spouting something about your innocence." He glanced up. "And now you're mad at Addie?"

"That's right—you didn't hear." Pearson sighed. He didn't relish airing the details of his humiliation, but his best friend had a right to know. "I'll tell you, but hold on to your hat." He sucked in a deep breath. "They think I'm the one who did it, Theo. They think I hurt Ceddy." The vile words soured his mouth.

"What?" Shock gripped Theo's features. "That's plain crazy. Who came up with that drivel?"

"Evidently Addie, Priscilla, and the reverend."

"Reverend Stroud?" This fact seemed to bother Theo the most. "I thought he was our friend."

"That's the worst part. He was trying hard to be a friend when he brought his suspicions to light. To tell the truth, when I consider all the strikes he had against me, I start to believe it myself."

Theo gave a disgusted grunt. "So how do you plan to do it?"

"Do what?"

"Prove your innocence."

Pearson sighed. "I don't know. I'll start by sitting lakeside and clearing my head. Maybe if I run the facts past, one by one, they'll start to make sense."

He stared at the blue sky through the pine trees filing by. "Ceddy Whitfield's a great kid, but the most important thing for me to do is steer well clear of him."

The carriage pulled to a stop in front of Reverend Stroud's humble little house. Climbing down behind Priscilla, Addie followed her past the rickety gate and through the front yard.

Absent of grass, the dark, moist dirt was a crisscrossed pattern of chicken scratches. Stiff-legged hens darted out of the way. Red-combed roosters sat on fence rails, flapping their wings in a brave display. Dodging a brood of chicks, Priscilla mounted the steps and rapped on the door.

Reverend Stroud opened to them wearing old trousers, one suspender fastened over a plaid shirt, and a surprised expression. He looked nothing like the man who smiled down from the pulpit each Sunday. He stepped aside with downcast eyes. "Come in, ladies. I believe I know why you're here."

"I'm afraid you don't, Reverend." The tears Priscilla held in check for so long found an outlet in the presence of her pastor. "It's Ceddy!"

she wailed. "He's gone, and this time he's not hiding under a bed. This time he may be in dire peril."

He glanced at Addie, and she gave a curt nod.

The scriptural admonition to give pastors double honor and high esteem for their labors pricked Addie's conscience. Swallowing her anger, she resolved to address her sense of betrayal later, in prayer to the Lord. "It's true, sir. He may be in the woods or somewhere past the garden fence, but he's nowhere on the grounds."

He motioned them inside then hurried to a kitchen chair, snagging his boots and dingy socks on the way. Struggling into them, he fired breathless questions. "How long has he been missing?"

"We thought he was sleeping," Priscilla said. "It could've been hours."

"Did you look in the servants' quarters?"

Addie gasped. "No! I don't know why, but we didn't. He could very likely be there."

"What sort of dire peril do you fear, Priscilla?"

"I believe he may have been taken." Her mouth hardened. "By Pearson."

His hands gripping the top of one boot, the reverend paused and glanced up. "Pearson was there?"

"Yes. And when he left, Ceddy was missing."

He lowered his head, rubbing his eyes with finger and thumb. "I just spoke to Pearson awhile ago."

"We know," Addie said, unable to keep the bitterness from her voice. "He told us."

The man's earnest gaze searched her face. "I hope you'll forgive me, Addie. I didn't tell him outright that you suspected him, but I didn't deny it."

She sank into a chair across from him. "That's just it, Reverend. I don't suspect him. I never did. I could never believe Pearson capable of harming a child."

Reverend Stroud heaved a heavy sigh. "I'm beginning to share your instincts, Addie." He shot a cautious look at Priscilla. "Forgive me, dear, but after listening to the man, watching his eyes, I think we've unjustly accused him."

"His eyes?" she spat.

The reverend nodded. "The window to a man's soul, remember? There's not a hint of darkness to be found in Pearson's."

Priscilla marched to the table. "Then how do you explain the fact that they've both gone missing?"

He held up his hand. "No one said Pearson's missing. He's merely gone to the lake for a few days, to nurse hurt feelings and devise a way to prove his innocence."

Her chin jerked up. "He's headed for Lake Caddo?"

"He and Theo both."

Whirling, Priscilla beat a path to the door. "Come, Addie. If he's bound for the lake, then so are we."

"Not so fast, dear lady," the reverend called. "Before you run off half-cocked, I'd suggest you slow down and allow us to look for Ceddy." His gaze jumped to Addie. "Starting with the servants' quarters."

THIRTY-SEVEN

Denny's turn had come at last. He may have opened his eyes that morning in a shabby boardinghouse flat he couldn't afford, with musty bedding and grime in the corners, but those days were over. Soon he too would fall asleep each night in a house with six bedrooms and satin-covered sofas in the parlor.

"We're still going up to the mansion, Den?"

The question pulled Denny from his pleasant daydream. "How else will we look for the rock, old boy?" In his present joyful mood, he couldn't summon an ugly name to spout.

Charlie twisted on the seat and pointed over his shoulder. "But we passed the carriage in town."

They had tiptoed past the landlord's room and slipped out the back door without paying their bill. Hustling over to the livery, they'd tossed their luggage in the rented buggy and headed out of town. Bouncing along Washington Street, they rode right by Miss Whitfield and the governess, going somewhere in a frightful hurry.

Denny beamed. "Most accommodating of them to leave, don't you think?"

Charlie studied his fleshy hands. "I'm trying to follow, Den, really I am, but it's paining me 'ead."

"You didn't see the boy with them, did you?"

Charlie shook his head.

"If he's there in the house, then our diamond is, too. Now the only thing standing in our way is that skinny maid."

Turning off the lane, Denny dashed past the circular drive and pulled in close to the back porch. As he approached the door, excitement simmered in his chest. He smiled at Charlie, touched his finger to his lips, and stepped inside the cool, shaded hall.

The house was quiet, the only sound the purring of a ceiling fan somewhere up ahead. Their backs to the wall, they slid along the railing until Denny could get a peek at the staircase and the areas beyond.

Nothing stirred. He'd never known a house where a boy lived to be so quiet. It seemed abnormal. But then, Ceddy was hardly a normal boy.

Motioning for Charlie to follow, he reached the landing in a few quick paces. Leaning, he peered upstairs, fully expecting to see scurrying shadows or hear some sort of movement. Raising his brows at Charlie, he placed his hand on the banister and took one cautious step.

A low growl shot fire through Denny's chest. He spun, nearly falling over Charlie in his haste.

Charlie, panic in his eyes, sat down hard on the bottom stair, as if he'd decided to take a rest.

The maid loomed behind them, an upraised knife in her hand. "Don't you all go up there, you hear? Turn around, now, and skedaddle."

On closer inspection—and Denny happened to be looking close—the knife turned out to be a letter opener. Not that it mattered. No doubt her twitching fingers, tightly clutching the handle, would gladly wield it to the same disastrous end.

"Calm yourself, little gal. There's no need to get fidgety."

"Uh-huh. I'm 'bout to show you fidgety." She tilted her head. "Go on, do like I say and leave."

Easing past Charlie, Denny raised his hand. "Dreadful sorry, but I can't go just yet."

She licked her bottom lip. "What you mean?"

"Listen, we're not looking to hurt anybody."

Her gaze drifted to the letter opener. "You ain't lookin' to hurt nobody? Is that what you jus' said?" Glaring, she lifted the makeshift weapon higher.

He took another sliding step. "There's something here that belongs to me, and I mean to have it. The sooner you help me find it, the quicker you'll be shed of us."

She blinked her confusion. "If you left a hat or cane or some-such here, why you don't knock at the front door and ask?"

"No hat or cane, darlin'. The item in question is far more valuable." He eased off the bottom step and moved to the side of the banister, giving her a clear shot at Charlie. "My friend here is about to go upstairs and have a look around, and there's nothing you can do to stop him."

Charlie's eyes widened.

Denny gave him a firm nod.

Gripping the railing with white-knuckled hands, Charlie started to climb.

Falling into Denny's trap, the maid lunged, aiming the crude knife at Charlie's back.

Denny's hand shot out and cruelly gripped her wrist.

She screamed, and the opener clattered to the floor.

Bending at the waist, he picked it up and held it to her throat. "Where's the boy?"

Her body heaved against him. "M–Masta Ceddy? What you want with him?"

He gave her a shake. "Answer the question."

"He ain't here."

"Sure he is."

"No, suh. I swear it."

"You want me to tell you how I know you're lying? Charlie and me just saw his old auntie and the hired girl in town. The brat wasn't with 'em."

Her chest rose and fell in a sob. "Don't you go callin' Little Man no brat."

Losing patience, Denny pushed the point a little harder against her skin. "Tell me."

She gasped. "Masta Ceddy gone missin' again, and we cain't find him."

Releasing her, he spun her around. "What do you mean 'missing'?"

"He runs off on occasion." A sudden thought sparked in her eyes. "Miss Priscilla gone for help. Half the county gon' show up here any minute. Search parties and such." Her throat bobbed. "It won't do for you two to be caught inside when they come."

Denny cursed and gripped her shoulder. "If you value your life, take me to his room." He shook her hard. "Go on! Which way?"

Stumbling over her feet, she struggled to the stairs, slid past Charlie, and clawed her way up the banister.

They fell in behind her and followed her to the first door on the right. Swinging it wide, she hurried inside and huddled in the corner.

Denny's gaze darted to the cheery quilt on the bed, the bright rugs, and the scattered toys. Confident she'd brought them to the right place, he took an anxious breath. "He had a rock when he came here."

She frowned. "A rock?"

"That's right." He made a circle with his finger and thumb. "About this big."

"Yessuh?"

His heart thudded in his chest. "White it was."

She nodded. "Yessuh?"

"Do you know where he kept it?"

She shook her head.

Bile rising in his throat, Denny held the letter opener over her head. "You'd best start figuring it out."

Leaping like a gazelle, she shot across the room to a large upright chest. Opening the lid, she tilted the contents onto the floor. Reaching for a shelf behind her, she swept several crates over the edge with her arm. They fell with a crash that emptied their contents. Dashing to the bed, she scrambled beneath it and pulled out several square display boxes. Crying now, she dumped them onto the mountain of stones in the middle of the room. "There be more in the closet," she panted. "You want me to fetch them?"

Denny stared in disbelief. Rocks of every imaginable color, shape, and size lay in a heap at his feet. "What the devil is this?"

"Little Man's collection, suh."

"This ain't a blessed collection. It's a quarry!"

Backing away from his shouting, she cowered next to the bed.

Denny hooked his thumb at Charlie. "Get started, mate. This lot could take all night."

"Right, Den," Charlie said, dropping to his knees.

Casting the maid a warning glare, Denny knelt to join him. "Best hurry, too. If what she said is true, we ain't got much time."

Delilah met the carriage before it rolled to a stop, waving her arms overhead and screaming.

Priscilla gasped and turned a sickly shade.

Addie bailed out the side without waiting for the driver's assistance and ran to grip Delilah's arms. "What's wrong? Have you found him?"

She wailed an answer Addie couldn't understand and fell sobbing onto her shoulder.

Fearing the worst, Addie turned flooded eyes to Priscilla. "I can't understand what she's saying."

Climbing down, Priscilla rushed to her maid and spun her around. "Delilah, get hold of yourself. Tell us what happened."

"They come in the house," she shrilled. "I took your letter opener and tried to make 'em leave, but they wouldn't go."

"Who?" Priscilla shook her. "Who came in?"

"Those two men. The same ones who come earlier today askin' for to let a room."

Priscilla flinched. "They came back?"

"Yes'm."

"Whatever did they want?"

Delilah stamped her foot. "Aren't you listenin'? They ain't made no social call. They broke in at the back door. Went up to Little Man's room. Threatened to kill me 'less I helped them find one of Ceddy's rocks."

A chill crept up Addie's spine. She suspected which stone they wanted. But why?

"One?" Priscilla's mouth lifted in a smirk. "Out of all he has? How curious. Did they find it?"

Addie knew the answer before Delilah spoke. Unless they had Ceddy, they hadn't located the white rock. She shuddered. Or her pendant.

"They ain't found it, but not for lack of trying. They tore up most every room in the house."

Her eyes wide, Priscilla stared over her shoulder at the mansion. "They ransacked my home? Where are they now?"

"They left once I told them Mr. Pearson mos' likely took Little Man."

Addie's stomach lurched. "Why did you tell them that?"

"I had to, Miss Addie." Her bottom lip trembled. "In all my days, I never been so scared. I jus' wanted them to leave."

Addie smoothed her back. "Don't fret now. In your place, I might've done the same."

Pressing her temples, Priscilla stared at the ground. "None of this makes a lick of sense. I can't keep up anymore. Ceddy's missing. Pearson's gone. Strange men are rummaging through my house. . ." Her frightened eyes begged Addie for answers. "What on earth is happening?"

"Calm yourself, dear lady," Addie said, taking her elbow. "Come inside, and I'll brew you a cup of tea."

Priscilla tensed. "I'm a little afraid."

"It's all right now," Delilah said. "They gone."

"I don't mean them." She sighed. "I'm scared to see the damage they've done."

Addie's fingers tightened on her waist. "We have to go in, Priscilla. Suppose they left behind a clue to finding Ceddy."

She inhaled sharply. "Do you think it's possible?"

"I don't know, but let's go see." Tugging gently, Addie coaxed her into motion.

Breathing harder as they approached the door, Priscilla allowed them to lead her inside.

Along the downstairs hall, drawers were pulled out, curio cabinets emptied. The parlor fared no better. Cushions from the sofa and chairs littered the floor, and a music box from the mantel lay in pieces.

Back in the hall, Priscilla's shoulders relaxed from around her ears. "It's awful, but nothing we can't put to rights."

Her eyes bulging, Delilah shook her head. "You ain't seen Masta Whitfield's den yet. They busted it up pretty bad and stole all his guns."

Priscilla gasped. "They took my brother's weapons?"

"Sho' did. Broke the glass and reached right in. Left nothin' behind but an empty case."

Priscilla moaned, and tears slid down her cheeks.

Delilah waved her hand. "That's nothing. Wait till you see up them stairs."

"Oh Delilah, don't tell me."

She shook her head. "I won't, 'cause I cain't describe it."

Clutching Addie's sleeve, Priscilla stared through the rails of the banister. "I can't bear this, Addie. Go with me, dear."

Addie squeezed her hand. "Reverend Stroud and his search party should be here soon. If he's able to round up men to look for Ceddy, surely he can enlist the women to help us clean up." She rubbed Priscilla's arm. "Just remember. . .the only things irreplaceable are our loved ones."

Priscilla nodded, a wistful glint in her eyes. "You're right, of course. And wise beyond your years."

Addie didn't feel wise. She just felt terrified for Pearson and Ceddy.

Upstairs, she crept over the threshold of Ceddy's room and groaned. Behind her, Priscilla cried aloud.

Ceddy's entire collection lay scattered over the floor in a rainbow jumble of rocks and stones. His bed had been stripped, the mattress slit open and the stuffing pulled out. They had dumped his clothing out of his drawers, smashed and broken his toys to bits. No books remained in the bookcases. They'd been pulled out and tossed aside, their spines cut open and covers ripped off. Ceddy's beloved collection boxes lay splintered and empty.

"Merciful heaven," Priscilla said. "What could be so important in a child's room?"

Her hands at her hips, Addie turned full circle. "It would have to be something quite valuable, wouldn't it?" Her gaze jumping to the broken boxes, she pointed. "Ceddy had a few precious stones in his collection, didn't he? A sapphire, an emerald, and a few others?"

Priscilla nodded. "Yes, but they were very small stones. Surely not worth much." She sighed. "Definitely not worth all this destruction."

Bending to pick up one shattered container, she blinked back tears. "These were far more costly in terms of sentimental value. Ceddy's father made them with his own hands."

Addie squeezed her shoulders. "I'm so sorry."

She lifted her chin. "We'd best go see the damage to the rest of the house."

Addie nodded. "Are you sure you're ready?"

She shook her head. "No, but I suppose we must. It can't be any worse than this."

Still hovering near the door, Delilah grunted. "I wouldn't place no wagers, Miss Priscilla. Them vicious dogs turned desperate by the time they reached your rooms."

Moaning, Priscilla let Addie lead her down the hall.

THIRTY-EIGHT

Pearson pulled the wagon to a stop. Puffing his cheeks, he blew a frustrated breath. "I don't want to push her any more, Theo. She's limping pretty bad."

They sat staring at the horse's twitching ears, as if waiting for her opinion on the matter.

Theo twisted his mouth to gnaw on the side. "The lake is only a mile or so farther. You don't think she'll make it?"

Giving it a few seconds' thought, Pearson shrugged. "We're talking about a horse, partner. If you want to know if the patch in the bottom of a dinghy will hold, I'm your man. But an animal. . ." He gave Theo a sideways glance. "You should know what to do. You have a horse."

Theo's finger shot up. "Papa has a horse. I just borrow him. He gets a limp, I take him home."

Pearson leaned forward to think. "She's been hobbled for a while now. If the extra mile will cripple her, I won't risk it. The liveryman will put her down. You want her death on your conscience?"

Theo held up his hands. "Then what are we supposed to do? If you haven't noticed, we're out in the middle of nowhere."

"I can see that."

"It'll be dark in a couple more hours."

Pearson squinted at the low-riding sun. "I see that, too."

"We need time to set up camp, build a fire, heat some food."

"I agree. Do you have a suggestion?"

"Yes, I say we press on," Theo bellowed, banging his fists on his knees.

Pearson caught his wrist. "Did you hear that?"

Theo's head swung around. "Hear what?"

"A voice."

Theo smiled. "Yes, mine. Echoing off the trees."

Pearson shook his head. "This was close by. Like the moan of a woman or child." Shifting his weight, he gazed behind him, a chill going up his back. "I'm almost positive I—"

Theo nudged him in the side with his elbow.

Irritated, he turned. "What?"

Struck dumb, Theo pointed.

It took Pearson a few seconds to see him.

A man had stepped out of the woods, so wild in appearance he blended with the surroundings. His hair, mostly dark but streaked with strands of gray, curled behind his ears and from under his hat. The beard and mustache he sported appeared dark at the roots but frosted with white. A pair of baggy denim pants covered his legs, and a shirt stitched together from hides draped his torso. He balanced a muzzle-loading shotgun over his shoulder.

It crossed Pearson's mind, a bit late, that they carried no weapons at all. He raised a hand in greeting, boasting a confidence he didn't feel. "Afternoon, sir."

The stranger stood ten feet away, as still as the tree he leaned against, watching them with a lazy smile. His eyes, older than his years, brimmed with wisdom. The warmth in their depths, clearly visible from across the way, eased Pearson's mind. The man glanced toward the west. "I reckon it still qualifies as afternoon. Won't be for long though." He pulled his hat lower and peered at the wall of trees. "You're a fair piece from civilization. If I were you boys, I'd get where you're going. This road will soon be thick with critters you wouldn't want to run into."

Theo cleared his throat. "Such as?"

"Bobcats. Coyotes. Black bear. You might stumble across a red wolf, though I doubt it. Nearly all of them have been killed out." He sniffed. "Sadly, your fellow man might prove the nastiest. It's not unusual to stumble across a no-account up to no good out here."

Pearson's pulse quickened. "You know a lot about the area, then?"

He pursed his lips. "More than most, I'd say."

Staring, Theo lowered his voice. "Um, that couldn't be—"

"Old Saint Nick himself?"

"Or the next best thing," he muttered, chuckling under his breath. "Like I said before, you're the luckiest man in Texas."

Pearson grinned. "And like I said before, I don't deserve it." Climbing down from the rig, he made his way through the underbrush with his hand extended. "Sir, would I happen to be in the company of the infamous Catfish John?"

The man clasped Pearson's hand, a slow smile lifting the corners of his mouth. "I won't bother to ask how you know my name. Sorry I can't offer you the same compliment, mister."

"That's understandable. I'm not legendary."

At this he laughed aloud. "It's a sad day if staying out of the way and minding your own business makes a man a legend." He turned to greet Theo, high-stepping over the tall grass. "Mind my asking where you fellows are from?"

"Galveston, originally," Theo said, "but right now we're staying in Marshall. We were headed up the way to Tow Head, but our horse fell lame."

Interest sparked in his eyes. "Up to Tow Head, huh?"

"Yes, sir."

He cut his eyes to Pearson. "Doing a little fishing, are you?"

Unable to hold his gaze, Pearson looked past his shoulder. "Well, not exactly."

Deep-throated laughter rumbled in John's chest. "As it happens, boys, I have heard of you. You're the two who've been asking about me and the *Mittie Stephens* from here to Marshall and back."

Feeling the warmth of a blush, Pearson nodded. "I was getting to that." He grinned. "We were hoping to ask you some questions."

Shaking his head, he brushed past them. "First let's have a look at your horse. I wasn't joking when I said you need to be on your way before nightfall." Catfish John lifted the horse's foot and placed his palm on the side of the hoof. Three seconds later, he lowered the leg and stood. "You're in luck. You've got a hot nail here, but I don't think it's a direct hit."

Theo shrugged. "What's that mean?"

"When the smithy shod this animal, he drove the nail too close to the quick. If I'm right, this one's not too bad. It's tender, but not likely to get infected."

Pearson braced his hands on his knees and leaned to stare at the hoof. "If you're wrong?"

"Then he's pricked the horse's flesh. This can go bad quick. She'll wind up with an abscess."

"What do we do then?"

"You shoot her—what else?"

At Pearson's stricken look, he chuckled. "You'll have to pull off her shoe. Allow the infection to drain. This kind of injury takes a long time to heal." He patted the horse's rear end, and she gave an answering shiver. "But I don't think it's that bad."

"So she can safely pull us as far as the lake?"

John nodded. "I'd say so."

Standing, Pearson breathed a relieved sigh.

Glancing toward the orange-tinted sky, Catfish John dusted his hands and shifted his gun strap. "I'll let you be on your way. The sooner you're camped in front of a fire, the safer you'll be."

Pearson tried to think fast. "Can we give you a ride somewhere?"

He smiled and pointed at the mare. "You're hardly in a position to ask. Besides, I have a mount tethered a few yards into the woods."

Determined not to let him get away, Pearson cast aside his pride. "Sir, we've been slogging through mud and swamp for weeks now and getting nowhere. I'm pretty certain if we'd found you sooner, you could've saved us a lot of sweat." He grimaced. "I know a man like you must be busy, but—"

Catfish John laughed. "I steer well clear of busywork, son, unless it's something I like to do."

Thinking fast, Pearson smiled. "That makes your time even more valuable, doesn't it? So I hate to ask, but could you spare us a few minutes? We'd sure like to ask some questions."

Chewing the ends of his mustache, Catfish John seemed to stall. "I suppose I should. Maybe once you hear me out, it'll save you more trouble than you think."

Pearson's heart surged. "That's our hope."

"Mine, too, but not for the same reason." He pushed his hat off his forehead. "First, let's get to your campsite and build a fire." Stalking toward the trees, he called over his shoulder, "Going after my horse. Be back directly."

Pearson spun toward Theo, rubbing his palms together. "You hear that, paisan? He'll be back directly." He clapped his cupped hands. "We found Catfish John!"

Theo grinned. "No, he found us. You think he'll really come back?"

"Sure he will. Don't even suggest otherwise." He pointed toward the rig. "Shuffle those boxes around and make yourself a place to sit. We can't ask the famous Catfish John to ride in the wagon bed."

Laughing, Theo hurried to lower the tailgate. Climbing into the bed, he shoved the parcels aside as he worked his way toward the front.

His hands stilled on a crate, and stunned surprise hit his face like a blow. "Whoa! What the. . . ?" Reeling, he fell on his behind, and his head whipped around. "Pearson? You need to see this."

Alarm chilled Pearson's blood. Running for the rig, he held his breath as he peeked over the side.

Ceddy Whitfield lay asleep beneath the seat with both hands curled under his chin. His rounded cheeks were flushed bright pink, and his hair was damp with sweat. He snored quietly, a string of drool from his mouth puddling on the wooden boards.

Tightening his grip until the rail creaked, Pearson gaped at Theo. "I guess you know what this means, paisan. I'm in a world of trouble."

The horrible men had pulled Addie's canvas bag off the top of her wardrobe and upended it on the floor. Grandmother's beads were there, kicked across the room like discarded trash, but the jasper pendant was gone. With all her heart, she prayed Ceddy would have it when they found him. If not, her chances of seeing the treasured pendant again were slim.

With greater fervor, she prayed they'd find him.

Reverend Stroud had come, bringing men to comb the woods. One look at the mess in the house, and he'd left again, returning with two wagonloads of chattering women. They were scattered throughout the mansion—with Priscilla running herself ragged trying to supervise all their activities at once.

Each time she found herself between tasks, she begged the reverend to take her to find Pearson, so she could see for herself if Ceddy was with him. The reverend talked her out of it by reminding her he was only one person. He couldn't stay and conduct a proper search and, at the same time, leave to take her somewhere else. He'd finally appeased her by promising to take her at first light.

Addie knelt beside Ceddy's bed, painstakingly matching shards of wood together like puzzle pieces. The boxes were far from perfect, and the glue would have to dry before he could replace the stones, but at least he wouldn't have to see them broken to bits. Remembering how the slightest change upset him, Addie fought the desire to smash the culprits the way they'd smashed Ceddy's things.

Delilah had helped her sort the rocks the way he kept them, as closely as she remembered at least. Staring at the mounds, Addie wondered how stressful it would be for him, seeing his collection in disarray. Especially when he realized the precious gems were gone. Her shoulders sagged. What sort of man stole from a child? Was any amount of monetary gain worth a single one of his tears?

She considered the missing white stone, Ceddy's favorite. Delilah confirmed that the intruders were looking for one suspiciously similar. Rummaging through the pile, she picked up a white rock, turning it over in her hand. It didn't look to be any different from the one Ceddy favored, the one the men tore Priscilla's house apart trying to find.

It may not look different, but the facts say it most certainly is.

Realization teased the dark corners of her mind. Ceddy placed his gemstones in perfect order on Aaron's breastplate on the Bible page. The only one he hadn't accurately matched was the diamond.

She gasped. Or had he?

Waltzing with the thought, she shook her head. Where would a little boy get a rough diamond of that size?

Struggling to her feet, she stared dumbstruck at the map of South Africa on Ceddy's wall. "Dear heavenly days," she said breathlessly. Clutching her skirt, she streaked from the room and barreled down the stairs, nearly tripping in her haste.

Standing beneath the ceiling fan, both hands filled with salvaged possessions, Priscilla turned at the sound of Addie's footsteps. "Oh my, slow down. It's very dangerous to run on the steps."

Reverend Stroud came toward them from the kitchen as Addie reached her. Panting for breath, Addie gripped Priscilla's shoulders. "I know what those men want—what they tore the house up trying to find."

"Yes, dear. Delilah told us. They were looking for stones from Ceddy's collection."

"Not just any stones. They're after the diamond."

Priscilla gave her an indulgent smile. "What are you saying, Addie? Ceddy didn't have a diamond. Just a few tiny gemstones, gifts from his grandfather. Hardly more than chips, really." She shook her head. "No diamonds."

Addie gripped her shoulders tighter. "What if I told you the large white rock he carried about was an uncut jewel?"

Her eyes flashed with disbelief. "I'd say you have a vivid imagination. You saw the size of it, dear. A gemstone that large would be worth a fortune."

Addie nodded. "Exactly."

The reverend studied Addie's face. "How would Ceddy get his hands on such a thing?" He tilted his head at Priscilla. "Could it have been your brother's?"

"No, Reverend. My brother wasn't the type to let an object of value go to waste."

Believing more in her theory by the second, Addie felt excitement rise in her chest. "I'd like to put forth the possibility that Ceddy brought it with him." She nodded firmly at Reverend Stroud. "When he came from South Africa."

"Nonsense," Priscilla said, though doubt muddied her tone. "If he had, his aunt Jane would've mentioned it."

Swiveling to face her, Addie raised her brows. "Not if she didn't know."

Priscilla opened her mouth to speak, but it froze into a gape. Her troubled gaze darted from Addie to Reverend Stroud. "It all makes perfect sense," she finally said. "That's why Pearson has tormented poor Ceddy. He's after the diamond, too."

Addie's jaw dropped.

Priscilla nodded firmly. "That's why he hurt my boy. . .trying to force information from him."

"Heavens, no. Pearson knew Ceddy kept the rock clutched in his hand most of the time. He even retrieved it that night it rolled across the floor and gave it back. Don't you remember?"

Priscilla's brows dipped in an ugly scowl. "He would in front of us, now, wouldn't he?"

Her heart an anvil in her chest, Addie clutched Priscilla's hands. "You've come to the wrong conclusion again. We're talking about the men who broke into the house today. Whoever they are, they somehow know what Ceddy has."

Addie pointed behind her. "I think the poor dear's out there now, hiding from those ghastly men." She bit her trembling lip. "We're going to find him, and when we do, you'll see that Pearson had nothing to do with his disappearance."

Priscilla fixed her with a cold stare. "Addie, I know how you feel about him. I was rather fond of Pearson myself, but—"

"Oh please," Addie interrupted, "don't speak in the past tense. You must still care about him."

Priscilla's mouth narrowed. "I don't know what those strangers were looking for, but they don't have Ceddy, and he's all that matters. I know in my heart he's with Pearson." Fisting her hands at her waist, she struck a stubborn pose. "Reverend, I need you to take me out there. I won't rest until I see for myself."

Matching her determination, he set his jaw. "Then you'll spend a restless night. I won't take a woman to such rough country after dark. If we haven't found Ceddy before morning, we'll strike out at first light."

Rolling from under the seat, the boy sat up and yawned.

Speechless, Pearson watched in disbelief. One peculiar little fellow had single-handedly ruined the possibility of proving himself to Addie.

Sleepy-eyed, Ceddy wrinkled his nose like he smelled something foul and smacked his lips as if he tasted something worse.

Pearson shook Theo's shoulder. "He's thirsty. Get him some water."

Theo snagged the canteen and shook it. It gave an answering slosh, so he scrambled over and held it out to Ceddy.

The boy stared blankly.

"Here"—Pearson crawled up beside them—"let me try."

He took the flask from Theo and opened the lid. Pulling Ceddy toward him, he cupped his hand under his chin and offered a drink.

Ceddy got a taste and drank heartily.

Wiping the boy's mouth with his shirt, he glanced back at Theo. "He has to be hungry, too. What do we have?"

Theo fumbled inside the crates but came up empty-handed. "All of this needs to be cooked."

Panic crowding his throat, Pearson rummaged in the box closest to him. "There has to be something he can eat. Didn't you get any bread? Or crackers?"

"I have a slab of venison jerky," Catfish John said, startling Pearson half out of his boots. He stood peering over the rail, watching Ceddy. "I didn't know you had a child with you."

"Neither did we," Pearson said grimly. "The little guy's a stowaway."

Humor flashed in John's eyes. "Your plight gets more exciting by the minute."

Pearson groaned. "I can't take much more excitement."

Sliding his shoulder pouch around, the man dug inside and handed a bundle to Theo. "There's enough jerky for all of you. Help yourselves."

Regret weighing his heart, Pearson heaved a sigh. "I'm afraid we'll have to cancel our little inquiry. I have no choice but to get this boy home straightaway."

Catfish John nibbled inside his cheek. "Aren't you forgetting something?" He jerked his thumb at the horse. "She won't make it, and it's a long walk to Marshall."

Pearson sagged against the wagon seat, pulling Ceddy with him. "In the flurry of finding the child, that little detail slipped my mind." He pleaded for good news with his eyes. "How long before she can make the trip?"

He shrugged. "Not more than a couple of days. A week if she's got an abscess."

Pearson's heart plunged. "Sir, the stakes of our plight just rose. I'm afraid my life is about to get very complicated."

John pointed at Ceddy with a grimy finger. "I take it there's a feisty woman somewhere who might be irked at you for this?"

"No, sir," Pearson said with a shudder. "Two feisty women."

"Even more deadly." Doing a poor job of hiding a grin, he climbed into the passenger seat. "I'm starting to be glad I accepted your invitation. I don't want to miss how this turns out."

Ruffling Ceddy's hair, Pearson climbed over the seat and took the reins. "You'd best rethink your position before it's too late."

A mischievous glint in his eye, Catfish John crossed his arms. "Not a chance."

Pearson urged the poor little mare onto the road at a slow, careful pace. Peering behind him, he couldn't resist a smile.

Theo and Ceddy sat like braves at a powwow, their peace pipes long strips of dried venison.

As they rode, Catfish John volunteered a lesson on the origins of Caddo Lake. "Legend has it she was fashioned by the New Madrid Earthquake of 1812. I reckon it could be true, since Reelfoot Lake in

Tennessee was formed the same way. Some folks disagree, but either way, the Great Raft caused an influx of water that filled the existing basin."

"The Great Raft?"

"A log jam creating a natural dam on the Red River, at least a hundred miles long before they busted it up in 1873."

Theo piped up from the rear. "Excuse me, sir. Do I call you Catfish, John, or Mr. John?"

Catfish John chuckled. "Plain old John will do."

"Well John, we've found plants out here that we've never seen before. I'd bet you can tell us the name of those bothersome weeds covering the lake bottom."

"Sounds like you've run into some coontail moss."

Theo grunted. "You could say so. Over time, we've hauled up enough with our drag to cover Texas."

John laughed. "I expect you've snagged your share of yonqupin, too. They're the lilies."

Theo rolled his eyes. "Oh yes, sir."

"What are the tiny, floating plants?" Pearson asked. "Like bright green lentils with stems?"

"Sounds like duckweed," John said.

"Duckweed," Pearson repeated. "Sticks to a fellow. I've come up wearing it like a shroud."

John nodded. "Gators do as well. They lurk in duckweed to get a jump on their prey."

Pearson grimaced. "We found that out the hard way."

Slapping his leg, John hooted with laughter. "So you've come up close and personal with Caddo's nastiest citizen?" Leaning away from Pearson, he seemed to take inventory. "I'm impressed with you fellows. It's been weeks since you started sniffing around for information. I figured you'd be long gone like the rest." He patted Pearson's back. "You have grit, I can say that much."

Pearson angled his head. "So you knew we were looking for you?"

John lowered his chin, mischief glinting in his eyes. "Let's say I had an inkling."

Theo leaned between them. "But we left word all over the docks stating exactly where we'd be." By the end of the sentence, his voice had risen to a soprano.

Pearson shoved him back with his elbow. "You'll have to excuse my friend. He gets as wound up as an old woman sometimes."

Looking ashamed, John twisted on the seat. "Sorry, fellas. If I got excited about every greenhorn treasure seeker who came asking about the *Mittie*, I'd spend all my time holding their hands. The truth is, you ain't the first to come looking for her, and I doubt you'll be the last."

Staring directly into his eyes, Pearson shrugged. "That may not be true since we're the most determined."

John seemed to weigh his words. "Well, son. . .that's good news and bad, considering."

"How is it bad?"

He held up his hand. "We'll save that conversation for later. The thing is, I trust you mean what you said." Shifting his pack around, he pulled out a drawstring pouch. "I think folks around here might've taken you boys too lightly. I'm starting to believe you would've found the *Mittie* by now"—tapping tobacco into a square of paper, he lifted twinkling eyes—"if you'd been looking in the right place."

FORTY

Addie hardly slept. Her disquieted spirit magnified every sound in the creaky old house tenfold, and she spent the better part of the night praying for Ceddy's safe return.

The few minutes she dozed were fraught with restless dreams. Only once, in the pitch darkness of the wee hours, did traitorous musings of Pearson's guilt invade her loyalty. With a thudding heart and quickening breath, she'd shoved them away.

She almost preferred the thought of Pearson having Ceddy. It seemed far less frightening than the boy wandering somewhere lost and alone. Yet that would make Priscilla's hunch right, and the repercussions were unthinkable.

A single memory of Pearson's russet eyes awash with grief was all it took to renew her faith. A man couldn't suffer such pain and then inflict it on another. Unlike Priscilla, Addie had gained entry into Pearson's beautiful soul. She bore personal testimony of his goodness, only no one cared to listen.

Her mind returned to Ceddy. For just a moment, she imagined him in his bed, curled beneath his special quilt, as bright and colorful as his rocks. Remembering the mattress tossed aside, its innards exposed, the quilt ripped into jagged pieces, Addie's heart broke.

Ugliness lurked behind such evil acts, something more sinister than thievery, as if the person responsible bore malice against the objects themselves. Or jealousy of Ceddy for having them.

A light rapping on the door startled her from her thoughts. Sitting upright, she pulled the covers up to her chin. "Who's there?"

"Jus' me, Miss Addie."

"It's all right, Delilah. Come in."

She peeked in, the lantern in her hand unable to light the deep shadows under her eyes.

Addie sighed. "I see you slept no better than me."

"Yes'm." Tiptoeing across the threshold, Delilah hurried to the window and pulled back the curtains. With only darkness outside, it did little good. "I mean, no, ma'am. I ain't slept worth spit for worrying about Little Man."

Addie let the covers slide and stretched her fingertips toward the ceiling. "Is it time to get up already? It feels like the middle of the night."

She nodded. "Miss Priscilla say if you insist on going, you best be dressed and downstairs lickety-split. She ain't gon' wait on you." She opened Addie's wardrobe and pulled out her plainest dress. "I believe her, too. She say she ready to go, and she ain't even hungry." Turning from shaking out the frock, she stared with bulging eyes. "Can you believe it?"

Addie couldn't, but it wouldn't be nice to say so.

When she imagined the pain driving the poor woman, her stomach lurched. "Oh Delilah. I'd pay dearly to go back in time to a few days ago. We were all so happy then."

Delilah shook her finger. "No, Miss Addie. Don't wish away time, not forward or back. God got every second planned, and we shouldn't go to meddling."

Tilting her head, Addie watched her face. "Every second? You really think so?"

She nodded firmly. "I know so."

Addie longed for such childlike faith. Unfortunately, her personality tended toward the meddling side. She swung her legs off the bed and felt for her slippers. "So you don't think He needs our help occasionally? To make things turn out all right?"

Delilah's eyes grew wide. "Go ask Abraham and Sarah. I s'pose if they had a do-over, they'd leave the 'turnin' out right' up to God."

Addie considered the story of Abraham, the biblical patriarch, and

Sarah, his wife. Instead of waiting for God to send them a promised son, they took matters into their own hands and arranged for another woman to bear a child with Abraham. Their efforts brought about disastrous results.

Probing with her toes for her house shoes again, Addie heard Mother's voice in her head. *"The ways of God are wonderful. . . . His generous heart unsearchable. . . . Keep watch at all times, and allow Him to orchestrate your destiny."*

It seemed simple. Trust in His goodness, watch for His hand in the affairs of her life, and then get out of His way.

Delilah swept Addie's slippers aside with her foot. "You don't need those. I'll fetch your stockings then help you with your frock and your outside shoes. Miss Priscilla gon' be stomping up them stairs any second hollering for you to hurry."

Delilah's prediction came true. Before she could help Addie fasten her dress, Priscilla blew through the door barking orders and clucking her tongue. "Not a dress, for pity's sake. Wear riding breeches at least."

"But we're traveling by wagon," Addie protested.

She pointed at her own split skirt. "We must be nimble and unfettered. No telling what we'll encounter out there."

By the time Addie selected and put on the appropriate attire, Priscilla was outside in Reverend Stroud's wagon. Delilah had just enough time to hand her a basket as she spun out the door. Carrying the food to the rig in the same basket from which she'd shared a picnic with Pearson, Addie felt her heart squeeze. She missed him desperately.

What would happen once they found him? Addie would be ever so glad to see him, but how would Priscilla react to finding her theory was wrong? Addie felt certain she clung to the notion out of desperation. After all, if Pearson didn't have Ceddy, who did?

"It's about time," Priscilla called as Addie hurried down the front steps.

Handing up the basket, she climbed into the backseat with a grimace. "I came as fast as I could, considering I dressed myself twice."

"Good morning, Addie," the reverend said.

"Morning, sir."

Priscilla patted his arm. "There's no time for social graces, Abner Stroud."

He cast a startled glance. "It's not like you to address me by my first name, Priscilla."

"Forgive me, but I'm a little distraught. You've kept me waiting hours too long to go to Ceddy's rescue, and there are still hours ahead of us." Her hand fluttered in the air. "Now please. . .carry on."

The reverend flicked the reins and started the horse in motion. Unable to contain the question, Addie leaned to tug her sleeve. "What will we do if Pearson doesn't have him?"

With a frantic shake of her head, Priscilla stared off into the woods. "That won't happen. It mustn't," she continued, her voice breaking.

Reverend Stroud slid his hand down her forearm and squeezed her white-knuckled fist. "We'll find him, dear lady."

She twisted to face him, her eyes pleading.

"The men are tirelessly searching. They've vowed to continue until young Ceddy is safely back in your arms."

Addie raised her hankie to muffle a sob as silent tears slid down Priscilla's delicate cheeks.

Pearson's eyes flew wide. As he stared at the cloudless morning sky, his mind scrambled for the answer to what had startled him awake. A gentle, sighing breath against his ear jerked his head around to the heart-jarring answer.

Ceddy lay asleep on Pearson's shoulder, one skinny arm across his chest. Smiling, Pearson cradled the boy's head with his palm, the thin blond hair the softest thing he'd ever touched.

The little fellow had definitely taken a shine to Pearson. Highly inconvenient in their present circumstances, but the fact surprised and pleased him.

Easing the boy to the blanketed wagon bed, he glanced at Theo gently snoring next to them, one gangly arm thrown over his eyes.

They'd offered to make room for John, but he'd pulled a bedroll out of his pack and spread it on a high spot, carefully winding a coil of rope around the edges.

"Why the rope?" Pearson had asked.

"Snake won't cross it," John explained.

The bedding still lay on the ground, but the man was gone. Pushing to his feet, Pearson scanned the horizon but saw no sign of him.

Theo sat up squinting. "Heard him rustling around before daybreak.

Figured he was leaving."

Climbing down from the buckboard, Pearson shook his head. "Not unless he left everything behind." Staring toward the water, he shrugged. "Maybe he's gone fishing."

"Good guess," Theo said, pointing with his chin. "Considering one of the boats is gone."

Pearson propped his hands on his hips. "Go find wood to stoke this fire. I'll get started on breakfast." He blew a frustrated breath. "John likely figures us for greenhorns. We've slept half the day away."

Ceddy slumbered right through the brewing of coffee and the sizzle of bacon and eggs—surprising since he'd napped so long the day before while tucked under the buckboard seat. The minute he awoke, he came to sit at Pearson's feet, scratching in the dirt for rocks and pebbles. Stretching his fingers, he wiggled them toward Pearson's coffee cup.

Drawing it away, Pearson shook his head. "Sorry, old man. None of this for you."

"I know just the thing." Theo pushed to his feet and hurried over to rummage in their supplies. Returning with a pot filled with sloshing liquid, he set it over the fire and stirred it with a metal spoon.

"What's that?" Pearson asked.

"Powdered milk, sugar, and chocolate mixed in water." Theo smiled into the swirling cup. "This way, he can have his own brand of coffee."

Testing the warmth with his finger, he poured out a cup for Ceddy. "There you go, big fella. See how you like it."

Ceddy took the cup and lowered his face, smelling first. Smiling with pleasure, he took a taste then several big gulps.

"I think your concoction is a hit, paisan," Pearson said.

Theo beamed. "Who doesn't like sugar and chocolate?"

Resting his back against a log, Pearson reflected on his conversation with John the night before. The man so skillfully avoided explaining his disturbing comment, Pearson might've thought he misunderstood. Except he knew he didn't.

Lucky for John, the outrageous remark went right over Theo's head. Had he heard John say they weren't dragging the right spot for the *Mittie*, the man would've gotten no rest from the relentless Italian.

If John really thought they were searching the wrong place, he didn't care to repeat it. He steered the conversation to their surroundings instead, seeming to relish the role of schoolmaster.

"The allure to Caddo is its mystery and beauty," he'd said, his eyes glowing with pride. He pointed out the trees as they neared the lake, some Pearson knew and some he didn't, calling their names like beloved children. "Those right there are water oak. The ones next to them are red oak, and the tall pine there is loblolly. We have pin oak, sweet gum, and river birch. Those on the water with sprawling trunks are red cypress."

Pearson learned the names of the fish they'd become acquainted with over the weeks—flathead catfish, blue catfish, channel cat, spotted bass, white perch, bream, and paddlefish.

John explained that the eggs of the paddlefish were sold up north for caviar. He said the massive creature that surfaced close to the boat, frightening Theo out of his wits, was likely an alligator gar, a type of fish that grew in excess of six feet.

Ceddy moaned, pulling Pearson from his thoughts.

He patted the boy's shoulder. "What's wrong, partner?"

Wincing, he groaned and clutched his stomach.

Concerned, Pearson pushed to his knees and bent over him, pressing his palm to his forehead. "Are you sick? You don't feel feverish." He met Theo's eyes across the campfire. "What's ailing him?"

Theo shot to his knees, shaking his head.

Writhing now, the distraught boy wailed as if in pain.

Comforting Ceddy the best he could, Pearson struggled to hold him still lest he hurt himself.

From out of nowhere, a wagon rattled into the clearing.

Pearson glanced up to see Priscilla Whitfield barreling toward them, a jagged stick in her hand. "Get away from him," she screeched, swinging with all her might.

Pearson sprawled backward, pulling Ceddy with him to protect him from the flailing stick. Twisting around, he shot to his feet, clutching the screaming boy.

Addie hunkered ten feet away, her pretty features limp with shock.

Addie squatted on the ground, her legs too weak to hold her. Her eyes met Pearson's across the distance, his filled with deep regret. The unthinkable had happened, despite her faith in him. Her glimpse into his soul had been a lie.

Priscilla saw Pearson for what he was. He'd used Addie's lack of experience to reel her in. Despite Delilah's admonishment against meddling in matters of time, she wished with all her heart to roll the clock back to the day she'd lost her heart to him. How had she been so blind?

"Addie?"

His mellow voice sought to work its magic, but Addie shot to her feet, shaking her head to escape his spell. "Give Ceddy to Priscilla this instant."

"Addie, please. . ."

"Let him go so his aunt can comfort him."

Pearson glanced at the sobbing boy as if he'd forgotten he held him. Placing him on the ground, he patted his back. "Go to your aunt Priscilla, Ceddy." He nudged him forward. "Go on, now."

Clutching his middle, Ceddy stumbled into Priscilla's skirts. Dropping to her knees, she gathered him close. "Oh darling, are you all right? Auntie was sick with worry."

Reverend Stroud came to stand behind Priscilla, one hand at her back.

Pearson's tortured gaze leaped to him. "Reverend, I know how this looks, but if you'll just listen, I can explain."

The reverend nodded at Ceddy. "The child being out here with you is all the explanation we need." His shoulders slumped. "I wanted to believe in you, son. I tried my best."

Holding his hands out to his sides, Pearson pleaded with his eyes. "I give you my word. I wouldn't lay a harsh hand on that boy."

Struggling to her feet, Priscilla guided Ceddy behind her. "You're lying," she shrieked. "Look at him—he's crying. What sort of evil man would harm a boy like my Ceddy?"

"Miss Whitfield, he didn't—"

She whirled. "Hush, Theo Bernardi. You're no better."

Howling, Ceddy rocked back and forth, his hands over his ears.

"You are a worthless, conniving weasel, Pearson Foster," she spat, her tone even louder. "Worming your way into decent people's lives, simply for gain. Your unbridled greed sickens me."

Ceddy stamped both feet and cried harder.

Taking his shoulder, Priscilla urged him toward Addie. "Take him, please, while I deal with these scoundrels."

Jerking away, Ceddy shot around Priscilla and rushed to Pearson, wrapping his arms around his waist.

Forced off balance, Pearson backed into the log and dropped to his rear. As if by instinct, he cradled Ceddy, drawing him under his arm. "It's all right, buddy," he cooed. "Don't cry. Everything will be fine. You'll see."

Snuggling closer, Ceddy pressed his cheek to Pearson's side.

The clearing froze to a haunting lithograph, the silver edges shimmering through Addie's tears.

Pricilla spun to stare at her, trembling hands clutching her mouth. Her eyes, visible above her fingertips, were wide with shock.

Pearson pulled his tender gaze from Ceddy and searched Addie's face.

She turned aside, unable to look at him. In his darkest hour, her fiercest trial, she'd failed them both.

"And there he was," Pearson said, squeezing Ceddy's thin shoulders. "Curled under the seat fast asleep without a care in the world." He raised his brows. "And he never made a sound the whole time."

Pearson sat around the fire with the others, brewing a fresh pot of coffee and relaying the story.

Priscilla, her eyes red from crying, stared in a daze at the flames. "Yes, he does that," she said vaguely. "He can lie for hours counting cracks in the floor."

"Anyway. . ." Pearson grinned. "I aged ten years when I saw him."

Reverend Stroud shook his head repeatedly and mumbled under his breath, reaching often to give his back a gentle pat.

Addie had perched on the log beside Theo, looking everywhere but at Pearson.

Ceddy played quietly in the dirt, making soft grunting sounds occasionally as if in pain.

Knowing Addie didn't drink coffee, Theo warmed a cup of his chocolate drink and placed it in her hands.

She glanced up. "What's this?"

He smiled. "Just taste."

She took a sip and gave an appreciative nod, but then a startled look crossed her face. "Is there milk in here?"

He nodded. "Made from powder."

Her long lashes fluttered, and her gaze snapped to Ceddy. "Did he have any?"

"I made it special for him."

She and Priscilla shared a meaningful look.

"He can't tolerate milk," Addie said. "It gives him a terrible stomachache."

Understanding flashed across Theo's face, and he blushed. "I'm sorry. I didn't know."

Pearson nodded. "That explains why he was crying."

Priscilla leaned toward Pearson and stretched out her hand. "Oh Pearson, please say you forgive me. I won't rest until I have your pardon."

Clutching her fingers, he gazed into her eyes. "I don't blame you, ma'am." Smoothing Ceddy's blond head, he smiled. "I'd react the same if my child was threatened."

Tears tracked down her cheeks. "I promise never to doubt you again."

"I hope you mean it." Pearson sighed, the pain of betrayal still fresh. "I'd do anything to keep your trust." He flicked his gaze to Addie, but she ducked her head.

Reverend Stroud placed his big hand over Pearson's and gave a firm shake. "I wish you could see into my repentant heart, son. I'm racked with grief over misjudging you."

"I won't say it didn't hurt, sir. Especially coming from you. But all I want now is a fresh start for everyone."

The reverend nodded. "It's far more than we deserve."

Watching Addie, Pearson felt a deep ache in his heart. Obviously suffering, she wouldn't forgive herself long enough to seek his forgiveness. He bore her silence for as long as he could. Proper or not, he was going to take her out of the others' hearing and settle things between them.

Gripping the log, he poised to stand. "Addie. . ."

She jumped like she'd been jabbed then raised her head. Before he could invite her on a walk, her attention shifted to something over his shoulder, alarm written all over her face.

Pearson turned.

The missing rowboat skimmed across the water, breezing toward shore. John, a stringer of fish in his hand, leaped to the bank and idly wrapped the towrope around a bush.

"It's all right," Pearson said, his hand going up. "It's only Catfish John."

Reverend Stroud whipped around. "Catfish John? You don't say!"

John glanced toward the newcomers and slowed his pace. Scanning the gathering, a big smile broke out on his face. "The feisty women you dreaded, I take it?"

Pearson grinned. "None other."

"I see they let you live. Have you been granted a pardon?"

"Yes, thankfully." He motioned toward the women. "Allow me to present Miss Priscilla Whitfield, Miss Addie McRae, and Reverend Abner Stroud."

John nodded. "Forgive me for not offering my hand." He glanced at the fish. "You wouldn't thank me."

Theo swung around the log and took the stringer from him. "I'll clean these for you."

John handed them over. "Thank you, young man. I hoped somebody would offer. I like catching fish. I just don't like cleaning them."

Pearson motioned for him to take a seat. "Let me pour you a cup of coffee. I know you must be hungry, too. We saved you bacon, eggs, and biscuits."

He accepted Pearson's offering with a hearty nod then squatted in front of the fire to eat.

Lifting her chin, Priscilla stared longingly at the skillet of leftovers. "I wouldn't mind having a plate, if there's enough."

"Of course, ma'am. Forgive my bad manners." He filled three plates and passed them to Priscilla, the reverend, and Addie.

She took one but didn't seem to find the food very appetizing.

"How did you find him, son?" the awestruck reverend asked, pointing at John.

Pearson blushed. "With my matchless tracking skills and bloodhound nose."

John grunted, and the reverend angled his head.

"All right then. He found us about a mile up the road, floundering like fish out of water. We had a lame horse and not a lick of common sense between us to decide what to do. John showed up and rescued us."

"Happens a lot out here," John said around a big bite. "More than you'd think."

Unable to contain his excitement, the reverend scooted to the edge of his seat. "Well, have you asked him all your questions? Is he going to help you find the *Mittie*?"

Pearson shifted his gaze to John, who seemed suddenly quite engrossed in his dish. "I've asked him a few things, but he's not been especially obliging. I suspect he's determined to avoid helping as much as possible."

Silence fell over the gathering.

Regret danced with irritation on John's face. "I'll only say this much because I've taken a shine to you, son. You haven't found her because you're searching miles from the actual site."

"What?" Theo rose from the water's edge and stormed toward them. "This is where the locals told us to look."

John sighed and set down his plate. "The fact is the history of Caddo wasn't chronicled very well, and most of the facts have been overblown for years. Some of the old-timers were masters at spinning a yarn, and now we're never sure what's completely true. That's why most tales and legends begin with 'It was once said,' 'The story I was told,' or 'As far as I know,' and so forth."

"So nobody really knows where she is?"

John puckered his mouth. "I wouldn't say that. But with limited information, it would be hard to nail down her location. And those who know aren't willing to tell."

"Why not?" several voices asked at once.

He smiled. "Unspoken agreement around the Caddo. To protect the site."

Reverend Stroud frowned and nibbled his bottom lip. "Why's that, John?"

Priscilla set down her cup. "Well, it's obvious, isn't it? Why should he reveal his leads to a possible fortune?"

John's head shot up. "Not so, dear lady. I'm afraid you've missed the mark."

Pearson offered to refill his cup. "Do you mind telling us why, then?"

Theo's ears turned bright red. "No matter the reason, it's not right. If they're not interested in raising her, they shouldn't stand in the way of those who are."

"Shouldn't they?" John asked, his voice hushed. "Sixty-one people died that night. When the fire aboard couldn't be put out, the captain gave the order to head for shore, but she grounded in shallow water. The forward part of the *Mittie* was in flames, the stern over deep water. Desperate, the pilot and engineer continued pushing for land. Unfortunately, this action dragged those who dove to safety into the turning wheels, crushing and drowning them."

Not a sniff, sigh, or shuffle of feet broke the silence that settled over the campfire.

Priscilla's cheeks held an unswallowed bite, and her fork stilled over her plate. "How utterly grim," she finally said, breaking the stillness. "And tragic. I never heard that account before."

"For most of them," John continued, "that site is their final resting place. People here feel that raising the *Mittie* is akin to robbing a grave."

An unexpected dagger of pain laced Pearson's heart. The storm that claimed his family's lives had also stolen his chance to stand over their grave sites and grieve their passing.

Before he accepted their terrible fate, he'd combed the island for weeks with other mourners, searching frantically for them. The rush of water that collapsed the wall of his house had carried their bodies out to sea. The most precious treasure he'd ever sought had slipped through his fingers forever. How would he feel if treasure seekers were to comb through their belongings in search of gold? He took a ragged breath and vowed to search for the *Mittie Stephens* no more.

Laying aside his dish, John stood. "I've enjoyed your company for too long now. I'd best be on my way."

Pearson stood with him. "Finish cleaning his fish, Theo, while I saddle his horse."

With a creel of skinned catfish and a bundle of bacon and biscuits tucked into his saddlebag, John prepared to take his leave.

Pearson offered his hand. "I can't thank you enough."

"Wasn't much. Just a little advice on a horse."

"Not that," Pearson said. "Thank you for setting me straight about the *Mittie*."

John grinned. "I hated to in a way. You seemed so determined."

Pearson hung his head. "Men who seek treasure can be a mulish lot." He shrugged. "I suppose we have to be. If not for you, I might've gone on dragging this spot forever."

John raised one brow. "Will you keep looking?"

Shaking his head, Pearson crossed his heart. "After the story you told? No, sir." He raised his right hand. "I give you my solemn word."

John gave his back a hearty pounding. "I'm glad to hear it. You just might've been the one to succeed." Swinging into the saddle, he took up the reins.

Pearson caught the horse's bridle. "You said we were looking miles away from the actual site. That means you know where she is."

He gazed fiercely into Pearson's eyes. "I have your word, then?"

"I said it, didn't I?"

John nodded. "The *Mittie* went down in Buzzard Bay on the southeast side, about two and a half miles from Swanson's Landing."

The name dashed cold water down Pearson's back. What had the old sailor in Rosie's Café said?

"At the midnight hour, just below Swanson's Landing, a steersman alerted the pilot that he'd caught a whiff of smoke."

Blast! He'd had the answer all along, but he'd barreled ahead of himself, too cocky and headstrong to slow down and remember. Some treasure hunter he was! Smiling at himself, he released John's horse and stepped back. "I suppose some things aren't meant to be."

Pushing back his cap, Catfish John saluted and rode away.

Swiveling on the ball of his foot, Pearson started toward camp. "But then, some things are." He strode purposefully to Addie and hauled her to her feet. "Come with me. We need to talk."

She took a quick breath but didn't resist.

Pearson glanced at Priscilla. "I trust you'll allow me to speak with Addie alone for a few minutes?"

"Of course. If Addie doesn't mind, that is."

"She doesn't," he said, pulling her away from the clearing.

They walked several yards down the road that led to Marshall.

Addie plodded in silence, her arms crossed at her chest.

Out of earshot of the rest, Pearson caught her shoulders and eased her around. "We're not walking to the gallows, you know."

She ducked her head and lifted one shoulder.

"Aren't you going to talk to me?"

"There are many things I want to tell you, Pearson. I just can't find the words."

He touched her rosy cheek. "Then don't say anything. It's not necessary."

She wagged her head. "I've utterly failed you. As a confidant, a friend—"

"Don't say that, honey."

"It's true. You're the one who shouldn't speak to me. I made you prove yourself over and over, yet it was never enough." She covered her face. "I'm so ashamed."

Shifting his weight, Pearson watched her and waited.

"I won't blame you if you never talk to me again," she continued. "In fact, I can't imagine why you've bothered now. I'm not worth your time."

He crossed his arms and rocked on his heels.

"If it makes you feel better, I had perfect faith in you all along." She sighed and buried her face deeper into her hands. "Until the moment I saw you with Ceddy."

Pearson stood quietly for so long, Addie peeked between her fingers. "Well? Aren't you going to respond?"

"When you're finished."

She blinked at him and lowered her hands. "With what?"

He waved. "Your apology. You see, men just blurt it out. Two little words and we're done. Females take the long way around." He chuckled. "We wind up at the same place; it just takes you women longer." Catching her hands, he pulled her to his chest and kissed the tip of her nose. "Let me know when you're through, so I can get on with forgiving."

Addie leaned into him, the smell of her hair intoxicating. "Oh Pearson, don't tease. This is serious."

He leaned to peer closely at her. "I'm completely serious. I need all the bad feelings between us gone, so we can finish our unfinished conversation."

Her breath caught. "Which one would that be?"

She knew exactly, but he wouldn't call her on it. He chucked her under the chin and grinned. "The one in the parlor. About living on an island."

"Oh yes." She sounded out of breath. "I remember now."

Pulling her hands to his mouth, he kissed her fingers. "I'd like to have your answer now, if you don't have anything else to do."

She pouted her lips. "First, kindly answer the question I asked you."

"Which was?"

"Why do you want to know?"

He released her hands and cupped her face. "Because I think it's time I went home." He trailed kisses along her chin. "And I want you to come with me."

Her eyelids drifted closed as she surrendered to his searching lips. "Is this an improper advance, sir?"

He shook his head. "There you go, falsely accusing me again." Her eyes flashed open, and he grinned. "This is a very proper advance, Miss McRae. I'm asking you to retire your last name and become Adelina Viola Foster of Galveston, Texas."

Her arms circled his neck and she pulled him close. "And my answer is yes."

FORTY-TWO

Ceddy rose from his place by the fire and wandered toward the wagon, drawn by the pattern of the wheels.

"Where are you going, darling?" Aunt Priss called. "Stay close, you hear?"

Ignoring her, he crawled into the shadowy space underneath, running his hands along the loop of wood. He counted the spokes as he went—one, two, three, four, all the way around until he reached fourteen.

Finished, Ceddy scooted to the next and then the next, tracing the circles as he went.

With all four wheels accounted for, he sprawled on his side under the wagon. In a daze, he stared toward the flickering campfire, spellbound by the pie-shaped pictures created by the spokes.

The drone of voices in the background soothed him. His eyelids fluttered, but he struggled hard against sleep.

"Here they are now," Priscilla said as Addie and Pearson rejoined them at the fire.

Addie's cheeks warmed, certain the others would take one look at her and guess she'd just received her first kiss, her first and only proposal.

They'd decided to keep the news a secret until they returned home.

Then they'd tell Priscilla and ask her to place a call to Addie's parents so Pearson could ask permission.

Pearson sat on the fallen log and patted the spot next to him. Blushing deeper, Addie sank down beside him.

"We were just about to tell Theo the news," Reverend Stroud said. "Now you can hear, too." He launched into the story of the break-in, how two men behaving like savages had threatened Delilah and tore the house apart. "I hate to tell you, son, but they were your friends, Denny and Charlie."

Pearson glanced at Theo. "They're no friends of ours, Reverend. Just hired hands. If you remember, we didn't trust them from the start."

"Yes." He nodded. "And Theo's premise that the criminal activity in town can be blamed on them is most likely correct."

"Thank you!" Theo said, slapping his leg.

"I'm sorry, Miss Whitfield," Pearson said. "If I hadn't hired them, maybe they'd be long gone by now. I hope they didn't take anything you treasure."

"It's not your fault, dear boy." She beamed over her shoulder at Ceddy. "In fact, God placed my greatest treasure in your hands for safekeeping." She winced. "I only wish He had advised me of the plan."

Addie gripped Pearson's arm. "They wouldn't have left if you hadn't hired them. Not without the one thing that brought them to Marshall."

Pearson frowned.

"The rogues stole a few tiny stones from Ceddy's collection. Oh, and some weapons—"

Pearson grimaced. "I hate to think of them with weapons in their hands."

"However, I think I know what they were after, what they chased Ceddy across the ocean for." Her face flushed red with excitement. "Only they came up empty because Ceddy has it with him."

Pearson peered across the clearing at the boy. "He doesn't have anything that I know of."

"If you check his pockets, I believe you'll find two very interesting stones. One is a jasper pendant that belongs to me. The other is a very large diamond."

Theo coughed, choking on his chocolate drink. "How could Ceddy have something that valuable that we've never seen?"

"We have." She gave Pearson a teasing look. "In fact, our treasure hunter held the diamond in his hands."

Staring blankly, Pearson scratched his head. "I'm sure that's something I'd remember."

She nudged him with her elbow. "It's that unsightly white rock he favors. Unless I'm mistaken, it's an uncut diamond."

Pearson looked skeptical. "If it's true, where did it come from?"

"Allow me to answer," Reverend Stroud said. "Before he came to live with Priscilla, Ceddy was a resident of South Africa. His parents were missionaries in a village near Pretoria." He lowered one brow. "Are you familiar with the diamond mines of South Africa, son?"

Interest sparking his eyes, Pearson nodded. "I know the Cullinan region. The largest rough diamond ever found was discovered there."

The reverend nodded. "Exactly."

Pearson searched out Ceddy under the buckboard and stared. "So you think he. . ."

"Would you recognize it for a gemstone, now that you know what you're looking for?" Priscilla asked.

"Yes, ma'am," Pearson said. "I'd like to think so."

"Let's find out." She twisted around to the wagon. "Oh Ceddy! Come here, please. Come to Auntie, darling."

Ceddy batted his heavy lids, fighting to keep them open. His name echoed in his ears, and he wanted it to stop. Moaning, he raised his head and searched through the slices of pie for the source of the noise.

Gasping, he snapped his eyes open. Sleepy no more, he felt fear churning in his tummy. Blinking fast, he looked through a different slice, hoping the picture would change. Panting, whining, choking, he scooted out the back of the wagon and crawled like a crab to the bank.

Hide! Need to hide!

His legs tangled with a length of rope on the ground. Clenching his mouth against a scream, he kicked his way free. Reaching the rowboat, he scrambled inside and ducked behind the seat.

His skin tingled. His chest ached. The hairs on his head prickled. He longed to peek, to see if they were coming, but didn't dare. Turning on his back, he lay very still in the rocking boat and watched an osprey soar.

"That's right, mum," Denny said, striding out of the woods. "Call the wormy little blighter out of hiding and save us the trouble."

The old lady's head whipped around so fast she nearly lost her teeth. Crying out, she latched onto the reverend.

Pearson leaped from the log and turned, easing the pretty little governess behind his back.

Theo, Pearson's mop-headed puppet, pushed himself off the ground. Both gents' eyes followed the pistol in Denny's hand.

Denny beamed. It felt good to have one up on them for a change. "Sorry we're late to the party. We'd have been 'ere sooner, but we ran into a little trouble in town. Seems our landlord don't appreciate the way we settle our accounts." He nodded at Miss Whitfield. "But he bartered for some of the items you so generously donated, missus, and was pleased to call off the sheriff once we offered them in trade."

She glared. "You devil. How dare you steal from me!"

Denny pointed at his chest. "How dare I?" He nodded at Charlie and laughed. "It was easy, weren't it, Charlie?"

Laughing, Charlie wobbled his direction, his shotgun waving wildly.

"Be careful, will ya?" Denny shouted, shoving the barrel aside. "Watch what you're doing."

"Sorry, Den. I ain't used to it yet."

Denny scowled. "Don't expect to be. I'm taking that thing away as soon as we sort this out." He faced his captive audience. "Speaking of which, I'd like to get the ball rolling, if you don't mind. Now where's the boy?"

"He's not here," Pearson said.

"Go on, don't take me for a mug. I heard the old cow calling him."

Miss Whitfield stood, defiance in her eyes. "You're going to leave my nephew alone. Do you hear me?"

Denny laughed. "Feisty, ain't she?" He pointed past her with the nose of his gun. "She was facing the wagon when she called for the brat, Charlie. Go take a gander."

The old girl balled her fists, her eyes wild. "Don't you go over there!"

Denny hooted. "I think we're onto something." He shoved Charlie's shoulder. "Don't listen to her. Just do like I say. Now go on."

Watching her carefully, Charlie lumbered past.

The little governess paled.

The old woman started to cry.

Pearson held up his hand. "Can't we talk about this, Denny? You seem to be a decent person at heart."

"No, he's not," the governess spat. "He's a no-account thief who's envious of Ceddy." She challenged Denny with her eyes. "Isn't that so, Mr. Currie? You're petty and small-minded enough to be jealous of a lovely little boy?"

He aimed the pistol. "Shut it, missy."

Pearson tucked her behind him again. "Hold on there, Denny. You don't want to add murder to your sins. Why not put that thing away before there's an accident?"

"Please don't hurt my Ceddy," Miss Whitfield called to Charlie.

Charlie looked inside the wagon bed, under the seat, and beneath the rig. He circled it once then came back scratching his head. "He ain't 'ere, Den."

Panic shot up Denny's throat. "Sure he is. He 'as to be." His fingers tightened around the pistol. That barmy nipper wouldn't do him over again or he'd wind up a nutter himself.

The four standing in the clearing passed worried glances.

Furious, Denny squared around to Charlie. "I ain't 'ardly in the mood for this, mate. We rode all night, and I've missed me kip. Don't make me come look for meself."

Charlie pointed behind him. "Look all you want. He ain't there."

Miss Whitfield skirted the log and took a few staggering steps toward the buckboard. "Then where. . . ?" Clutching her throat, she screamed, her howls echoing off the trees.

Risking Denny's pistol, Pearson ran to her. "Priscilla, what's wrong?"

She pointed a trembling finger at the bobbing rowboat, floating forty yards out on the lake.

He gripped her arm. "Ceddy?"

A gulping sob escaped, and she nodded.

"Can he swim?"

She shook her head.

The governess moaned and covered her mouth.

Charlie spun and stared at Denny.

"Don't stand about like an 'eadless chicken," Denny shouted, breaking into a run. "Go after 'im, you witless dolt."

Charlie held out his hands. "How?"

He waved his arm toward the bank. "The second boat."

Pearson and the other men poised to lunge, but Denny trained his pistol on them. "Get back before I drop you where you stand."

They raced for the other vessel and jumped aboard, Denny pushing off with a mighty shove before he wobbled his way to the seat. "Don't just sit there, Charlie. Row!"

Charlie snatched up the oars and leaned into them, skimming the boat easily across the water. Shouts and screams reached them from the bank, but Denny focused on only one thing.

A brilliant future awaited him less than ten yards ahead. At last, Denny Currie would have exactly what he deserved.

Ceddy lay very still in the bottom of the boat. His hair, swirling in a shallow pool of water, tickled the back of his neck, but he didn't feel like laughing.

Holding his breath, he squeezed his eyes shut against the voices in the distance—far away but scary—and tried to think of Mummy. He smoothed his cheek with the back of his hand the way she used to, but it didn't feel the same.

The middle of his chest swelled like a puffer fish, and he nearly cried out.

Must be quiet, Little Man. Must be careful to be quiet.

Mummy! I'll be good, if only you'll come and get me.

The words were muddled sobs in his ears.

His eyes flashed open. Water lapped against the side right next to his ear.

Not safe.

He shook his head.

Not safe. It's not safe.

A hard bump, and the boat rocked under him.

Ceddy's heart squeezed, and a scream rose in his throat as Charlie's fat fingers latched onto his arm.

His leering face appeared overhead, close enough to touch. "We got 'im now, Den." His head turned, long hairs growing from inside his droopy ears. "He's ours now."

Ceddy's trembling fingers slid down to his pocket and cupped the two big stones. Drawing them out, he slammed the side of Charlie's face as hard as he could swing.

Charlie's eyes rolled back. Wobbling briefly over Ceddy's head, he slumped.

Straightening both arms, Ceddy blocked him, shifting his weight to the side.

Charlie slid between the two boats with a terrible splash and disappeared.

"Charlie?" Mr. Currie bawled. "Where are you, mate?" He stood up in the other boat, towering over Ceddy. "What happened? Where'd he go?"

Moaning, Ceddy scrambled over the seat to the other end and perched on the side.

"Where's Charlie?" Denny screamed. "Where is he?"

In a rush of splashing water, Charlie shot up between them, both hands madly grasping for the boats.

Cursing, Mr. Currie did a curious dance before he toppled.

Ceddy bounced high off the end and hit the water on his back.

FORTY-THREE

Pearson raced to the bank and dove. Cold water closed around his head as Addie's frightened screams echoed in his ears. Rising to the surface, he swam, demanding more from his body than he ever had in his life. With every stroke, he pushed harder, his mind consumed by thoughts of Ceddy sinking beneath the murky lake.

Charlie flailed near the rowboats, the whites of his eyes shining. There was no sign of Denny.

"Help us," Charlie whimpered, reaching out his arm. "Please help Den. He can't swim."

Three feet away, Pearson drew a breath and flipped, diving toward the bottom with hearty kicks. His heart sank as he realized Charlie's thrashing had stirred the muddy bottom. Mushrooming silt billowed toward him, impossible to see through.

His chest ached and his head pounded. Frustration swelled inside him in crushing waves.

He hadn't been there for his family, but he was present this time. He kicked harder, driving toward the bottom.

Please God. . .help me save him.

Ceddy drifted down. He kept his mouth shut and held his breath the way Daddy taught him, but he longed to cry for help. Little fish darted past, and he reached for them, but then he fell into a black cloud and had to close his eyes.

The stones in his other hand shifted, and one began to slip. He swiped his thumb across it and felt the pointy end of Miss Addie's jasper.

Bloodstone. Heliotrope. Banded quartz.

He saw her sad face, wet with tears. Latching onto the escaping jasper with both hands, he let the diamond slide away.

Pearson broke the surface of the water and drew a gasping breath. He sighted off the stern of the boat Ceddy fell from and dove toward the deep again. Charlie's pleas to save Denny followed him down, but his only thought was of Ceddy.

His eyes useless within the foggy churn, Pearson relied on touch, spreading his arms and groping in all directions. One second before he shot to the top for more air, the barest tip of his finger connected with soft, swirling hair. With a strong thrust, he lunged. Scooping Ceddy's limp body from the lakebed, Pearson pushed off, kicking furiously.

Arms reached for them as they rose. A dripping wet Theo and Reverend Stroud leaned over the side of the boat ready to pull Ceddy aboard.

"Is he all right?" Priscilla shrieked from the shore.

Praying he'd be able to tell her yes, Pearson lifted Ceddy toward the men.

Gripping his wrists, Theo jerked him up and laid him on his side in the boat bottom. His little body heaved and water rushed from his mouth.

Pearson pulled himself into the boat and crowded close, briskly rubbing Ceddy's back. A final trickle poured from his lips, and he started to cough.

Cheers rose from Theo and the reverend, echoed by Addie and Priscilla.

Racking sobs spun Pearson toward Charlie.

He slumped in the other boat, one hand over his eyes. "Don't you even care about poor Denny?"

Pearson shared an ominous look with Theo. "Get Ceddy to the women."

Theo nodded.

Pearson stood on the seat and brought his arms overhead. Launching himself overboard, he plunged for the third time into the muddy Caddo Lake. Using the same method as before, he skimmed the bottom, feeling his way with his hands. Coming up empty, the need to breathe forced him up top.

Charlie's crying had become hysterical. "Where is 'e, Mr. Pearson? Where's me best mate?"

"I'll find him, Charlie," he called and then plummeted again.

Halfway down, in a spot where the mud had settled, something solid bumped his back. Spinning, he came face-to-face with Denny, tangled in coontail moss. The long, twisting weeds held him like a bug in a web. His tortured eyes stared, and his mouth gaped in a soundless scream.

Swimming around behind him, Pearson pulled hard on the collar of his shirt, ripping him free. With very little hope of reviving him, he hauled him toward the light.

Addie rushed into the shallow water and helped haul the rowboat to shore.

Priscilla danced on alternating feet as the men lifted Ceddy and hurried to place him in her arms. She sank to the ground under his weight, cradling him on her lap. "Don't cry, darling. Hush now, Auntie's here."

Kneeling beside them, Addie murmured comforting words while wrapping Ceddy in her shawl and picking bits of debris from his hair.

"We almost lost him," Priscilla said, meeting Addie's eyes. "But for Pearson, he'd be down there still." Visibly shaken, she rocked Ceddy. "And after the way I treated that young man, I'm so ashamed."

"We have to forgive ourselves," Addie said, patting her back. "It's what Pearson wants. All we can do now is try to make it up to him."

Ceddy lifted his arm toward Addie, something clenched in his fist.

Firing a questioning glance at Priscilla, she opened her hand. The jasper pendant fell into her palm, the stone cool against her skin. Gripping it tightly, she shed tears of gratitude. "Thank you, honey," she whispered. "Thank you for keeping it safe."

Struggling away from Priscilla, he staggered over and fell against Addie, sinking to his knees in her lap. He stroked her cheek with the back of his hand and shook his head. "Nuh. N–nuh."

Priscilla covered her mouth with her hand. "Oh Addie. . .I don't believe it. He's comforting you. His mama used to soothe him the same way." She shook her head. "It's the first time in his life he's done such a thing."

The first boat reached the bank in a jubilant celebration. Pearson rowed the second to shore in a tragic shroud of grief.

Denny's body lay in the bottom of the boat, his head cradled in Charlie's lap. The big man cried softly, sniffling and running his sleeve under his nose.

Pearson had sacrificed Denny for Ceddy, but there'd been no other choice. Still, it grieved him to the depths of his soul.

Rowing in ten yards down from the others, he leaped to the bank where Theo and the reverend met them and tied up the boat.

Charlie gathered Denny's body and prepared to stand, but Reverend Stroud held up his hand. "Leave him here for now, son. We don't want the boy to see him."

Stretching out his arm to brace Charlie, the reverend helped him to dry land. Charlie winced and probed a gash beneath his left eye, the skin around it swollen and bruised.

"That's a nasty cut," Pearson said. "Did it happen when you fell from the boat?"

Charlie shook his head. "The little nipper smashed me in the face." He pouted a bit. "With Denny's diamond."

Pearson's head came up. "A diamond? Are you sure?"

"I'm sure, all right. Saw it coming from the corner of me eye." He held up his fingers in a circle. "Great white stone about this big around."

So Addie was right.

Pearson patted him on the back. "We'll find a doctor in town to look at you," he said, then ran to join Addie and Ceddy.

Ceddy lay cuddled in her lap, his arms wrapped around her waist. Longing to offer comfort, Pearson massaged his shoulder. "Is he all right?"

Tears in her eyes, she nodded. "He's quite shaken, but I think he'll be fine."

"That was a close call."

"Entirely too close," Pricilla whispered, her voice choked. "Thank you, son." A startled look crossed her face. "Heavens, that sounds so inadequate to express what my heart feels."

Pearson smiled. "It's plenty." He reached for Addie's hand and frowned. "What's this?" he asked, his fingers fumbling with the large stone.

"My jasper pendant. It's very precious to me. It belonged to my grandmother." She smiled down at the boy's wet head. "Ceddy kept it safe for me."

Pearson turned it over in his palm. "It's very nice. I'm glad you got it back." Remembering, he lifted his head. "Where's the diamond?"

"He doesn't have it."

"Sure he does. He bashed Charlie with it."

Her brow creased. "Priscilla searched his clothing. It's not on him."

"Do you suppose he hid it?" Theo asked.

She shook her head. "He would've hidden them together."

"Then where?"

She shrugged. "I can't imagine." She stared at the lake. "You don't suppose he dropped it?"

They shared a look before Pearson stood.

Combing the ground, he retraced their steps to the bank, searched inside the boat and in the shallows beneath it. Finding nothing, he and Theo rowed out to the spot where Ceddy went down.

Steeling himself to return to the cold water, Pearson dove repeatedly and groped along the bottom. He searched until exhaustion forced him to quit.

Back onshore they held a meeting to decide what to do. Reverend Stroud agreed to stay behind with Charlie and the body while they used his wagon to take Ceddy and the women home. Pearson promised to send Theo back with the sheriff, a fresh horse, and the liveryman to tend his wounded animal.

"Are you sure you can handle things here, Reverend?"

He made a face. "Of course."

"I don't think Charlie's dangerous without Denny's influence, but be careful just the same."

The reverend tossed a look over his shoulder. Charlie sat on the log by the fire, staring into the flames. "He's a broken man, son. I think he's harmless." He nodded at the shotgun he held and patted the pistol at his waist. "But just in case, I think I'll be fine."

Pearson gave him a wry smile. "No swashbuckling involved, but you're finally getting your adventure."

He nodded at Charlie. "Yes, but I regret that it's under such tragic circumstances."

Seeking the heavens for guidance, Pearson approached Charlie and sat beside him on the log. "I can't tell you how sorry I am about your friend. I wish things had turned out better."

Charlie sniffed. "It ain't your fault. You 'ad to bring up the lad." He turned with tormented eyes. "It's on me, what 'appened to Denny. I upset the boat and 'e fell." He wiped his nose on the back of his hand. "Denny fell and 'e couldn't swim a stroke."

Pearson tightened his hand on his shoulder. "It's not that simple, Charlie. Denny fell because he was standing up."

Charlie blinked at the fire. "Yeah? Den always told me not to stand up in the boat."

"That's right. And he drowned because he got tangled in the weeds. If not for that, he would've bobbed to the surface and held on to the boat until we pulled him in."

Charlie faced him, his eyes pleading. "So it ain't my fault?"

Pearson shook his head. "It's not your fault."

His plump bottom lip trembled. "Denny was me best mate."

"I know, buddy. I know." Standing, Pearson gave him a gentle shake. "Will you be all right?"

He stared up at Pearson. "I'm going to jail, ain't I?"

"I don't know. I suppose that's for the sheriff to decide. But if I can do anything to help you, just send for me."

Charlie's eyes narrowed. "You'd do that for me? After what we done?"

"Sure I will." He lifted his chin at Reverend Stroud. "So will the reverend. Just remember that, all right?"

Tears flowing freely, he nodded.

Addie touched Pearson's arm. "We're ready to go."

Over her shoulder, he saw Priscilla in the wagon, cradling Ceddy and trying to keep him warm. Theo sat in the driver's seat holding the reins.

Behind Pearson, most likely buried in lake-bottom mud, lay the biggest treasure he'd ever sought. In front of him stood the most valuable.

Glancing at the boat that held the body of poor Denny Currie, Pearson suppressed a shudder. Just like he'd said to Catfish John—some things weren't meant to be.

Addie stood at her bedroom window, watching Pearson and Ceddy in the garden. Pearson chased him through the hedges, deliberately allowing him to escape. Catching up to him occasionally, he'd lift him high and swing him in the air. Ceddy's delighted squeals echoed across the yard.

"Isn't that a wonderful sound?"

Addie turned to smile at Priscilla, standing on the threshold. "Yes, it is. A glorious sound."

She crossed the room and joined Addie at the window.

Outside, Pearson strode back and forth with Ceddy chasing at his heels like a clumsy, flop-eared puppy.

Priscilla placed a hand at Addie's back. "I want to thank you for sharing your good news with me. It's an honor, especially knowing you told me before you telephoned your mama."

Addie leaned into her. "We wanted you to know. Besides, since we're having the wedding in Marshall, I'll need your help to make plans. Mother can't come until the day before the wedding."

"And your daddy?"

She beamed as brightly as the light in her heart. "He's coming with her. They're bringing my sisters as well."

Priscilla nodded. "Well, your news was a fresh breath after the ugliness of the other day. We needed something happy to focus on." She patted Addie's waist. "I can't tell you how proud Reverend Stroud is that Pearson asked him to officiate."

"He's a good friend and a wonderful pastor."

"That he is."

Addie sobered. "As happy as I am, I'm very burdened at the same time."

Priscilla's mouth dipped into a frown. "Goodness! Why? A bride shouldn't be burdened."

"I'm going to miss you all so fiercely when Pearson and I leave for Galveston." She choked back her tears. "Especially Ceddy."

Priscilla tugged her arm, drawing her to the bed. "Sit down, dear. I have something I've needed to discuss with you, but I couldn't find the right time. I suppose you just gave me the perfect opening."

Addie watched expectantly while Priscilla settled onto the bed next to her and clasped her hands in her lap.

"Adelina McRae, the changes you've wrought in my great-nephew are nothing short of miraculous. He's alert, receptive to touch. He's making eye contact more and more, and the biggest blessing of all, he's becoming affectionate. This morning he looked me full in the face and smiled." She beamed. "It came and went so fast, I thought I'd imagined it, but my heart says I didn't. It's as if you reached inside him and turned a switch."

Addie squirmed with pleasure. "I feel sure the change in his diet was the key."

"I wholeheartedly agree, but how did you know that simply removing dairy and sweet foods would bring about such a change?"

"Well, I—"

"It's a gift, Addie, the incredible instincts you have."

Addie's cheeks warmed from the undeserved praise. "Yes, it's exactly that. . .a gift. So I can't really take the credit. I pray over all my charges, and I truly feel God gives me special insight into each child." A sweet smile stole over her face. "However, it's different with Ceddy. God has also given me a special love for him."

Priscilla sat quietly for a minute then adjusted her skirt and swiveled toward her. "I was going to wait to bring this up when both you and Pearson were present, but if you're going to provide me with such an ideal opportunity, how can I delay?"

She gripped Addie's hands. "What would you say if I asked you to take Ceddy with you?"

Addie studied her face. "You mean to Galveston?"

"Yes."

Confusion crept over her. "Well, of course. We'd love to take him for a visit."

Gnawing the side of her mouth, Priscilla squeezed Addie's fingers. "I don't mean for a visit, dear. I mean permanently."

Addie felt doused with cold water. "You're not serious."

Priscilla stared at their hands. "Ordinarily, I'd never ask, never intrude upon your new life." Her dewy lashes fluttered, and she looked up. "But we both know Ceddy is no ordinary child. He needs special attention. You and Pearson are so good with him, dear. So good *for* him. He's blossoming under your nurturing care." Her bottom lip trembled. "I love him desperately. And I'll miss him terribly. But I want the best for him." She tightened her grip. "Naturally that would've been his parents, but Ceddy was cheated out of a life with them. The next best thing is you and Pearson."

Addie took a moment to probe her heart. She wouldn't accept without knowing her true feelings about taking on such a responsibility. What she found within her soul was pure joy.

"I can't think of anything I'd want more, but I'll have to speak to Pearson before I give my answer."

Priscilla's eyes lit up. "I understand."

Addie angled her head. "What about the rest of your family? Won't they object?"

She waved her hand. "Let me handle the wolf pack. I've learned how to manage them over the years." She shrugged. "Besides, I have legal guardianship, left to me by both parents. With that comes the right to make important decisions on Ceddy's behalf."

Patting Addie's knee, she stood and walked to the window. "If I decide to assign his custody to a trusted teacher to further his education, who can argue the point?"

Addie followed her to the window seat and gripped her frail shoulders. "I'm honored, most of all because I know what a sacrifice you're making. You're going to be lost without him."

A sob shook her. "More than you know." She caught Addie's hand. "But we must face reality. I'm not getting any younger." She laughed through her tears. "And that little scamp is more than I can handle alone."

Pointing down at the yard, she chuckled. "And here he comes. You'd better ask Delilah to draw his bath."

Addie sighed. "I'm surprised he'll go near water after his close call."

"So am I, dear. So am I."

Pearson chased Ceddy onto the porch, swatting him just before he jerked open the screen and barreled inside.

Delilah met them with a smile. "Whoa there, Little Man. Where you be to go?"

Giggling, Ceddy slipped behind her skirts to hide from Pearson.

She twisted around, tried to pull him away, but then gave up with an indulgent smile. "How you this afternoon, Mista Pearson?"

He grinned and stretched out his arms. "Couldn't be better, Delilah. It's a beautiful day."

"Yessuh. That old sun be shining bright."

Peering behind him, he frowned. "It is? I hadn't noticed. I'm so happy, this day would be beautiful in a downpour."

Her laughter echoed in the foyer. "I reckon it would, what with you and Miss Addie planning your nuptials and such."

He ducked his head to peer down the hall. "Where is my bride? I've come to call on her."

Herding Ceddy, Delilah led Pearson into the downstairs foyer. "Go on and sit in the parlor. I'll fetch her."

Pearson took a seat on the sofa and ran his hand along the padded arm. The last time he'd been in the room, he'd almost told Addie he loved her. Stunned, he realized that though they were engaged to wed, he'd still never told her. Chuckling to himself, he determined to correct the grave oversight the minute he saw her.

"There you are, Delilah," Addie said from somewhere in the hall. "Priscilla wants you to draw Ceddy a bath."

"I'm two hops and a jump ahead," Delilah said. "Me and Little Man on our way right now."

"Good. Mr. Pearson didn't leave, did he?"

Pearson's insides warmed at her anxious tone.

"No missy. He waitin' for you right there in the parlor."

With no further ado, the door burst open and his breath caught.

Addie stood on the threshold, as fresh and radiant as the day she stepped off the train in Marshall. A wide ribbon in a dark coffee shade cinched her middle, setting off her tiny waist against the beige dress. The neckline plunged lower than he'd ever seen on her, a large bow in the center adding a touch of respectability. Dangling strands of pearls crisscrossed the top of her bodice, swinging each time she moved. Gracing him with a broad smile, she crossed the room with a pleasing swish of layered skirts. A fragrant cloud of magnolias reached him before she did.

He rose to meet her. "Honey, you're beautiful."

She paused then stretched out her hands. "I give you permission to greet me that way from now on."

"I'm certain I will. I won't be able to help myself."

She giggled like a girl. "Can I expect this sort of flattery when I'm old and gray?"

"I promise."

Gazing into her bottomless brown eyes, he remembered the vow he'd just made. "I love you, Addie. Did you know that?"

She stirred in his arms. "I should hope so, since you asked me to be your wife."

He kissed her nose. "I didn't want there to be any misunderstanding on that score."

She beamed. "I love you, too. I have for weeks and weeks."

He nodded. "I knew it all along."

She swatted his arm, and he jumped back, laughing. Recalling the main reason he'd come to see her, he reached into his vest pocket. "I almost forgot. I took the sheriff with me to the rooming house where Denny and Charlie stayed. The sheriff informed the landlord they'd paid him in stolen goods, a fact I'm sure he already knew. It wasn't hard to convince him to surrender Priscilla's things."

He held out his hand. In his palm lay Ceddy's stolen gems. "Can you see that these get where they belong? I know how upset he's been at their loss."

Addie ran her finger over the dazzling stones, a topaz, a sapphire, an emerald, an amethyst, and. . .a small but brilliant diamond sparkled in their midst. "Oh Pearson, he'll be so pleased."

He grinned. "It's not as big as his last specimen, but it'll fit better in his collection box."

She picked up the gem. "Where did you get it?"

Lowering his eyes, he toyed with the buttons on her puffy sleeves. "The landlord of the rooming house has a collection of his own. I saw the diamond and offered to trade him."

Catching his eye, she lifted her brow.

He shrugged. "I had no more use for a couple of rowboats, oars, and a sturdy lift rig—a Yale & Towne hoist and pulley to be exact."

She melted against him and pressed her cheek to his chest. "You're the dearest man in the world."

He smiled against her hair. "Not really. I just care a lot about that little guy."

They swayed in silence for a blissful bit, and then Addie raised her head. "Do you, Pearson?"

"Do I. . . ?"

"Care about Ceddy."

His brows dipped in the middle. "Very much."

"Enough to raise him as our own?"

He held her at arm's length, dread dampening the excitement he felt. "Oh honey. . .get that notion right out of your mind. Priscilla would never allow it."

"It was her idea."

He gave his head a little shake. "I don't understand."

"She's decided we're the best thing for him. She wants us to take him to Galveston."

He gripped her arms. "Really? Oh Addie, it's a wonderful idea. Galveston is a great place to raise a boy. I'll take him fishing, teach him to sail a dinghy, we'll search for treasure together." He finally inhaled. "He'll love it there."

Addie laughed. "May I take that as a yes?"

He hugged her to his chest. "Absolutely yes! Tell her we accept."

Grasping his hand, she squeezed. "I'm so glad you feel that way. I was afraid you might say no."

He pulled back enough to peer into her face. "Why would I even consider saying no?"

A spark of humor lit her eyes. "Well, he *can* get into trouble on occasion."

"That's all right. So can I. Just ask Theo."

Addie turned. "Maybe I'd better. Where is he?"

He sobered. "He's taking Charlie to Reverend Stroud's house. The reverend's taking him in."

"Oh, I'm glad." She took his hand and pulled him toward the sofa. "Come sit down and tell me all about it."

Seated next to her, Pearson found it hard to concentrate, but he gathered his thoughts and continued. "Since Priscilla decided not to press charges—"

"Once you persuaded her not to, you mean," she interrupted, smiling proudly.

"Charlie's not a bad person at heart. He's a follower. With the reverend agreeable to mentoring him, it seemed the perfect plan. Let him follow a good man for a change."

"It's a wonderful idea." She picked up a pad and pen from the low table. "Speaking of ideas, I need some from you on the wedding preparations. There are a thousand little details to attend to."

He placed his hand over hers. "I've been meaning to tell you. You'll have to plan without me for a few days. I have preparations of my own to make."

She blinked her confusion.

"I need to prepare you a place to live. To do that, I have to leave for a few weeks."

She leaned back and stared. "You're leaving Marshall?"

"Yes, honey. You see, my parents' house"—he swallowed hard—"my house now, I suppose, was repaired and remodeled after the storm, but it hasn't been lived in since. I have no idea what condition it's in. I'm sure it needs to be cleaned and aired out at least."

She pouted her lips. "I don't want you to go."

He squeezed her hand. "I'll be back before you can miss me."

"Impossible. I miss you already."

Laughing, he drew her close. "Keep yourself busy planning our wedding. I'll just show up and say 'I do.'" He took the pad she'd scratched in and flipped to a clean page. "Right now I need a list of everything you want laid in stock in your new home. I want everything perfect for my new wife."

FORTY-FIVE

Pearson slid off his boots and socks and walked to the edge of the rolling surf. The pull of the ancient tide stirred the sand between his toes, drawing it away in a rush. With the same force, Galveston Island had drawn him to return to his childhood home, a lure he could no longer resist.

Turning his face to the wind, he breathed deeply. The pungent salty air smelled like home.

More than anything, he longed to have Addie standing by his side. There were many things to show her, things to teach her about life on the coast, and he felt anxious to start.

He had two challenges yet to face before he could relax and enjoy the promise of a new beginning. First, he had to tell Pearl he'd be bringing a wife to the island. Second, he had to overcome the pain of walking into his house for the first time since the disaster. The thought of either confrontation had kept him lingering too long on the shore.

Theo, hungry and eager to see their friends, had gone ahead of him into the café. Brushing the hair from his eyes, Pearson picked up his boots, squared his shoulders, and walked up the beach. Time to brave the first hurdle.

Drawing a steadying breath, he pushed open the door and stepped inside.

Rosie squealed from across the room and rushed at him. Throwing her fleshy arms around his neck, she peppered kisses on his cheek. "If you're not a pleasant sight! I told Theo if you didn't come through that door soon, he'd have to leave my soup alone and go find you."

Pearson gave her a crushing hug. "I missed you, Rosie."

Pulling away, she propped her hands on her hips in mock indignation. "You did not, or you would've come home before now."

He leaned close to whisper. "I wouldn't have left in the first place, but somebody sent me on a treasure hunt."

She winced. "Theo told me the outcome. Sounds like a bigger dead end than Lafitte's gold."

He slung his arm around her neck. "Don't worry. I don't regret going." She didn't know it yet, but it was the best decision he'd ever made.

Theo sat at a table across the way, dipping thick-sliced bread in a steaming bowl.

Pearl flitted around him, filling his glass, passing the salt, laughing and talking the way she always did. When she glanced toward Pearson, her dimples flashed briefly in a quick smile.

He waved, but she didn't respond, intent on serving another bowl of soup to Theo. He must've been mistaken. She hadn't seen him yet.

Dread was layered like ice around Pearson's heart. He had to hurt Pearl, break her heart, and he'd rather sever an arm. "Listen, Rosie. . . there's something I need to tell you."

"You can tell me anything, darlin'," she bellowed in her usual boisterous tone.

He shushed her. "I'd rather say this to you first. I may need your help breaking it to Pearl."

Interest flashed in her eyes. "That serious, is it?"

"Just the happiest news of my life." He glanced toward Pearl. "But not everyone in this room will think so."

"Oh," she whispered. "You mean Addie."

"Theo told you?"

She nodded. "He told us both."

Pearson cringed. "Pearl knows?" It explained why she hadn't returned his wave.

Pearl swept past, and he ducked behind Rosie. "I despise the thought of hurting her. Was she very upset?"

Rosie snickered behind her chubby hand. "She's trying to be strong, honey."

Returning to Theo's table with a saucer of bread, Pearl giggled with delight at something he said.

Pearson took another peek. "Well, she's putting on a brave face, that's for sure."

Rosie patted his arm. "I hate to disappoint you, sweetheart, but Pearl's fickle heart has moved on."

"What?" Pearson gaped at her. "In just a matter of weeks, she's already tossed me aside for someone else?" He grinned. "My ego is getting a lashing lately."

Rosie chuckled and slapped his arm. "I thought you knew. Pearl falls for a different fella every week." Leaning in, she fought a smile. "It gets worse."

He shook his head. "How could it?"

"Her new interest happens to be a friend of yours."

Pearson touched his chest. "Of mine? Rosie, I don't have that many friends around here, except for—" He spun to stare at Theo, sopping up Pearl's attention along with the soup. "Theo?" His voice grew shrill at the end. "It can't be."

Rosie nodded, her eyes twinkling. "Not a week after you left, she realized it wasn't your absence she grieved. Pearl couldn't get Theo out of her mind. She missed his constant smile and teasing ways." She made a face. "His full lips and dreamy eyes. . . Her observations, not mine."

"Not a word about me?"

"Um, yes, there was the one thing. It seems Theo has much nicer hair."

Pearson's head reeled. "Well, I'll be. I suffered terrible pangs of guilt for nothing?"

Rosie patted his back. "Sorry, honey. I suppose you did."

Sobering, she lowered her voice and tilted her chin at the flirting couple. "I sure hope Theo feels the same. Just between you and me, this time, I think it's serious."

Hours later, Pearson stood on Broadway Street outside the big house where he'd been born. His heart pounded and his mouth felt dry, but memories of the good times he'd shared with his family swirled in his head, dulling the pain he'd dreaded.

Staring down the sidewalk, he saw his brother, shouting with laughter over learning to pedal a bicycle. His dapper father strolling home with his walking stick. His smiling mother pushing his sister in a pram.

He saw a Christmas tree in the window, a wreath on the front door. Busy Saturday mornings raking leaves and painting fences. Lazy Sunday afternoons sipping lemonade together on the portico.

These things he could look forward to again, only this time shared with Addie and his own rowdy brood, beginning with Ceddy. The promise of such a future filled him with hope and a great sense of expectation.

Pearson had an odd sense of his family drawing near, surrounding him with loving arms to celebrate new beginnings. Such thoughts might be fanciful, but God's presence, urging him toward a life filled with blessings, was achingly real. The time for crushing grief and the burden of guilt had passed. At last he could move on.

Drawing a deep, refreshing breath, he began by taking the wide front steps two at a time and striding confidently across the broad front porch.

At the door, he smiled and patted his front pocket. If the extensive list inside was what it took to make Addie happy, he'd make sure to furnish her new home with every item. He only hoped it wouldn't take long. His heart yearned for Marshall and his wedding day. The day he would finally make Addie his bride.

The minute Tiller McRae's boot heels touched the station platform in Marshall, Texas, he wanted to snatch up his eldest daughter and book passage home to Canton.

As if she'd read his mind, Mariah gripped his arm and held on tight. Was she anxious to see Addie, or were her thoughts running similar to his?

"Do you see her?" Mariah shouted over the huffs of the steam engine and the other shouting voices.

Tiller shook his head. "Hard to see anything in this churning mob." He glanced at the smallest of their wide-eyed traveling companions. "Hold tightly to the girls, Mariah."

Gathering them under her shawl, she shaded her eyes and peered in the distance. "She said she'd be here."

"Then she will," Tiller said.

Thomas and Hope Moony appeared in the passenger door behind them. Holding tightly to the rail, Dr. Moony stepped to the ground then turned to help his granddaughter.

Tiller offered his hand as well then scowled at Dr. Moony. "This is your fault, you know."

The doctor shot him a good-natured smile. "I should by now. You've reminded me often enough."

"Credit where credit is due, sir. If not for you passing Miss Whitfield's letter to my Addie, I'd be home in the garden, not waiting to meet the stranger who's marrying my daughter tomorrow."

Hope gave a merry laugh. "I'm the one who should be angry, Mr. McRae. With my wedding planned for months, I'm appalled that Addie will beat me down the aisle."

Tiller snorted. "She wouldn't be if I had my say-so."

Carrie tugged on his coattail. "Father, where's Addie?"

He leaned close to her ear. "She'll be along, ladybug. You just stay close to Mother. And hold your sisters' hands."

Drawing his friends and family away from the noisy train, Tiller allowed his gaze to sweep the crowd. His heart stilled when he saw her, disbelieving what his traitor eyes were telling him. "I sent my baby to Marshall and got back a woman."

Mariah clutched his sleeve. "Where?"

Struggling against the lump rising in his throat, he pointed. "There."

Addie hurried across the platform, reminding him very much of her mother at that age. Mariah once had the same youthful spirit, the same happy smile—he cringed—the same glow of a woman in love.

The man trailing behind her didn't seem quite as happy.

Tiller grunted. "He's much too old for her, Mariah."

She nudged him.

"What happened to his hair?"

"Tiller McRae! Lower your voice."

Squealing, Addie rushed to him, his little girl again for just a moment. "Father, it's so good to see you."

"You, too, honey."

Too quickly, her arms slipped from around his neck and she moved on. "Mother, I missed you so."

Mariah held her for as long as Addie stayed still but stepped back and smiled while she leaped in circles with her sisters and then Hope.

"How could you, Addie?" Hope said, beaming. "It's ill mannered to steal my thunder."

"I'm ever so sorry! I never planned it, I assure you."

Dr. Moony touched her arm. "Let me have a look at you, child."

She turned into his embrace. "Hello, Dr. Moony. I'm so glad you could come."

"My, but you're lovely, Addie. You'll be a beautiful bride. I'm so grateful Priscilla invited me to share your happy day."

A cloud passed over her face. "She didn't exactly invite you, sir. You're meant to be a surprise."

His bushy brows shot to the sky. "Come again?"

Easing free of him and the topic, Addie returned to the tall stranger standing awkwardly off to the side. Hooking her arm through his, she walked him over and presented him proudly. "Dear ones, this is my Pearson."

Looking a little surer of himself after Addie's enthusiastic endorsement, he offered Tiller his hand. "Mr. McRae, it's nice to meet you."

It took all of Tiller's grit to be cordial. "Likewise, young man. I've been eager to get a look at the man who's about to run off with my daughter."

Mariah cleared her throat. "Pay no attention to him, Pearson. He still sees her in pigtails."

The line of his shoulders relaxed, and his tight smile became a hearty grin. "Mrs. McRae, how nice to see you again."

"Likewise, dear." She caught his hand. "If I told you I knew from the start that you were the one for my Addie, I don't suppose you'd believe me."

He gave her a little wink. "I certainly would. I suspected the same myself."

Tiller suppressed a groan. "If you two are done with the reunion, I'd like to get the girls away from this throng."

"Of course," Pearson said. "Come right this way. Miss Whitfield sent her carriage."

Herding the little ones, Tiller and Mariah fell into line behind Hope and the doctor. Tiller leaned to whisper in Mariah's ear. "I'm not sure I like him. Too swaggering for my taste."

Her mouth twitched. "I seem to remember a cocky young rogue who didn't pass muster with my family at first."

Tiller sniffed. She'd struck below the belt, as usual. "All right. I'll give him a chance."

Dr. Moony touched Addie's elbow. "Do you mean to say Priscilla doesn't even know that I'm coming?"

She gave him a reassuring smile. "Don't worry. I promise you'll be fine. She'll be positively thrilled at the news."

Addie tucked her lips and took a calming breath through her nose. It would be fine, wouldn't it? Truthfully, she'd had misgivings all morning about meddling. A great many years had passed since the two were close friends. Dr. Moony had enjoyed a successful marriage. Seen the birth of his children and grandchildren. Lost a wife. Suppose the things they shared in common so many years ago they'd long since outgrown? Glancing at the fretful man in the backseat of the carriage, she reminded herself it was too late for second thoughts.

At the mansion, she and Pearson led their guests through the great hall and into the parlor. While they took their seats, Addie stood at the threshold, watching for their hostess.

Delilah pushed out of the kitchen with a tray of coffee and her special scones, and Addie hurried to meet her. "Where's Miss Priscilla?"

"She still upstairs. Told me to fetch these refreshments."

"And Ceddy?"

"He's napping."

Dashing by Pearson at the parlor door, she pointed inside. "Entertain them," she whispered, "while I go for Priscilla."

"What?" he said hoarsely. "Addie, no."

Ignoring his frantic expression, she waved him inside. "You'll do fine. I'll be right back."

Feeling she'd left him alone to face the gallows, she hurried upstairs to a reckoning of her own. She knocked at Priscilla's door and waited for her soft-spoken invitation to enter.

Priscilla turned from straightening her sash in the mirror. "Your parents are here. I saw them from the window." She smiled. "You must be so happy to see them."

"Oh yes, I am. Aren't you coming down to meet them?"

"Of course, dear. I'm on my way now." She took Addie's arm. "From the window, your sisters looked like precious little ladies stepping down from my carriage. And that red-haired father of yours cuts a handsome figure." A tiny crease gathered between her brows. "But I'm curious. . .who was the older gentleman and the pretty young girl?"

A chill coursed the length of Addie's back. "Priscilla, um, that was Dr. Moony and Hope."

Her steps faltered and she froze, one hand on the doorknob. "No, it's not, Addie. Don't tease."

Addie swallowed. "I'm afraid it's true."

She shook her head. "Impossible."

"I hope you don't mind. I invited them as a surprise."

The truth dawned on her in waves, slowly eroding the doubt in her eyes. "That stoop-shouldered old geezer downstairs is Thomas Moony?" She touched her forehead. "The man with thinning hair?"

Addie nodded.

Spinning, she hurried across the room to her mirror and gaped at the pale image staring back. Trembling fingers lifted a lock of her white hair. "My heavens, it's true. We really are that old."

Addie gulped. "Are you upset with me?"

Her likeness glanced at Addie. "Only for forcing me to accept my own mortality, dear. You see, my Thomas is ageless and handsome, forever a dapper twenty-year-old boy." Tears glistened in her eyes. "When I'm with him in my memories, I'm forever young, too."

Addie cringed. Mother's meddling ways were nothing compared to this. "Please don't cry, Priscilla. I'm a horrible toad, and I can't believe what I've done to you."

Turning, she caught Addie's shoulders. "No, dear. Don't be silly. It caught me off guard, that's all." She wiped her eyes. "You've given me a wonderful surprise, and I'm very, very grateful. It will be wonderful to be with Thomas again after all these years." She smiled. "Under all the bags and wrinkles, we're still the same people, aren't we?" She patted Addie's back. "Let's you and I go greet our guests."

Downstairs, Addie opened the parlor door, afraid of what she'd find. She needn't have worried.

Her parents sat together on the sofa, holding hands and chatting quietly with Dr. Moony. Hope and Pearson sat across from each other in the matching chairs, attempting to talk with three little magpies sitting at their feet.

By the gleam in her eyes, Carrie had fallen under Pearson's spell. She sat with her arms propped on his knees, drinking in every word.

Dr. Moony rose as if pulled from the top with a string. His appreciative gaze fixed on Priscilla, growing more admiring with every step he took in her direction. Evidently, he held no memories carved in stone. "Priscilla, I don't believe these old eyes."

She held out her hands. "Thomas, what a nice surprise. Welcome to my home."

He caught her fingers and held on for several long minutes, studying her glowing face. "My, my. Forgive me for saying so, but you're as pretty as ever."

She lowered her lashes, her cheeks flushing bright pink. "Go on with you, Thomas Moony. I see you haven't changed a bit."

Addie smiled at Pearson. He grinned up at her and winked. Perhaps she'd inherited Mother's flair for successful meddling after all.

Addie stared at herself in the looking glass, magically transformed into a bride. Unlike most girls, she hadn't given much thought to her wedding day. She'd focused too strictly on breaking free of her overprotective parents and forging her own destiny, never dreaming how important it would one day seem. Whispering a prayer of gratitude, she thanked God for looking past her stiff-necked independence and intervening in the affairs of her life.

Mother stood behind her, fastening Grandmother's beads around her neck. Today, as promised, they would become hers. "There's so much history bound up in this ancestral necklace," she said. "Someday we'll sit together, and I'll tell you all about it."

Addie smoothed her fingertips over the jasper pendant. "Since you saw them last, there's a lot of excitement bound up here, too." She grinned. "Some of it I may never tell."

Mother's brows rose. "Such as?"

"Suffice it to say, if not for Ceddy, our tradition would've ended with you."

"Speaking of traditions. . ." Holding up one finger, Mother spun to the bed. Returning with a small rawhide bag, she reached inside and held up a pair of shoes. "These are your grandmother's wedding slippers. She got married in them, and so did I. Unless you object, I'd like you to keep with this custom as well."

Addie touched the butter-soft leather and sighed. "They're exquisite."

Mother helped her slip them on. Then they both stared at Addie's reflection in the mirror.

"You're a vision, honey." Sudden tears flashed in her eyes. "I got married in black, did you know that?"

Tearing up herself, Addie shook her head.

"We were still in mourning for your grandfather." She smiled. "It sounds scandalous, I know, but at the time, it wasn't. And it turned out to be the most wonderful day of my life."

Addie swiped at an escaping tear.

"I remember gazing in a mirror much like this one—without the gilded edges, of course—wishing my parents were alive to see me wed." Mother wrapped her arms around Addie's neck. "I'm grateful to God you have a large loving family to witness your day."

"So am I," Addie said. "More than I can say. But I wish Miss Vee had come."

"So does she, but she's far too frail to travel. I promised to persuade you and Pearson to visit Canton soon."

Addie turned to rest her head on her mother's shoulder. "You were right, you know. About everything."

Laughter rumbled in Mother's chest. "Wait and say that again in your father's hearing."

"Oh, but it's true. You saw Pearson's character right from the start, despite his unusual appearance. And you said God had amazing gifts in store for me." She smoothed her mother's back. "I can't imagine a more precious gift than a life shared with Pearson."

A knock came at the door. Mother opened it to Father's stunned face.

He scratched his temple then shook his head at Addie in wonder. "Look at you, little missy. You're a bride."

Addie ran into his embrace. "I love you, Daddy."

His arms around her tightened. "You haven't called me that since you were three." He lifted her chin. "Are you ready? They're waiting for us downstairs. I think your young man is getting anxious."

"Has Reverend Stroud arrived?"

He gave her a wry grin. "I'm afraid so. And I can't find another reason to put things off."

Addie nudged him from one side, her mother from the other.

"Whoa there, soldiers. Hold your fire. I can tell when I'm defeated." He held out an arm for each of them. "Shall we?"

Priscilla met them at the foot of the stairs, her eyes aglow. "Addie, you're a lovely bride."

Addie smiled. "All thanks to you."

Mother wrapped her arm around Priscilla's waist. "Addie's right. You've done a wonderful job with her wedding dress and trousseau. And the garden is prepared beautifully. I owe you for my daughter's happiness today. Thank you for stepping in when I couldn't be present."

Priscilla hugged her back. "It was a joy. Addie's become the daughter I never had."

Delilah appeared in the background, her eyes red and swollen from crying. "Excuse me, Miss Priscilla. I done pack all Little Man's bags, like you said. And I tucked in the family Bible like you say to." She sniffed, her dark eyes jumping to Addie. "Miss Addie, you gon' take good care of him for me, ain't you?" Her bottom lip trembling, she wiped her eyes on her sleeve. "Missin' that chil' gon' be the death of me."

Addie pulled her into a hug. "Don't cry, Delilah. You'll see him again soon."

Laughing, Priscilla patted her arm. "Heavens, Delilah, you're taking on worse than me. I told you I'd take you along when I visit with Addie this fall."

Touching Addie's shoulder, she smiled. "We're sending his collection boxes along in his trunks, but the rest of his rocks will be shipped to you later." She rolled her eyes. "I hope you have ample room."

Fidgeting beside her, Father caught her eye. "Are you ready, honey?"

She grinned at him. "That's the second time you've asked. Are you hoping for a different answer?"

He shrugged and took her hand. "You can't blame a man for trying." He ushered her outside the back door into a wonderland of muted light.

Priscilla and Delilah had fashioned hundreds of luminaries and placed them throughout the garden. Chairs lined the yard, overlooking the gazebo where they would take their vows.

Priscilla pointed across the lawn. "How do you like his hair?"

Pearson, so handsome in his suit he took her breath away, leaned against the gazebo rail talking to Reverend Stroud.

Addie gasped. "I've never seen it so. . .controlled."

Priscilla nodded. "Delilah helped him comb it." She patted Addie's shoulder. "Enjoy it while you can. With all the carrying-on he did while she smoothed it out, I doubt he'll ever submit to it again."

Theo, who had arrived that morning from Galveston, stood in the company of a rather loud woman Addie didn't recognize and a pretty young woman who clung to his arm.

Ceddy sat in a circle of little girls, all trying to talk to him at once.

Raising his head, Pearson spotted her. Excusing himself, he loped across the yard.

The burnt-sugar eyes she loved, as clear as a handblown demijohn, latched onto her, and she couldn't pull away.

"You're beautiful."

"Thank you." She giggled. "So is your hair."

Bowing slightly, he offered his arm. "Are you ready to marry me?"

Addie winked over her shoulder at her father. "Yes, I am."

Near tears, she leaned for a last hug from her mother and father as their little girl. The next time they embraced, she would be Mrs. Pearson Foster.

Winding her arm through his, she let him lead her off the porch. Through a heady haze of bliss, Addie saw joyful friends and family, bright blue Texas skies, and an endless horizon.

Reverend Stroud smiled brightly as they approached. Stepping into the gazebo ahead of them, he turned wearing his minister face. "Shall we begin?"

Standing stiffly beside her, Pearson nodded.

A bundle of happy nerves, Addie barely heard the reverend's opening words. He awoke her from her daze by calling her name.

"Adelina Viola McRae, do you take Pearson to be your wedded husband, to have and to hold from this day forward, for better, for worse, for richer, for poorer, in sickness and in health, to love, cherish, and to obey, till death do you part, according to God's holy ordinance?"

Addie bit back a mischievous smile. The truth was, she'd take Pearson any way she could get him. This time, of course, in order to make it official, she would say so.

SCONES

Sift one quart of flour; add half a teaspoon of salt, a teaspoon of sugar, a tablespoon of lard, one beaten egg, two teaspoons of cream tartar, one of soda, and a pint of sweet milk. Mix to a thick batter, drop in squares on a very hot, greased griddle, and bake brown on both sides. Serve with butter and honey.

The Good Housekeeping Woman's Home Cook Book
Arranged by Isabel Gordon Curtis (Chicago: Reilly & Britton, c. 1909)

COBBLER

Make from any sort of fruit in season—peaches, apples, cherries, plums, or berries. Green gooseberries are inadvisable, through being too tart and too tedious. Stone cherries, pare peaches or apples and slice thin, halve plums if big enough, and remove stones—if not, wash, drain well, and use whole. Line a skillet or deep pie pan—it must be three inches deep at least, liberally with a short crust, filled rather more than a quarter-inch thick. Fit well, then prick all over with a blunt fork. Fill with the prepared fruit, put on an upper crust a quarter-inch thick and plenty big enough, barely press the crust edges together, prick well with a fork all over the top, and cook in a hot oven half to three-quarters of an hour, according to size. Take up, remove top crust, lay it inverted upon another plate, sweeten the fruit, then dip out enough of it to make a thick layer over the top crust. Grate nutmeg over apple pies, or strew on a little powdered cinnamon. A few blades of mace baked with the fruit accent the apple flavor beautifully. Cherries take kindly to brandy, but require less butter than either peaches or apples. Give plums plenty of sugar with something over for the stones. Cook a few stones with them for flavor, even if you take away the bulk. Do the same with cherries, using say, a dozen pits to the pie. Serve cobbler hot or cold.

Dishes and Beverages of the Old South
By Martha McCulloch-Williams; decorations by Russel Crofoot (New York: McBride, Nast & Company, 1913)

EASY FRUIT COBBLER

1 stick butter
1½ cups sugar
1 cup flour
1½ teaspoons baking powder
⅔ cup (or a little less) evaporated milk
Blackberries, dewberries, or peaches
Cinnamon

Melt butter in a 9x13-inch baking dish. Mix ¾ cup of sugar, flour, and baking powder together. Stir in milk. Pour over butter. Add berries (I usually smash mine with a fork first), pouring evenly over batter. Sprinkle with rest of sugar and a little cinnamon. Bake at 350 degrees for 30 minutes or until browned. Delicious with vanilla ice cream.

Courtesy of Cooks.com

Marcia Gruver is a full-time writer who hails from Southeast Texas. Inordinately enamored by the past, she delights in writing historical fiction. Marcia's deep south-central roots lend a Southern-comfortable style and touch of humor to her writing. Through her books, she hopes to leave behind a legacy of hope and faith to the coming generations.

When she's not plotting stories about God's grace, Marcia spends her time reading, playing video games, or taking long drives through the Texas hill country. She and her husband, Lee, have one daughter and four sons. Collectively, this motley crew has graced them with eleven grandchildren and one great-granddaughter—so far.

Discussion Questions

1. After the tragic deaths of his family, Pearson Foster is angry with God, yet he carefully patterns his moral behavior after God's commandments. Christians often go through the motions of a committed life, but their hearts are missing from the equation. Whether their posturing stems from fear, pride, or deeply ingrained habits, how do you suppose God views this behavior in His children?

2. Dreaming of a life more exciting than safe and respectable Canton, Mississippi, Addie McRae longs to escape the confines of her hometown and the bonds of her overprotective parents. However, her initial foray into the outside world leaves her cowering behind her mother like a frightened child. Why are we often braver with our feet on familiar sod than we are on the other side of the fence?

3. Despite their humble beginnings, Addie's parents provided her a life of affluence and safety. Therefore, the rough-and-tumble appearance of Pearson Foster and his friend frighten her and make them seem untrustworthy. Even after she comes to know Pearson better, it's easy for her to jump to conclusions about him. How often do we judge a person based on his or her appearance? Is this practice wholly wrong or, depending on the circumstances, could it have some merit? How important are first impressions?

4. With the facts lined up so convincingly, it was easy to misunderstand Pearson's interest in Addie's mother. Have you ever, due to extenuating circumstances, appeared guilty of a wrongdoing you didn't commit? How did it make you feel to be accused?

5. Denny Currie is a bitterly unhappy man, displaying harsh, cruel treatment toward his sidekick, the only person who cares about him. Sick with greed, Denny believes that lack of wealth is the only obstacle to the life he covets. What do you think is actually the root cause of his unhappiness?

6. As Pearson leans into a renewed relationship with God, he breathes an unusual prayer: *Help me to forgive You.* What seems on the surface to be a forward, sinful request, Pearson's plea rises from the depths of his pain. How do you think God responds to such a prayer?

7. After believing Pearson to be a bold lothario devoid of a gentleman's conscience, Addie reaches a turning point in her feelings for him. Catching a glimpse at his upright, decent soul, she's determined to trust him unconditionally. Yet when seemingly irrefutable evidence makes him look guilty of cruelty and greed, Addie's newfound trust puddles at her feet. How often do we jump to conclusions and allow circumstances to persuade us away from the truth?

8. Miss Whitfield's remembrances of Dr. Moony didn't grow old along with her. Her first glimpse of him as an elderly man disturbs her and brings home the truth of her own mortality. She makes the decision to put aside her cherished memories of him in favor of forming a new relationship. Is there an outdated memory of someone or something you've held for far too long? If given the chance, would you cling to treasured memories or trade them for something more tangible?

9. Pearson's return to his childhood home in Galveston triggers healing; allowing him to lay aside old ghosts and deal with his grief. When we avoid confronting our pain, do we extend our misery unnecessarily?

10. Priscilla Whitfield is charged with the daunting task of raising an autistic child. Despite her willing heart, in an era where autism is little understood, Priscilla might have bitten off more than she can chew. Do you approve or disapprove of the way she handled Ceddy's welfare in the end?

Other books by Marcia Gruver:

Texas Fortunes Series

Chasing Charity
Diamond Duo
Emmy's Equal

Backwoods Brides Series

Raider's Heart
Bandit's Hope